PRAISE FOR
THICK AS THIEVES AND
#1 *NEW YORK TIMES* BESTSELLING
AUTHOR SANDRA BROWN

"Bold and bracing hard-boiled crime thriller *Thick as Thieves* [is] perhaps [Sandra Brown's] most ambitious and best-realized effort ever...A tale steeped in noir and nuance that's utterly riveting from the first page to the last." —*Providence Journal*

"[*Thick as Thieves* is a] taut novel of romantic suspense...A final twist will catch readers by surprise. Good pacing, smooth prose, inventive action scenes, and a touch of hot romance combine to make this a winner. Brown consistently entertains." —*Publishers Weekly*

"[Brown] is a masterful storyteller, carefully crafting tales that keep readers on the edge of their seats." —*USA Today*

"Suspense that has teeth." —Stephen King

"Brown deserves her own genre." —*Dallas Morning News*

"Sandra Brown proves herself top-notch." —Associated Press

"A novelist who can't write them fast enough." —*San Antonio Express-News*

"Brown's storytelling gift is surprisingly rare." —*Toronto Sun*

"Sandra Brown is a publishing icon." —*New York Journal of Books*

THICK AS THIEVES

THICK AS THIEVES

SANDRA BROWN

GRAND CENTRAL
PUBLISHING

NEW YORK   BOSTON

Grand Central Publishing
Hachette Book Group
1290 Avenue of the Americas, New York, NY 10104
grandcentralpublishing.com
twitter.com/grandcentralpub

First trade paperback edition: March 2021

Grand Central Publishing is a division of Hachette Book Group, Inc. The Grand Central Publishing name and logo is a trademark of Hachette Book Group, Inc.

The publisher is not responsible for websites (or their content) that are not owned by the publisher.

The Hachette Speakers Bureau provides a wide range of authors for speaking events. To find out more, go to www.hachettespeakersbureau.com or call (866) 376-6591.

LCCN: 2020938337
ISBNs: 978-1-5387-5192-3 (paperback), 978-1-5387-5191-6 (ebook)

Printed in the United States of America

LSC-C

Printing 1, 2021

Prologue

That night in 2000

T alking about it is the surefire way to get caught."

He let the statement settle, then looked each of his three companions straight in the eye one at a time, using the deliberation rather than additional words to serve as a warning.

The huddled quartet was coming down from an adrenaline high. It hadn't been a crash landing but a gradual descent. Now that they were no longer in immediate danger of being caught red-handed, their heartbeats remained stronger than normal, but had slowed to a manageable rhythm. Breaths gusting into the humid air were just as hot, though not as rapid as they'd been.

However, what hadn't let up, not by a single degree, was the tension among them.

They couldn't risk being seen together tonight, but before going their separate ways, they must forge an understanding. If, during the process of creating that bond, a threat was implied, so much the better. It would discourage any one of them from breaking the pact to keep their mouths shut. One stuck to the vow of silence, or else.

"Do not talk about it." The speaker's hair was a paprika-colored thatch that grew straight up out of a sidewall. A freckled scalp showed through the bristle. "Don't tell any-damn-body." He made five stabbing motions toward the ground to emphasize each word.

Somewhat impatiently, the oldest of the group said, "Of course not."

The one vigorously gnawing his fingernails spat out a paring while bobbing his head in assent.

The fourth, the youngest of them, had maintained an air of cool detachment and remarkable calm throughout the evening's endeavor. A laconic shrug conveyed his unspoken *Goes without saying.*

"One of us boasts about it, or drops a hint, even joking, it'll have a domino effect that could—"

"You can stop going on about it," the oldest interrupted. "We got it the first time, and didn't need a lesson from you to start with."

The ditch in which they were hunkered was choked with weeds, some thriving, some lying dead in the mud, having drowned during the last hard rain. The ravine was four feet deep and made for an ugly scar that cut between the narrow road and a listing barbed-wire fence demarcating a cow pasture that reeked of manure. Without a breeze to disperse the odor, the sultry atmosphere kept it ripe.

At the center of the circle formed by the four was the cause of the resented lecture: a canvas bag stuffed with stolen cash.

It was a hell of a lot bigger haul than they had anticipated, and that unexpected bonus had been both exhilarating and sobering. It made the stakes seem higher, which wound the tension tighter.

Following the rebuke about unnecessary lessons, no one moved or said anything until the young, aloof one reached up and ground a mosquito against the side of his neck, leaving a smear of blood. "Nobody'll hear about it from me. I don't cotton to the idea of jail. Already been there."

"Juvie," the redhead said.

"Still counts."

The older one said, "Only a fool would blab about it. I'm no fool."

The redhead thought it over, then nodded as though reassured. "All right, then. Another thing. We see each other on the street, we act the same as always. We don't go out of our way to avoid each other, but we don't get chummier, either. We recognize each other on sight, maybe we're well enough acquainted to speak, but that's it. That's why this will work. The only thing we have in common is this." He nudged the canvas bag with the steel-tipped toe of his boot.

The other pair of cowboy boots in the circle weren't silver-toed. They weren't worn for show but lived in. This wasn't the first time they'd been caked with mud.

The pair of brown wingtips had sported a shine before sliding down into the ditch.

The navy blue trainers had some mileage on them.

"Six months is a long time to wait to divide it up," the eldest said, eyeing the carrot-top. "In the meanwhile, why do you get to keep the money? We didn't vote on that."

"Don't you trust me with it?"

"What do you think?"

If the one with the gingery thatch took offense, he didn't show it. "Well, look at it this way. I'm the one taking all the risks. Despite our pledge not to talk it up, if one of you lets something slip, and somebody who wears a *badge* gets wind of it and starts snooping, I'm the one holding the bag."

The other three hadn't missed the emphasis he placed on that certain word. They exchanged glances of patent mistrust toward the self-appointed banker, but no one argued with him. The youngest gave another one-shouldered shrug, which the redhead took as consensus.

"Once you get your share," he said, "you can't go spending cash like crazy. No new cars, nothing flashy, nothing—"

The older one cut him off again, testier than before. "You know, I could well do without these instructions of yours."

"No call to get touchy. Anything I tell you is a reminder to myself, too." The redhead fashioned a placating smile, but it wasn't in keeping with his eyes, which reflected the meager moonlight like twin straight razors. He then turned to the nail-biter, who was running out of fingers on which to chew. "What's the matter with you?"

"Nothing."

"Then stop with the nervous fidgeting. It'll single you out like a red neon arrow."

The older seconded that. "He's right. If you come across as nervous, you had just as well confess."

The nail-biter lowered his hand from his mouth. "I'll be okay." His Adam's apple forced down a hard swallow. "It's just...you know." He looked down at the bag. "I still can't believe we actually did it."

"Well, we did," the redhead said. "And when you report for work on Monday morning and are informed that the safe was cleared out over the weekend, you've got to pretend to be as shocked as everybody else. But don't overreact," he said, raising his index finger to underscore the point.

"Just a soft 'holy shit' will do. Something like that to show disbelief, then keep your trap shut. Don't do anything to call attention to yourself, especially if detectives start interviewing all the store employees, which it's certain they will.

When your turn comes, you stay ignorant and innocent. Got that?"

"Yeah."

"*Got that?*" demanded the older.

"Sure. I know what to do." But even as he acknowledged his responsibility, he dried his palms by running them up and down his pants legs, a gesture that didn't inspire confidence among the other three.

The older sighed, "Jesus."

The nervous one was quick to reassure the other three. "Look, don't worry about me. I've done my part, and I'll continue to. I'm just jumpy, is all. Out here in the open like this." He made a sweeping motion with his arm that encompassed the pasture and deserted stretch of country road. "Why'd we stop out here, anyway?"

"I thought we should come to an understanding," the redhead said.

"And now we have." The oldest one started up the embankment and gave the nervous one a warning glare. "You had better not screw this up."

"I won't. By Monday I'll be okay." He wet his lips and formed a shaky grin. "And six months from now, we'll all be rolling in clover."

As a group, they climbed out of the ditch, but the adjourning optimistic prediction didn't pan out.

By morning, their plan had been shot to hell.

One of them was in the hospital.

One was in jail.

One was in the morgue.

And one had gotten away with the haul.

Chapter 1

Present day

Lord, Arden. I had counted on it being run-down, but..."

Lisa expressed her dismay with a shudder as she stepped through the back door into the kitchen and surveyed the conditions in which Arden had been living for the past five months.

Arden trailed her sister inside and pulled a chair from beneath the dining table. As she took her seat, she noticed that the tabletop had defied the recent polishing she'd given it. Before yesterday, she had fretted over those nicks and scratches. Today, she couldn't see what possible difference they made.

Lisa was rattling on. Arden tuned back in. "Have you had that stove checked for a gas leak? It could be a safety hazard. Is there a functioning smoke or fire alarm?"

"They're called Braxton Hicks. Think of them as practice contractions. But it'll be a month or so before you start to experience them. And when you do, they're no cause for alarm."

That's what the OB had told her on her last prenatal checkup.

But yesterday's contractions weren't Braxton Hicks. They'd turned out not to be a rehearsal, and they'd caused a great deal of alarm in the produce section of the supermarket.

She forced her thoughts away from that and back to Lisa, who stood in the center of the kitchen, elbows tucked into her sides as though afraid she might accidentally make contact with a contaminated surface.

"You told me you were occupying only a few of the downstairs rooms. What about in here?"

Lisa went over to the open doorway and looked in at the formal dining room and, beyond it, the living room. Two decades ago, they'd been emptied of all furnishings except for the upright piano that stood where it always had. Arden had been surprised to find it still here, but she supposed that it had remained for the same reason Lisa hadn't taken it with them when they vacated. How does one cart off something that large?

"I suppose the rooms upstairs are as empty as these," Lisa remarked. "Doesn't appear as though you've been in here at all." She gave the staircase a sweeping glance, then turned back into the kitchen. "Where are you sleeping?"

Arden nodded toward the room off the kitchen. Lisa gave the partially open door a push with the knuckle of her index finger.

It was a square and featureless space with a square and featureless window. Their mother, Marjorie, had used it as a catch-all to store Christmas decorations, castoff clothing bound for Goodwill, their dad's rarely used golf clubs, a portable sewing machine, and such.

When Arden moved in, she'd decided to set up a temporary bedroom in here rather than use her old room upstairs, saving herself from having to go up and down the stairs as her pregnancy advanced and she grew more ungainly.

That was no longer an issue.

When the first pain gripped her, Arden dropped the apple she'd been testing and splayed her hands over her distended abdomen. Although the sharp and unexpected contraction robbed her of breath, she gave a cry of fright.

"What's the matter, honey?"

She turned toward a voice filled with concern. She registered a pleasant face framed by gray hair, a blue-and-white-striped blouse, and kindly eyes. Then another pain seized her, meaner than the one before. Her knees buckled.

"Oh, goodness. Your water broke. You're going into labor."

"No! I can't be. It's too early."

"How far along are you?"

"It's too early!" Her voice went shrill with panic. "Call 911. Please."

Lisa was commenting on her drab, makeshift bedroom. "I simply don't understand why you chose to come back here and live like this."

Arden had furnished the room with a twin bed, a nightstand and lamp, and a chest of drawers that she had assembled herself over the course of two days. She remembered feeling a great sense of accomplishment and had imagined herself assembling a crib soon.

The mirror that Arden had mounted on the wall above the chest reflected Lisa's dismay as she came back around, shaking her head slowly and regarding Arden as she would an indecipherable ancient transcript.

"Is there anything to drink?"

Without waiting for an answer, Lisa returned to the kitchen and checked inside the refrigerator. "Good. Diet Coke. Or would you rather have something else? Does the ice maker work?"

Arden tried to keep up with Lisa's brisk thought processes, but her mind was fettered by vivid recollections.

"You'll be all right. Lie back. Take deep breaths."

A young woman in yoga attire had responded to the older lady's shout for help. She eased Arden down until she was reclining in the supporting arms of another stranger who'd taken up position behind her. Kneeling at her side, the young woman continued to speak to her in a calm and soothing manner. But nothing she'd said helped, not with the pain that assailed her, not with the despair that was equally intense.

Desperate, she shoved her hands between her thighs in an effort to hold inside the life that her body was prematurely trying to expel.

Lisa located the drinking glasses in the cabinet in which they'd always been and poured them each a drink. Bringing them to the table with her, she sat down across from Arden.

She sipped from her glass, then reached out and covered Arden's hand with her own. "Baby sister."

Lisa whispered the endearment with affection, caring, and concern. All of which Arden knew to be genuine. Lisa was as baffled by her life choices as she was annoyed.

She said, "From the moment you called me yesterday, I've been in a tizzy. I don't know how much you remember of last evening, but when I got to the hospital, you were in hysterics one minute and near catatonic the next. I was beside myself. Then this morning, trying to get you out of there..."

"What's your name?"

At her side and bending over her, the EMT had replaced the yoga-clad woman. He was young and fresh-faced.

"Arden Maxwell."

"Arden, we're going to take care of you, okay? How far along are you?"

"Twenty-two weeks."

His partner, who looked like a career bodybuilder, was taking her vitals. They asked everyone who'd congregated around her to move aside, then lifted her onto the gurney, and rolled her out of the store.

The midday sun was directly overhead. It was blinding. Her vision turned watery.

She blotted tears from her eyes now.

Lisa must have noticed, because she stopped enumerating the aggravations associated with being discharged from the hospital. "What I'm leading up to is that this is the first chance I've had to tell you how sorry I am. Truly, truly sorry, Arden." She stroked Arden's hand.

Fresh tears welled up in Arden's eyes. She looked into her untouched glass of Coke where bubbles rose in a rush to the surface, only to burst upon reaching it. Something vital and alive, extinguished faster than a blink.

In the ambulance, her jeans were cut away. She was draped. When the young-looking medic examined her, his smooth brow wrinkled.

She struggled to angle herself up in order to see what had caused his consternation, but the bodybuilder kept her pressed down, a hand on each of her shoulders, not unkindly, but firmly.

"My baby will be all right, won't she?" Arden sobbed. *"Please. Tell me she'll be okay."*

But, thinking back on it now, she believed she'd known even then, on a primal and instinctual level, that her girl child would never draw breath.

"You probably won't believe this," Lisa continued as she rubbed her thumb across Arden's knuckles, "but I admired you for electing to have the baby. Oh, don't get me wrong. I was appalled when you told me about it and what you planned to do. Coming back here to live and raise the child. *Here* of all places?"

She took a look around as though seeking to find an explanation for the inexplicable written on the faded wallpaper. "It's masochistic. Does this self-inflicted punishment have to do with the baby's father?"

Arden picked up her glass and tried to hold it steady as she took a sip of Coke. The glass clinked against her lower teeth. She set it back down.

In a hushed tone, Lisa said, "Is he married, Arden?"

She cast her eyes downward.

Lisa sighed. "I figured as much. Did he even know you were pregnant?"

She took Arden's silence as a no.

"Just as well," Lisa said. "You're under no obligation to tell him now. If he didn't know about the child, he doesn't need to know about its fate. That episode of your life is behind you. You can start afresh. Clean slate."

Again she covered Arden's hand and pressed it affectionately. "First thing on the agenda is to get you away from here. I want you to move in with me until you figure out what you want to do with your life." She gave Arden time to respond, but when she didn't, she continued. "Since Wallace died, the house seems so empty."

Lisa's husband, who had been much older than she, had died two years earlier. No doubt their huge, rambling house in an elite neighborhood of Dallas did feel empty.

"I'll give you all the privacy you wish, of course, but Helena will be delighted to have you there to fuss over. She and I will pamper you until you're completely recovered." She smiled and patted Arden's hand again before checking her watch.

"You can't have much to pack. If we get away soon, we'll be there by dark. Helena will have dinner waiting." She was about to leave her chair, when she paused. "And, Arden, you're not under a deadline. Give yourself time to think things through. Really think through an idea before you act on it. Don't rush headlong into something.

"In all honesty, I had a bad feeling about your move to Houston, and, at that point, I didn't even know about your relationship with this married man. Granted, the job held promise, but your pulling up stakes and relocating seemed impulsive and doomed from the start."

The attending physician in the ER clasped her hand. "Ms. Maxwell, I'm sorry."

"No."

"Your daughter was stillborn."

"No!"

"Don't blame yourself. Nothing you did caused it. It was an accident of nature."

Doomed from the start.

Feeling as though her breastbone was about to crack open, Arden pushed back her chair and went over to the sink. Opening the blinds on the window above it, she looked out at the backyard in which Lisa and she had played.

The fence was missing slats. The grass had been overtaken by weeds. Her mother's rose bed, to which she'd given so much tender loving care, was a patch of infertile dirt.

She sensed Lisa moving up behind her even before her sister encircled her waist and rested her chin on her shoulder so she could share the view through the window. "I remember the day Dad brought the swing set home for you."

It was still anchored in the ground with concrete blocks, but it was rusty, and the chain was broken on one of the swings.

"I was around twelve years old, so you would have been two. There was a little seat for you with a bar across your lap."

Lisa rubbed her chin against the knob at the crest of Arden's shoulder. "You were too young to remember that, but surely you remember when I taught you how to skin-the-cat."

Lisa had been almost too tall by then, but she was athletic enough to demonstrate how easy it was. She'd spotted Arden on her first fearful attempts, then had challenged her to do it on her own.

Her palms damp with nervous sweat, she'd braced herself on the crossbar, taken a deep breath, and somersaulted over it. But she fell short of making the full rotation. Her hands slipped off the bar, and she'd landed hard on her butt.

Pride smarting as much as her bottom, she'd fought back tears. But Lisa had insisted that she try again.

"Tomorrow," Arden had whined.

"No. Right now."

On the second try, she'd succeeded. Lisa had practically smothered her in a bear hug. She recalled now how special Lisa's approval and that congratulatory hug had been.

The family had celebrated her feat with dinner out at the restaurant of her choosing: McDonald's, of course.

That had been a happy day, one among the last happy family times that Arden recalled. Their mother's fatal accident had occurred within months.

But losing her hadn't been as sudden and unexpected as their father's abandonment.

This past March marked twenty years, twice the age she had been when Joe Maxwell left his two daughters, never to be seen again. His desertion remained the pivotal point around which Arden's life continued to revolve.

It did no good to speculate on how differently Lisa and she would have turned out as individuals, or what kind of futures they would have had, if he hadn't forsaken them. He had.

Softly, sympathetically, Lisa said, "You've been through a terrible ordeal, and I don't want to pressure you when you're so vulnerable. But, Arden, this isn't the place to recover. Believe me, it isn't. You were younger. You can't appreciate how bad it was after Mother died. Or maybe you can, but you've blocked it from your memory. I haven't. I remember.

"When Dad disappeared, and I moved us away from this town, I swore it would be forever. People who lived here then will remember us. Why subject yourself to gossip and speculation? To say nothing of the fact that this house is literally falling down around you." She flipped her finger over a chip in the Formica countertop.

"So many times, I've thought about selling it, but I would get sentimental, think of Mother in these rooms, cooking in this kitchen, humming as she folded laundry, and I couldn't bring myself to let it go. Though God knows we could have used the money, selling it would have made severance with Mother seem so final. Besides that, the house belonged to you, too. Selling it wasn't a decision I felt comfortable making for both of us."

She took a deep breath. "But now I wish I had gotten rid of it, so you wouldn't have made this dreadful mistake of moving back. You've deluded yourself into seeing this place as *home*. It isn't. It hasn't been for twenty years, and, without your child, it never will be.

"I'm your only family. I'll nurture you until you decide what you want to do from this point forward."

She gave Arden a quick, hard hug and held on for a moment longer before letting go.

Arden turned to face her. She kissed her sister's cheek, then crooked her pinky finger, and Lisa linked hers with it. After their father's desertion, they'd begun doing this often. It symbolized that they had only each other, and that their bond was unbreakable.

They kept their fingers linked, smiling wistfully at each other, then Arden pulled her hand free. "Are you finished, Lisa?"

"Finished?"

"Finished telling me where I'm going to live and what I'm going to do with my life from this point forward. If you're done, please leave." She took a bolstering breath. "If not, leave anyway."

Arden was still awake when she heard the car approaching on the road.

She glanced at the clock on her nightstand. It read a few minutes past one a.m. The drive-by was a little later than usual tonight.

Immediately after learning she was pregnant, she'd made plans to leave Houston. Within a week, she had resigned from her job, paid out her lease, emptied her condo, and made the move back to her hometown.

Although Penton was a county seat, most of the county was rural, so the "city" itself was small, and it had a thriving grapevine. Anyone familiar with the Maxwell family's history would naturally be curious about the recent occupant of the house that had remained uninhabited for so long, and it hadn't taken long for word to get around who the resident was.

She had grown accustomed to motorists slowing down and coasting past the house.

She wasn't bothered by the daytime gawkers.

But one came at night. Every night. By now she recognized the sound of his car's engine. She even found herself listening for it. Too often, she didn't fall asleep until he, or she, had driven past. It wasn't the kind of close to each day that she wished for. It didn't feel like a benediction.

Of course she hadn't breathed a word of this to Lisa, who had predicted that Arden's taking up residence would resurrect the suspicion, rumor, and speculation about their father and the crimes he was alleged to have committed before disappearing.

As usual, Lisa was right, but Arden sensed that this particular passerby wasn't motivated strictly by curiosity and the hope of catching a glimpse of the infamous Joe Maxwell's youngest daughter. These nightly rounds had a predatory quality that made her uneasy.

But just today hadn't she determined she would no longer yield to intimidation?

She threw off the covers, got out of bed, and went to the window, keeping well behind the wall so she wouldn't be seen. It seemed sensible and cautious not to let the person in that car know that she was aware of him.

The house was set too far back off the road for her to make out more of the vehicle than its headlights. As it came even with the house, it slowed to a crawl, as it did every night, and didn't resume its speed until having driven past.

As she watched the taillights go around a bend and out of sight, she told herself that maybe she was letting her imagination turn something innocent into something ominous. That purring motor could belong to a night worker who was making his way home after his shift.

But she didn't know of any businesses out this way, and what kind of job would require a seven-day workweek? He came past the house on weekends, too. He hadn't missed a night in months.

The regularity of it felt compulsive and sinister.

Trying to shake off her uneasiness, telling herself that she was being silly, she returned to bed. But turbulent thoughts kept her awake.

Lisa hadn't gone quietly.

For half an hour after Arden had made her declaration of independence, Lisa had argued with her. "If Wallace were still alive, he would side with me."

Arden had no doubt of that. She'd liked her brother-in-law, who had been a good surrogate father—more like a grandfather, actually—after he and Lisa married. A successful commercial real estate developer, the even-tempered Wallace Bishop had routinely negotiated deals that left both sides feeling they had come out favorably. Numerous times he had mediated disagreements between the sisters, but, in order to maintain marital harmony, he had leaned toward Lisa's side.

But even though Lisa had invoked his name, Arden had remained steadfast in her decision to stay, giving Lisa no choice except to ultimately relent. As she left, she'd said, "I only want you to be happy, Arden."

"I want me to be happy, too."

Now, as she lay in the dark, staring at the ceiling, she conceded her sister one point: For most of her adult years, she'd been moving at a frenetic pace but getting nowhere. She hadn't discovered her path. She'd been directionless and without purpose.

Reflexively, she ran her hand over her abdomen, missing the small mound that had been so wonderfully new, yet had soon become endearingly familiar.

The baby had given her purpose.

"As it is . . ." she whispered.

Grief suffused her, but she refused to give it a foothold. She couldn't let her mind, her heart, center on the loss of the baby. If she did, bereavement would immobilize her.

She had to get on with her original plan. Just like learning to skin-the-cat, she must do it, on her own, and now.

Exhausted as her body was, her mind continued to churn, busily mapping out a plan of attack on a house that had stood neglected for twenty years.

Until her own dying day, she would mourn the daughter she had lost, but she felt a sense of urgency to act, to move, to *live* before it was too late.

That last thought gave her pause.

Too late for *what?*

Chapter 2

The name "L. Burnet" was stenciled on the metal mailbox mounted on a post at the entrance to a gravel driveway. Although the road to get here had been bumpy, narrow, and roundabout, Arden had arrived at her destination.

Up to this point, the two months since the loss of the baby had been busy, but discouragingly unproductive. She hoped this call on L. Burnet would change that.

She turned into the driveway, pulled up behind a dually pickup truck, and let her motor idle as she assessed the house. The architecture was Acadian, which was unsurprising since the state line with Louisiana bisected Caddo Lake, and the lake was within shouting distance.

The white-frame, one-story structure had dark green shutters and a matching tin roof. It was scrupulously tidy and aesthetically pleasing. A porch with a low overhang ran its width. The only thing on the porch was a varnished wood rocking chair with a tall slat-back and wide armrests. Landscaping was limited to dwarf evergreen shrubs that bordered the edge of the porch on either side of a set of recycled redbrick steps.

She turned off her car. When she got out, her ears were assaulted by a high-pitched whine coming from behind the house. She walked around the tank-size truck and followed a footpath worn into the grass. It led her around the left side of the house to the backyard, which was studded with tall pine trees.

A sizable outbuilding matched the house's white exterior and green tin roof. Its double garage door was raised. She made her way over to the opening and looked inside. The source of the racket was a buzz saw. The man operating it had his back to her. The noise was earsplitting.

"Excuse me?"

He gave no sign of having heard her and remained bent over the worktable, ably cleaving a length of lumber down the middle.

She raised her voice. "Mr. Burnet?"

When he didn't respond, she decided to wait until he'd finished. When he did, he straightened up, surveyed his work, then, much to Arden's relief, switched off the saw.

"Mr. Burnet?"

As he came around, he pushed a pair of safety goggles up to his forehead. Upon seeing her, he reacted in a manner she couldn't quite specify, and it had been so fleeting that if she had blinked, she would have missed it.

She said, "I hope I didn't startle you. I called out, but you didn't hear me above the racket."

He held her gaze, gave her a slow once-over, then turned away to set the saw on the worktable. He pulled off the goggles and a pair of suede work gloves and placed them beside the saw before facing her again. "I heard you."

She didn't know what to say to that. If he'd heard her, why hadn't he acknowledged her presence?

"My name is Arden Maxwell." She walked toward him and stuck out her right hand.

He looked at it as though a handshake was a new experience for him, then reached for a faded red shop rag and used it to wipe sawdust off his forearms before shaking hands. He did so economically, almost curtly. "What can I do for you?"

She gave an uneasy laugh. "A lot, I hope."

He didn't return her smile, only cocked his eyebrow.

And somehow that added an unintended innuendo to what she'd said. She was quick to explain. "I saw your ad. On the internet. I Googled local contractors, and you were listed."

"Um-huh."

That was all he said, displaying no particular interest in whether or not he could secure her as a customer. She plunged on. "I called yesterday and left a voice mail, asking that you return my call. I guess you missed it."

"I got it. I've been busy."

She looked beyond him at the newly halved board. "Yes, I see. Well, I had another errand to run in town, so I decided to try and catch you here, since it was on my way."

"On your way?"

She gave another light laugh. "A *winding* way. Granted, you are off the beaten path, and I almost missed the turnoff. But I found you."

"Lucky I was here, or you would have come all this way for nothing."

"I consider it a stroke of luck, yes."

"Well, now you're here, what do you need?"

"I have a home project, a rather extensive one. It will require considerable time and a lot of hard work."

Finished with the rag, he tossed it down onto the worktable. "How many contractors did you call before me?"

Abashed, she ducked her head. Then, realizing she owed

him no explanation, she again met his gaze, which was cobalt blue and unwavering behind an unfriendly squint. He was younger than the image she'd formed in her mind, but she figured that the threads of gray in his dark hair, the squint lines, and the unsmiling mouth added years to his actual age.

His physique certainly wasn't that of a man settling comfortably into his middle years. No paunch overlapped the waistband of his jeans. Well-defined biceps stretched the short sleeves of his black t-shirt. He was tall and lean and, overall, looked as tough as boot leather and as cuddly as a diamondback.

"He was a soldier, you know."

"No, I didn't know."

"Afghanistan. Iraq before that."

"He was in combat, then?"

"Oh, yeah. He saw action, all right. Might have spent a little too much time at war, if you know what I mean. But he's all right. Not dangerous, or crazy, or anything."

In the ad, a former client of Mr. Burnet's had left his name as one to call for a reference. Arden had. In addition to his endorsement of Burnet's craftsmanship and trustworthiness, he'd volunteered the information about his military service.

In truth, she *hadn't* known what he'd meant by his comment on Burnet's spending too much time at war. Now, she wished she had asked him to elaborate.

Maybe war had left L. Burnet taciturn and borderline rude. Or perhaps he was standoffish by nature. But, as long as he could do the work, she didn't care whether or not he had an engaging personality. She wasn't hiring someone to entertain her.

His stare was piercing, but she didn't detect any madness behind it. Quite the contrary. She sensed intelligence, acute attentiveness, and a perceptiveness sharper than an average person's. Little would escape him, and that was a bit discomfiting. However, she was willing to take her chances that he was of reasonably sound mind.

But—and this was the bottom line—what really recommended him was that over the course of the past two months, she had interviewed many contractors, and he was the last on her list of candidates for the job.

Thanks to the trust fund her late brother-in-law had established for her, she could afford to hire anyone. However, as a matter of principle, she wanted to finance this project using money she had earned, which put a ceiling on how much she could comfortably spend.

In answer to his question, she said, "Honestly, Mr. Burnet, I've consulted several others who were qualified."

"They couldn't fit your project into their schedules?"

"I couldn't fit them into my budget."

"So you called me."

"Please don't take offense. The comments posted online said that you do good work, that you're dependable, and that you're a one-man operation. At first, I didn't see that as an advantage."

"Now you do?"

"Yes. Because you don't have a crew, I thought perhaps you would be a good choice."

He propped his butt against the worktable and hooked his thumbs into the front pockets of his jeans. "You thought I'd work cheap."

So much for diplomacy. His stance was challenging if not downright belligerent. The placement of his hands was a none too subtle assertion of masculinity. He seemed set on being blunt. To all of the above, *Fine.* "All right, yes, Mr. Burnet. I thought you might work cheap. *Er.*"

"No doubt I would. But I'm not the guy for the job."

She gave a short laugh. "Before you determine that, couldn't you at least hear me out?"

"Waste of time."

"How do you know?"

"An extensive project that would take considerable time? Lots of hard work? Sounds like what you have in mind is a complete overhaul of your house."

"More or less."

"I don't do complete overhauls."

"Would you at least come and see—"

"I've seen it."

Her heart gave a bump of alarm. She had identified herself by name on the voice mail but had said nothing about the location of her house. The vehicle that came past her house each night sprang to mind. "You know where I live?"

He bobbed his square chin.

She studied him for a moment, then said slowly, "When you turned around and saw me here, you recognized me, didn't you?"

Another brusque nod.

"How?"

"Somebody had pointed you out to me."

"Where?"

"I think it was in the fried pie shop."

"I didn't even know there was a fried pie shop."

"Oh. Well, then it must've been somewhere else."

"Why was I being pointed out to you?"

He pulled his thumbs from his pockets and pushed away from the table, then glanced aside for several seconds before coming back to her. "You're the lady who had the... emergency... in the grocery store."

Her breath hitched, and instinctively she took a step back. "Oh."

The recollections swarmed her, blocking out light and sound, everything. Her mind unreeled the memories at warp speed, but they were as distinct as though it had happened yesterday instead of two months ago.

She recalled being jerkily conveyed from the ambulance into the ER, the rapid-fire questions of the medical personnel, the pervasive antiseptic smell, the biting coldness of the stirrups against the arches of her bare feet, the kindly voice of the nurse asking if she would like to hold her daughter. Her lifeless daughter.

She didn't know how long she stood there, remembering, but, as the kaleidoscope of memories receded, she realized that she was slumped forward, hugging her elbows. Her skin had turned clammy. Self-consciously, she straightened up and swiped a strand of hair off her damp forehead with the back of her hand.

She became painfully aware of him, standing motionless and silent, watching her. To avoid eye contact, she looked around and took stock of the workshop. Fluorescent tubes augmented the natural light pouring in from four skylights. Two ceiling fans as large as airplane propellers circulated from the ends of long rods. She could identify some of the tools of his trade, while the purposes of other apparatus and pieces of machinery were unknown to her.

A large draftsman's table occupied a far corner. A light fixture with a perforated metal shade was suspended above it. Next to it was a desk with a computer setup. Except for the sawdust on the floor beneath the table where he'd been working, everything was neatly arranged and appeared well maintained.

Finally her gaze returned to him.

He shifted his stance slightly, the soles of his boots scraping against the floor and disturbing the sawdust. "Sorry about..."

He made a small hand gesture in the general direction of her midsection.

"Thank you." She didn't dwell on that. "So when you listened to the voice mail yesterday, you recognized my name."

"Yeah. Rumor had been circulating for months that the youngest of the Maxwell girls was back. Living out there alone. Expecting a baby."

In all the time she'd been back, this was the first time she had come face-to-face with the gossip about her. "Do you know the rest of it?"

"Don't know who or where the baby's father is."

She ignored the implied question. "Are you acquainted with my family's history?"

"I grew up here." He said it as though that were explanation enough, and it was. Everybody knew her family history.

"You ever learn where your dad went, what happened to him?" he asked. "Did the money ever turn up?"

She didn't address those questions, either. "Are you open to discussing my project, Mr. Burnet?"

"I told you. Discussion would be a waste of time."

"You won't even consider it?"

"Don't know how plainer I can make it."

"Are you afraid that being associated with the youngest Maxwell girl will dent your reputation?"

The corner of his stern mouth twitched, but it couldn't be counted as a real smile. "My reputation is already dented. The thing is, your project would involve more work than I take on at any one time. I specialize in small jobs. Ones with a short shelf life. That way, I'm not overcommitted or overextended. I don't like being tied down. I'd rather keep my work schedule flexible."

She crossed her arms and looked him up and down. "That sounded like bullshit."

"It was."

Chapter 3

W hen the ball game ended in the tie-breaking tenth inning, the crowd at Burnet's Bar and Billiards had begun to thin out. Now, only a few customers remained in the popular lakeside watering hole, which seemed on the verge of toppling into the opaque water of Caddo Lake at any given moment. But since it hadn't slipped from its pilings in the forty years that it had been there, no one worried too much about that happening.

Of the eight pool tables, only one was currently in use. A hotly contested tournament among a group of very vocal and rowdy young men was winding down.

A man and woman, seated across from each other in one of the dark, semi-private booths, had been engaged in a hushed but heated argument for the past hour. Seeming to have called a tenuous truce, they left the booth and headed for the exit. The woman flounced out ahead of the man, who punched the exit door hard with the heel of his hand as he followed her.

"I think she's got the advantage, and he's in for a rough

night," the bartender remarked to the only drinker left seated at the bar.

Without much interest, Ledge said, "Looks like." He remained hunched over his near-empty glass of bourbon. The color of the liquor reminded him of something he didn't want to be reminded of. Arden Maxwell's eyes were that color. Hair the color of corn silk. An abundance of loopy curls.

"You're entitled to a free refill, you know."

Ledge looked from his glass to the bartender. "How's that?"

"Last holdout of the night gets a top-off on the house."

"Oh, yeah?"

"New policy."

"Since when?"

"You want it or not?"

Ledge pointed into his glass. "Make it a short one."

The bartender refilled his glass without benefit of either ice or water. He set the bottle aside, draped his towel over his shoulder, and leaned down, setting his elbows on the bar to bring himself eye to eye with Ledge. "You rarely stay this late. Bad day?"

"It was okay."

"Tell me another."

Ledge took a sip of his freshened drink. The whiskey had just the right amount of sting and felt damn good going down. Real good. Too good. Which was why he always paid for his drinks, even though the Burnet who owned the place was his uncle Henry, who had reared him.

Running a tab kept track of his consumption. He had self-imposed this accounting and was afraid to suspend it. He never took a bottle of hooch home with him, either.

"You go see Henry today?"

Ledge shook his head.

"I know it was bad the last time you went."

"And the time before that."

The billiard balls clacked. Half the young men around the pool table reacted with groans of defeat and expletives, the other half with whoops of victory and expletives.

When they quieted down, the bartender said, "May not seem like it, Ledge, but Henry's still in there somewhere. One of these days he may surprise you with a spark of recognition."

Ledge didn't agree, but he nodded as though he did. He wouldn't shoot down Don's wishful thinking.

Don White had worked alongside his uncle in the bar for as far back as Ledge could remember. More than merely the bartender, Don had been entrusted with the bookkeeping and other facets of the business.

When Henry's Alzheimer's had progressed to the point where he could no longer be relied on to carry out even routine, everyday functions, Ledge had offered to let Don buy him out. Don wouldn't hear of it.

Ledge said now, "Changed your mind yet?"

"Since yesterday?"

"Well?"

"No. Stop asking."

"I'll let you pay it out over four years. Five if you need more time."

"I'll continue running this place like it was mine, you know that. But Burnet's will belong to Henry Burnet for as long as he's drawing breath. After he's gone—"

"He *is* gone, Don."

"Ask me again, after. Then we'll see."

Don was sixty-something. The story was that days before his wedding to his high school sweetheart, she'd been killed at a train crossing.

Ledge didn't know the particulars, because, in all the time

he'd known the man, Don had never referred to either her or the tragedy that had taken her. But the lady must have been special, and the love of Don's life. He was friendly with women customers. Over the years, plenty had gamely encouraged more than friendliness. But if Don had ever had a date, or even a hookup, Ledge was unaware of it. His life was the bar. He had adopted Henry and Ledge as his family.

From an objective observer's viewpoint, they must appear to be a sad, sorry trio of men.

Hell, from Ledge's viewpoint they did.

"I miss the old cuss," Don said of Henry. "Miss his bad jokes."

"Me too."

Don turned his head to look at a framed picture hanging on the back bar. "I remember the day he hung that picture of you up there. He was so proud."

Henry might have put the photograph on proud display, but Ledge hated the damn thing. A buddy of his had taken the picture with his phone as they were preparing for a mission. Ledge had been geared up, face painted, armed to the teeth, looking like a post-apocalyptic badass.

His buddy had emailed him the picture and told him to forward it to his uncle. *Maybe he'll hang it up in his bar. Brag to his customers about his nephew, the scourge of the Taliban.*

Ledge raised his glass to his mouth and spoke into it. "He didn't come back."

Don came around to him. "Sorry?"

"The guy who took that picture. He didn't make it home." Ledge tossed back what was left of the bourbon.

The subject ended there, and each became lost in his own thoughts until Don muttered, "Oh, hell. Look who just sauntered in."

Before Ledge could turn around and check out the

newcomer, he slid onto the stool next to Ledge's. "Hey there, Don. Ledge. How's it hanging?"

Ledge kept his expression impassive, but mentally he was swearing a blue streak. This just wasn't his day. First that unheralded face-to-face with Arden Maxwell. Now he was having to suffer the presence of this son of a bitch.

Rusty Dyle, taking him unaware like this, was grotesquely reminiscent of a Saturday morning twenty years ago.

Spring 2000—Ledge

Friday night had been a raucous one at Burnet's Bar and Billiards. Ledge and his uncle Henry hadn't gotten to bed until after three o'clock, when they'd finished sweeping up.

It was a rainy morning, a good one for sleeping in, but Ledge's seventeen-year-old stomach had growled him awake. Rather than rattle around in the kitchen and wake up his uncle, who needed the shut-eye, he drove into town to the Main Street Diner for breakfast.

He was enjoying his food and the solitude when, without invitation, Rusty Dyle slid into the other side of the booth, snatched a slice of bacon off his plate, bit into it, and crunched noisily.

Ledge's impulse was to lash out, verbally and physically. But in juvie you learned not to react, no matter what was going on around you. You didn't take sides in a fight that didn't involve you. You didn't provoke a guard who would love nothing better than to be given an excuse to whale into you. You didn't respond when the shrink asked about your childhood, whether or not you thought you'd gotten a fair shake or had been dealt a shitty hand.

The first time the counselor had asked, Ledge had told

him he hadn't minded his unorthodox childhood at all. He couldn't miss parents he didn't even remember. He loved his uncle, who had taken him in and raised him as his own son. He had the highest respect for Henry Burnet.

The counselor had frowned like he didn't believe a word of it. Ledge saw no point in trying to convince him of what was the solid truth, so he had shut down and made subsequent sessions frustrating for the counselor by not answering a single question. He hadn't "shared" a goddamn thing with the asshole.

Reticent by nature, he had come out of juvenile detention even less inclined to reveal what he was thinking. That applied especially to his take on Rusty Dyle. Nothing would give the jerk more pleasure than knowing the extent of Ledge's contempt for him and his spiked-up, red-orange hair.

"Big breakfast there, Ledge. Feeding a hangover?"

"I'm not hung over." Ledge kept his attention on his short stack and fried eggs.

"Oh, right. It wouldn't do for you to get caught drinking illegally." He guffawed and polished off the bacon. "But you are looking a little ragged around the edges this morning. Must be on account of Crystal. She give you a hard ride last night?"

Ledge fantasized jamming his fork into the side of Rusty's neck, right about where his carotid would be.

"Hell knows she's good at it," Rusty said, man-to-man. "When she gets going, that gal can plumb wear you out, can't she?"

Ledge knew for a fact that Crystal Ivers had never had anything to do with Rusty Dyle, which galled Rusty no end. His taunts were intended to get a rise out of Ledge, goad him into defending Crystal's honor. The hell he would. Her honor didn't need defending.

"Piss off, Rusty."

"You'll regret saying that when I tell you why I'm here."

"I don't care why you're here."

"You will. Finish your food."

Though he'd lost his appetite, he wouldn't give Rusty the satisfaction of having spoiled his breakfast. He ate. Rusty made meaningless chitchat. When Ledge pushed his empty plate aside, Rusty posed a seemingly irrelevant question.

"How much hard cash do you reckon Welch's takes in during any given week?"

Ledge looked out the window at the rain, which had increased to a steady downpour. "No idea."

"Quarter of a mil."

"Good for the Welches."

"Know how much it rakes in on a holiday week?" Leaning toward Ledge, he whispered, "At least twice that."

Welch's was a family-owned, sprawling warehouse of goods that had weathered the onslaught of big-box store juggernauts because of its loyal customer base. It was also a one-stop shopping outlet for tourists to the lake. The store's inventory included everything from car jacks to Cracker Jacks, butterfly nets to Aqua Net.

"I'm going to take it."

While gauging how wet he was likely to get if he made a dash for his car, Ledge had been only half listening. "Take what?"

"Welch's cash till."

He turned back to Rusty in time to catch his wink. "You heard right. And I could use a guy like you."

Ledge listened to the rest of Rusty's outlandish spiel, believing that he was being set up as the butt of an elaborate practical joke. He even looked around the diner to see if he could spot any of Rusty's like-minded cronies who were in on the prank and waiting for Rusty's signal to spring the trap.

But he didn't see any familiar faces, and by the time Rusty paused and asked, "What do you think? Are you in?" Ledge realized that he was serious.

"Are you insane?"

"Listen." Rusty inched closer to the edge of his bench. "The week before Easter is always a big one for the store. Huge. It runs specials and sales all week. Not counting credit card sales and personal checks, it takes in a shitload of cash."

"Which an armored truck picks up."

"On Monday. Ask your uncle Henry. I'll bet his place is on the same route."

Ledge didn't have to ask. He knew.

"That leaves everything the store has raked in that week in a vault over Easter Sunday. Praise Jesus!" Rusty added, laughing under his breath. "And, before you ask, they don't mark the bills or put them in bags that explode with blue paint. They band them by denomination, that's all."

"Where'd you get this information?"

"My inside man. His name's Brian Foster."

Rusty went on to describe the guy. Ledge scoffed. "The store's second-banana bean counter? He sounds like a loser."

"He is. He's doing this to spite his hard-ass boss, who's always on his case. Also to prove that he has a pair."

Ledge again snorted skeptically, but Rusty wasn't discouraged. "We can't do squat without Foster. He'll get us into the store and open the vault."

"There is no *we*, Rusty. Forget it."

"Don't say no until you hear me out."

"I've already said no."

"Okay." He patted the air. "You're worried about Foster's reliability. Understood. True, he's scared of his own shadow. But see? That makes him easy to intimidate. To control. Do our bidding."

"What it makes him is a screwup waiting to happen."

"He can open the vault."

"While you pose for the security cameras."

"All the store cameras are dummies." He flashed a grin. "Foster told me that old man Welch is too cheap to spring for the real thing."

"I wouldn't take this Foster's word on anything."

Rusty mimed firing a pistol at him. "Me neither. So I got verification from another source."

"From who?"

"Someone else who's familiar with the store. You know the Maxwells? Lisa was Miss Everything. She graduated a couple of years ago. There's another girl. A lot younger. The mother got killed in a car wreck."

"I know the family you're talking about."

"Well, the daddy, poor ol' Joe, lost his wife like that," he said, snapping his fingers, "and got saddled with two daughters to raise. Which would bring any man to drink. It did Joe, and now he's a full-fledged drunk. It's a well-kept secret that everybody knows."

"Not me." Ledge had been racking balls in his uncle's place since he was tall enough to see over the pool table. To his knowledge Joe Maxwell had never darkened the door.

As though reading his mind, Rusty said, "He's a closet drinker. Doesn't do it publicly so his daughters won't be disgraced. He let his insurance business slide until he had to shut it down. Since then, he's been moving from job to job. Guess where he last worked."

Ledge didn't have to guess. He saw it coming. Welch's store.

"Stocking shelves. Mopping the restrooms. Shit detail," Rusty said. "A few months ago, he got fired for being rude to a customer and using foul language. Now, you would think Joe would be out for revenge, wouldn't you?"

"I don't know the man, and I can't read minds."

"Well, see, I can," Rusty boasted, flashing his canny smile. "Joe has turned into a short-tempered drunk, but he's not entirely without scruples. I was afraid that stealing from his former employer might be pushing the envelope."

Rusty explained how he had gotten around Joe Maxwell's conscience. Ledge was dismayed and disgusted by his arm-twisting tactics.

"Came down to money, as everything does," Rusty said. "I waved around the bills he owes to everybody, from the electric company to a shabby liquor store across the state line. Those overdue invoices worked as good as a handful of magic wands. When someone's desperate enough, they'll agree to anything. Anyhow, as of yesterday, I got verification of everything Foster had told me about the store and its chickenshit security. We're good to go."

"With those two as your accomplices?" As a motive, Ledge thought desperation sucked as bad as proving you had balls. "You're crazy."

"More like crafty." Rusty tapped his sidewall.

"You've explained why the other two are doing it. Why are you? Did your daddy cut off your allowance?"

Rusty's father was Sheriff Mervin Dyle, the most corrupt law officer that money could buy. Taking graft was his sideline, and it was a lucrative one. He collected dirt on everybody, hoarded it, and used it on an as-needed basis to bend or break local politicians, judges, law officers, school board members, clergymen, business owners, and anyone else who, in his opinion, needed comeuppance. Being a believer in equal opportunity for all, Mervin also preyed on those who had no influence whatsoever.

His corruption was well known, but nobody did anything about it for fear of reprisal, which was Machiavellian and often medieval. Rusty, Mervin's only child, was upholding the family tradition. Bullying came as easily to him as breathing.

Rather than taking offense at Ledge's remark about his allowance being cut off, he grinned. "Why am I doing it? For the hell of it. Just to see if I can get away with it."

It was such a chilling, amoral comeback that Ledge had no problem believing it. "Well, count me out. I want no part of your stupid scheme. And no part of you."

"You would turn down a quarter share of half a million dollars?"

"I *am* turning down a quarter share."

"I realize it's small potatoes. Not like it's five million, or something. But it's good pocket change, right? A portable amount. Easily spent on Mickey Mouse stuff a little at a time so nobody notices you're suddenly flush with cash."

Into it, he leaned forward. "It's a good-for-starters amount. A practice run. We'll see how it goes. Then . . . ?" He bobbed his eyebrows. "We could aim higher."

"I wouldn't go in league with you for any amount."

"Well, that's just thick-headed, Ledge. Think of all the dope you could buy."

Ledge gave him a fulminating look.

"Hell, with that kind of money, you could bankroll your own meth lab."

"Go fuck yourself." To hell with the rain; he reached for his keys and scooted to the end of the booth.

Rusty said, "After I've shared the plan, you don't really think I'll let you walk away, do you?"

"Watch me." He stood.

"You go along, or I burn down your uncle's crappy red-neck bar."

Ledge froze in place and looked back. Rusty remained smiling and smug. "Well, not me personally, of course. But I know a couple of wetbacks who'd do it for fifty bucks and a bottle of mescal."

He leaned back against the vinyl of the booth and stared pensively into the middle distance. "That would be such a damn shame, wouldn't it? Your uncle Henry has been pouring his heart and soul into that place for years, trying to make a better life for you, his poor orphaned nephew. It's a shithole, but losing it would probably kill him."

He then refocused on Ledge, who actually felt the skin on his face growing taut as he glared at Rusty with loathing. "He's not getting any younger, ya know." After a beat, Rusty said, "Now sit the fuck down."

Ledge slid back into the booth and leaned across the table. "Why me?"

"I have my reasons."

"Crystal? Is this about her?"

Rusty snorted. "That whore? Take her. God knows everybody else has."

Not for an instant did Ledge buy into the dismissive attitude Rusty tried to sell. Crystal had rejected him, and, pure and simple, Rusty couldn't stand it. But Ledge let it drop this time. "You've got your two insiders. I don't have anything to contribute. You don't need me."

Rusty placed his hand over his heart. "But I do, Ledge, I do need you. In case something goes wrong and we get caught, you'll serve a very useful purpose." He widened his grin. "I may need a scapegoat, and you're an established criminal."

Chapter 4

As Rusty settled more comfortably on the barstool, Ledge greeted him with a mere hitch of his chin.

Don took a swipe at the bar in front of Rusty with his towel and forced a smile. "Name your poison."

"Nothing, thanks. I'm driving." He said it unctuously.

"Working late tonight?" Don asked.

"Working late every night. Daytime, too." He added a wink and gave Ledge a sly grin. "Anyhow, I saw Ledge's truck outside. Been a while. Thought I'd drop in, say hi, see what he's up to these days."

Taking the hint, Don said, "Let me know if you change your mind about that drink." After shooting an apologetic glance toward Ledge, he moved to the far end of the bar and made himself look busy.

"How're you getting on, Ledge?"

"Fine."

"Your uncle any better?"

"No worse."

"Well, I guess that's good."

"Not really."

Rusty's red hair had been dulled by gray at his temples, but his insufferable, superior attitude hadn't mellowed a whit. Ledge couldn't bear to be in his company. He stood up and reached toward his back pocket for his wallet. "I gotta shove off."

"What's your hurry?"

"It's late."

"Not that late. Sit a spell." Rusty tipped his head down toward Ledge's barstool. "I want to talk to you about something."

He didn't need to ask Rusty what was on his mind, because he already knew. This confrontation had been inevitable since the day Arden Maxwell had turned up in Penton. He was surprised Rusty hadn't ambushed him sooner. Now that he had, at least he no longer had to dread it. He sat back down, not in concession, but in order to get the conversation over with as quickly as possible.

But Rusty seemed in no hurry to commence. He swiveled around toward the group of young men who'd wrapped up their tournament and were counting out currency to the winner.

Rusty called out, "You boys having fun over there?"

They ceased what they were doing, but none answered.

Rusty homed in on one of them. "Well, lookee who we've got here. Hawkins. I thought you were in Huntsville. Dogfighting, wasn't it?"

"Got screwed over by the system."

"The system, huh?"

"Lousy public defender made me take a plea bargain. I got two years."

"You're already out?"

"Paroled for good behavior."

"Good behavior, my ass," Rusty said. "Won't last. You'll go back."

Before the young man could retort, one of his buddies grabbed him by the arm and towed him out, the others hot on their heels.

As the door shut behind them, Rusty came back around on his stool, chuckling. "He ran a chickenshit operation out of an old barn belonging to his twin brothers. Whole tribe of white trash. Probably inbred. Name of Hawkins. Know them?"

"No."

"Well, anyway, Dwayne there was born to be wild. Reminds me of somebody else I know."

Ledge said nothing and kept his gaze forward, but out of the corner of his eye, he could see Rusty's deliberately provoking grin as he called to Don, "Maybe I'll have a Dr Pepper after all. And be generous with the ice."

With smug amusement, he continued to stare at Ledge's rigid profile while his drink was being poured. Don delivered it but didn't tarry. Rusty discarded the straw and drank directly from the glass.

He emitted a honking burp without covering it. "Well? What about it?"

Ledge didn't say anything.

"Don't play dumb. You know what, or rather *who*, I'm talking about." He leaned toward Ledge and lowered his voice. "They're baaaaack. At least one of them is. Unfortunately, it's not the old man."

Rusty leaned in a little closer. Ledge recognized the transparent attempt to intimidate him and didn't move a muscle. "What do you think about her coming back here to roost?"

"Not a damn thing."

"No?" Rusty angled back and took another drink of his

Dr Pepper, eyeing Ledge over the rim of the glass. When he lowered it, he said, "I find that hard to believe."

"Believe whatever the hell you like. It's a free country."

Rusty barked a cynical laugh. "Nothing comes free. Who would know that better than a war hero?"

Ledge glanced down the bar toward Don, who'd been polishing the same highball glass for the past several minutes, shooting furtive, worried glances in their direction.

"Must say," Rusty continued as his finger drew a trail in the condensation on the outside of his glass, "that was quite a scene she created in the supermarket."

Ledge looked at Rusty with repugnance. "She *created*? She didn't choose the timing or the place to lose her baby."

"You know what I mean. It was a *scene*." He proceeded to describe it to Ledge. When he finished, he nudged Ledge's arm with his elbow. "I have the nitty gritty, *all* the details, on good authority. But even if someone hadn't reported it straight to me, word of it spread faster than the clap."

"You would know," Ledge muttered.

Rusty grinned, took another drink, and with see-through casualness checked a loose cuticle on his thumb. "Her big sister showed up at the hospital later that evening. Did you know that?"

"No."

"Oh, yeah. Ordering everybody around. Pushy bitch. Just like she always was."

"I didn't really know her."

"No, guess not. Y'all didn't run in the same crowd." Rusty made a point of taking a look around the bar, ending on the strand of colored Christmas lights draped along the back of the bar. "Around town, Lisa Maxwell was always a golden girl." He paused. "*You*, by contrast, were raised in the back room of this pool hall."

This was the type of goading at which Rusty Dyle excelled. Ledge had expected it, but he was damned if he'd let Rusty get a rise out of him.

Instead, he looked at his wristwatch. "I'm off."

"Hold on." Rusty clamped his hand around Ledge's forearm. Ledge looked down at the restraining hand and kept looking at it until it was removed. But his silent warning didn't dissuade Rusty, who hissed, "We need to talk about this."

"No. We don't."

"How come you think she came back here? Why now?"

"I have no idea."

"Just seems peculiar," Rusty said. "In this great big *free country* of ours, wouldn't you say it's odd she picked here to nest?"

"She wanted her kid to grow up in the same house she did. What's peculiar about that?"

"Nothing. Except that she's no longer having a kid. So why's she sticking around?"

"I guess she likes it here."

"Guess she does. She's planning on fixing up the place."

Despite his determination not to react, Ledge's heart rate hitched. "How do you know?"

"She's been calling around. Getting estimates." Rusty winked. "I've been keeping tabs on her goings-on."

The thought of Rusty keeping tabs on Arden Maxwell chilled Ledge to the bone. This afternoon, she'd stood her ground with him when he was being his most contrary self. She was no pushover. But he knew Rusty's character. Or rather, his lack of it. He knew the treachery Rusty was capable of.

"Twenty years ago, she was still in grade school," Ledge said. "If you're thinking she knew anything about where her daddy got off to with that money, you're wrong."

"Am I?" Rusty leaned in again. "Think on this. The woman hasn't held a job since she left Houston—six, seven months ago—and moved here. She's got no visible means of support, but she's going to renovate that big ol' house, which will take some serious coin. Makes me wonder where she's getting the financing."

"Her sister."

"Could be. She married up. Way up. Big shot in Dallas. Then he croaked a couple years ago, leaving her not only his fortune but the reins to his company. Which is why I can't see her funding a reconnection to our little burg over here in the sticks."

In order to try to dismantle Rusty's interest in Arden and her unexpected return to town, Ledge groped his mind for other explanations. "Maybe Arden did so well at her former job, she doesn't need to work. Not for a while, at least."

Rusty shook his head. "Not likely. She sold fancy clothes at the Neiman Marcus in the Galleria. Top-dollar goods, but she worked on commission only. She didn't cash out as the retiring CEO."

"Generous alimony."

"She's never been married."

"You know that as fact?"

"Hell, yes. I checked."

Arden had deliberately dodged his probing about the identity and whereabouts of her baby's father. Admittedly, he was curious, but, for Rusty's benefit, he feigned indifference. "Then she's got a well-heeled boyfriend."

"There hasn't been a man around since she got here."

"You've been watching?" Ledge asked, maintaining his casual tone.

Rusty didn't admit to that but thoughtfully scratched his cheek. "Maybe he dumped her when he found out about the kid. He paid her off, wished her luck, then sent her on her way to have the baby alone."

"Or maybe he was a loser, and she dumped him."

"Maybe. But that brings us back to her unknown source of income." Rusty leered, whispering, "Take a wild guess."

"I'll leave the wild guessing to you."

"Okay, how's this? Daddy's had it stockpiled all these years, and has just now divvied it up."

"If that were so," Ledge said, "she could do better than to move back here."

"Money doesn't stretch as far as it used to." Rusty shook an ice cube from the glass and into his mouth. Crunching it, he said, "I intend to keep a close eye on Miss Arden Maxwell and her spending habits." He playfully socked Ledge's arm. "Same as I've kept a close watch on you, buddy."

Although Ledge wanted to deck him for touching him, he did nothing except fix a hard stare on him. "And same as I have on *you*. Buddy."

Across the short distance separating them, the two adversaries glared at each other and, in that moment, came to a meeting of the minds: The gloves were coming off. For all these years, the two of them had waged a silent war. As of now, it had been officially declared.

Don, seeming to sense the volatility of the moment, ambled over and asked Rusty if he wanted a refill.

"No thanks." Without breaking eye contact with Ledge, Rusty pushed himself off the stool. "Like I said, I just dropped in to see what Ledge has been up to." Then he flashed his crocodile grin and ambled out.

He was clear of the exit and the door had closed behind him before Don released his held breath. "You two look at each other, and smoke comes out of all four ears. Are you ever going to tell me the origin of this longstanding animosity?"

"No. But you didn't have to keep fingering that sawed-off shotgun under the bar."

Smiling wryly, Don said, "How'd you know?"

"I know."

"I probably wouldn't ever use it," Don said, "but looking at that bastard's back just now, it did cross my mind what a prime target it would make, and I don't think many in the county would mourn the passing of our illustrious DA."

Ledge continued to stare at the door through which District Attorney Rusty Dyle had exited. "One of these days I'll probably have to kill him." Then turning to Don, he added, "But when I do, I'll be looking him in the eye."

Chapter 5

———◆———

Fresh from the shower, Arden had just finished dressing when someone knocked on her front door. Looking out the window of her temporary bedroom, she was astonished to see the enormous black pickup in her driveway.

She considered not going to the door, but he would know that she was at home because her car was there. Besides, avoidance would make her look cowardly. She pushed her feet into a pair of flats. On her way out of the room, she gave herself a quick check in the mirror above the dresser and resented herself for caring about her appearance even to that extent. Her hair hadn't completely dried, and because she hadn't slept well, she looked peaked. But there was nothing to be done about it now.

As silently as possible, she approached the front door, peered through the small diamond-shaped window in its center, and was startled to be met by her own reflection looking back at her from the dark lenses of his sunglasses. He was looking straight into the window as though he'd been waiting for her face to appear.

Coolly, and with a dash of spite, she repeated the question he'd asked her yesterday. "What can I do for you?"

"Let's talk about your overhaul."

"You said discussing it would be a waste of time."

He pulled off the sunglasses. "I've rethought that."

She stepped away from the window and out of the view of those piercing eyes. She extended his wait overlong before flipping the lock.

When she opened the door, his head was tilted back. He was looking at the eaves and lightly tapping the sunglasses against his thigh. "You've got wood rot."

"That much I could have told *you*."

"Your doorbell doesn't work."

"Again. I already know that."

He lowered his head and looked at her; she looked back, hoping that her stare was as steady and held as much challenge as his. Neither moved or said anything, and she was beginning to think that this standoff would continue indefinitely when he folded the stems of his glasses and slid them into the breast pocket of his plain white oxford-cloth shirt.

"I've reconsidered taking the job."

"What changed your mind?"

"My bank statement. I balanced my checking account this morning."

She didn't know if he was joking, or trying to be charming, or if he was telling the bald truth. His expression gave away no clues.

With indecision, she caught the inside of her lower lip between her teeth. Her sleepless night had been the result of worrying over what her next step should be, since his flat refusal yesterday had left her with no remaining prospects. None that she could afford. He had made this conciliatory move, and that counted for something. Each still had the option of saying no thanks to the other.

Hoping that she wouldn't live to regret it, she opened the door wider and motioned him in.

The empty living area seemed to shrink the instant he stepped inside. His cuffs had been rolled back almost to his elbows. His shirttail was tucked into a pair of jeans, which, like yesterday's, had been softened and faded from many washings. They were worn with a belt of tooled brown leather. The antiqued brass buckle had a military insignia. But he no longer had a military haircut. In back, his dark hair was long enough to brush against his collar.

Boot heels thumping on the hardwood floor, he advanced into the room and took a slow look around. "You play the piano?"

She had anticipated a comment, not a question, and it took her off guard. "No. Well, a little. I was taking lessons when—"

At her abrupt stop, he turned his head and looked at her expectantly.

Amending what she'd been about to say, she said, "I gave up music lessons when my sister and I moved away."

"Hmm. Too bad you didn't pick back up after you got resettled."

"I regret now that I didn't continue, but other things had to be given priority."

He went over to the staircase and stepped up on the first tread with only one foot. It squeaked. So did the second step. As he backed down, he ran his palm over the bannister. "This is nice wood. Worth salvaging, I think. It could be sanded and revarnished. Maybe a lighter stain?"

She gave a noncommittal "Umm."

Returning to the center of the room, he turned in a tight circle as he surveyed the ceiling. "The crown molding has possibilities, but I won't know if it's worth keeping until I get a closer look at it, and I didn't bring a ladder today."

"I'm not particularly attached to it."

"What about that chandelier?" He pointed to the fixture in the dining area. "Does it have any sentimental value?"

"None."

"Good. I'd pitch it. It's too large for the space."

He gave the fireplace mantel the same rubdown he'd given the bannister. Stepping back and assessing the fireplace as a whole, he said, "The brick is boring. Another material would add some character."

He went over to the row of front windows and inspected the sills. Sliding a pocketknife from his back jeans pocket, he picked at the splintered wood with the tip of the blade. "All these window frames need to be replaced. If you go with wood again, it's more labor intensive and therefore more expensive. Or you could go with prefab, but that still requires some carpentry. I'll figure it both ways. How many windows in the house?"

"I've never had cause to count them."

"I'll need that number before I can give you an estimate." He closed the knife and pushed it back into his pocket. He flipped all the light switches on the wall plate, matching them to the fixtures they controlled. "What took priority?"

"Pardon me?"

"You said you quit music lessons because other things had to be given priority. Like what?"

"Like food and shelter."

Her curt reply brought him around to look at her. "When your dad skipped out, nobody stepped up and took you in? A relative? Foster parents?"

"No."

"Weren't you too young to fare for yourself?"

"I was ten, but my sister was already in her second year of college. She'd been commuting to and from Commerce, but had to drop out when she became my legal guardian."

"Tall order for a college coed."

"Yes."

"She must be one tough cookie."

Arden laughed lightly. "To say the least."

"Always an overachiever, I guess."

That comment took her by surprise. "You knew Lisa?"

"She was several classes ahead of me, and I was far beneath her notice, but I knew who she was. Everybody did. Hard not to know the homecoming queen."

Arden smiled. "That was her senior year. I think everybody in town went to the parade."

"Not me."

"Oh?"

"No, I wasn't into all that."

"What about the football game when she was crowned?"

"Missed that, too." He opened the door to the storage area beneath the stairs and poked his head inside.

"You weren't into football, either?"

He backed out of the closet. When he went to shut the door, he tested the squealing hinges. "Love football. Playing and watching."

"They why did you skip the homecoming game?" She shot him a teasing grin. "Couldn't get a date?"

"Couldn't get out of juvenile detention."

He stopped fanning the door and turned to face her. She gaped at him and waited for a punch line that never came. "You were in jail?"

Appearing rather blasé, he raised a shoulder.

"What did you do?"

"Got caught smoking weed. Back then, it was a big no-no."

She nodded absently. "Was that your only offense?"

Not so blasé, he said, "At the time."

She was digging herself in deeper, but she couldn't help but ask, "How long were you in for?"

"Long enough." He stayed still, looking directly into her eyes, then abruptly turned away. "I notice you don't have a security system."

"No."

He went over to the front door and fiddled with the lock. "This dead bolt is ancient. It wouldn't keep out anybody who wanted in. You learn about these things in juvie."

It disturbed her that he could refer to his criminal past so nonchalantly. Could she trust his reference? For all she knew, the man she had spoken with was a former cellmate.

As had happened yesterday when she realized that he knew who she was and where she lived, her thoughts went to the car that drove past each night. Including last night. And here this stranger, who looked like he could split a board in half without a saw, was testing the strength of her lock.

She blurted out, "I'm thinking of getting a dog."

He crouched near a wall, ran his fingers along the cracked baseboard, scraped at its peeling paint with his thumbnail. "You don't have an alarm system; if all your locks are like this one, they're useless; and you live out here by yourself. Do you have a weapon?"

"Weapon?"

"A gun."

"No."

"Then I'd say a guard dog is a good idea."

"I don't want a guard dog. I want a pet to keep me company."

He stood up slowly and started walking toward her, dusting his hands together as he came. When he got to within a couple of feet of her, he stopped. "I wouldn't think you'd lack for company." Then, "Let's go upstairs."

A sensation purled through her midsection.

But if she'd read a hidden invitation into his statement, she was mistaken. There wasn't any guile in his eyes, nor a trace of suggestiveness in his tone when he added, "I need to see the layout of the rooms."

"Of course." She turned away and started up the stairs, him following. She wished she'd dressed in her baggy jeans.

But if he'd taken notice of any aspect of her appearance, he didn't act as though he had. As she showed him from one room to the next, he was scrupulously professional and businesslike. He asked pertinent questions, pointed out problem spots, and offered suggestions on how to remedy them.

"See how the floor is buckled? You have a roof leak. Rain's getting in and running down inside the walls."

He frowned as he assessed the fixtures in both bathrooms. "I'd bet these look good compared to the pipes."

"One of the other contractors I interviewed foretold of a plumbing disaster."

"No argument from me."

In her old bedroom, he surveyed the ceiling. "Careful. That light fixture is barely holding on." He curved his hand around the side of her waist and moved her from beneath it.

"Thanks," she said, trying not to sound flustered.

He removed his hand a bit more slowly than necessary to save her from potential injury. Still looking down at her, he said, "I think I've seen all I need to."

When they returned to the landing, he paused and, with his hands on his hips, looked back down the long hallway. He studied it for a time, then, as though talking to himself, said, "It has possibilities."

He pondered for a moment longer, then turned and motioned that she should precede him downstairs. When they got to the first floor, he struck off for the kitchen. Once there, he took only a cursory look around, as though the outmoded appliances and cabinetry didn't warrant a more thorough inspection.

"What's in here?"

"That's where I—"

She stopped because he had already drawn up short on the threshold of the catch-all room. She hadn't yet tidied up when he arrived. The unmade bed and her nightgown, which she'd left lying on it when she went to shower, made it evident that this was where she'd slept. It was a private space, not intended for anyone else's eyes.

Especially not his.

Feeling as though more of her had been exposed than her bed, she wanted to edge around him and jerk the bedspread up for concealment. Instead, she pretended to be unaffected and offered him coffee, hoping he would decline.

Still looking into the room, his back to her, he said, "Yeah. Thanks."

The one modern appliance she had bought since moving in was a coffee machine that made various brews. Sensing that he had turned back into the kitchen, she asked if he had a preference.

"Nothing fancy. Just black coffee."

She tipped her head toward the table. "Have a seat."

He didn't sit. He crowded in beside her at the counter to look out the window above the sink. He had to duck slightly. "That cypress grove blocks any view of the lake. Ever thought of thinning it out?"

"It's so far from the house, I hadn't given it any thought at all."

"Huh."

"What?"

"Nothing. How much acreage do you have?"

"Nothing significant. Twenty maybe?"

"Some would consider that significant."

She didn't see that the size of the property had relevance, but he seemed to make a mental note of it, then walked over to the back door and tested the lock as he had on the front door. It rattled when he jiggled it. He muttered something, but Arden didn't catch what he said. He pulled open the door and looked out.

"Anything in the garage?"

It was detached from the house. A few days after moving back, she'd looked inside it, but, as remembered, it had been cleaned out. "Lisa and I had no use for tools, the lawn mower, and such. She either sold or donated everything." She didn't say, *Including Dad's car*. Arden had cried when the new owner drove away in it.

She carried two mugs of coffee to the table. He joined her there. She had never considered the chairs around the table as being too small until he sat down in the one across from her. She remembered being struck by the proportions of the rocking chair on his front porch.

He didn't use the handle on the coffee mug, but picked it up by placing his fingers around the rim. He sipped from it between his thumb and index finger. All this without taking his eyes off her.

"Who owns this place?"

"What do you mean?"

"Whose name is on the deed? Yours or your sister's?"

"Both. We own it fifty-fifty. After our mother died, Dad

had a local attorney draw up a will. He told us it was only a precaution. Should anything happen to him, Lisa and I would be provided for."

"So this will has been executed?"

She nodded.

"He's dead, then?"

"Declared to be. Wallace had—"

"Who's Wallace?"

"My late brother-in-law. He kept a regiment of lawyers on retainer. Now Lisa does."

"The lawyers had your father declared dead?"

"We waited for ten years before petitioning the court. It's a process, but at the end of it, his estate was probated. Lisa and I got clear title to the house, which we needed in order to sell it."

"But you haven't. How come? Did you always plan to come back?"

"No. Lisa certainly didn't. But she stalled on selling it for sentimental reasons. I didn't give it much thought while I was trying to establish myself."

"As what?"

"As anything," she said on a light laugh.

"Such as?"

"Well, let's see. My first job out of college was in public relations. I wrote press releases for a promising new record label in Nashville. It folded. I worked as an assistant to the curator of a New Orleans art gallery. She ran afoul of the IRS. I and a friend invested in a cupcake bakery. It went bankrupt, and so did the friendship." She stopped ticking off her failed attempts at a career and gave him a wan smile.

"You get the idea. Anyway, every once in a while, Lisa would circle back to the subject of putting the house up for sale, but she never acted on it. It had no priority. Out of sight, out of mind, I suppose. Anyway, here it's sat for all this time."

"Going to seed." He looked around the kitchen, but eventually his gaze returned to her. "Why now? Why come back and take this on?"

"None of your business."

He snuffled at her sharp rebuke. "Actually it is. If I start this project for you, and it turns out that the house doesn't even belong to you, and I get sued by somebody, I'll be up shit creek. See, I don't have a regiment of lawyers on retainer."

"I'll email you a copy of the deed."

"Are there any house plans to go with it?"

"I don't know."

"Blueprints would be helpful."

"I'll see that you get copies of everything." That would take some finagling. She hadn't yet broached the idea of renovation with Lisa, and she predicted that her reaction would be negative. On steroids.

As though reading her mind, he said, "What about your sister? Is she onboard? The house is half hers. What's she think of your project?"

"You ask a lot of questions, Mr. Burnet."

"I'm careful that way. Do you have your sister's thumbs-up?"

"In all honesty she didn't warm to the idea of my coming back here, to this town."

"Why?"

She gave him a pointed look. "I'm sure you know why."

"Yeah, I guess I do. You've got a lot to live down. I admire you for trying. But I gather your sister doesn't feel the same."

"No, she doesn't. After the loss of my baby, she urged me not to stay. I won out."

He looked at her for so long and with such intensity, she had to will herself not to squirm.

At last, he said, "Tell me what you have in mind."

"What I had in mind when I came here was to make a home for my daughter and me. Lisa's former bedroom was to have been the nursery. I was going to turn my parents' bedroom into a playroom with a built-in mom-office tucked in under the sloped ceiling in the corner."

"Good use of otherwise wasted space."

"That was the idea. And that room gets a lot of sunlight." She'd fantasized scenarios of her playing with her gurgling baby girl while dust motes danced around them.

Now, thinking back on the many domestic tableaus she had imagined, she slid her hand beneath her hair and massaged the back of her neck. Quietly, she said, "For obvious reasons, my needs have changed."

He sat there without saying anything, abnormally still, and she wondered if his ability to remain like that for an extended period of time had been a facet of his military training. It would certainly be of benefit to a soldier. But it was unsettling to anyone who came under his scrutiny while he was at it. At least to her it was disquieting.

Eventually he reached for his mug and took another sip of coffee. "Do you have a particular style in mind?"

"Something different."

"From what?"

"From what it is."

"That would entail a clean sweep."

"I realize that."

His long legs had been stretched out at an angle to the table, ankles crossed. He pulled them in now, placed his forearms on the table, and leaned toward her. "Forgive my bluntness. Can you afford this?"

"I won't know until you submit an estimate."

"Right." He thought it over. "I'll make up a list of things. Not the pretty, sexy stuff. The basics. Wiring. Plumbing. Roofing. Like that. I'll attach a high-end estimate, as well as a low-ball one. Pricing will depend a lot on your choice of materials.

"If you don't like my ideas, if you can't afford to have the work done, if you decide your sister's advice was sound and move back to Houston, all you owe me is a hundred bucks for putting in the time. Sound like a plan?"

She swallowed, but her voice still came out huskily. "Mr. Burnet? How did you know I had moved here from Houston?"

There was the merest flicker in the blue eyes before he shrugged off her question. "It's general knowledge."

She shook her head. "I haven't told a single soul."

"That's the scuttlebutt. Beats me how it got around. I don't even remember who told me."

"Like you don't remember where you were when I was pointed out to you."

He gave a huff, trying to blow it off. "Is that a big deal?"

"I don't know. Tell me why anyone would be discussing *me* with *you*."

He raised his arms at his sides. "Everybody and his grandmother has been discussing you. Because of the . . . event."

"The *event* being my personal tragedy."

"Which you suffered in public. Gossip thrives on other people's miseries."

"Yes. It does." She pressed the heels of her hands to her temples. "Just like when my father abandoned us."

"Did he abandon you?"

"What would you call it?"

"Flight."

She lowered her hands and glared at him.

Not that it had much effect. He said, "It's generally believed that he wasn't deserting you, so much as he was escaping capture."

"Is that what you believe?"

"Facts point that way. The night he went missing, Welch's store safe was cleaned out, and an employee died under mysterious circumstances. The money was never recovered, that suspicious death is still unexplained, and Joe Maxwell was never seen again. So, yeah, I'd say he's cloaked in mystery, and, like it or not, so are you."

Raising her voice, she said, "Well, I don't like it."

"Then you should have stayed gone."

She shot up out of her chair, shoved it aside, and stalked from the room. When he caught up with her, she already had the front door pulled open. "You told me yesterday that you aren't the man for the job. I couldn't agree more. Thank you for coming out this morning, but—"

He reached past her shoulder and pushed the door shut.

The suddenness of his movement alarmed her. She backed up to the adjacent wall. Her heart was thudding. "Have you been driving past this house every night?"

His chin went back a notch. "What?"

"You heard me."

"Yeah, I did." Moving slowly, he raised his hands shoulder high and took several steps backward, away from her. A cleft formed between his eyebrows. "Someone's been driving past your house?"

"Every night. Almost from the day I moved in. Even before I lost the baby."

"Have you reported it?"

She shook her head.

"Why not?"

"At first I didn't think much of it. I passed it off as

curiosity-seekers. Then after the emergency in the super-market, I didn't want to send up a flare and call further attention to myself."

He digested that, then said, "Have you made out what kind of car it is?"

She took a breath. "Is it you?"

"Why would I be driving past your house every night?"

"That's not an answer. Is it *you*?"

"No."

A simple denial. No embellishment. No telltale expression. Ergo, a perfect lie. A perfect liar. "Is lying another skill you honed while in juvenile detention?"

His jaw clenched.

She wasn't going to be deterred by his apparent anger. "The marijuana was your first offense, but it wasn't your last, was it?"

"No."

Her breathing shallow, she asked, "What other crime did you commit?"

Chapter 6

That night in 2000—Ledge

Stopping along the roadside minutes after pulling off a burglary, to conduct a meeting with your accomplices, in a ditch no less, was just one of the reasons that this whole escapade of Rusty's design was all kinds of ways fucked up.

During the planning stages, Rusty had charged Ledge with the task of driving them, and he had been okay with that. In fact, he wouldn't have had it any other way. If escape became necessary, he figured he knew more back roads than the other three. He certainly trusted himself over any of them to keep a cooler head in a tight situation.

"It only makes sense for us to convene in the parking lot of your uncle's bar," Rusty had told him during one of only three covert meetings they'd had in advance of the burglary.

"It will be hopping on a holiday Saturday night. Cars and pickups will be coming and going from happy hour till after last call. Our cars won't be noticed in the overflowing lot. You're in and out of there all the time. Christ, you live there.

So nobody will think twice about you leaving and returning an hour or so later."

As Rusty had predicted, the theft itself had been incredibly easy to pull off. When Foster opened the vault, Rusty had exhaled a short laugh. "That's a fucking lot of Easter bonnets and chocolate bunnies."

They didn't stand around congratulating one another, though. They'd hastily stuffed the banded bills into one large canvas bag provided by Foster. As they'd left with it, Ledge had halfway expected an ambush. At any given heartbeat, he'd feared spotlights hitting them, SWAT officers swarming, and a cop with a bullhorn shouting for them to drop facedown and place their hands behind their heads.

It hadn't happened. Ledge had driven them away while the same mean-looking cat that had been eating from a pile of garbage when they'd arrived was still eating from it when they'd left. Not even he had scurried for cover behind the row of dumpsters behind the store.

But now, after having made a clean getaway with their haul, when they were halfway between Welch's and the bar in the middle of freaking nowhere, Rusty told him to pull over.

"Pull over? What the hell for?" Ledge spoke for himself as well as for the two in the back seat, who shared his incredulity and were vocal about it.

"Just do it," Rusty said, squelching their chorus of protests. "We need to lay some ground rules before we split up."

The car was still rolling to a stop on the shoulder when Rusty opened the door and got out, taking the money bag into the ditch with him. The back of Ledge's neck began prickling with apprehension, and it lasted the whole while they were huddled in that damn, stinking ditch. While pretending to be cool and unruffled, he'd kept a close eye on Rusty. Ledge wouldn't put it past him to whip out a pistol and shoot the three of them right there.

As it turned out, he'd only wanted to assert his authority. The son of a bitch.

Strangely, though, Ledge felt even more uneasy now as they were climbing out of the ditch. Foster slipped, and Ledge had to lend him a helping hand. He didn't like not having his hands free, and for a fleeting moment, it occurred to him that Foster's bumbling might have been a ruse to distract him.

But all Foster did once he made it up the slope was to thank Ledge. Without further mishap, the four of them piled back into the car.

But the tension inside it was palpable. At least among three of them. Rusty appeared to be untroubled. Riding in the passenger seat, he whistled softly through his teeth and used his fingers against his knee to drum out a beat only he could hear.

They didn't meet a single vehicle as they took the turn-off toward the lakeshore and Burnet's. Ledge drove to the farthest, darkest edge of the parking lot where tree limbs were so low, the Spanish moss hanging from them brushed against the windshield.

He pulled to a stop but left the motor running. In an atmosphere of hostility and mistrust, he said, "Nobody followed us, but we'd better scatter quick."

"I agree," said Rusty. "I've said everything that needed saying."

"You said more than needed saying."

The complaint had been muttered, but Rusty heard it. "Hey, Ledge," he said conversationally, "why do you think it is that Joe doesn't do his drinking here? Why doesn't he give your uncle Henry his business? Do you reckon he thinks nobody knows he's an alky?"

The back door slammed hard enough to rock the car.

Angrily, Ledge said to Rusty, "Why not just lay off?"

"I didn't mean any offense. Truly," Rusty said with exaggerated earnestness. Then he looked into the back seat and changed his tone to a threatening one. "Foster, if you fuck up, we're all fucked."

"I won't. I promise." The accountant scrambled out and disappeared into the maze of vehicles.

Rusty opened the passenger door and pulled the canvas bag from the floorboard. He patted it affectionately and grinned across at Ledge. "Well, see you around, partner."

Moving faster than Rusty could blink, Ledge's right arm cut an arc across the console, his fingers locking around Rusty's wrist like bands of iron. "Hear me, and hear me good, you prick. You had better hope that nothing bad happens to my uncle or this place, because if something does, I'm gonna assume you're behind it, and I'll come after you, and I will kill you."

Knowing he'd made himself understood, he released Rusty as swiftly as he'd grabbed him. Rusty appeared too shocked, too afraid maybe, to move. Then he climbed out with the bag and closed the door.

Ledge put the car in gear and drove away, out of the parking lot.

Although he realized that his uncle and Don could use an extra pair of hands on such a busy night, he couldn't face them just yet. They would know right away that something was bothering him, and when they probed him for a reason, he would have to lie, and they would detect that, too.

His getting caught smoking pot and having to go to detention had come as a disappointment to his uncle. But Henry had been unwavering in his support. They had weathered that dim chapter in Ledge's life without Henry losing all faith in him.

So God forbid that Henry ever find out what he'd done tonight. Sick over the mere thought of that possibility, he headed back toward town and Crystal's house. He could shelter there with her for a while. She didn't require him to make conversation.

The squad car's flashers didn't come on until it was right on his tail, and the lights nearly blinded him, causing him to swerve toward the shoulder.

He braked hard and skidded to a stop in the gravel.

His heart began racing. His breathing turned choppy. Mentally chanting, *No way they could know. No way they could know,* he watched the two sheriff's deputies in his side mirrors as they approached, one on each side of the car. He placed his hands on the steering wheel at ten and two.

The one who came to the driver's side shone a flashlight in his face. "Hey there, Ledge." He kept the beam of his flashlight on Ledge's face, while the other, on the passenger side, swept his over the interior of the car. Ledge wondered if there was mud from the ditch on the floorboard. *Shit!*

"Keep your hands where I can see them, Ledge," the deputy instructed. "Open the door slow, and get out."

"What did you stop me for?"

"Get out," he repeated.

Ledge did as ordered. "Why'd you stop me?"

"Assume the position."

"You gotta be kidding."

"Do I look like I'm kidding?"

"I wasn't even speeding."

"Assume the position!" the officer shouted.

Ledge turned and placed his hands on the roof of the car and set his feet wide apart. While the deputy was patting him down, the other was rifling through his glove box. "There's nothing in there," Ledge said.

"Where are you keeping your stash these days?"

"I don't have a stash."

"What? You gave up smoking dope for Lent?"

"I gave it up after being put in jail only for sharing a joint with friends at a party."

"Every druggie has a sob story." The deputy said to his partner, "Pop the trunk."

Ledge said, "There's nothing in there but a tire iron and a spare."

"You wouldn't lie to us, would you?"

"No."

"Well, we got a tip saying you were selling out of your car on the parking lot of your uncle's bar."

"That's bullshit."

"Somebody saw you chatting with a group of people inside your car."

Ledge broke a cold sweat.

"Have you graduated from using to dealing, Ledge? Were you having a get-together with customers, or competitors?"

He knew not to say anything more. Some lessons learned in juvie were valuable.

"Give us names, Ledge. Who were you meeting with?"

My accomplices.

The deputy prodded him in the spine. "Cat got your tongue? What have you been up to tonight, Ledge?"

From the opened trunk, the second deputy chortled. "Unless he can come up with a real good alibi, it's back to jail he goes for dealing."

"I'm not dealing."

"Then you must be planning on staying high every day for the rest of your life."

The deputy frisking him whistled. "I hope you have a good lawyer and a better alibi."

Ledge dropped his head forward and snorted a bitter laugh.

The deputy jabbed his backbone again. "You think that's funny?"

No, there was nothing funny about it. But, at the very least, it was ironic.

He had a killer of an alibi.

He'd been stealing half a million dollars.

Chapter 7

In reply to Arden's question about his criminal history, Ledge was accurate, if not quite truthful. She had asked what crime he'd *committed*. It wasn't the one he'd been arrested for.

"A lot of smoke was found in a bag in the trunk of my car. More than one would have on hand for personal use. I was booked for possession with the intention to sell."

"A more serious offense," she said.

"And I was two years older. Not quite eighteen, but charged as an adult."

"Were you guilty?"

"I was set up."

"Isn't that what all criminals say?"

"I'm not all criminals. It happens to be the truth."

Gazing up at him were wide eyes the color of a smooth, expensive bourbon, the kind that warmed the belly. Only a few minutes ago, her eyes had been sparking with anger. Now he saw in them only apprehension.

Small but telling, involuntary, feminine motions—hooking

her hair behind her ear, shifting her weight from one foot to another, wetting her lips—were indications of her uneasiness. He made a lot of people uneasy. But usually it didn't bother him. With her, it did.

"Are you afraid of me?"

Without equivocating, she said, "I haven't made up my mind."

"If you're that unsure, it means you are. I sensed it the minute I darkened the door. You've been on edge the whole time I've been here. How come?"

"Well," she said around a mirthless laugh, "because somebody is coming past my house every night, and that's creepy."

"I ask again, why would I do that?"

"I can't come up with a single reason."

"Then why have you singled me out as a suspect?"

"Because before we had exchanged two sentences yesterday, you treated me with hostility."

"I wasn't hostile. Inhospitable, maybe."

"Why?"

"Not many people just show up at my house." Especially not Joe Maxwell's kid. Joe Maxwell's kid all grown up and…and filled out.

"I had called."

"Not to say that you were coming. And when you got there, you admitted that I was your last resort."

"Which should have made you want to win me over."

"Not my style."

"You've made that apparent." She studied him, her brow furrowed. "What did you do in the military?"

"How'd you know about that?"

"The man I called for a reference told me. He said you fought in the Middle East."

"That's right."

"What branch of the service?"

"Army. Special Forces."

"What was your specialty?"

"Killing the enemy."

She took a swift breath. "I see."

"No, you don't. And if I tried to describe the warfare I engaged in, it would scare the living daylights out of you." Realizing that his heavy-handed tone was probably doing that already, he modulated it. "I apologize for yesterday. Sometimes I come across as rude when I don't mean to be." She gave him a look, and he added, "Okay, and sometimes I mean to be.

"But you don't have to be afraid of me. I'm not the creep driving past every night. If I was, and up to no good, why haven't I attacked you in the hour I've been here?"

When she failed to respond, he became annoyed. "Look, if you can't get past this, I don't want to work for you. I'm not going to sign on to do the project and then be constantly on guard for fear of spooking you."

"Like slamming a door."

He raked his fingers through his hair. "Sorry about that. I reacted too quick. Comes from soldiering in a war zone when your ass could get capped at any second."

He took a wider stance and was about to say that he was over having to defend himself, but reasoned that belligerence would only increase her apprehension. He needed her to hire him so he could keep an eye on her. He needed to act as a buffer between her and Rusty, at least until Rusty backed off the notion that she had stacks of stolen cash lying around.

He changed tactics. "I can do the job. There's a lot here to work with, and the job would be a welcome change from mending sagging porches and getting closet doors to hang straight. So? What's it to be?"

She looked down at the floor. He stared at the crown of her head while she deliberated for what seemed like ages.

When she raised her head, she said, "I'll sleep on it."

That pissed him off. He figured she was now being either coy or stubborn.

"You've got until noon tomorrow to let me know." He reached for the doorknob, then halted, and with exaggerated slowness, turned it gently and pulled open the door.

Looking piqued, she asked, "What happens at noon?"

"I start accepting the jobs I've put on hold."

She gave a curt nod.

Straddling the threshold, he reached into his back pocket for his wallet and took a business card from it, passing it to her. "Sometimes I don't hear the shop phone. Call the second number. That's my cell. It'll vibrate."

He stepped out onto the porch and slid on his sunglasses.

"Ledge?"

He came back around and saw that she had read his name aloud off the business card. Looking up at him, she said, "Until now, I didn't know what the ell stood for."

"Ledge Burnet? Where did you dredge up that name?"

"I met him yesterday."

"How did that come about?"

"I went in search of him at his place of business."

"The pool hall?"

"Pool hall?"

Lisa laughed shortly. "Let's back up and start over."

After seeing Ledge Burnet off, Arden had replayed his visit

in her mind several times and concluded that, although fear might have been an overreaction on her part, she did have reason to be leery of him.

He'd lied about learning through the grapevine that she had moved here from Houston. The only person who knew that was the OB to whom she had been referred by her doctor in Houston. His practice wasn't even in Penton, but in the nearest larger city of Marshall. Neither he nor anyone on his staff would have disclosed patient information.

Someone else was Ledge Burnet's informant. But who? And why would he be reluctant to identify him or her?

Then there was the matter of the door locks. He'd paid a lot of attention to their insufficiency.

That sudden move when he'd slammed the door behind her had been startling, but even when he was sitting perfectly still, his sheer physicality was intimidating.

On the flip side, she couldn't think of a reason why he would be cruising nightly past her house. It had seemed to trouble him that someone had been. When he'd started his pickup truck as he'd left, the rumble of its engine wasn't the one she heard each night.

Nevertheless, before awarding him the job, she wanted more information, and she had no one else to ask about him except Lisa. She'd needed to check in with her sister anyway. They hadn't spoken for several days.

"If you're talking about the boy I'm thinking of," Lisa said, "he was riffraff."

Boy? He was definitely no longer a boy. She also thought Lisa's terminology was a bit over the top. "He said that he was beneath your notice."

"I knew who he was, but only because of his reputation," Lisa said. "His *bad* reputation. I think he was incarcerated at least once."

"He must have turned things around at some point. He served in the military for years."

"So he's reformed and living in Penton?"

He was living in Penton. Arden wasn't certain that he'd undergone a reformation. "What was that about a pool hall?"

"You should remember the place. We had to drive past it to get to Mabel's."

The family's Friday night tradition had been having dinner at Mabel's on the Lake. "All-you-can-eat catfish for twelve ninety-nine," Arden murmured. "Mabel lost money on Dad. He could pack it away."

Lisa laughed again. "We had some good times."

Then their mother had been killed, and all that had changed.

After a short lull, Lisa said, "Anyway, Ledge Burnet. That beer joint that looks like it's growing up out of the lake? It belongs to Ledge's uncle. Or at least it did. It may have collapsed by now."

"Burnet's Bar and Billiards!" Arden exclaimed with sudden recollection. "He's that Burnet?"

"He and his uncle lived on the premises."

"Just the two of them? What about his parents?"

"God knows. I never heard mention of them. Only him and his uncle and that bar. Not exactly a healthy environment for a boy to grow up in, which I guess explains his brushes with the law."

"He has his own business now." Arden fingered the white business card with his name and contact information printed in a no-nonsense font in bold black ink. No flourishing logo. Nothing gimmicky. No frills. Very much like the man.

"What kind of business?"

Lisa's question pulled her from musing over what the right

kind of physique could do for a plain white shirt and blue jeans. "Uh, he's a contractor. Of sorts."

"Of what sort?"

"Carpentry. Home repairs." She minimized the scope of the job, needing to work up to suggesting a complete renovation. "He works alone."

"You interviewed this former jailbird to do repairs on our house?"

"I didn't know he was a former jailbird when I interviewed him."

"Well, now that I've told you—"

"*He* told me. He was very straightforward about it." Less straightforward about how he knew her recent history.

"He sounds like a glorified handyman," Lisa said, "and he can't be the only one in Penton."

"No, but he's affordable, and he comes highly recommended."

That was a stretch. She'd obtained only one reference. She didn't know just *how* affordable he was because she hadn't yet seen his estimate. One could wonder then why she was trying to sell Lisa on him when she wasn't sold herself.

"Arden," Lisa said in the manner that always preceded a lament. "Please pack up and leave there. Tonight."

"We've been over this. A thousand times."

"I've done as you asked. I backed away and cut you some slack. I've tried to be understanding and supportive of your insistence on staying there. If that's what you thought would make you happy, I wanted it to work out for you."

"I feel a 'however' coming."

"However, I'm afraid it will be—"

"Another venture doomed to failure."

"The prospects aren't looking good. For chrissake, you're hiring a convict."

"I haven't decided on him."

"What repairs are we talking about? How extensive will they be?"

"Update the plumbing. Replace some light fixtures. He's going to come back to me with options, so nothing's been decided yet."

Lisa hesitated, then said quietly, "I could alleviate your having to decide anything."

"That sounds like a veiled threat."

"You could think of it that way, or you could think of it as my providing a safety net to prevent you from making another bad decision."

"Out with it, Lisa."

"The house is half mine. Plumbing, rewiring require city inspections. I don't wish to become ensnared in civic red tape in that crappy town."

It was as though Ledge had forecast that Lisa might take this position. "For twenty years you've ignored this house, but now that I've taken an interest in it, you're up in arms."

Lisa sighed. "You're right. Never mind my personal aversion to that place. How costly will these repairs be?"

"I've received estimates that were over budget. Burnet hasn't submitted his yet."

"What was your budget?"

"That's my business."

"Are you dipping into your trust fund from Wallace? Or is your married boyfriend helping you financially?"

Arden saw red. "I'm hanging up now, Lisa, before we say things we'll regret."

"Hold on. I'm sorry. That was totally uncalled for." She paused and took a breath. "I promise not to be so testy, if you'll not be so hasty."

"As I said, nothing's been decided yet. I told Mr. Burnet that I would sleep on it and let him know tomorrow."

"Do you really think he's reputable?"

"He hasn't given me a reason to think otherwise."

"I've given you several."

"You would judge him today based on what he did as a teenager? You, *we*, of all people should know how it feels to be looked upon with prejudgment and suspicion."

"True, but I would feel better if I knew about his present standing in the community. Is he a stable and upstanding member of the community? Is he a member of the Chamber of Commerce? Is he married? Does he have a family?"

Arden didn't have the answers to those questions.

Lisa was ahead of her. "I'll see what I can find out about his current status."

"I wish you wouldn't."

"I'll be discreet. In the meantime, please promise me that you won't sign a contract with him, or make a down payment, or do anything that will commit you. Not until we've had another chance to discuss it. I don't want you to make another mistake."

"If you're referring to my baby, Lisa, she wasn't a mistake."

"I didn't mean—"

But Arden hung up, too angry to listen to any more.

It was a lively place. Happy hour was in full swing. Brooks & Dunn were pumping through the speakers. There was noisy activity at all the billiards tables. Several men were clustered in front of a large-screen TV, watching a baseball game. At a table running along the far wall, a group of senior ladies, wearing feather boas and gaudy tiaras, were having a giggly, grand time.

Arden had to wait for several minutes before a barstool became free. She quickly claimed it. The bartender acknowledged her with a jerk of his chin as he filled two mugs with tapped beer. He swapped a few words with the couple he served, then made his way down the bar to her.

"Hi, there." With a magician's smooth skill, he removed the last patron's glass and swiped the bar clean with a white towel. "First time in?"

"How did you know?"

"Because I've never seen you before, and I would remember. Welcome. My name's Don."

"A pleasure." She didn't give him her name, but she shook the hand he extended.

He slid a cardboard coaster in front of her. "What can I get you?"

She looked over at the table of ladies, who were laughing so hard, several were dabbing tears from their eyes. "Birthday party?" she asked.

He grinned. "Bachelorette party. The one with the spangles on her blouse is the bride. She's getting married on Saturday."

Arden laughed. "First marriage?"

"Second. She and the groom have known each other since they were kids. Married, had families, lost their mates a year apart. Found new love."

"That's certainly something to celebrate. Pour me a glass of the same wine."

He winked. "I'll pour you a better one."

He removed a bottle of wine from the refrigerator under the back bar and showed her the label. Although she didn't recognize it, she nodded approval. He poured enough for her to sample. "Light, crisp and very good," she said. "Thank you."

He filled her glass, but, after checking to see that he wasn't needed by another customer, he stayed. "Are you with the naturalists group?"

She shook her head.

"There's a two-day symposium on ecosystems and conservation going on over at the civic center. I thought maybe you might be in town for that."

"No."

"You live here or roundabouts?"

"I've been here for a few months. I've considered making it permanent."

"I hope you do, and that you become a regular customer."

"It looks as though you don't lack for—"

She spotted the framed photograph on the back bar, and it stopped her cold. The bartender turned his head, then came back around. "If it was enlarged it would look like a movie poster, wouldn't it?"

"A Mad Max movie."

He chuckled. "That's the owner's nephew. Without all the gear, he looks only a little ferocious. In fact, ladies of all ages pine after him."

Arden took a sip of wine. "What does his wife think of that?"

"He's never married. Soldiered for a long time, then when he got home, there were other things to see to. Top off that glass?"

"No, I'm fine, thank you."

"Let me know when you need another." He excused himself to attend two men in angler hats who'd just come in. He called them by name and asked if they'd had any luck on the lake.

Well, she'd had one of Lisa's questions about Ledge

answered. Although Lisa had probably learned Ledge Burnet's marital status before she had.

"Excuse me?"

Arden turned. One of the ladies from the bachelorette party was standing behind her, smiling tentatively. "Ms. Maxwell? I thought it was you."

Arden regarded her for several moments before recognition dawned. Gray hair. A blue-and-white-striped shirt. Pleasant face and kind eyes. "You're the lady who helped me in the store."

"I wasn't sure you would remember me." She smiled and stuck out her hand. "Lois Miller."

Arden shook her hand, then clasped it between hers. "I remember how extremely kind you were that day."

"I didn't learn who you were until after." She paused as though about to say more before thinking better of it. Arden was relieved she didn't bring up her family or her return to Penton.

"I'm glad you came over and introduced yourself, Mrs. Miller. I've regretted not knowing how to contact you so I could thank you."

"I was so sorry to hear about your baby. I wish there was something I could have done to—"

"There was nothing to be done. It couldn't have been prevented. Your presence of mind and kindness were very helpful."

"Oh, I didn't do anything. Not like that young woman who calmed you down with deep breathing."

"She was dressed in yoga clothes. I would like to thank her, too. Do you know who she is?"

"No. I'm sorry, I don't." She looked remorseful, then her face brightened, and she motioned to the picture on the back bar. "Ledge was the only person there I recognized."

Arden's insides went into a free fall. Stunned, she divided a look between the photograph and the well-meaning woman's smiling face. "Ledge?" said huskily.

"Ledge Burnet. The soldier in the picture. This is his uncle Henry's place."

"Yes. The bar…bartender told me who he is." She swallowed dryly. "He was in the store that day? Are you sure?"

The older woman gave Arden an odd look. "Well, yes, honey. I can't claim to be closely acquainted with Ledge, but he's hard to mistake. And he was right there the whole time. It was him holding you till the paramedics arrived."

He was *there*? *Holding her*?

"I thought for sure you would remember him."

Absently, Arden shook her head. "No." *Holding her*?

"Well, with what you were going through, that's understandable." She reflected a moment. "He was ready to throttle a man who took your picture on his cell phone. After they wheeled you out, Ledge bore down on him, dropped a few f-bombs, and threatened to stuff his phone where the sun don't shine. He hung around, too, with several of us, waiting till we got word. Again, I'm very sorry."

"Thank you."

A fresh round of laughter erupted from the party table. Lois Miller looked over her shoulder in that direction, then said to Arden, "We're telling naughty jokes. That one must've been a doozy."

Arden worked at holding her smile steady. "You had better rejoin the party before you miss another one."

She patted Arden's shoulder. "I'm glad we got to chat. And really glad to see you looking so well." She glanced at the picture. "If you come out here often enough, you're bound to run into Ledge. You'll have a chance to thank him, too."

Chapter 8

———◦◉◦———

Rusty rolled off his wife and flopped onto his back. She took a lot more effort than she was worth. After giving himself a couple of minutes to regain his breath, he swung his feet to the floor and bent down to retrieve his discarded trousers and undershorts, then got up and started for the bathroom.

From her side of the bed, she asked, "You're getting up?"

"Go back to sleep."

"I was hardly asleep."

"Could've fooled me." He shut the bathroom door.

Judy called something through it, but he caught only the bitterness behind the words, not the words themselves, and they didn't matter anyway. He took a shower just long enough to wash off his sweat, then dried hastily and went back into the bedroom.

Judy had turned onto her side, her back to him, the sheet pulled up over her shoulders. He took a pair of track shorts and a t-shirt from his chest of drawers and put them on, then headed for the door.

From the depths of her pillow, Judy mumbled, "Joey has a playoff game tomorrow at four-thirty."

Joey was their oldest. He was a freshman in high school and already hoping for a college baseball scholarship. Rusty was hoping he would get one, too. Joey's sister and little brother were close behind him in age. Having to funnel money into three institutes of higher learning at the same time made Rusty want to drive his fist through the wall.

He said, "I'll make it if I can."

Judy flopped onto her back and came up on her elbows. "If his team wins that game, they'll play for the championship."

"I'll be there *if I can*."

"Asshole."

"Love you, too, sweetie."

"I know what you do in your man cave."

"You don't know shit and never have."

"You lurk on porn websites. It's pathetic."

"Take a look in the mirror, see how your tits have gone south and your ass has spread. *That's* pathetic."

"While you've got your hand in your pants and dreaming about Crystal Ivers, think about what she's doing to Ledge Burnet." She licked her lips.

He slammed out of the room, her disparaging laughter trailing him.

Judy had been a freshman looker when she was introduced to him at a fraternity party at Stephen F. Austin. When he learned that her family owned a fleet of logging trucks that did a thriving business in timber-rich East Texas, he regarded her not only as a pretty and sought-after coed, he saw dollar signs.

He moved quickly to secure her and her family's affluence. They got engaged over Christmas break. By the time he'd graduated in the spring, he had wooed her into dropping out of college and marrying him. He'd told her she didn't need a college education to be Mrs. Rusty Dyle. Dumb her thought he was joking. Down the overly decorated aisle of First Methodist they had marched. Joey was born before their first anniversary.

Determined not to let her taunts ruin the remainder of the night for him, he made his way down the darkened upstairs hallway. No lights shone beneath their kids' closed doors. He went downstairs, and, out of habit, checked to see that the alarm was set, although he set it religiously.

He'd had the elaborate security system installed after a prosecutor in a neighboring county had been gunned down by a disgruntled ex-con recently released. Broad daylight. Middle of the street. In cold blood.

Rusty's daddy always told him that if he played the game right, he would be the Big Dick that everyone was afraid of and that nobody would dare to cross. He hoped his legion of enemies had gotten that memo.

He went into his study, the room Judy had dubbed his man cave. He locked the door behind him, poured himself a neat vodka, booted up his computer, and settled into his soft leather chair to enjoy the evening's entertainment.

But Judy's ridicule had soured him on it tonight.

On his way home from work, he'd driven the route that took him past Crystal's place. She owned two corner lots in the center of town that backed up to each other. Crystal's Hair and Nail Salon faced the commercial street, her house faced the residential one.

She ran a successful business, having made more of herself than one would expect from a woman with such a mucky background. Judy was one of the few women in town who wasn't a loyal customer of the salon. His wife wouldn't wipe dog shit off her shoes on the doormat of the place.

Other women, though, flocked to it, none seeming to remember or care about the rumors that had circled Crystal like turkey buzzards when she was younger. The hell of it was that Crystal seemed to care the least of anybody about those rumors. Over time, she had developed an elegance and poise that Rusty resented. Her newfound confidence, in combination with the provocative allure she'd always had, only made her more desirable...and unattainable.

Burnet never had been bothered by the gossip about her.

Her salon was closed when Rusty had driven past tonight, so he'd turned the corner to the front of her house. Through the window blinds, he had detected the flicker of a television. There had been two cars in the driveway, Crystal's and Marty's.

A while back, Crystal had invited a friend, who'd needed a place to stay following a nasty divorce, to move in with her. Rusty delighted in the thought of Burnet's reaction to that arrangement. Up till then, he'd had Crystal all to himself, anytime he wanted her. His truck hadn't been out front when Rusty drove past this evening.

He snickered at the thought of Burnet being deprived. Bet he wished he'd married Crystal when he got out of the army. Everybody had expected it. Rusty had spent months after Burnet got home dreading it. He still did. But it hadn't happened. Burnet wasn't in sole possession of Crystal yet. Not officially anyway.

Nevertheless the images that Judy—that bitch—had conjured up enraged him. Crystal and Burnet. Naked and sweaty. Her begging for more, more. Him obliging.

If that wasn't reason enough to want to kill Burnet, he was also now edging in on the Maxwell girl. Arden.

Oh, yeah, Ledge Burnet had been right there with her when she slipped her kid in the produce aisle.

During their conversation in the bar last night, Ledge had acted uninterested in Joe's youngest, even after Rusty disclosed that he knew Ledge had been there during her emergency situation. Burnet had dismissed his involvement, of course. He was a fucking hero, after all. Modesty went with the territory.

But Rusty wasn't dumb enough to believe that Burnet's being Johnny-on-the-spot that day had been a coincidence.

According to people who witnessed the incident and told Rusty about it later, Burnet and Arden had entered the store separately, hadn't looked at each other, hadn't spoken. They had appeared to be totally unaware of each other until she went to the floor. He was told that Ledge happened to be nearby and did what any decent human being would do. Someone had said, "Ledge helped out, is all."

"Bullshit," Rusty said now as he took a gulp of vodka.

It had been reported to him today that Burnet had been seen on the road that led to the Maxwell property. He'd been headed back toward town, but where had he been? Wasn't much else out that way except the Maxwells' place.

The timing of it couldn't be pooh-poohed, either. Last night he and Burnet had had a lengthy discussion about Arden, and *today* Ledge had been within a couple miles of her house, when his was on the other side of town?

"No. Uh-huh," Rusty muttered as he refilled his glass. "I wasn't born yesterday."

But what did the Maxwell girl think of Burnet? During the months she'd been back, Rusty hadn't heard of her making any local friends, socializing, or mixing or mingling anywhere. It seemed she kept pretty much to herself out there and lived like a nun.

Well, she had fucked somebody, hadn't she? But who? And where was her baby's daddy now? He remained a mystery. In fact, a *lot* of mysteries swirled around Miss Arden Maxwell, the chief one being the whereabouts of her thieving father, who had made off with Rusty's half a mil.

Folks thought Joe had gotten off scot-free.

But in Rusty Dyle's book, nobody got off scot-free.

———◦———

The clock on Arden's nightstand read eleven twenty-two. Her drive-by had made his round, but still she couldn't sleep.

She was so angry over what she'd learned from the unwitting Lois Miller that she punched her pillow extra hard as she turned onto her side and tried to find a more comfortable position.

From the top of the dresser, an oscillating fan blew a gentle stream of cool air across her. It also provided a lulling white noise. She closed her eyes and willed herself to relax by engaging in a meditative exercise that eased tension out of muscles.

But two minutes into this sleep-inducing drill, a noise shattered her concentration and jerked her bolt upright.

The fan hummed; it didn't clank.

When the sound came again, she threw off the sheet and slipped out of bed. She crept to the door that connected to the kitchen, where the range light shed a soft glow. The door stood ajar. She peered through the crack.

Ledge Burnet was standing just inside the back door, leaning with his back against it, arms folded, ankles crossed. "See how useless that lock is?"

His arrogance made her want to kill him. She raised her right hand and aimed her pistol at him. "What the hell are you doing here?"

"Proving my point." Upon seeing the pistol, his natural

squint had narrowed. Otherwise he remained exactly as he was.

"Get out of my house."

"You lied about having a gun."

"Well, I wasn't going to announce it to a potential intruder, and I was right to be suspicious of you."

"Do you know how to use it?"

"Yes."

"Who taught you?"

"I had lessons."

"How long ago?"

"When I bought the gun."

"And when was that?"

"A few years ago I worked in an art gallery in the French Quarter. Sometimes I had to close up for the night. I thought—Why do you need to know?"

"Because the gun under review is in your hand, and it's aimed at me."

"Because you broke into my house."

"Put the gun down. You're not going to shoot me."

"What are you doing here?"

"I told you. I—"

"You could have proven your point about the locks this morning. Why wait until this time of night?"

"So the lesson would be more effective." He frowned. "But if I'd known about the gun, I might have revised my plan."

"By calling ahead?"

"No, by coming through an unlocked window and catching you in bed."

She was ashamed of the images that sprang to mind. They were totally out of keeping with the situation. "Why are you dressed like that?"

"It's camouflage."

"I know what it is. Why are you wearing it?"

"Why does anybody?"

"And the face paint?"

"It's dirt, not paint. The moon came out. I used what was available." He unfolded his arms and lowered them to his sides. "Set the gun down."

"Not yet."

"You're not going to shoot me."

"Don't be so sure."

"I'm certain you won't."

"Oh? How's that?"

He tipped his chin down toward the firearm. "The thumb safety's on."

She reacted by looking down at the pistol. The instant she did, he sprang forward, grabbed her wrist, and literally shook the gun out of her hand and into his waiting palm. She uttered a soft cry. As he released her wrist, he swore viciously.

Glaring at her, he pointed down to the pistol. "This particular model doesn't even *have* a thumb safety." He popped the clip out, then worked the slide. As a round was ejected, he cursed again. "It did, however, have a bullet in the chamber. You could have killed me."

"Which would have served you right for scaring me half to death."

"Yeah, well, you scared me, too." He set the pistol and clip on the table. "Don't touch those." Going over to the sink, he turned on the faucet, bent over to wash the soil off his face, and ripped several paper towels from the holder.

"There's a trash can in the cabinet under the sink," she said.

He used the towels to dry his face and hands, then tossed them, and turned back to her. "You really shouldn't have—"

Before he could finish, she interrupted. "Why didn't you tell me you were in the supermarket that day?"

Chapter 9

*W*ell, *fuck.*

He didn't say it out loud. He didn't say anything for fear of giving away more than she already knew.

"Do you deny it?" she asked.

"No."

"Why didn't you tell me?"

"I thought it might make you uncomfortable."

"It made me uncomfortable learning it from someone other than you."

"What difference would it have made if you'd known?"

"Exactly!" She jabbed her index finger toward him.

When she did that, her breasts moved beneath her nightgown, and that drew his eyes to them, which made her aware of something he'd been keenly aware of since she'd confronted him: She didn't have many clothes on.

In fact, the nightie was it.

"Don't leave until we've had this out." She went into the bedroom and slammed the door behind her.

He ran his hand over his mouth and chin and around the back of his neck. He should have anticipated this. She was bound to find out sooner or later. He'd been busted. He had just as well face the music.

He opened the refrigerator and helped himself to a bottle of water, uncapped it, and chugged it.

When she came back into the kitchen, she was wearing a pair of Christmas-plaid pajama bottoms, a gray hoodie zipped up to her chin, and fuzzy slippers. A knight of the round table couldn't have been better armored. She set her cell phone—decisively—on the table near the pistol. He supposed that both were to serve as warnings that he had better not get out of line.

"Want some water?" he asked.

"No."

He placed his empty in the trash can. When he came back around, she looked ready to launch.

"I went to your uncle's bar this evening."

"I get the feeling you didn't just stumble upon it."

"No. I went there on a fact-finding mission."

"Facts about me? Why didn't you ask?"

"Because I didn't want to be lied to."

He figured he had that coming.

"I met Don," she said. "He was very pleasant."

"A job requirement."

"We had an enlightening chat."

"Don didn't tell you that I was in the store that day, because he doesn't know. You must've chatted with someone else."

"Lois Miller."

"Don't know her."

"Well, Lois knows you. You're hard to mistake."

He couldn't account for the emphasis she placed on that, although she looked him up and down as she said it.

"You should remember her. Seventy-ish. You were right there with her. The whole time, she said. You, she, and another woman. Younger. Dressed for yoga. Is any of this jogging your memory?"

He ignored her sarcasm. "I remember."

"So?"

"The older lady hovered. The younger one went into action. She helped you to lie back. I was there to sort of..." He held out his hands, palms up. "Keep you off the floor."

She looked at him curiously, making him wonder just how descriptive this Lois person had been. Had she told Arden that he'd rested her head in the hollow where his rib cage divided, that his hands had cradled her shoulder blades while that younger woman coached her on breathing?

He remembered looking at the gray-haired lady to get her read on what was happening and receiving only a worried frown and a sad shake of her head.

That might have been when he'd slid his hand from beneath Arden's back long enough to brush a silky, stray curl off her cheek. The sequence of events during that eternal wait for the ambulance ran together and blurred in his memory, but he remembered the feel of her hair. Too well.

"Lois told me that you attacked a man for taking my picture."

"Attacked? No."

"Verbally."

"He was a jackal."

It had been a crass invasion of Arden's privacy for the guy to take her picture in those circumstances, but Ledge conceded that he might have overreacted. Unknowingly, the fellow had triggered a memory of Afghanistan. Pinned down and helpless to prevent it, Ledge had watched as men photographed soldiers already dead, their bodies butchered post-mortem, some American, some their own countrymen.

"No mercy for jackals," he mumbled.

He could tell by Arden's expression that she didn't grasp the subtext, but she didn't deviate from the subject. "You stayed in the store with Lois and a few others, waiting to find out..." She let the rest go unspoken.

"It seemed the decent thing to do."

She was still regarding him in that curious, almost wary, manner. "Well, this explains how you recognized me yesterday when I came to your shop," she said. "But it makes me wonder why you didn't take credit for your involvement that day."

"Because only a prick would take credit."

"That's the only reason?"

"Sensitive subject like that, I didn't want to embarrass you."

She nodded, but not like she wholeheartedly accepted that explanation. Shaking off the pensive demeanor, she drew herself up straighter. "My visitor drove past."

"When?"

"A couple of hours ago."

"Damn. I got here an hour too late."

"You've been lying in wait?"

"Down there by the road, hoping I'd catch him at it."

"That explains the camo getup."

"For all the good it did me. Are you sure it was your regular?"

"Yes, I recognize the sound of the motor."

"What's it sound like?"

She gave a shrug of confusion. "A car. But it does have a distinctive sound."

He tried to make sense of that, but it escaped him.

"Where's your truck?"

"Parked in the cypress grove." He thumbed in the general

direction. "I used a road that brought me in from the west to the back of your property. I walked from there."

"So I wouldn't know you were here."

"So *he* wouldn't know."

"I doubt he would have spotted you. Out there in the dark, you would have been well concealed."

Had she put on that ungodly outfit to conceal herself from him? If so, she'd been too late. He'd gotten a tantalizing eyeful while she was waggling that nine-millimeter at him. Underneath her short nightgown, the dips and distentions had been impossible not to notice, and even more impossible to ignore. As was the disturbance they'd created below his belt.

"Well?"

He realized she had continued talking while his mind had drifted to shapely bare legs and a slipping shoulder strap. "I'm sorry, what?"

Exasperated, she said, "Did you come here tonight to see if the bogeyman was real or a figment of my imagination?"

"I believe he's real."

"Thank you for taking my word for it."

"I didn't. Animal instinct."

"Oh, really? Is your animal instinct so reliable that you always act on it?"

He waited a beat. "Not always." Another beat. "Bad as I want to."

His suggestiveness wasn't intentional. Or maybe it was. But in any case, the words caused a subtle but definite shift, not only a straying from the topic of discussion, but a change in the current between them, a thickening of the room's atmosphere. He felt the increase of air pressure in every cell of his body. The ticking of the wall clock seemed to be keeping beat with something other than passing seconds.

She must have sensed it, too, because she didn't say anything, or move, and her eyes stayed locked with his, as though any reaction might trigger something uncertain and unsafe.

Then her cell phone jangled, and she jumped like she'd been scalded.

She shuffled backward away from him and glanced down at the phone where it lay on the table. "My sister. I'd better get it." She picked up the phone and clicked in. "Hi."

"Were you asleep?"

Still looking directly at him, Arden said, "No, I'm wide awake."

The voice coming through the phone was as clear as a bell to him, but Arden didn't retreat to conduct the conversation in private, so he didn't retreat to grant her privacy. He propped himself against the counter and watched Arden closely, hoping to gain a clue as to why she seemed to have such a complex relationship with her sister.

Lisa said, "Well, what I have to tell you certainly won't help your insomnia."

"Then can it keep until morning?"

"You need to hear this now." Arden looked ready to protest, but Lisa didn't give her a chance. "After we talked today, I had one of our people who runs background checks on potential employees do one on Ledge Burnet. She discovered something startling."

Arden blinked several times, but otherwise remained as she was.

Lisa took a deep breath. For effect, he thought. Then she said, "This guy is bad news. He was arrested on a drug charge—"

"I already know that."

"But did you know that his second offense occurred on the same night that Dad disappeared?"

Arden's lips parted in shock. By an act of will, Ledge kept his expression impassive.

"The same night, Arden," Lisa repeated with emphasis.

Arden swallowed. "Are you sure?"

"It's a matter of record. I had one of our legal team double-check."

Her lips remained open. She was breathing through them. "I fail to see—"

"Think about it." Lisa sounded as though she wanted to shake her. "In Dullsville, USA, where big news is who catches the largest bass of the month, in a single night a major burglary and a likely murder took place, both of which our father was alleged to have committed. That same night, this prior offender was out and about dealing drugs. Only marijuana, but still."

Arden continued to stare straight into his eyes as she pieced together the components. "But what...what possible connection could there be?"

"I have no idea," Lisa said. "But at the very least it's a bizarre coincidence, wouldn't you say?"

Arden didn't say anything, only continued to search his eyes.

Lisa pressed on. "Furthermore, when he came clean with you about his criminal record, he didn't say, 'Oh, and by the way, get this. This is a weird coincidence.' Wouldn't that have been the time to mention it?"

Arden gave it thought, then said, "We didn't learn about the burglary and the allegations against Dad until the following Monday. If Ledge was in custody over the weekend, maybe he never knew about the coincidental timing, either."

"I'd find that very unlikely." Lisa paused, then said, "No, he had to have known. Everyone did. Even if he was in jail, news like that would have been circulating. He had to have known," she insisted.

"And it's suspicious that he didn't make reference to it when the opportunity presented itself. He owned up to his crime, but left out the most interesting aspect. He didn't want you to know, or he would have told you. I think you should be asking yourself why."

In a barely audible voice, Arden said, "I am asking myself why."

"Well, good! That's wise. You should have nothing more to do with him, at least not until we've had a chance to explore the matter."

"I'm supposed to let him know by noon tomorrow whether or not I'm hiring him. I owe him that courtesy."

"You don't owe him a damn thing."

"I'll handle it on my terms, Lisa."

Her sharp tone surprised Ledge and silenced her sister. Temporarily. Then Lisa said, "All right. I'll leave it to you, but please call me after you've spoken to him."

"I will. Good night."

Arden disconnected and set the phone on the table, but she never took her eyes off him. After a silence the length of a freight train, he opened his mouth to speak, but she raised her hand.

"I don't want to hear it."

He did as she asked and held his silence, giving her time to determine just how irrelevant, or dire, the implications of this discovery were.

"Did you know about—" She broke off and gave a dry laugh. "Of course you knew." She crossed her arms, hugging her middle. "I thought we'd met as strangers. But that's not so, is it? We have a night in common. A night twenty years ago that drastically impacted both our lives. You knew that, but withheld it from me. Why?"

"What relevance does it have?"

"That's what I would like to know," she said, raising her voice in anger. "So would Lisa. She's right. If it weren't relevant, you would have said something about it. The fact that you didn't is even more troubling than the coincidence itself. If it *was* a coincidence. Did you know my dad?"

"Knew who he was. Knew his situation."

"You mean his being a widower with two daughters?"

"His reputation as a drunk."

"Of course," she said gruffly. "Was he a customer of your uncle's?"

"I never saw him in the bar. Never."

"That night—"

"I was in jail over that weekend and didn't learn that your dad had been linked to the burglary until, as you said," he said, motioning toward her phone, "the next week." *True.*

She tilted her head, seeming to assess his trustworthiness. Rightfully. His truth had missing parts.

She said, "I don't believe for a minute that it was a coincidence you were in the supermarket that day. What were you doing there?"

"Buying food and toilet paper."

"Damn you! Don't be cute. How did you come to be in the produce section when—"

"I followed you into the store."

She inhaled a swift breath and on a soft expulsion asked, "Why?"

The time for playing it cool had passed. He pushed himself away from the counter and faced her squarely. "As I told you, someone had pointed you out to me. But not in the pie shop, and not *after* you had lost your baby. It was earlier on. You must not have been back in town for long, because you were in the post office to rent a mailbox. I was there to pick up a package. The woman working the counter caught me looking at you, and—"

"Why were you looking at me?"

He tipped his head down in a manner that asked, *Really?* "Come on."

Self-consciously she glanced aside before coming back to him.

He continued. "The postal worker asked if I remembered the scandal about Joe Maxwell, and I said, 'Vaguely,' and she told me you were his daughter. Long lost. Now living in Penton again. That's how I came to know who you were."

"That's the truth?"

"Swear to God."

"If it was that innocent, then why have you been hush-hush about it?"

"I didn't tell you this morning because you were already freaked out over your ghost driver."

"How do I know you're not lying now about the post office?"

"You had on blue jeans with holes in the knees. Red t-shirt. You hooked your sunglasses in the neck of it while you were filling out the form for the mailbox. Your ponytail—high, on the top of your head—was lopsided. Your pregnancy wasn't obvious yet, so I didn't know about that until later."

"You saw me again?"

"Couple of times."

"When, where?"

"Around. And so did a lot of other people."

"A lot of other people haven't broken into my house in the middle of the night."

She said that with heat, and he couldn't say he blamed her. But he didn't defend himself.

"I suppose that on one of these Arden sightings, you noticed my baby bump."

"Yeah, but by then, I'd already heard you were pregnant."

"From whom?"

"I picked it up in the hair and nail salon."

"While getting your roots done?"

With utmost patience, he said, "A friend of mine owns it. A squirrel had nested in the attic insulation and chewed up some wiring. I was asked to trap and relocate the squirrel, and repair the damage. While I was up there—"

"You overheard that Joe Maxwell's daughter was pregnant."

"But no daddy to be seen. Juicy stuff. That kept them going for a good half hour."

"Oh, I'll bet," she said with disgust.

"Can I ask you a question now?"

"If it's about my baby, no."

"About that chat with your sister."

"What about it?"

"You didn't tell her about going to my uncle's bar to conduct your own recon. You didn't tell her about Lois what's-her-name and the shocking secret she had revealed. You didn't tell her that I was standing six feet from you. How come?"

"I didn't want her to panic."

"Why aren't you?"

"Why aren't I what?"

"Panicked."

"I don't know." Her bafflement appeared to be genuine and self-directed. "I really don't. You have a criminal record. You break into my house looking like Rambo. You've piled lie upon lie, until I don't trust anything you say. God knows what other secrets you're harboring. Honestly, I don't know why I didn't shoot you when I had the chance."

She took a firmer stance in the ridiculous slippers. "But I warn you that if there's a next time, I will. I'll act on my own animal instinct."

She had just as well formed a fist around his cock. He tried to talk himself out of what was a really, *really* bad idea. But himself wasn't listening.

He covered the distance between them in two strides, cupped her jaw with one hand and the back of her head with the other, tilted her face up, and melded her mouth with his.

His tongue slid past her lips and burrowed deep. Somehow, God knew how, he kept his hands where they were instead of exploring the hollows and hills he'd charted through the thin cotton nightgown.

He ended the kiss long before he wanted to and while he was still able.

Angling his head back, he looked deeply into her eyes, then released her abruptly and turned away. He yanked open the door through which he'd entered and, as he went out, said, "By noon tomorrow."

Chapter 10

The memory care center in Penton hadn't met Ledge's rigid standards, and, besides, he hadn't wanted his uncle to be an object of curiosity or pity with townsfolk who had known him before his affliction. Instead, he'd placed him in a highly rated facility in Marshall.

The days began early there. Ledge arrived as the sun was just clearing the treetops. He was greeted by a staff member who told him that Henry was up and dressed.

"He's watching the news until breakfast is served, which isn't for another ten minutes."

"Can I trouble you to bring a tray to his room?"

"Of course, Mr. Burnet."

Every day of Henry's life that Ledge could remember, he'd worn Levis, western-cut shirts, and cowboy boots. These days it was pull-up polyester pants, a zippered jacket, which, as often as not, didn't match his pants, and slip-on sneakers.

He was sitting in the La-Z-Boy that Ledge had given

him for his birthday, staring vacantly at the small flat-screen TV that Ledge had had installed last Christmas. The audio was muted.

"Morning, Uncle Henry." He dragged a chair nearer the lounger and, as he sat down, asked if anything interesting and worth repeating had occurred in the world overnight. Of course no reply was forthcoming, but while Henry continued to stare unresponsively into the TV, Ledge chatted on about nothing consequential.

One of the catering staff delivered the breakfast tray. "Need any help?" the lady asked Ledge.

"We're good. Hey, do we have you to thank for the flowers?" He'd noticed a fresh-looking bouquet on top of Henry's bureau.

"Wish I could say so. They're sure pretty. Buzz if you need anything."

Despite Henry's illness, he still had a good appetite. When he reached for a slice of toast, Ledge stayed his hand. "I haven't buttered it yet." Henry yanked his hand free, picked up the toast, tore off a bite, and crammed it into his mouth. Wryly, Ledge muttered, "Butter's bad for your cholesterol, anyway."

As he assisted Henry with his meal, Ledge kept up a one-sided conversation, eventually working his way around to Arden Maxwell. "She took it upon herself to do some recon on me. Went to the bar and chatted with Don. I called him as soon as I got home from her place last night. She hadn't told Don her name, but when I described her, he remembered her right off. She's got this unusual pairing of pale blond hair, but brown eyes." Under his breath, he added, "Somehow it works."

He wiped a missed bite of oatmeal off Henry's jacket. "Yeah, I kissed her, but don't make a big deal out of it, all right? It didn't amount to anything. Not really. I mean...Oh, hell, I'm lying to you, too."

He set aside the spoon and dragged both hands down his face. "I'm stacking up lies like firewood, and I hate that like hell. But I can't tell her about that night." He looked hard into his uncle's eyes, willing them to show understanding, empathy, something. They were blank. Which was why he could speak with such candor.

"I'm not just covering my own ass, either. I can't tell her without creating a shitstorm around her, and she's just come through a terrible one. The loss of her baby and all."

Henry picked up the juice box and sipped at the straw without mishap.

"She and her sister Lisa have this weird chemistry," Ledge continued. "If I were to tell Arden everything, all of it, and Lisa found out, there's no telling what she would do.

"But what really scares me? Arden is already on Rusty's radar. I can't caution her, or explain to her the reason for the caution, without implicating myself, not just for the burglary, but for Brian Foster's murder. Let's face it, his was no accidental death."

He made another unsuccessful attempt with the oatmeal.

"I would like to think that my deployments balanced the scale. You know, good and evil. Criminal on one hand. Protector of freedom on the other. But guilt over what I did that night eats at me, Uncle Henry. Bad.

"But even if I wanted to tell somebody to clear my conscience, or to save my soul, I couldn't. I *wouldn't*. Not because of the repercussions to myself. But because of the blowback on you. See," he said, and paused to take a deep breath, "I never want anyone to think badly of you because of me. Anything bad I ever did was *not* your fault. No matter what happens, never think that. Promise me. You didn't fail me. I failed you."

He ran his hand over the top of his uncle's head. Through the thinning hair, he noticed age spots that had recently appeared. Henry's eyebrows, which had always been dark and expressive, were mostly gray now, and they never conveyed an emotion. The creases in his face became more deeply etched between Ledge's visits. His body was following the path of his mind, deteriorating incrementally but inexorably.

For all his fighting skills, Ledge was powerless to repel this ravaging enemy.

As he stroked his uncle's head, he felt an unmanly welling of emotion. "I hope you don't mind, but I've taken to carrying your pocketknife."

Henry had never been without it. He had kept it sheathed in a leather scabbard attached to his belt and utilized it several times a day to open cases of liquor. It had broken Ledge's heart to have to take it away from him. It had broken his heart even more to realize that Henry hadn't missed it, when it always had been like an extension of his hand.

The pocketknife was a connection to Henry that Ledge could maintain when none other existed. If there was a single benefit to his uncle's condition, it was that he would never know about Ledge's crime. The last memory Henry would have of him wouldn't be that he was a thief and deceiver, but a decorated soldier.

"Don didn't think you'd mind if I started carrying your knife," he said, his voice rough with emotion. "He said you'd like knowing that it was in my safekeeping."

Just then the door was pushed open, and a young black man breezed in. "Hey, Cap'n, they told me you were here."

Ledge had to clear his throat before he could speak. Grumbling, he said, "I've told you not to address me that way."

George was one of the physical therapists on staff. "Naw,

now, we've talked about this. Once an officer, always an officer. To me you'll always be Cap'n Burnet."

George executed a crisp salute. Ledge gave him the finger. George laughed, then they fist-bumped. This was their script and routine every time they saw each other. Over the time that Henry had been a resident, the therapist and Ledge had become well acquainted and liked each other. They had their military service in the Middle East in common, and, taking into account George's occupation, Ledge admired the man's seemingly inexhaustible cheerfulness.

He squatted down in front of Henry's lounger. "How's my main man this morning?"

"He ate a good breakfast. All except the oatmeal." Ledge made another swipe at the damp spot on Henry's jacket.

George looked at the contents of the bowl and winced. "I'd have spit it out, too, Henry." He patted his patient on the knee and stood up.

Ledge asked, "How's he doing?"

"Good."

"No bullshit, George."

"I wouldn't insult you with bullshit. Your uncle's still strong. He does his exercises when I coach him through them. Oh, every once in a while he balks, but nothing I can't handle with a little persuasion."

"Any belligerence? Violent outbursts?" Ledge had dreaded asking about this, afraid of hearing the worst. "I've been warned that can happen."

"Can," George said, nodding. "But not necessarily. No signs of it yet, so don't invite trouble." George hesitated, then said in a softer tone, "You don't have to come see him quite so often, you know."

"I want to. I miss him."

"All I'm saying is, if you were to cut back on the visits,

no one would hold it against you. Especially not him. He won't know."

"But I would."

George gave a rueful smile. "Fuckin' hero, through and through."

"Knock it off."

"Okay. Carry on with your visit." Over Ledge's shoulder, he addressed Henry. "See you in PT. No slacking today."

As he was on his way out, Ledge said, "Oh, George. Thank whoever put the flowers in here. Both of us appreciate the gesture."

"Wasn't anybody on staff," George said. "Dude brought them to Henry yesterday."

"Dude?"

"Had metal tips on the toes of his boots. Said he was a friend of yours."

Ledge's jaw turned to granite. "Dude said wrong."

Chapter 11

The forty-minute drive from Marshall took Ledge only twenty-five. When he stalked into the office of the district attorney, the receptionist turned away from her computer, and, recognizing him, smiled. "Hi, Ledge."

"Ms. Raymond."

His thunderous expression and tight tone of voice caused her smile to falter. "What brings you here this morning?"

"The DA invited me."

Flustered, she shuffled the paperwork scattered across her desk and consulted a large calendar. "I don't have you—"

"It was an open invitation."

Without slowing down, he strode past her desk, made straight for the interior door across the anteroom, and practically tore it off its hinges. Rusty was seated behind his massive desk. Propped up on the corner of it were the obnoxious boots, crossed at the ankles. He was talking on his cell phone. Seeing Ledge, he grinned with what looked like supreme satisfaction.

"I'll have to get back to you." He ended his call and dropped his phone onto his desk. "Ledge."

"Cocksucker."

"Mr. Dyle?"

Ledge didn't turn around, but evidently Ms. Raymond had followed him as far as the doorway but had stopped short of coming in. Rusty raised a calming hand to her. "It's okay. He's rude as all get-out, but as long as he's here, I'll spare him a minute."

Ledge heard the door being quietly closed behind him.

Rusty remained leaned back in his leather swivel chair, but lowered his feet to the floor and linked his fingers over his middle. He had developed a paunch, all the more noticeable because the rest of him had remained slender. "Well, after that grand entrance, what can I do for you?"

"You can wipe that shit-eating grin off your face."

The grin only spread wider. "How come you're in such a high snit this morning?"

"Twenty years ago, I warned you to stay away from my uncle. The warning stands."

Again, that infuriating, taunting grin. "You didn't like the flowers? I thought they were pretty. Picked them out myself."

"Stay. Away. From. Him."

"I went to see a sick old man who doesn't know up from down. Trying to be nice, mend fences, show compassion."

Ledge rounded the desk, planted his foot on the edge of the leather cushion between Rusty's wide-spread knees, and shoved with all his might. The chair rolled back on its casters and banged against the wall with such impetus it knocked a brass plaque off its hook and onto the floor.

The back of the chair sprung upright and virtually catapulted Rusty out of it. He came up swinging, his right fist making impact with Ledge's cheekbone. His skin split like a ripe tomato, but fury made him numb to the pain.

He lunged for Rusty, closed his hands around his throat, and propelled him backward until the DA crashed into the window blinds and bent several of the thin metal louvers. It was a miracle that he didn't go through the panes of glass.

"I swore I would kill you," Ledge said through clenched teeth. "If I do it now, it'll save me the trouble of having to do it later." He squeezed his fingers tighter.

Rusty was clawing at the back of Ledge's hands, but Ledge didn't relent. Rusty's eyes bugged. His face turned so florid, it clashed with his hair.

The door came open. "Ledge!" The ruckus had brought Ms. Raymond back. "What in the world? Let go of him!"

Ledge stared murderously into Rusty's eyes, but released him immediately, flung his hands up, and stepped back. Rusty stumbled forward. Planting his palms flat on his desk, he leaned over it as he coughed and gasped, making sounds like death rattles.

"Mr. Dyle? Are you all right?"

Rusty raised his head and glared at his receptionist, croaking, "What does it look like?"

She stood on the threshold, wringing her hands. "Should I call 911? Security?"

Rusty responded with a curt negative shake of his head.

She looked at Ledge with uncertainty, her gaze drawn to the gash on his cheekbone, which was mute testimony that Rusty had given as good as he'd got. Almost.

Ledge said, "We had words, is all. Things escalated in a hurry. Apologies for the commotion. And I'm sorry for my language earlier."

"Never mind that. It's all right." But her voice trembled. Rusty was still hacking. Ledge was bleeding. The situation was far from all right, but she seemed at a loss as to how to set things right.

Finally, she said to Ledge, "All these years you've been back, you've stayed out of trouble. It would be such a shame if you picked up where you left off way back when. Don't do that, Ledge."

"I won't."

She looked at him with silent appeal, then looked over at Rusty, who had brought himself to his full height, normal breathing nearly restored. He readjusted his necktie and yanked on the hem of his suit coat. Tipping his head toward the anteroom, he ordered Ms. Raymond to leave. After giving Ledge a reluctant glance, she backed out of the office, pulling the door closed as she went.

As soon as Rusty was sure she was out of earshot, he hissed, "You son of a bitch. How dare you lay a hand on me. I ought to have you locked in a cage *under* the jail and leave you there to rot."

"You do that. My one phone call will be to the attorney general."

"Send him my regards. He and I played golf during my last trip to Austin."

"He won't be so chummy when I tell him about Welch's and the unsolved murder of Brian Foster."

Rusty rolled his eyes. "Give me a fucking break. You're not about to do that. You can't even drop a hint without implicating yourself."

"I have a rock-solid alibi. I was in police custody, remember? Tactical error on your part, Rusty, to have me arrested with weed in my trunk. I couldn't have killed Foster because I was in lockup. But where were you? Where did you get off to after the four of us split up? Who could vouch for your whereabouts later that night?"

Rusty gave a pugnacious roll of his shoulders. "Don't rattle your saber at me, soldier boy." He scoffed. "You're not going to confess to that burglary. It would ruin your reputation as a war hero. It'd tarnish your chest full of medals."

Because of the heartache it would have caused his uncle, Ledge hadn't thought he would ever admit to committing the burglary, either. But after seeing Henry today, he had accepted the inevitability of his decline. He was never going to improve. He would never be cognizant again. Every trait that had made him Henry Burnet was irretrievably gone.

The one saving grace of the tragedy was that he would never know about Ledge's crime. He was free now to own up to it.

He'd done some serious soul-searching about this decision, even before Arden's return to Penton had put additional strain on his tenuous coexistence with Rusty. Ledge was sick of the dance they'd been dancing, where each was constantly waiting for the other to make a misstep and trip himself up. He was ready to face whatever consequences came of confessing his culpability, so long as Rusty was made to suffer them, too. He wanted to take this motherfucker down.

"You think I care about those medals?" he said. "The only thing they're good for is to remind me of dead guys. Those I killed. Buddies I watched die bloody. My uncle no longer knows my name, or his. Don will take over the bar, no matter what." He raised his shoulders. "So, if I were to have a heart-to-heart with the AG, I would catch some flack, but nothing major, because I don't have anything to lose. While *you*..."

Ledge looked around at the framed photos of Rusty with politicians and C-list celebrities, the plaques and certificates and civic awards, the homages Rusty had paid to himself. He snorted with contempt as he came back around to his nemesis.

"You'd be stripped of all this, of everything you hold near and dear."

"Do you actually believe I would stand by and let that happen?" Rusty asked in a silky voice. Then he *tsk*ed. "Ledge, Ledge, in all this time, haven't you learned anything?"

"I've learned that you'll stoop to anything. Foster was a soft target. Easy to dupe, easy to bully. You told me so yourself that morning you corraled me in the diner. I know you killed him."

"You'd have better luck trying to prove I shot Kennedy. Or Lincoln."

"True. Mother Nature lent you a helping hand that night."

Rusty flashed a smile as he raised his hands at his sides. "So where does that leave you? Exactly nowhere. You're hamstrung. Admit it."

Privately, Ledge did, although he didn't concede it out loud. "A big hang-up I can't figure out is how Joe Maxwell got that bag of money. When? Where? You wouldn't have handed it over without putting up one hell of a fight. Is that how you got injured and wound up in the hospital?"

"See, Ledge?" he said, winking. "You're not the only one with an alibi. In the wee hours, I was being treated in the ER."

"Hospital records will be tough to dispute."

"Oh, I can do better than hospital records." He rolled his chair over to its rightful place behind his desk and resumed the complacent position he'd been in when Ledge arrived. Except this time, he stacked his hands on the top of his head. "You want to know who can vouch for my whereabouts that night?" He snickered, his smile sly and provocative. "Ask your girlfriend Crystal."

Chapter 12

Lisa's assistant knocked once on her office door, then pushed it open. "I know you asked not to be disturbed."

Lisa, who'd been reading over the previous quarter's financial report, removed her reading glasses and, with an edge, said, "What is it?"

"Your sister."

"What about her?"

"I'm here." Arden stepped around the assistant and entered the office.

Lisa dropped her eyeglasses onto the desk and came to her feet. "What in the world are you doing here?"

"Can you spare me a few minutes?"

"Of course." Lisa came from around her desk and gave her a warm hug. "I'm delighted to see you, but surprised. Did you make the drive this morning? You must have left Penton awfully early."

"Even the drive-through at the bakery wasn't open yet."

"And after you had such a late night. Were you able to get any sleep? Do you want coffee?"

"In answer to the first question, not much. No thank you on the coffee. I stopped a couple of times along the way."

Lisa said to her assistant, "Everything is on hold until further notice."

"You have a meeting at—"

"Move it back an hour."

"If someone's schedule doesn't allow for the change?"

"Then they're to rearrange their schedule to allow it."

"Yes, Ms. Bishop." The woman, seemingly accustomed to Lisa's directives, smiled at Arden, then withdrew and pulled the door closed.

Lisa took Arden's hand and led her to a seating area in a corner of her expansive office. The Bishop Group occupied the two top floors of a glassy contemporary high-rise, which Lisa's late husband had developed. The glitzy skyline of downtown Dallas was on full display outside the wall of windows.

Inside, the office was exquisitely furnished and decorated with treasures from around the world, which Lisa and her late husband had acquired on their frequent trips abroad.

As Arden took her seat, she said, "I know you're busy, so I'll be as brief as possible. But I didn't want this to keep any longer, and I didn't want to tell you over the phone."

"You look upset."

"Apprehensive."

"All right, apprehensive. Is this about Ledge Burnet? You told him he won't be working for you, and he didn't take it well?"

Arden still felt the imprint of his lips on hers. The pressure points where his large body had aligned with hers quickened with the memory. "No. That call to him is pending. But I do need to tell you something troubling that I should have shared weeks ago. Months, actually."

They had taken adjacent chairs. Lisa reached across the space separating them and clasped both Arden's hands in hers. "You're scaring me."

"It's not *that* scary. Just—"

"Tell me, Arden."

She took a steadying breath and told Lisa about her nightly drive-by. As she talked, she watched Lisa pale, the color literally draining from her face. But to her sister's credit, she didn't interrupt. By the time Arden had finished, Lisa was visibly shaken.

"Someone's been stalking you, and you didn't tell me?"

"It's not exactly stalking."

"What would you call it?"

"I don't know, but not stalking. I haven't seen the person, so I don't even know that it's a man. It could be a woman."

"Whoever it is, he, she is spying on you."

"Monitoring."

"There's a negligible difference between the words I'm using and the ones you're substituting. When did you become aware of the *spying*?"

"Shortly after I moved back."

"Good God, Arden. I cannot believe you're just now telling me."

"Please don't lecture me about my timing. You were already dead set against my moving into the house, I didn't need you harping over another issue. Besides, I didn't want to add to your worry."

"Well, I'm worried now."

A quarrel over semantics, or anything else, would be contrary to why she'd come seeking Lisa's opinion and counsel, so she took a moment to let them both cool down before resuming.

"At first I thought that our property was on someone's route to and from work. Something like that. But now..." She rubbed her forehead. "It's gone on for so long, the person is so dedicated to it, I don't know what to think. Who would be that interested in me?"

"Someone glaringly obvious springs to mind." Lisa's arched eyebrow was as eloquent as if she'd actually named him.

Arden said, "I'll admit, I wondered."

"What made you wonder?"

"When I contacted him, he knew who I was and where I lived even before I told him." Before Lisa could speak, she rushed to say, "But then if everyone who knows who I am and where I live were to drive past the house, it would be a nightly parade."

"That doesn't make him innocent."

"I realize that." She didn't dare tell Lisa about Ledge's being in the supermarket or of his unorthodox visit to her house last night. Once again, she found herself staving off her own misgivings and, rather, defending him, even to herself. "But nor does it make him guilty."

"Have you accused him?"

"I inquired. He denied it."

"But he would, wouldn't he?"

Arden gave a noncommittal shrug.

"Have you reported it to the police?" Lisa asked.

"I've been reluctant to."

"Why?"

"*Because* it could be, and probably is, someone who routinely drives that road and slows down to gape out of curiosity. *Because* I don't have a description of the car, or the person, and I'm disinclined to sit on the roadside and wait for him to come by so I can get a description."

Nor was she prepared to camouflage herself as Ledge had.

"*Because* the individual has never stopped or posed any overt threat. And *because* if I did report it, it would create another brouhaha, and I don't want to draw any more attention to myself." Softly she added, "Mainly that."

"Why mainly that?"

Arden sat back in her chair, leaned her head back, and glanced over at the expansive bookcase. Most of the shelves held leather-bound, signed limited editions and museum-worthy artifacts. On one of the shelves, in a five-by-seven silver frame, was a picture of the Maxwell family. It was a posed portrait that their mother, Marjorie, had insisted on having made. *Before you girls get any older,* she'd told them.

In the picture, they were dressed in their Sunday best. The four of them were smiling and appeared happy, both individually and as a unit. None of them had an inkling of how terribly wrong things would go.

"Do you suppose he's still alive?" Arden asked quietly.

Lisa left her chair quickly and went over to the wall of windows, keeping her back to Arden for at least a full minute. When she came back around, her hands were tented in front of her mouth. There were tears in her eyes.

Slowly she lowered her hands but kept them clasped at chest level. "The day after you lost the baby, when we were talking there in the kitchen, you asked me why I hadn't sold the house. All the reasons I gave you were valid. But what I didn't add, because it seemed—and is—so ridiculous and immature, is that I thought he might come back one day."

She blotted a tear and shook her head. "Not for good, not to stay, or to reunite with us, but just to..." Frustrated with her inability to find the right words, she raised her arms at her sides. "I held out the faint hope that if we kept the house, it would be an irresistible draw for him."

Arden got up, went to Lisa, and the two of them hugged,

rocking each other. With that embrace, all their differences ceased to matter. When they eventually broke apart, they linked their little fingers.

"Not so ridiculous or immature," Arden whispered. "That faint hope has been lurking in the back of my mind, too. Could Dad be the person *monitoring* me? Do you think that there's any possibility?"

Lisa hugged her close again. "Don't break your heart, don't break mine, by counting on it."

Chapter 13

That night in 2000—Rusty

Sitting on his bed in his room at home, Rusty gingerly rubbed his bruised wrist.

Goddamn Burnet.

Rusty's taunt as he was getting out of the car with their haul had struck a nerve in Ledge, and his reaction had been swift and scary. Rusty was rarely taken by surprise like that, but Ledge had attacked with such ferocity, speed, and strength, he'd been too astounded to defend himself or counterattack. Ledge's grip had felt powerful enough to crush his bones. Rusty supposed he should be relieved that he hadn't.

That Ledge had that ability and advantage over him grated like an iron file. In hindsight, he should have arranged to have the bastard killed tonight. His only deterrent, which he hated to admit even to himself, was the fear that if he attempted it and failed, it was likely that he would have been the one to die.

When Ledge had told him that if anything went awry with Henry, he would hunt him down and kill him, he had believed it right down to the toes of his steel-tipped boots.

If somebody else had threatened him that way, he'd have gotten a good laugh out of it and then annihilated the reckless fool. But there was something about Burnet that induced a deep-seated and unremitting terror. Maybe it was that steely blue stare of his. It could be downright eerie, calculating, cold-blooded, like he had resolved to mess you up bad, but in his own good time.

Whatever Ledge's fearsome quality was, it had intimidated Rusty into making other plans for him tonight, and he celebrated that decision now, because the alternate scheme had been executed without a hitch.

Several days earlier, he'd driven over into Louisiana and bought the marijuana himself. He had then intercepted the wetback who tended his mother's flower beds as he was piling his tools into the bed of his piece-of-shit pickup and threatened to sic immigration on him if he didn't grant Rusty one small favor.

The marijuana got planted in Ledge's car. To demonstrate what a nice guy he was, Rusty had given the Mexican a doobie for his trouble.

Tonight, immediately after he and Ledge had parted company, using a burner phone he'd called the sheriff's office with an anonymous tip that Ledge Burnet was selling weed out of his car on the parking lot of his uncle's bar.

"There were some people with him in his car. I didn't see who. Anyhow, he drove out alone, headed toward town."

That's all it had taken.

Ledge was in lockup. It was unlikely he would be granted bail. If his case went to trial, conviction would be a slam-dunk. Even if Ledge made a plea bargain to avoid trial, both his immediate and long-range futures included incarceration. He had been removed, if not permanently, then for a good, long time.

Rusty could now proceed to his next chore of the night.

He rotated his wrist a few times to work out some of the soreness and keep it flexible, then reached for his phone and made one of the most important calls he would ever make.

"Foster? It's Rusty. Are you still awake?"

"Are you kidding? Who could sleep? I was about to—"

"Listen," he interrupted, almost breathless with urgency. "Whatever you were about to do, forget it."

"Why? What's happened?"

"It's Burnet. He's been hauled in."

"To jail?"

"Yes to jail! Where'd you think?"

"Oh, God! How did they catch him? Was it his car? Somebody saw his car behind the store?"

Rusty pictured him peeing his pants.

"No. His arrest didn't have anything to do with the burglary. The dumbass was stopped for a busted taillight, something stupid like that. While the deputies had him pulled over, they searched his car. Guess what they found."

He told Foster the rest of it. He spoke in a rushed whisper, not only to convey urgency but to keep from waking up his parents in their bedroom down the hall. His daddy was a class-A crook, but it wouldn't go down well with him that Rusty had stolen roughly half a million dollars.

That was, not unless Mervin got a hefty chunk of it.

Rusty freely acknowledged that he'd been spoiled rotten. He couldn't remember a time when he'd demanded something that he didn't ultimately get. His mother was sweet and doting and thought the sun rose and set on her boy. She was also clueless to a laughable extent. He manipulated her unmercifully.

His dad had a loud bark, but he hailed from the school of Boys Will Be Boys. Not so secretly, he got a kick out of Rusty's misbehavior. The more unsavory the misdeed, the more it tickled his dad. Rusty's shenanigans, the more outlandish the better, showed a creative streak that his dad took pride in.

However, Rusty had no delusions about the depth of Sheriff Mervin Dyle's affection and indulgence. It wasn't bottomless. It wasn't even skin-deep. If it came down to protecting Rusty or preserving his own position of power, his dad would give him over without hesitation and not waste an instant of regret over it.

Cutting Mervin a large slice of the pie would be Rusty's only bargaining chip. He wouldn't use it unless it became absolutely necessary, of course, and, if all went according to plan, it wouldn't. He would be able to keep the Welch's take all to himself, and neither parent would be the wiser.

If all went according to plan. There were still hindrances to success that must be eliminated. Which brought him back to Brian Foster. "What concerns me," Rusty said, "is what Burnet will do or say."

"What do you mean?"

"He'll try to cut a deal. I'm afraid he'll rat us out in exchange for a lighter drug charge."

"He wouldn't do that."

"In a heartbeat."

"The four of us made a pact."

"Pact," Rusty snickered. "You think a promise matters to that guy? You don't know him like I do. He's surly. Resentful. Believe me, he would betray us."

Foster moaned an appeal to the almighty. "What are we going to do?"

"Well, first, we're not going to panic. Burnet won't parley until he's talked to his lawyer. My guess is that their meeting won't take place till morning, and maybe not till Monday, 'cause tomorrow's Easter. But, in case I'm wrong, we need to hide this money. Tonight. Now."

"Right, right. Hide it."

"Where should we meet?"

"Meet?" Foster's voice rose an octave. "You and me?"

"I'm not doing this alone, Foster."

"But—"

"If something happened to me, nobody would know where the money was stashed."

"What could happen to you?"

"Anything. Jesus! I could have a car wreck, fall in a fucking sinkhole. Anything. But what really scares me? If Burnet talks, he'll give me over first, and it won't matter that my daddy's the sheriff. They'll be after me. I can't be caught with this money.

"If Burnet is granted bail, he'll come after me. He'll want to shut me up. Probably all of us." He built in a strategic pause. A little longer. Then, "Look, never mind. I'll figure it out for myself."

"No, wait. Give me a sec to think."

Rusty smiled but made himself sound put out. "Well, think fast. I've got to move on this."

"I'll help you."

"If you're afraid, if you're going to be whimpering like a little girl the whole time—"

"No, I'm all right. Just nervous. But I don't think Burnet will break the pact. I really don't."

"Think what you want. I'm counting on him selling us out. Which means..."

"What?"

"Well, I'm thinking that in addition to hiding the money, we need a fall guy."

"Someone to take the blame?"

"That's what fall guys do, Foster."

"I know, I know, but—"

"We may not need one, but we should have it set up in case Burnet double-crosses us."

Foster ruminated on it for so long that Rusty was ready to scream by the time he said, "Yeah, okay. It's probably a good idea. But who?"

"The town drunk, otherwise known as Joe Maxwell."

Chapter 14

Ledge sat with his legs wide apart, hands loosely clasped between his knees, head down, staring at the floor and wishing to God he could rewind the clock to when he'd woken up this morning and live today over again. Maybe then he wouldn't be behind bars, sharing space with a stinking urinal.

But, hell, he probably would be. As Rusty had so accurately pointed out: In all this time, he hadn't learned a damn thing.

"Burnet!"

Ledge raised his head. A deputy was unlocking the cell door. Ledge knew him to be a veteran of the sheriff's office, long in the tooth and a heart attack waiting to happen. Perpetually short of breath, he wheezed when he talked. "Get your ass out of here. You're free to go."

"How come?"

"Do you care?"

"I haven't even called a lawyer yet."

"Then I guess this visit is on the house. Come on, move it. My pizza's getting cold."

Ledge quit arguing and stepped out of the cell. The deputy caught him by the sleeve. "It'll piss me off good if I see you back in here."

Ledge pulled his arm free. "Shouldn't have been in here today."

"Debatable. From what I've heard, anyway. But the DA thought it over and didn't deem your offense arrest-worthy after all."

"He's all heart."

The deputy gave a gruff snort. "Another deputy will meet you at that door and escort you out." He pointed Ledge toward the end of the corridor, then shot a glance up at the security camera, leaned closer to Ledge, and whispered, "Do yourself a favor. Steer clear of the turd. You understand what I'm saying?"

Ledge bobbed his chin. "Thanks. A beer is on me the next time you come into the bar."

"Wife's got me off it." He slapped his potbelly. "Says I'm getting fat."

Ledge smiled at him before heading down the hall.

The deputy called after him, "Keep your nose clean."

Ledge didn't turn around, but waved his hand in acknowledgment.

He was processed out and returned his belongings. In the parking lot where he'd left his pickup, he found Don White leaning against the front fender. Ledge scowled as he approached him. "What are you doing here?"

Equally cantankerous, Don replied, "I was about to ask you the same."

Ledge used his fob to unlock the doors of his truck, went around, and got in on the driver's side. Don hiked himself up into the passenger seat. "Lord, it's an oven in here. Start the engine, get some AC going."

Ledge gave him a sour look. "Nobody invited you." But he did as ordered, because his truck had sat in the sun for hours, and the interior *was* an oven. Soon, cooler air was whirring through the vents.

Don situated himself more comfortably in his seat.

Under his breath, Ledge said, "Here it comes," which Don ignored.

"This morning," he began, "when I got up, I had a voice mail from you, telling me that you were going to see Henry. Nothing out of the ordinary. Then midday, I got a call at work informing me that you were in jail. I'm having a hard time believing what I was told happened in between times."

"Who called you?"

"Well, not you. I had to hear about your altercation with the district attorney through the grapevine. I was also told that if you didn't have the good sense to call a good defense lawyer, I should do it in your stead, because you were likely to need one. By the time the tale got around to me, Dyle was said to be seeking the death penalty."

"I'm glad you brought up 'work.'"

"Out of everything I've said, that's what you picked up on?"

"Well, since you won't take the bar off my hands, I do still own the place. Who's covering for you?"

"Don't worry about it. I cashed in a favor or two. Unlike you, I have friends I can call for help in times of need."

"I have friends."

"Name one."

Ledge was about to say Crystal but stopped himself. Crystal had never told him—*never told him*—that Rusty had been with her that night. It was a betrayal that cut him to the quick. Learning that had bothered him a hell of a lot more than being jailed.

Of course Rusty could have been lying, but Ledge didn't think so. He'd seemed way too sure of himself, too goddamned smug, and the claim could be too easily denied or confirmed. By Crystal.

He tabled thoughts on that for now, and, instead of naming her as a friend, he claimed George.

"The physical therapist at the center? That George?"

"Yeah. Hell of a guy. He and I talked this morning."

Don downshifted his aggravation level. "How was Henry?"

Ledge aimed one of the AC vents at himself, slumped in his seat, and laid his head back. He described Henry's condition, then filled Don in on everything that related to Rusty. Except for his parting shot about Crystal.

"The bastard knew how I would react when I heard he'd brought the flowers, that he'd actually been in Henry's room. I could have killed him on the spot. Stormed into his office, scared the receptionist. You know Ms. Raymond?"

"Alicia."

Ledge looked at Don askance.

"Every once in a while she pops in for a drink."

Ledge raised an eyebrow. "Does she?"

"With Mr. Raymond."

"Oh. Well, she'll need a drink or two tonight. When I left Rusty's office, she looked ready to cry, said she'd put me on her prayer list. Rusty must've called courthouse security the second my back was turned. Two deputies stopped me right there." He used his nose to point out a spot just beyond the grill of his truck.

"I was arrested for assaulting a public official. Mirandized. Hand restraints. The whole shebang. The chickenshit didn't have the guts to do it while I was there in his office, looking him in the eye."

"He's a son of a bitch."

Ledge huffed a laugh. "That's what he called me."

"He's wrong," Don said, his vexation back. "You're a *stupid* son of a bitch."

"If I'm so undesirable, why did you even bother coming down here?"

"Because although I haven't made even the short list of your friends, I was worried about you."

"Well, you can stop worrying. I'm out."

"For the time being." Don paused to take a breath and rein in. "Tending bar, I hear stuff, you know. Rusty Dyle has it in for you. He's a snake. You know it. Why do you let him get to you? He goads you with a bouquet; you play right into his hands. My advice—"

"I didn't ask for any—"

"—would be to have it out with him once and for all. Settle whatever it is between you two. Rumor is it's Crystal."

Even hearing her name set his teeth on edge. "She's part of it, but it's way more complicated than that." Don didn't say anything, but Ledge sensed his interest. He turned his head toward him. "You'll have to take my word for it, Don."

"Can't talk about it?"

"No. But I will tell you this. Rusty isn't fucking around. We're not in a pissing contest for playground dominance. He had me locked up today so I would have time to think about all the ways he could hurt me if he took a mind to, and his weapons of choice are the people close to me. So keep that shotgun loaded and handy."

"Don't worry about me."

"I do." He gave him a wry grin. "You *are* a friend."

"And you are a pain in the ass," Don grumbled, but with evident love. "Unfortunately, when Henry hired me, he told me that you came with the job." He opened the passenger door and climbed out. "See you at the bar?"

"Since you've got backup, I think I'll call it a day and go home."

Don regarded him with concern. "Ledge—"

"I'm good."

"No, you're not. I haven't seen you this low since just after you got back from Afghanistan, and I had to tell you about Henry's frequent memory lapses. Tough time for you."

That was putting it mildly. He had survived two bloody wars with barely a scratch, only to come home and be felled by that news. As soon as they'd swept up after his welcome-home party, he'd gone on his first bender. He'd stayed away for days, finally stumbling home like the proverbial prodigal.

Henry had met him with a heavy heart but open arms, hugging him tightly, weeping with relief, telling him over and over again that he would do whatever it took to heal Ledge's wounded spirit. But in the cruel game of give-and-take that Fate often played, as Ledge had improved, his uncle had declined.

"That was a tough time," he said. "But I didn't know how good I had it. I'd give anything if Uncle Henry was half as cognizant now as he was then."

"Me too, Ledge."

Both were quiet, then Don asked, "You gonna be all right?"

"Yeah."

"You're sure?"

Ledge assured him with a nod, but only because he didn't want to lie to his friend out loud.

———◇———

"Ya know," the guy working the cash register drawled, "you can get this for free out at your own place."

Ledge fixed his iciest stare on him. "I like to support the local economy." He didn't wait for a sack but grabbed the bottle of bourbon by the neck and carried it out to his truck, which he'd kept running while he went into the liquor store.

He was breaking all kinds of rules today. Even self-imposed ones.

The trees along the curving lake road were cloaked in Spanish moss, which could look either beautiful or bleak. This evening it resembled tattered winding-sheets hanging heavily from the branches. The surface of the lake was as still as death. The cypresses growing up out of it, looking like life-forms from fantasy fiction, made for stark silhouettes against a glowering dusk.

The entire landscape appeared haunted and forbidding, adjectives that also described his frame of mind.

Gravel peppered the underbelly of his truck as he took the turnoff to his house at an unsafe speed. The potholes seemed to have deepened since he'd driven over them at dawn on his way out. He hit them deliberately now, punishing the shocks on his truck. He narrowly missed flattening an armadillo stupid enough to cross the road in his path.

He rounded the last curve, his house came into view, and he braked suddenly, causing the seat belt to catch across his chest.

Her car was in his driveway.

"Fucking perfect."

Chapter 15

———◆◈◆———

Ledge turned in. Arden had parked to the side of the drive, so as not to block his spot. Thoughtful of her.

She wasn't inside the car.

It had grown dark enough for him to realize that as he'd headed out this morning, he hadn't left any lights on inside the house, but there was a glow coming from behind it. He took the bourbon with him as he got out of his truck and followed the path around to the back. The workshop's garage door was up, but no overhead lights were on.

Because it was partially dark inside, it took him a moment to spot her. She was standing with her back against the drafting table, silhouetted against the shaded bulb suspended above it. It made a halo of her hair.

He went over to a table where he kept a coffee machine and fixings. He broke the seal on the bottle and poured a goodly portion of sour mash into a coffee mug, then shot it.

"The deadline was noon," she said.

"Time got away." He poured another drink and shot that one, too.

"I called you several times."

He poured more liquor, looked down into it, then turned and raised the mug. "Drink?"

"Yes, please."

He was surprised she accepted, but she didn't come over and take it. She made him walk all the way across the shop to deliver it to her. He extended her the mug, handle toward her. She hooked it with her fingers. "Thank you." She took a sip. "You must've had a full day?"

"You could say."

She used the mug to point out the raw wound on his cheekbone. "What happened there?"

"Bee sting." He ignored the look she gave him and tried to keep his focus off her plush, whiskey-damp lips. "You came all the way out here to give me your answer in person?"

"You gave me no choice. I'm a woman of my word, and I had promised that you would have my decision by noon. But you didn't answer your phone or return my calls. I called the bar and was told by the person who answered that you hadn't been in all day. There's no email address on your business card. I didn't know how else to reach you."

She took another sip, then ran her finger 'round and 'round the rim of the mug. He felt that spiraling touch low in his belly and had to stifle the groan that tried to push its way from his throat. He told himself it was the booze hitting rock bottom on an empty stomach, but he knew better.

She was saying, "I don't get the impression that you've been on tenterhooks to hear my decision. On the contrary, you've led me to believe that you don't give a damn one way or the other."

"Not really, no."

She looked up at him with challenge. "You're a liar."

"Busted. It wasn't a bee sting."

"You're lying about not giving a damn." She indicated the table behind her. "These drawings are of my house."

Going through his mind was a litany of military-born, illustrative obscenities. But he made a motion of indifference. "Couldn't sleep last night. I did some doodling."

She set the mug down with a thump on the most convenient level surface, which was his computer desk, then turned to the drafting table and began sorting through his drawings.

She selected two of them and positioned them side by side. "Variations on how to widen the upstairs hallway. This one, turning it into more of a gallery. Very detailed, down to the molding around the recessions cut into the walls.

"This," she said, pointing to the other, "takes out a wall altogether, and, by doing so, opens up the extra bedroom and converts it into a sitting area/TV room. These aren't doodles at all."

She slid forward a sketch. "The front elevation. The windows enlarged. The porch expanded. Or, as you've designated it here, the veranda." She looked at him for comment. He didn't say anything, but she wasn't deterred.

She pulled another drawing to the forefront. "Reconfigured master bath. There's another for the layout of a modernized kitchen." She ran her fingertips over the drawing, then faced him. "They're brilliant."

"Thanks."

"When did you study architecture?"

"I didn't."

"Where did you learn to do this?"

"It's just something I know how to do." She was frustrated by his answer and showed it. "I see it in my head," he said, not knowing how else to explain it. Motioning toward the computer, he added, "CAD helps."

"Why are you repairing squirrel damage and getting closet doors to hang straight when you can do this?"

"Hanging closet doors is honest work."

"Yes, but it's also a waste of obvious talent."

He picked up the mug she'd set aside and drained it. "How long have you been here?"

"A while."

"Making yourself at home. Going through my stuff."

"Why are you so angry?"

"I don't like people meddling in my business."

"Well, you've had a heyday meddling in mine," she said loudly. "Imagine my surprise when I got back from Dallas this afternoon to find a locksmith's van parked in my driveway."

Shit. In light of everything else that had happened, he'd forgotten about that. He'd called a locksmith from his truck immediately after leaving the memory care center. It had scared him to think that if Rusty chose to, he could get just as close to Arden as he had to Henry. Not that door locks would protect her, but he'd acted on a compulsion to take at least one preemptive action.

But he'd gotten snagged by something else she'd said. "You made a round trip to Dallas today?"

"To talk over something with Lisa."

"Something you couldn't talk over by phone?"

"You're getting me off the subject. Why did you take it upon yourself to order new locks for me?"

"Because you didn't take it upon yourself. You needed stronger door locks, and now you have them."

"He said you told him that it was an emergency."

"If something had happened to you, at least I would have

a clear conscience. I'd have done my best to protect you from an intruder."

"The only intruder I've had was *you*."

"And you should be damn glad it was me," he shouted.

In the sudden hush that followed, he could hear her breathing as she forced it to slow down. Then, speaking quietly, she said, "He gave me a receipt. He had already charged your credit card. I'll pay you back."

"Whenever," he mumbled.

"Thank you."

"You're welcome."

After another laden silence, she said, "It didn't really qualify as an emergency."

That's what you think. Rusty fought guerilla-style. He struck without warning and in nefarious ways. Likely, she would never see him coming, and it sickened Ledge to think how creative Rusty could be, he who had no scruples.

She seemed a lot smaller here in his cavernous workshop than she had in her kitchen. The glow of the light fixture gave her a fairy-like quality. She looked even more delicate and vulnerable than she had in her insubstantial nightgown. Her hair looked softer, her eyes larger and more innocent.

But he realized that it wasn't the setting or the lighting that made her look more fragile here and now. It was her contrast to him. Big and mean him, shouting, incautiously slamming back shots, trying to keep a leash on rampaging lust.

He needed to get her away from him. "What have you decided about the house?"

"Who is Crystal?"

He didn't actually reel backward a step or two, as though he'd taken a blow right between the eyes, but that's what it felt like. Vulnerable, fairy-like, fragile? Like hell. She was a steamroller.

He didn't answer her question.

"The reason I ask," she said, "is because when I called the bar, and you weren't there, it was suggested by the person I talked to that I should check with Crystal, that you might be with her."

"I wasn't."

"She's...?"

"A friend."

"With benefits?" When again he didn't respond, she said, "Given that you kissed me last night, it's a fair question."

He gave a precise nod. "Who was your baby's father, and why isn't he with you?" He arched his brows and looked at her expectantly. "What? You're allowed to ask fair questions, but I'm not?"

"I just don't want some woman I've never even met coming at me and accusing—"

"Ain't gonna happen. Not unless you tell."

"I have no intention of telling anyone."

"Me neither. So we've got no problem."

She propped her hands on her hips. "Well, I disagree. It's a problem for me if you're cheating on—"

"*Cheating*?" he repeated with incredulity. "It was only a kiss."

In the face of such a blatant distortion of fact, they held each other's stare longer than they should have, and, at some point during it, she lowered her hands from her hips. In the end, he couldn't say for sure who looked away first, but it was awkward.

She turned to face the drafting table and neatly stacked the drawings. "You have a great eye for design, and, even though it irritated you for me to say so, your talent is being wasted. But..." She took a breath. "I won't be going with your ideas."

It crushed him to hear that, for so many reasons, most

of which he couldn't rationalize. But rather than show his disappointment, he made a gesture of dismissal. "I guessed as much."

"I will, however, be using your services. If you're still available."

"Doing what? Rehanging your closet doors?"

"Removing them. You see, I've changed my mind about restoring the house. I want you to take it apart. Piece by piece. Board by board. Nail by nail. Tear it down. To the ground."

Chapter 16

Ledge stood there looking at her for what seemed an interminable amount of time. Then he turned, saying over his shoulder, "I haven't eaten all day," and walked out of the workshop.

Arden didn't know what to make of his exit, but she couldn't leave things up in the air, so she followed. As an afterthought, she went back for the bottle of bourbon.

He entered the house, and lights came on inside, illuminating the steps leading up to the back door. He'd left it standing open. Not quite an invitation, but not a lockout.

She went inside. His kitchen was surprisingly modern. It certainly showed hers up.

He was standing in the open door of the refrigerator and didn't turn when she closed the back door to let him know she had followed him in. He sailed a deli package from the fridge onto the granite countertop, then a second landed there with a plop. After taking some items from the shelves in the door, he bumped it closed with his hip.

As he set a butter dish and jar of mayonnaise on the counter, he said. "Grilled cheese?"

"No thank you. But you drank my whiskey." She lifted the bottle.

"Glasses are up there."

She took a glass from the indicated cabinet and poured herself an inch of the liquor. "You?"

"No thanks." He turned on the griddle section of the range and dropped a slab of butter on it. "Bad idea to drink straight bourbon on an empty stomach." The butter began to sizzle. He came around to face her. "Makes your belly burn like hellfire. Makes your brain go to mush."

He came toward her and, with the back of his hand at her waist, eased her out of his path. "For instance..." He went into a walk-in pantry and emerged seconds later with a loaf of bread in one hand and a bag of potato chips in the other. He tossed the latter onto the dining table.

He hefted the loaf of bread in his hand as he came to within inches of her. "For instance, I thought I heard you say you wanted me to tear your house down."

In defiance of his thunderous expression, she casually took a sip of the whiskey. As she lowered the glass, she said, "You look like you're gauging the weight of that loaf of bread. Are you going to hurl it at me?"

He muttered something foul as, this time, he sidestepped to go around her without touching.

He kept his back to her and said nothing more as he slathered a slice of bread with mayo, then piled on slices of cheese he took from the two deli packages. He laid the stack carefully on the griddle in a pond of melted butter, which had filled the kitchen with a mouthwatering aroma that made her stomach growl.

He turned only his head to look at her.

Abashed, she said, "Maybe I'll have a sandwich after all."

He built her one and laid it on the griddle beside his. He topped them with slices of buttered bread and stared at them as they cooked.

She said, "Aren't you going to ask—"

"Not yet."

She set her drink on the table. "Would you like for me to set the table?"

"Plates are up there."

With a brevity of words, he told her where to find things, and when the sandwiches were ready, they sat down across from each other. He plucked a paper napkin from the holder in the center of the table and began to eat.

She followed suit. The sandwich was delicious, and she told him so. "What kind of cheeses did you use?"

"One's yellow, one's white."

That was the extent of their mealtime conversation.

When he'd demolished his sandwich and several handfuls of chips, he wiped his mouth and hands, balled up the napkin, uncapped his bottle of water, took a long drink from it, and returned it nearly empty to the table. Folding his arms across his chest, he stared at her for ponderous seconds, then said, "What the *fuck*?"

"I know it seems an odd—"

"No. No, odd would be you wanting to put statues of cartoon characters along the expanded veranda. That would be *odd*. This," he said, stabbing the table with his index finger, "seems calculated."

Of all the words she had anticipated—crazy, fickle, addlepated, just plain dumb—calculated wasn't among them. "Calculated?"

"Yeah, planned. Devised to make a fool of me." His eyes were as hot as twin blue flames.

At a loss, she said, "Why would that have been my intention, when I didn't even know you?"

"Who sent you to me?"

"What?"

"Who. Sent. Y—"

"I heard you. I just don't know what you mean by it. Nobody sent me to you."

"I'm supposed to believe that you picked me at random."

"I did."

"Off the internet?"

"Why do you doubt that?"

"Nobody referred you? Or suggested me to you?"

"No. But what difference would it have made if some-one had?"

"You had never heard of me before you saw my name in that list of contractors?"

"No," she said with force. "But clearly you suspect other-wise. Why?"

"Because this sounds like a cruel practical joke played by someone of my acquaintance who thrives on this sort of shit. You might have been an unwitting partner—"

"I didn't partner with anybody."

"Who have you talked to about me?"

"No one except the bartender, Don, and the woman, Lois, I met there. She approached me, not the other way around."

"That's it?"

"Yes. Well, no," she said, correcting herself. "Lisa."

"Right, right. Sister dear. I overheard her opinion of me. She advised you to keep away. But here you are." He extended his arms from his sides in a grand gesture that encompassed the room and beyond. "Why didn't you take your sister's advice and have nothing else to do with me?"

Before she could speak, he held up a halting hand. "You

know what? On second thought, I don't care what your game is. You want your house leveled, get somebody else. I suggest a wrecking crew. Efficient. Cost effective."

"I considered doing just that. But I don't want the demolition to be noticed. I don't want anybody to know what I'm doing until it's done."

He laughed shortly. "Now *that's* odd. But, whatever. I'm out. Thanks for wasting my time. The hour spent on the walk-through. The—"

"You came to me for the walk-through, remember?"

"—estimates I worked up."

"Which you haven't submitted."

"I was going to bring them over to you in the morning."

"Was that when you were going to show me the drawings?"

"I hadn't decided."

"My decision isn't a reflection of your ideas. They're excellent. The finished product would've been beautiful."

He shrugged off the compliment.

"You put a lot of thought and time into those drawings. I'll compensate you for doing them. And, as we agreed, you'll get one hundred dollars for working up the estimates on the basic repairs."

"Keep your money," he said angrily. "We'll be even-steven if you tell me why you changed your mind."

"I'll answer as I have to all your personal questions. None of your business."

His features turned even more fulminating. "Right. It isn't. As of now." He scraped back his chair and carried his empty plate to the sink. "Hate to be rude, but today's been a bugger. I'm going to bed."

She made no move to leave.

Acting indifferent, he said, "Turn out the lights before you go."

"First, talk me through that night when you were arrested and my father disappeared."

———◦———

Ledge had gotten no farther than the doorway leading into the rest of the house when Arden's words stopped him cold, with the exception of his heartbeat, which spiked.

He took a moment to school his features before turning around. She had remained exactly as she'd been, except that now her hands were on the table, clasped so tightly her knuckles were white. She seemed to have braced herself to hear whatever was coming, no matter how unsavory it might be.

He steeled himself and, without inflection, asked, "What do you want to know?"

"Were you selling marijuana that night?"

"No. I told you, I was framed."

"By whom?"

He questioned the wisdom of full disclosure, but reasoned that if he was honest on some points, he could hedge on the more consequential ones.

He said, "You got peeved because I was unreachable today, but other than that question about Crystal, which was obvious fishing about my love life—"

"You flatter yourself."

"—you didn't ask why I couldn't be reached."

"Are you going to tell me?"

"If I don't, it'll sound worse coming from somebody else."

"Does it relate to what we're supposed to be talking about?"

"Roundaboutly."

"Well?"

"I spent the better part of the day in jail."

She reacted as though he'd told her that Martians had

landed. He returned to the table and resumed his seat across from her. "I was arrested after getting into a scuffle."

She recovered enough to ask, "With...?"

"The district attorney." Judging by how flabbergasted she looked, he thought her reaction was genuine.

"Where did this altercation take place?"

"In his office at the courthouse."

"Are you serious?"

"Yes."

"Who started it?"

"Me."

"What in the world were you thinking?"

"I was thinking of beating the crap out of him."

"Over what?"

"We go way back. Bitter dislike for each other. We've had an ongoing grudge since we were kids."

"What provoked you today?"

"That's personal and irrelevant."

"I doubt that."

He frowned. "Enough to say, he's a sneaky bastard. He plays dirty pool and pulls dirty tricks. I thought he might be the one in cahoots with you on this house business."

"I'm not in cahoots with anybody, and I don't know the district attorney. What's his name?"

Looking directly into her eyes to test her reaction, he said, "Rusty Dyle."

"I remember a Sheriff Dyle from when I was little."

"Mervin. Now deceased. Rusty is his son. Ever run across him?"

"I wouldn't have had occasion to."

"Hmm." He continued to watch her closely. She seemed curious, interested, but didn't appear to be lying.

"You want to know about that night I was arrested?" he

said. "It was Rusty who put the weed in my car. I can't prove it. I don't know how he managed to do it without my knowledge, but I'm certain he was behind it.

"I don't know if he bribed those two deputies who arrested me, or if he tipped them anonymously, but it makes no difference. He saw to it that I got caught with enough evidence to make it look like I was dealing. I wasn't. God as my witness, Arden."

Looking startled, she angled back in her chair.

"You don't believe me?"

"No. I do. It's just, that's the first time you've called me by name."

Her name had been constantly pinballing inside his head for the past couple of days, so it surprised him now to realize that he hadn't addressed her by it. But he didn't comment on it. What was he supposed to say? That he'd sighed her name, moaned it, in more than a few lurid fantasies?

She indicated his cheekbone. "That looks more serious than a scuffle."

He drew a breath, let it out. "It was."

"Does it hurt?"

"It's a dull roar. The whiskey helped."

She pushed her glass across the table toward him. "You're welcome to the rest."

"No, thanks. I've done all the bingeing I'm going to do tonight."

"Well, you did have a bugger of a day."

"Jail, you mean?"

She nodded.

"I was left to stew for several hours. Wasn't that bad."

"Did you post bail?"

"No, Rusty had a change of heart. Declined to press charges."

"That was decent of him."

He scoffed. "Decent, my ass. It was self-serving."

"In what way?"

"I don't know yet," he said grimly. "But I'm sure I'll find out."

"Dirty pool."

"Count on it."

He wondered if now was the time to tell her that he suspected Rusty of being the party surveilling her house every night. If he did, though, she would press him to explain why he would think that. He couldn't tell her without wading into the deep end. He could get in over his head real fast.

And he would be inviting more trouble for himself and everyone around him if he pointed the finger at Rusty, and the accusation was later proven to be false.

For a while neither of them pursued the topic, then Arden said, "Back to that night before Easter, were you locked up?"

"For the next several nights, in fact. I wasn't arraigned until Wednesday of the following week. They kept me in a holding cell. Old-fashioned. Off to one side of the squad room. Uncle Henry came as soon as he was notified and tried to bail me out. They gave him the run-around. He was beside himself.

"For my part, I was livid, because I knew Rusty had set me up. I already had one strike against me. Who would believe me over the sheriff's son? I spent that first night thinking up ways to eviscerate him. Finally I exhausted myself and fell asleep.

"The next morning, I woke up to a lot of chatter and activity. The squad room was buzzing. Human body parts had been discovered by early-morning fishermen in the root system of a grove of cypresses on the lakeshore. The remains were eventually identified as Brian Foster's."

"The man my father allegedly killed."

"Yeah."

He couldn't tell her how anguished he'd been to hear about that gruesome discovery. He'd had a discomfiting intuition that the dismembered parts would turn out to belong to one of his accomplices.

That was, one of the two other than Rusty.

"All day Sunday," he said, "there was a lot of coming and going in the squad room. Sheriff's deputies. Game wardens. State troopers. Organized chaos. Nobody had been reported missing, so they didn't know where to start to identify the victim. Had this been a terrible accident? Or a homicide? Easter ended with nothing concrete to report. No clues."

"What about you?"

"Me? I was fed, let out to use the bathroom, but otherwise ignored."

"You weren't questioned?"

"No. I'd already refused to talk without a lawyer. The one my uncle had called to represent me had begged off until Monday because of the holiday. Besides, my little possession charge took a back seat to the grisly discovery at the lake."

Choosing not to expand on Foster's fate, he settled an incisive look on Arden. "Your turn. What are your recollections of that Saturday? Was your dad around?"

She nodded. "All day. Lisa and I had shopping to do for Easter dinner. Dad was in the garage tinkering on something when we left for town, and was still puttering when we got back a couple of hours later. She and I dyed Easter eggs, upholding the tradition in honor of our mother. The three of us had an early supper. Dad left soon after."

"What time was that?"

"Still light, but not for long."

"Did he say where he was going?"

"To the cemetery to tend Mother's grave. Before he left, he kissed me on the top of my head and patted my shoulder."

She placed a hand on her shoulder to mark the spot. "That was the last time I saw him. That's it."

Quietly he said, "That's not even close to being *it*."

"Well, it's all I have firsthand knowledge of. We didn't know he hadn't returned home until the next morning when Lisa sent me upstairs to tell him that breakfast was ready. He didn't come home on Sunday. Lisa and I ate the Easter ham without him."

"Did you report him missing?"

"No."

"Why?"

"After my mother was killed—you know she died in a car wreck?"

"Heard that. I don't know the circumstances."

"Her name was Marjorie. She'd gone to see a former college classmate in Fayetteville, Arkansas. As she was driving back, she ran into a band of freezing rain and sleet, hit an icy patch, skidded into the back of a eighteen-wheeler."

Her eyes turned reflective. "Dad told us that she hadn't felt a thing, that she'd died instantly. Lisa never questioned or disputed him, but I seriously doubt she believed the instant-death story."

"Did you?"

She brought him back into focus. "I wanted to. With all my heart. But I'm almost certain that Dad knew better and had lied in order to spare us."

"Maybe. But maybe not."

"I guess I'll never know," she said wanly. "In any case, she was suddenly gone. Essentially, so was Dad. He was never the same. Before, he drank an occasional beer. Two at most. I guess you could say that he began drowning his sorrow.

"He fooled himself into thinking that he covered it well, that no one knew, not even Lisa and me. But of course we did. That

Easter weekend wasn't the first time he had left us without notice and stayed away from home for days at a stretch."

"Was he drinking that Saturday?"

"At the time, I didn't think so. I remember being glad of it. I was wishing for an Easter without Lisa and me pretending not to notice that he was drunk. Functioning, but drunk. We had to do that a lot."

With the tip of her finger, she traced the wood grain pattern of the table. "In hindsight, I suppose he was steadily drinking all day. But when he gave me that goodbye kiss, I didn't smell liquor on him."

Ledge asked when she'd learned about the store burglary and Foster's death.

"Dad still hadn't returned by Monday. Lisa was on spring break from college, but because she had to take care of me, there were no trips to Padre or Cancún for her. She planned to spend that week working on a paper that was due when classes resumed. The school bus picked me up that morning as usual." Ruefully, she added, "I didn't know it then, but that was the end of my *usual*. Forever.

"When the bus dropped me off that afternoon, there were several squad cars parked in front of our house. The officers had come to question Dad about his whereabouts on Saturday night."

Ledge said, "The burglary at Welch's had been discovered that Monday morning when employees reported for work. Only one was unaccounted for."

"Mr. Foster," she said. "Dad's employment at the store was short-lived. He didn't take his dismissal well, called it unjust. He was particularly bitter toward Mr. Foster."

"Why?"

"His termination had come from higher-ups, but it was Foster who'd hand-delivered Dad his severance check."

"Huh."

That was a previously unknown fact that Ledge tucked away for further review.

"According to people who witnessed the exchange," Arden said, "Dad was verbally abusive to Foster."

"So, when the human remains found in the lake were identified as his, and Joe Maxwell and the stolen cash were nowhere to be found..."

She raised a shoulder. "The logical conclusion was that Dad was the culprit, that possibly he'd coerced or blackmailed Mr. Foster into opening the store and the safe, then killed him."

"That's the logical conclusion, yes. But do you believe it?"

"No." When he continued to look hard at her, she repeated the denial. "Dad drank. He would get emotional and senti-mental, but never violent. Not once. It wasn't in his nature."

"Sober, maybe."

She gave a stern shake of her head. "Even drunk. He was maudlin, but never mean."

"It was well known that he was struggling financially."

"That's true," she said. "It's *possible* that Dad had become desperate enough to clean out the store safe with Brian Foster's help. I could almost accept that. But I don't believe Dad could have killed him afterward. He didn't have it in him to kill anybody, no matter the circumstances."

"Arden," he said softly, "with half a million dollars at stake, circumstances can turn ugly in a heartbeat."

Chapter 17

That night in 2000—Brian Foster

"…in addition to hiding the money," Rusty said, "we need a fall guy."

"Someone to take the blame?"

"That's what fall guys do, Foster."

"I know, I know, but—"

"We may not need one, but we should have it set up in case Burnet double-crosses us."

"Yeah, okay," Brian said. "It's probably a good idea. But who?"

"The town drunk, otherwise known as Joe Maxwell."

Disbelieving that Rusty could be serious, Brian switched his cell phone from one damp hand to the other.

For days leading up to tonight, he had been a nervous wreck.

Actually, since the day Rusty Dyle had approached him with his heist scheme, Brian had been teetering on the borderline of a complete meltdown. It wasn't as though he and the sheriff's son were close friends who had been blood brothers since childhood and trusted each other implicitly.

They had met only a few months ago, and it had been Rusty, with his engaging swagger, who had suggested that they "hang out." That invitation to camaraderie was a startling and flattering first for Brian. Nobody had ever asked him for companionship. He didn't have an appealing personality. Indeed, it was blah, which was a drawback to making friends, or so his mother had hammered home to him. Daily.

Her assessment had been shared by his first employer, who, after Brian had been on the job for only three months, had called him into a closed-door meeting, during which he had described Brian as "unprepossessing," and then had fired him for failing to show initiative. He didn't foresee the likelihood of Brian acquiring a go-getter spirit. Ever. Basically: Make yourself scarce.

That having been his first job after graduating junior college, it was an inauspicious launch of his professional life.

Following his dismissal, he had spent an anxious month of unemployment before seeing the online notice of an open position in Penton, Texas, for Welch's Mercantile. Never having heard of either, he had looked them up on the internet.

Both the town and the position at Welch's had seemed to Brian to be as unprepossessing as he. But for a young man who'd grown up in the Steel Belt, the geographical area with its dense pine forests and mystical-looking lake held some allure. Also, it promised escape from the only house in which he had ever lived, with his pipsqueak father and domineering mother.

He had submitted his application, figuring that a relocation to Texas was about as adventurous as he was likely ever to get.

Little had he known then.

He survived the rounds of interviews conducted over the

telephone and was awarded the position. He packed his car to the gills and made the move. He signed a lease on a duplex whose best feature was that the rent included a cable hookup.

The hearty friendliness of the people, as well as their accent, would take some getting used to. He had a virulent gastrointestinal experience with his first Tex-Mex meal. But the mystifying lake, whose lore included a sasquatch, lived up to the pictures he had seen online. His new situation held promise.

That was dashed on his first day on the job.

His boss had shaken his hand, welcomed him to the accounts receivable/payable department. Then, with badly capped teeth glittering, he had said, "You mess up, you're history."

He was a strutting, bandy-legged tyrant to whom management and terrorism were synonymous. Brian was a perfect target for his scornful putdowns. Within a week of his employment, Brian had become miserable.

However, he couldn't—wouldn't—pack up and go home and have his mother tell him, "I told you so." He resolved to tough it out for as long as he could stand it, telling himself that there would come a day.

That day had come in early January.

He had returned to the store from his lunch break when he'd collided, literally, with a young man with spiky orange hair.

"Hey, sorry, man," he'd said. "Didn't see you. This damn thing." He'd shifted the cumbersome box from beneath his left arm to beneath his right. "My mom sent me to get a refund." He'd snorted contempt. "My dad's idea of a romantic Christmas present for her. Pots and pans. Seriously? Even I know better."

Unable to think of anything else to say, Brian remarked that the cookware set had been on sale through Christmas Eve.

"Probably was when my old man bought it. Last minute, you know. Anyhow, she sent me to bring it back. Didn't know there would be such a damn long line."

He'd leaned in a little closer and lowered his voice. "I thought about walking the box back to the housewares section and just leaving it there on the shelf, screw the refund. But they've got cameras everywhere," he'd said, glancing up at the ceiling. "If somebody saw me do it and wondered *What the hell is he up to?*, I'd have to spend time explaining. Just as well stand in line."

"The cameras aren't real. They're for show."

"Get out!" the young man had exclaimed in a stage whisper. "They're fakes?"

"Yes."

"You're shittin' me."

"No."

"How do you know? Do you work here?"

"Accounting."

"A bean counter, huh?" He had said it with good humor, not like he was deriding Brian. "You must be really smart. Me and numbers? Forget it. PE and lunch are my standout subjects."

PE and lunch had been Brian's worst two hours of the school day, but he chuckled as though he shared the joke.

"How long have you worked here?"

"I signed on just in time for the Christmas season."

"Oh, man. How bad did that suck?"

Brian was enjoying being talked to in the vernacular. Although the stranger was a few years younger than he, he was conversing with him in the casual manner of one man to another, and that rarely happened to Brian. Correction: It never happened to Brian.

However, as much as he was enjoying it, he remembered the

time. "Well, I'm due back from lunch. Have a nice day." He'd been about to move off when the young man waylaid him.

"Say, listen. Could you help me out here? Since you're an employee, you could jump this out-of-sight line, right?"

"Well, I—"

"Just carry this box behind the counter like it's your business. I've got the receipt. My old man paid cash. Should be a no-brainer to get the money back. What do you say?"

Brian had hesitated and was still considering it when the kid had nudged him with his elbow. "Grandpa Welch probably wouldn't appreciate a new employee telling a customer that the security cameras are bogus."

A wave of dizziness swept over Brian. He had actually felt the blood draining from his head. He heard his mother calling him a dumb bunny.

But then the young man had thrown his head back and laughed. "You should see your face," he'd chortled. "I'm harmless. Swear I am. My old man is the sheriff."

Brian's knees had gone weak with relief.

"Had you going there, didn't I?"

Brian had tried to laugh at the teasing, but achieved only a squeaky sound.

"I'm sorry. Really. Now, what about doing me this little favor?"

Brian heard himself say, "Sure."

Bravely, he'd jumped the line of disgruntled customers. Even the employee working the counter gave him grief until Brian had told her that he was acting on behalf of the sheriff's son.

"Rusty?"

Brian wasn't sure what to make of the way she raised her penciled brow and gave a sour-sounding harrumph.

He returned to where he'd left the young man waiting and

counted out his refund. "The lady at the counter said your name is Rusty."

"Rusty Dyle. What's yours?"

"Brian Foster."

"I don't forget favors, Brian. Thanks." After pocketing the refunded money, he'd given Brian an assessing once-over. "Got a wife?"

"No."

"Live-in girlfriend?"

"No."

"You gay?"

"No."

"Great. Let's hang out. What's your phone number?"

Brian's boss had been waiting for him at his desk, fuming over his lateness. Brian calmly had said, "I'm a few minutes late because I was doing a favor for Sheriff Dyle's son. If you have a problem with that, I suggest you take it up with him."

He had never felt more like a man.

Rusty had phoned him the very next day and invited him to meet at a spot on the lake. "You've turned twenty-one, right?"

"Almost twenty-two."

"Awesome. You get to buy the six-pack."

They had three more beer-drinking sessions before Rusty broached the subject of the burglary. He'd prefaced it with: "This might sound crazy. Hell, it *is* crazy. But what's life all about if you don't take a few risks?"

Brian had risked his livelihood—everything—in order to pull off the burglary. He was already dreading Monday and the playacting he would have to do. And now Rusty was asking him to take yet another risk.

They'd gotten away clean. Then that broody boy with the blue eyes had gotten himself arrested, and Rusty was convinced that he would betray them. Rusty wanted Brian to help him hide the money.

Brian wanted to throw up.

How had he gotten himself into this mess? After tonight, and for the rest of his life, he would be a *criminal*. Him. Dull, drab, blah Brian Foster. Nobody would believe it of him. His mother wouldn't believe it of him. *He* didn't believe it of himself.

Maybe this was a bizarre and elaborate nightmare from which he would soon wake up.

But Rusty had also said that they needed to set up Joe Maxwell as their fall guy.

Brian didn't know Mr. Maxwell well. When he'd been fired from Welch's, Brian had had the misfortune of having to give him his severance check. Taking his anger out on Brian, Joe had given him a tongue-lashing that had been heavy on expletives.

But a few days later, Mr. Maxwell had called to apologize for his outburst. "I'm sorry I created that scene. It wasn't your fault I got canned."

Coworkers had enlightened Brian to Mr. Maxwell's lamentable history, being left a widower, losing his business. Given the circumstances, Brian had thought the apology was most decent of the man.

While Brian was thinking back on that phone call, and the moral fiber Joe Maxwell had exhibited by making it, Rusty had been enumerating all the traits that made the older man the perfect scapegoat.

Rusty called him a loser who had nothing going for him. The more Rusty talked, Brian gradually came to realize that Rusty was also characterizing Ledge Burnet, who'd already served a stint in juvenile detention. He was bound for jail for the second time, and he hadn't even graduated high school yet. With even more clarity, Brian realized that he could fill in his own name each time Rusty made a disparaging comment about the down-and-out Mr. Maxwell.

That's when it dawned on him that they all three would make ideal patsies for Rusty Dyle, whose immunity was practically guaranteed because his father was not only a high-ranking public official, he was also the most corrupt.

Rusty ended his speech by saying, "So let's meet there, okay?"

Brian was dumbstruck by a disturbing realization: He was the last person anybody with half a brain would choose as an accomplice to shoplift a pack of chewing gum, much less to pull a grand heist like this.

Beyond gaining entrance into the store and opening the safe, what purpose did he serve? His mother would say, "That of chump, stupid."

Rusty shouted in his ear. "Brian!"

He'd been dumbstruck by the revelation and had to swallow several times before acknowledging Rusty.

"What the hell? I thought we'd gotten disconnected."

"No, I'm here," Brian said huskily.

"What do you think?"

He swallowed again. "I think it's really unfair to Mr. Maxwell. He—"

"Okay, okay, never mind about that now. We'll cross that bridge *only* if and when we need to. Top priority now is to hide this money. Remember where we knocked back that first six-pack of Coors? I'll meet you there in half an hour. Lots of places along that channel to stash it. See you there." Then he was gone.

Brian used three of his allotted thirty minutes just sitting there, staring at his phone.

Finally he moved, but only his thumb, to scroll through his call log. It didn't amount to more than a dozen calls, mostly to the pizza place that delivered. But among the calls was the one Joe Maxwell had placed to him a few weeks earlier.

He took a deep breath and tapped on it.

Mr. Maxwell must have seen that it was Brian calling, because he answered in a hushed, but surprised, voice. "Foster?"

"Yes, it's me. We need to talk, Mr. Maxwell. Like right now."

Chapter 18

Ledge carried Arden's empty plate to the sink and returned the sandwich makings to the fridge. "Want anything else?"

"No thank you. Were you convicted of the drug charge?"

He went back to the table and sat down. "The subject was your dad."

"It *was*. I told you all I know. I want to hear what happened after your arrest."

"The case never went to trial. My lawyer negotiated a plea deal for me. Misdemeanor possession instead of a felony charge. He argued that the deputies had stopped me without probable cause. Which was true.

"It galled me to admit to doing something I hadn't done, but they had the evidence, so I took the deal. I was resigned to spending at least a few months in county. But when it came time for sentencing, the judge called me, my attorney, and my uncle into his chambers. He offered me an alternative."

"The army?"

"Good guess. The judge was a Vietnam veteran, very pro

military, a hawk. He told my uncle that boot camp and a tough drill sergeant would have me whipped into shape in no time. It was quite a recruitment spiel, and Uncle Henry recognized the advantages. But he bargained for the charges to be dismissed."

She sat back in her chair and shook her head with dismay. "You must have been so relieved."

"Relieved, yeah, but I wasn't let off the hook. Both my uncle and the judge put the fear of God in me. They warned me that if I didn't apply myself, there would be hell to pay."

Laughing quietly, she said, "I can't believe it."

"At the time, it was hard for me to take in, too. Everything happened fast. I was a couple of months shy of graduating high school, but passed all the exams and got my diploma. Next day, I was sent to basic training."

"Applied yourself and returned twelve years later a hero."

He shook his head and, speaking low, said, "Don't mistake me for a hero."

"People say you are."

"Those who say that don't know."

Frowning with concentration, she said, "Well, I know one thing."

"What's that?"

"You're unlike anyone else I've ever met."

He wanted to ask her in what way he was unique, but was afraid of how she would answer. He broke her thoughtful stare to glance down at his watch. "It's late." He stood up. "I'll lead you home."

"That's unnecessary."

"The road is tricky in full daylight. In the dark, if you don't know it well, you could wind up in a bayou."

"I'll manage."

"Argument over." He went to the door and pulled it open.

A few minutes later, her headlights were in his rearview mirror. If she fell too far behind, he slowed down until she caught up. When they reached her house, he got out of his truck and, despite her protests, walked her to the back door.

"These new locks are impossible," she said as she worked the key into the slot.

"They're meant to be."

"For a bad guy, not for me." The lock snapped, she swung the door open and poked her head inside. "See? No intruder lying in wait."

He gave the small of her back a nudge, then followed her in, went around her, and checked out the rooms on the first floor, switching lights on, then off, as he made his way.

They met at the bottom of the staircase. "You didn't look up there." She pointed to the dark landing above.

"An intruder would have had to come in on the ground floor. Nothing's been disturbed."

"As noted earlier, you've been my only intruder." She gave him a brief smile, then lowered her gaze to the placket of his shirt. "Will you be coming to work in the morning?"

"Not to restore, but to destroy?"

Still addressing his shirt, she said, "I suppose I do owe you an explanation for the switch."

"Your sister told you last night you didn't owe me a damn thing."

"Well, she's wrong."

"Okay. I'm listening."

"I'll do my best to explain, but even I'm conflicted."

"Over what?"

"It's hard to put into words."

"I don't know that many anyway. Make it simple."

She tugged her lower lip through her teeth. "It sounds

so banal, but I came back to Penton to get closure. This house represents sorrow and heartache to me. If it comes down—"

"It won't fix a damn thing. I don't mean to interrupt, but, look, the house is a house. It's made of destructible materials. All the shit that took place in it when you were a kid will be with you for the rest of your life. It's not inside the house, it's inside *you*. Curse it, accept it, and then turn your back on it."

"I can do that with the shit I *know*," she said. "It's what I *don't know* that plagues me."

All of a sudden he was wary of where this might be going. He backed away from her and leaned against the newel post. "What you 'don't know'?"

"I moved back here needing answers. But not only have they eluded me, the longer I'm here, the more questions I have, the more gaps I see that need filling."

She folded in on herself as she sat down on the second step of the staircase. She didn't say anything for a time, but rubbed her thumb across her other palm, studying the faint network of lines as though trying to gain insight from their intersections.

"I still feel like that ten-year-old girl caught up in a crisis. The grown-ups are speaking in euphemisms to shield me from harsh realities. I've been given the outline, but not the whole story. I feel that the parts I'm missing are the ones I should know." She looked up at him and shook her head. "Never mind. I don't expect you to understand."

On the contrary, he understood perfectly, and his conscience was killing him over it. He was missing elements of that night himself, but those he had intimate knowledge of, he had intentionally kept from her. How much longer could he sustain that secrecy? Every day she was here upped the odds that she would discover the active role young Ledge Burnet had played in the course her life had taken.

Better to drive her away now, when she disliked and distrusted him only a little, and before Rusty got wind of her interest in the events of that night.

Salving his conscience by telling himself that his lying was for her own good, he lied again. "You're right. I don't understand. You came here to get closure. Didn't work. You're miserable. Why not call it quits and leave?"

"You sound like Lisa."

"God help me, but she has a point. Have you asked her about those gaps that bother you?"

"Of course, but Dad's disappearance affected us differently. It changed her life profoundly, yes. But she was grown, mentally and emotionally, already independent of him. Anytime I bring up my ambiguity, she tells me I should do as she did. Put it all behind me and move on."

"I agree with that advice. It can't be healthy, hanging around a place that pains you. Just go."

"With nothing resolved?" She shook her head. "Relocating wouldn't achieve anything. You said so yourself. The uncertainties that devil me aren't within the house, they're—"

"Forget what I said. It was horseshit. What do I know? I'm no shrink. But maybe that's what you need."

"I've had therapy. Lisa couldn't afford it until after she married Wallace. He was a godsend in so many ways. He and Lisa formed a happy twosome. I was a—"

"Fifth wheel?"

"They did nothing to make me feel that way. But their togetherness compounded my feelings of what the therapist called 'displacement.'"

"Was the counseling helpful?"

"Some. But it's obvious it didn't rid me of all my issues. I won't be rid of them until I get some answers."

Fuck. Back to *answers*. Answers to questions that, if asked, would put her in danger from Rusty.

"Arden, listen, I'll do whatever you want me to. I'll either take this place apart or redo it. But I need to get going on it, because I've got other jobs waiting. Decide tonight what you want me to do, and then clear out tomorrow."

"Clear out?"

"The earlier the better."

"Where am I going?"

"Houston? Dallas? How the hell should I know? Choose a place."

"I'm not going anywhere."

He squared his stance. "Whatever I do to the house, you can't be here while I'm doing it. Especially if I tear it down."

"I'll wait until the last minute to move out."

"It'll be a mess."

"It's already a mess."

"Yes, but nothing like it will be. You have to leave."

"If I leave, people will start wondering—"

"They're going to wonder no matter what. Besides, you won't know what they're wondering, because you'll be gone."

"You never indicated that I would have to vacate."

"Yes, I did."

"No you didn't. Not once." She came to her feet, bringing them almost eye level to each other. "This is the first I've heard of it."

"Then that was an oversight on my part. Sorry. But I'm telling you now. You can't stay. It's my work site, I make the rules."

She thought on it. "Well, I guess I could rent a lake cabin nearby."

There were dozens of vacation rentals within a ten-mile radius of Penton. For his peace of mind, that was too close. "Wouldn't your sister put you up?"

"She's offered."

"Well, there you go. That was easy."

"But I don't want to stay with Lisa. I want to be close enough to check on the progress each day."

"My progress? On the house? No."

"Why not?"

"Be reasonable. You can't be popping in and out of here while walls are coming down."

"It's my house."

"And my liability."

"Don't you have liability insurance?"

"A good question. A little late for you to be asking, though."

"Do you?"

"Yes, but it's for crap. It wouldn't cover a hangnail."

She was about to say something but stopped herself and looked at him with sudden suspicion. "You're making this up as you go along, aren't you?"

He just looked at her.

"You are," she said. "You're trying to get rid of me. Just like you did when I came to your workshop that first day. You're throwing out bullshit and hoping I'll accept it."

He should have known that she would see through the ruse. He relaxed his combatant posture, swore under his breath, and gave a realigning roll of his shoulders. "Yeah, I am."

"Why?"

"It would be better if you left town, that's all."

"Better for me or for you?"

"Both."

"Why don't you want me here?"

"Because you could get hurt."

"How could I get hurt?"

"All kinds of ways."

"For instance?"

"You mean besides your nightly drive-by?"

"Who so far has only driven past. Why do you fear I'll get hurt?"

"Christ." He lowered his head and focused on the one stair step between them. "Because I would be seeing you every day, but having to keep my hands off you." He looked up at her from beneath his brows and spoke from the heart. "And I don't think I can do that."

The silence between them stretched out, and, correspondingly, the sexual yearning she felt low and deep continued to tug at her until she took the next step down. Which was all the urging he needed.

He curved his arm around her waist and pulled her against him as their mouths sought each other. Last night's kiss had stunned her. She'd had no time to think, to react, before it was over. However, for all its brevity, it had left her shaken, breathless, and irrationally aroused.

Throughout the day, she'd caught herself analyzing that kiss, the manly spontaneity that had sparked it, the bold lustiness of it, and its startling, erotic effect on her.

But all her analyses had left her no better prepared for this kiss. She might have invited it, but he immediately took charge of it. Taking unrestricted possession of her mouth, he slid his tongue along hers. She responded with an involuntary, shivery movement of her breasts against his chest.

A low growl emanated from his throat. His hands grazed the sides of her breasts before coasting down her rib cage to bracket her hips. His fingers tensed, pressing into the curve of her bottom and holding her still as he pressed against the notch of her thighs.

But only long enough for her to respond with a subtle grinding motion against him, and then he retreated and brought his hands up to her face. He cradled it between his palms as he broke the kiss. His eyes moved over each of her features and then stayed intent on her lips. He brushed her hair off one cheek, then rested his scruffy one against it and spoke, feverishly and roughly, directly into her ear.

"I want to be skin to skin with you. So bad it's killing me." His kept his lips there for seconds more, his breath unsteady and hot. Then he aligned his forehead with hers. "But I can't, Arden." Lightly, he bumped his forehead against hers as he repeated it. "I can't."

He released her, turned and walked away, through the kitchen and out the back door. It was the click of that blasted lock that spurred her. She hurdled the bottom step and dashed toward the kitchen. She undid the lock and flung open the back door, then charged after him.

"Wait a minute!"

He stopped and turned. She didn't slow down until she came to a dead stop no more than a foot in front of him. "I won't keep doing this. No more good night kisses."

He raised one shoulder in a negligent manner that made her want to smack the scratchy cheek that minutes ago had been nuzzling hers.

He said, "I *can't* keep doing it. You *won't* keep doing it. Problem solved if you would pack up and leave tomorrow." He motioned toward the house with his chin. "But for tonight, get back inside and lock the door."

"Go to hell and take your damn locks with you."

"I don't know what you're mad about. I could've carried

you into that nun's cell of sleeping quarters you've got, and we'd be hard at it by now. Hell, I could've had you on the staircase. By leaving, I was trying to do the right thing. You should be thanking me."

"Thanking you? For using me to get a cheap thrill, to cheat on your girlfriend, make her jealous, whatever? No. But I do have something to thank you for."

She flung her hand toward the house. "You opened my eyes about the house. Build it up, tear it down, the mysteries will still be there. Like freaking ghosts. But I'm going to rid myself of them."

She pulled herself up straighter. "Your services won't be needed after all, Mr. Burnet. The house will stay as is, indefinitely, while I look for answers somewhere else."

She turned.

"Arden, wait. Stop. Will you wait a goddamn minute?" he shouted. "What do you mean you'll look for answers somewhere else?"

She kept walking, went inside, and slammed the door behind her, taking great pleasure in locking him out with the hardware he'd provided.

Chapter 19

Ledge knocked. "It's me."

Seconds later, Crystal opened her front door and greeted him with a smile. "Well, you've made yourself scarce lately. To what do I owe this unexpected pleasure?"

"Where's Marty?"

"Working the three-to-eleven shift."

She stepped aside, and he went in, saying, "Don't bet on it being a pleasure to see me."

"You're in a mood?"

"And then some."

"Does it have to do with that gash on your face?"

"That's the tip of the iceberg."

"Sounds ominous."

"It is."

He made his way into the living room, where he plopped down in the center of the sofa, laid his head back on the cushion, and dug the heels of his hands into his eye sockets. "Jesus, what a mess."

"Henry?" she asked with worry.

"Well, that, yeah. But not in particular tonight."

She claimed the corner of the sofa and curled her legs up under her hips. "What's going on?"

He lowered his hands and rolled his head to the side in order to look at her. Time and maturity had changed her features only slightly. She maintained the exotic—some called it bewitching—quality she'd had the first time he'd noticed her.

Fifth grade. Recess. She'd been standing off to one side of the playground, alone. She hadn't been included in any of the horseplay or games. She hadn't attempted to join any. She'd spent the entire twenty minutes of freedom looking confined, standing alongside the cyclone fence, shrinking against it any time another kid came near, as though afraid she would be noticed and challenged for taking up space.

Ledge had had his share of experience with that kind of social ostracism. He'd been the only kid in his grade who didn't have at least one living parent. His uncle was raising him, and his "home" was the ell annex of a bar and pool hall. That had made him different, which meant he might just as well have had leprosy.

However, even at that age, he'd been tough enough, sizable enough, to pose a threat to the elementary school kingpins like Rusty Dyle.

But this girl with skinny legs and breasts just beginning to bud on her narrow chest appeared too timid to defend herself against a butterfly. His feelings of protectiveness began that day, although he hadn't even known her name yet.

They were in different classrooms, but after that recess, he'd made it his business to find out that her name was Crystal Ivers. He'd kept an eye on her in the cafeteria and on the playground, ready to jump in if anybody bothered her.

No one did. She was ignored. Which in many ways was worse.

Then one windy day after dismissal, he'd spotted her chasing down the contents of her notebook, which she'd dropped on the sidewalk. He'd run to help. Between the two of them, they'd managed to collect all the scattered sheets of paper.

He'd walked over the ones he'd caught and handed them to her. She'd thanked him in a voice he could barely hear as she'd stuffed her schoolwork back into her notebook and, using both thin arms, secured it against her chest. Shyly, she'd met his gaze then given a furtive look around.

To begin a dialogue, he'd said, "You're in Miss Henderson's class." Then he thought that was a dumb thing to say. Like she didn't know whose class she was in. "My name's Ledge. Ledge Burnet."

She'd shot another quick look over her shoulder. "I'm not supposed to talk to boys."

Then, like a flash, she'd taken off, walking hurriedly down the sidewalk still hugging her notebook. When she reached the corner, the passenger door of a parked maroon pickup swung open, and she'd climbed in.

Ledge hadn't approached her again, although they were always aware of each other at school, never speaking but making brief eye contact any time their paths crossed.

He hadn't been a member of the cool crowd commandeered by Rusty, but Henry had seen to it that he participated in sports and other school activities. He cultivated a small but tight circle of friends.

As he got older, he'd been much sought after by girls. His aloofness notwithstanding, and probably because of it, he'd been considered the catch of all catches. He enjoyed an enviable amount of action, but the choice of a partner was always his. No one girl had ever been able to label him "hers."

By contrast, Crystal was a nonentity. She wasn't a member of any school group, never attended a ball game, dance, or private party. Ledge never had understood why. Until the day he'd found out why. And on that day, he'd almost killed her stepbrother.

She always had possessed an uncanny ability to read him, and as she scrutinized him now, she said, "You're strolling down memory lane, aren't you?"

"How can you tell?"

"Because you're wearing the same ferocious scowl that you were when you caught me hiding in the culvert."

By then, they'd been sophomores in high school. During the intervening years, Crystal had turned into a beauty. She had a Native American gene somewhere in her ancestry that was manifested in her slanted hazel eyes and high cheekbones. Her breasts had filled out to a solid C. Her legs were no longer skinny, and she was no longer ignored. She had the attention of the male student population.

Ledge had overheard Rusty Dyle telling his cronies that he'd like to get his hands on the Ivers chick's ass, which was the best one in school, bar none.

Ledge had wanted to clock him, but instead he had pretended not to have heard the remark. Any reaction from him would have been noticed and acted upon by Rusty, more than likely to Crystal's detriment.

She had developed a reputation for being a go-to girl if you were looking to get laid or blown, but Ledge attributed the rumors to jealousy from the girls who started them, and to the wishful thinking of boys who fueled the rumor mill. How could she be giving away easy sex when she was never in the company of peers?

One day he'd seen Crystal rushing out of the cafeteria during lunch period, obviously upset. On impulse, he'd left his unfinished lunch and went after her, following her out of the building and off campus.

He'd stayed at a distance behind her, until he saw her leave the sidewalk and slip-slide down a steep ravine. He'd run to catch up and discovered her sitting in a concrete culvert, her back to the damp, curved wall, head bent over her raised knees, crying so hard her body shook.

When he spoke her name, she'd jumped and was about to scramble to her feet. He'd put out his hand in a steadying gesture. "Go ahead and cry if you need to. I'll just sit here with you. Okay?"

Slowly, he lowered himself into a crouch in front of her. She watched him with wariness, but when he didn't make a move to touch her, she'd replaced her head on her knees and cried herself out.

When she finally had run dry, she raised her head and wiped tears off her bloated, splotchy face. "Go away. You'll only make it worse by being here."

"Make what worse?"

"The things they say about me."

"Who says?"

"Everybody."

"Screw them."

She gave a bitter laugh. "They say I do." Settling her forehead on her knees again, she'd spoken softly, but stressfully. "I don't do those things they say. Why would I want to? I hate it. It's awful. It hurts."

The words seeped into Ledge like a vile and oily venom. He thought about her strict isolation, and the maroon pickup truck that transported her to and from school, remembered clearly her saying with a tremor in her child's voice, *I'm not supposed to talk to boys.*

"What hurts, Crystal?"

Though her head still rested on her knees, she gave a negative shake. "I can't tell."

"You can tell me."

"So you can blab it to everybody else."

"I wouldn't do that."

She raised her head and looked at him skeptically.

He said, "I swear I'll never tell anything you ask me not to. Who hurts you?"

Her eyes filled to overflowing with fresh tears, and, in a raw voice, she whispered, "My stepbrother."

A surge of red-hot rage consumed him. "He abuses you? Like, touches you?"

"It started out that way. Now..." She couldn't go on, but her expression had spoken volumes.

Ledge settled back on his rump and didn't take his eyes off her face as she'd told him the whole sordid story.

It had started when her stepfather died. His son continued to live with Crystal and her mother. Her mother was aware of his molestation, but she was too afraid of him to do anything about it. They lived in terror of him. His name was Morg Young.

Morg Young was a regular at the bar, one who Henry and Don had just as soon do his carousing someplace else. He picked fights, was generally disorderly, and, once, Henry had tossed him out for harassing a woman who had neither invited nor welcomed his attention. Ledge would never have connected that redneck lowlife to Crystal, who had a different last name.

Now, Ledge reached across to the corner of the sofa and covered her knee with his hand. "To this day, I wish I had killed him."

"You very nearly did."

He had been too young to serve liquor, but often, after he

had finished his dinner and homework, he'd helped out in the bar by sweeping, washing glasses, unloading cases of product, anything that needed doing.

That night around ten o'clock, Morg Young had come in alone and, after getting a beer from Don, had sauntered over to the billiards area and asked those standing around the tables which one of them was ready to lose some money. He'd played several games and stayed until closing. He had been one of the last customers to leave.

Unnoticed by his uncle and Don, Ledge had gone into the stockroom, then slipped out the back door. He caught up with Crystal's abuser just as he was about to climb into his truck.

Five minutes later, Ledge was again pushing the broom across the barroom floor. A customer who had bid everyone a good night and left rushed back inside, breathless. "Guess Morg spouted off to the wrong man tonight. He's lying out there by his truck, beat to a pulp."

Henry rushed outside to assess the situation. Don called 911. As in the wake of all violent emergencies, the next half hour had been eventful. In the midst of it, Don had noticed Ledge's bloody, swollen knuckles and had looked at him with alarm.

Ledge mumbled, "He had it coming."

Don had held his gaze for a moment, glanced over at Henry and, particularly, at the pair of sheriff's deputies who were questioning him about who Morg had been playing pool with. Coming back to Ledge, Don said querulously, "Aren't you supposed to be studying for an algebra test?"

Taking the hint, Ledge had gone to his room and lay on his bed, staring at the ceiling for almost an hour before Henry came in. He'd sat down heavily on the foot of the bed, and looked at Ledge's bruised hands.

"How'd you get crosswise with that horse's ass?"

"I didn't."

"Then why'd you send him to the hospital?"

"There's this girl in my grade. Crystal. She's his stepsister. Today, I caught her crying. She talked to me. Personal like." He stared hard into Henry's eyes, and what he had sworn to Crystal not to tell, he compelled his uncle to interpret.

"Morg messes with her?"

Ledge didn't say anything, but he didn't have to.

"Jesus." Henry had dragged his hand down his face and contemplated the gravity of the situation. "The girl's name is Crystal?"

"Ivers."

Henry repeated her name as though committing it to memory. "Is she your girlfriend?"

"Not like that."

"This wasn't secondhand information? She told you herself?"

Ledge just looked at him.

"Are you sure she's telling the truth?"

The question had so angered Ledge, he'd glared at his uncle.

"Okay, okay." Henry had tugged on his chin thoughtfully. "Could he point you out as the guy who attacked him?"

"I made sure he didn't see me."

"Did anybody?"

"I don't think so."

"I don't think so, either. The man who found him said the parking lot was empty except for his car and one other, and no one else was around."

"What will happen?"

"I don't know. Let me think on what I'm going to do about this. I should turn you in. On the other hand..." He sighed and rubbed his forehead. "I understand why you did it. I'd be tempted to myself." He pondered it for a moment longer, then said, "For the time being, keep your head down, your mouth shut, and pray that the son of a bitch doesn't die."

"I wish he would."

"No, you don't, Ledge," Henry had said, sounding angry for the first time. "No, you don't. It's ugly what he's done. Damn ugly. Disgusting and criminal, and he should never see the light of day for the rest of his miserable, perverted life. But you can't be his judge and jury. You can't go taking matters into your own hands."

"Nobody else did."

"No, but...but...Aw, hell. There's no arguing with you when you think you're right. In that respect you're just like my brother was." He'd spoken with both gruff annoyance and affection.

"Please promise me that from now on, when you want to set a wrong situation right, you'll talk it over with me first. We'll figure out a way to fix it that doesn't involve you drawing blood. Promise?"

That was the second promise that Ledge had been called upon to make that day. He'd upheld his promise to Crystal never to reveal her secret. To an extent. He hadn't told about Morg out loud. But he'd intimated enough that his uncle had read between the lines.

Although he and Ledge had never mentioned it again in all the years since, Henry must have reported the abuse to CPS, the cops, something, because when Morg had recovered enough to be released from the hospital, he'd left it manacled and in police custody.

Crystal and her mother were persuaded by the authorities to testify against him. He stood trial and was convicted. Only three months into his prison sentence, another inmate had done the world a favor by jamming a shiv into Morg's left kidney, killing him.

Ledge could justify fudging a bit on his promise to Crystal, because it had served to liberate her and her mother from the degenerate. However, he'd flat broken the promise he had made his uncle Henry. After leaving the diner on that rainy Saturday morning, he should have gone straight to Henry and told him about Rusty's mad plan to burglarize Welch's. He hadn't. That had been costly bad judgment, which he was still paying for.

To this day. To this moment.

Crystal covered his hand resting on her knee with her own. "Memory lane is a dangerous neighborhood, Ledge. Why don't you stay out of it?"

"I wish I could. I can't."

"What's happened? What's the matter?"

He pulled his hand from beneath hers. "The night I got arrested for the second time, when all that weed was found in my car? Remember?"

Caution clouded her eyes. "What about it?"

"Was Rusty with you that night?"

Her expression became guarded. "That was twenty years ago."

"I know exactly how long ago it was, Crystal. Please answer the fucking question."

She hesitated, then left the sofa, went over to a bar cart, and uncapped a bottle of bourbon.

"I don't want a drink."

"It's not for you, it's for me." She poured and carried the glass of neat whiskey over to him. "But you'll probably need one, too."

He took the glass from her but didn't drink from it. She returned to the bar and poured another for herself. "Yes, Rusty came to my house that night. My old house. Mother was asleep. He knocked on my bedroom window and threatened to raise a ruckus that would wake the dead if I didn't let him in."

"What time was that?"

"Lord, Ledge, I don't remember."

"Try."

"Why is it so important?"

"*What time?*"

"Late. One, one-thirty. Thereabout. And I couldn't swear to that. I was too astonished by the condition he was in."

"What condition?"

She gave him a withering look. "Like you don't know."

Matching her pique, he thumped his untouched drink onto the coffee table. "Please stop making me repeat my questions. Describe his *condition.*"

She took a quick sip of her whiskey. "He was all banged up. His jaw had a fist-sized bruise. Here." She pressed her knuckles against her jawline in front of her ear. "His lower lip was split open. His left arm was black-and-blue, swollen twice its normal size. I assumed that it was broken. An assumption that was later confirmed. He was in a lot of pain. Anxious. Sweating profusely."

The more she told him, the more incredulous Ledge became. She wasn't describing Rusty as Ledge had last seen him that night, getting out of his car and taking the canvas bag of cash with him. He hadn't been battered and bruised. He'd been his whole and healthy, arrogant, asshole self.

"Did he tell you what had happened to him?"

Her eyes remaining on him, she said softly and with empathy, "Yes, Ledge, he did. There's no need for you to pretend anymore. I know what you two did that night."

Chapter 20

That night in 2000—Crystal

W hat in God's name happened to you?"

After letting Rusty in through her bedroom window, Crystal spoke in a stage whisper out of fear of waking up her mother. Morg was gone for good, but her mother still slept fitfully.

Rusty shouldered Crystal aside and went to sit on her bed, cradling his arm against his abdomen. "Get me something to drink."

"I don't have any alcohol."

"Nothing? None?"

"Nothing. None."

"Who doesn't keep a bottle for emergencies?"

"Since Morg was put away, Mother's gone apostolic."

Rusty swore under his breath. "Percocet?"

She shook her head. "Nothing like that. Your arm looks broken. You need a doctor."

"No."

"But—"

"Not now! Okay?" He grimaced with pain. "You must have aspirin. Advil?"

"I'll drive you to the ER."

"For godsake, Crystal, will you give it up? I can't go right now."

"Why not?"

"Because I can't."

"What happened?"

"Your boyfriend happened, that's what."

"Ledge?"

"Ledge," he repeated, mimicking her astonishment. "You gotta have a fucking aspirin."

"Shh! All right."

She left the room and slipped down the hallway, moving as silently as possible past her mother's closed bedroom door. Using only the nightlight in the bathroom, she took a bottle of Advil from the medicine cabinet and rinsed out the toothbrush glass. She made it back to her bedroom without being detected.

In her absence, Rusty had switched on the bedside lamp. In its dim glow, he looked ghastly. He had smeared the blood dripping from his mouth across his chin. Drops of blood speckled the front of his shirt. He continued to hold his left forearm against his middle.

With his uninjured hand, he lifted his shirttail and inspected the damage done to his midsection. There were abrasions. A large, dark bruise had blossomed between the bottom of his rib cage and his pelvic bone.

"Rusty, you need to go to the emergency room."

He dropped his shirttail and reached for the bottle of Advil. He popped off the top with his thumb and shook several tablets into his mouth. Crystal passed him the glass of water. He drank it all and set the empty glass on the nightstand, where there was a framed school picture of Ledge.

"Sweet," Rusty said, glowering up at her.

She had always tried her best to avoid Rusty and the sly manner in which he looked at her, implying an intimacy that had never existed. Gossip about her sexual escapades had been started by him. He had boasted of encounters that had never occurred.

All of that now made her self-conscious of her dishabille. She pulled a cotton housecoat on over the short pajama bottoms and t-shirt she'd been sleeping in. She clutched the robe to her, arms folded over her torso. "What did Ledge have to do with this?"

"Everything. The bastard." He looked at her with mad, feverish eyes. "But I can't report his assault on me without incriminating myself. So he'll get away with it and only be charged with selling weed."

"He doesn't sell weed."

"And the pope doesn't wear a beanie."

"Ledge smoked that one time and got caught. That's it."

"You believe that? He only tells you what you want to hear so you'll fuck him."

"That's not true."

He snorted a dismissal of her incensed denial. "Tonight, he was dealing out of his car on the parking lot of his uncle's shitty bar. I...I..." He looked aside, then came back to her. "I had supplied him some of the goods."

Her lips parted in dismay.

"Surprise!" he said. "The sheriff's kid peddling pot. Who'd've thunk it?" He shifted his arm slightly, winced, swore, took several stabilizing breaths. "Anyhow, Burnet and I got into a dispute over the division of our profit. When we couldn't reach a fair and reasonable agreement, he came at me with fists flying. I guess it comes from being raised in a pool parlor, but he doesn't fight fair."

"You're saying Ledge did this to you?"

"Haven't you been listening?"

"I don't believe you."

But despite her assertion, she did. She believed him, and that made her apprehensive and afraid for Ledge. She sat down on the same side of the bed as Rusty but kept her distance.

She thought back to what Morg had looked like the night she and her mother were summoned to the hospital and informed that he'd undergone emergency surgery to repair a ruptured spleen. Their assumption was that he'd been in a terrible car wreck, but when told that he'd been attacked on the parking lot of Burnet's Bar and Billiards, she'd known who had thrashed him.

Only a few hours earlier she had told Ledge about Morg's abuse. Ledge hadn't ranted, hadn't taken an oath of vengeance for her, hadn't pledged he would put a stop to it.

Rather, he'd remained motionless and silent, simply staring into the near distance, his eyes radiating an intense, white heat. Then he had come to his feet and offered to walk her as far as the corner near the school where Morg was due to pick her up.

In the hospital waiting room, she and her mother were questioned by a sheriff's deputy. When asked if she knew anyone who held a grudge against her stepbrother, she was trembling on the inside but had lied with remarkable composure. "No, sir. No one."

Now, as then, her concern was more for Ledge than for his victim. "Is he as banged up as you are?"

"You're worried about him?" He looked at her with contempt. "I told you, he doesn't fight fair. He walked away with barely a scratch, if any." He reached for the glass on the nightstand and spat bloody saliva into it. "He left me there like this and sped off with what was left of our stash and the money we'd made. But I got the last laugh."

When he chuckled, it was an ugly, evil sound. Pinkish bubbles formed between his swollen lips. "Not long after he left me bleeding, he got busted. Caught with what we hadn't sold. As we speak, he's in lockup."

She made to leave the bed in a rush, but Rusty's good arm shot out and caught her wrist. "Where do you think you're going?"

"To the jail."

"Like hell you are." He pulled her back down onto the bed. "You and I are staying right here. Where I've been all night."

"All night? What are you talking about?"

"Why, Crystal, honey, I've been with you since around nine-thirty, when your mama turned in for the night. No more than five minutes after her bedroom light went out, I tapped on your window, and you let me in. The prints of my boots will be outside your window under those scraggly bushes, and right there under the window on your rug."

She pulled on her arm, but he held fast. "If your jailbird sweetheart tries to implicate me in his little sideline business, I have a rock-solid alibi. You. We were screwing each other's brains out."

"You filthy piece of crap. We were doing no such thing."

"Okay, then. We weren't screwing. You were sucking me."

She looked at him with disgust. "I will never lie to protect you."

"Yeah, you will."

"Like hell, and you can't make me."

"Crystal, dear, you will go along with whatever I say. Want to know why? Because, so far, in order to save face, I'm willing to lie to anybody who asks how I wound up in this sorry state.

"But if Ledge squeals on me, and you side with him, I'll be forced to tell the truth. In which case, Ledge will be charged not only with dealing weed, but also with assault and battery. Maybe even attempted murder." He snickered with regret. "In case you didn't know, that's serious shit."

"It would be your word against his," she said. "Besides, your injuries aren't life-threatening. A split lip, a broken arm? You're hurt, but hardly knocking on death's door."

"Oh, wait. You thought I was referring to this little fender-bender he inflicted on me?" He touched the center of his chest with his fingertips. "No, honeybun. I was talking about the near-fatal assault he wreaked on your sorry stepbrother."

Crystal felt the earth giving way beneath her. "How did you know it was Ledge?"

A slow grin spread across Rusty's features. "I didn't. But I do now."

Chapter 21

W hen Crystal told Ledge that he could drop the pretense, that she knew what Rusty and he had done that night, she hadn't been referring to the burglary.

Not at all.

As she related her account of Rusty's visit to her house, Ledge was by turns incredulous and enraged. Rusty had spun quite a tale. He'd left Crystal convinced that if she denied he had been with her much of that night, it would be Ledge who suffered the consequences.

But beyond the personal ramifications, this previously unknown information painted an even blacker picture of Rusty and what he might have done that night after he and Ledge had parted.

I have a rock-solid alibi. But where were you? Where did you get off to after the four of us split up? Who could vouch for your whereabouts later that night?

He'd baited Rusty with that this morning as part of his chest-thumping threat to go to the attorney general and try to get the cold case of Foster's questionable death reopened. From the moment Ledge had learned of it, he'd suspected Rusty of having had a hand in it, though he'd figured it would have been from a distance, that Rusty would have had someone else do his dirty work.

But maybe not. The burglary hadn't left him anxious and sweaty. He'd come away from that humming a tune. It hadn't left him bleeding and broken, either.

When Rusty came to Crystal's house with an urgent need to establish an alibi, he had been incapacitated, and Foster was dead. There was only one logical conclusion to draw from that. At least to Ledge's mind. He would need more than supposition before he started slinging accusations.

First, he must set the record straight with Crystal. "Everything Rusty said about selling marijuana that night was one big, fat lie."

"It was found in your car, Ledge."

"But I didn't put it there. I sure as hell wasn't in a dealing partnership with Rusty. If I'd had an intention to peddle it, I wouldn't have done it on my uncle's property. Risk implicating him? No way in hell."

He pushed himself off the sofa and began restlessly prowling the room. "I didn't beat up Rusty. I didn't break his arm, but I'd like to break his neck now for making you believe that I had." He stopped meandering and faced her. "Do you believe me?"

"I want to."

"Not good enough, Crystal."

"After what you did to Morg—"

"I don't deny that. I never did. But *this* I did not do."

"Did you see Rusty that night?"

"Yes."

"Where?"

"Out at the bar. On the parking lot."

"What were you two doing together?"

He never wanted her to be placed in a position of having to lie for him, so he skirted around the whole truth. "What he and I are always doing when we're together. Wishing we could eat each other's liver. We pawed the ground, but that's as far as it went. Not a single punch was thrown. I left him and was on my way into town to see you when I was pulled over. The officers found the pot. I was arrested.

"I didn't see Rusty again until I came home on leave just before my first deployment overseas. We spotted each other in passing and from a distance. We didn't even acknowledge each other.

"We didn't speak until years later, after my discharge. He strolled into the bar one night while I was there. He made out like we were long-lost buddies and asked if I'd heard the good news that he was the district attorney. I told him he was the only person who thought that was good news. I wasn't kidding.

"He advised me not to get too used to the idea of being seen as a hero, that he couldn't wait for me to screw up again and give him a chance to prosecute me. He wasn't kidding, either. Then he gave me that smirk of his and left. I swear that's gospel."

"All right. But why did he come to me that night and tell such a lie?"

"He needed you as his alibi. He told you so himself."

"But an alibi for what?"

Cautious in his reply, he said, "I think the answer lies in who banged him up."

"He was in bad shape, Ledge. It was a serious fight."

"Um-huh. Over something Rusty didn't want anyone to know about."

Crystal's expression became increasingly troubled. "So he made up that lie about you, the marijuana, to shift blame."

"Knowing that you wouldn't *want* to believe it, but that you just might because of my prior possession charge, and because of the pounding I'd given your stepbrother."

"God, how easily he manipulated me."

"He's good at it. He knew you would never contradict his version of the events that night, not to the police or to anyone, for fear that I would be the one who paid the penalty. Your loyalty to me was his single ace, and he played it. He banked on that loyalty."

Which brought him to another matter. The one that hurt. He went over to the sofa, braced his hands on the arm of it, and bent down until he was on eye level with her. "Why didn't you ever tell me about this, Crystal? I had to hear it from Rusty. Today."

Her gaze shifted to the wound on his cheekbone. "Is that how you got that?"

"Technically I got that before he told me."

"You two were fighting today?"

"Doesn't matter," he said curtly. "What does matter is that you never told me about his late-night visit. Not in twenty years. That doesn't seem like an oversight. Why didn't you tell me?"

"You were going into the army. Why borrow trouble? What difference had it made? None."

"It made a difference to me when the dirty little secret came out today."

"It wasn't dirty. Nothing happened between Rusty and me."

"Then why keep it from me? It feels like a betrayal."

"It wasn't."

"Then what would you call it?"

"Common sense," she shouted. "You would have gone ballistic. I was afraid of what you would do to him."

"I'd have killed him."

"Exactly! Given the choice again, I still wouldn't tell you. I'd rather prevent you from doing something rash and stupid."

"Like I did to your rapist stepbrother? Would you rather I hadn't interceded and let the abuse continue?"

She looked as though he'd struck her.

He pushed himself up, turned away from her, hung his head, and put his fingers to his temple. "Shit, I'm sorry, Crystal. I'm sorry. That was an awful, terrible thing to say."

"Never mind it. You're upset."

"I am, yeah." He faced her again. "But that's no excuse."

She gave him a gentle smile. "I forgive you, okay? Tell me why you're upset. Why are we arguing over this? It happened a long, *long* time ago. You, me, Rusty, we're different people now."

"You and I, maybe. Not Rusty."

He sat down in the center of the sofa, planted his elbows on his wide-spread knees, bowed his head, and shoved all ten fingers up through his hair. "I'm angry over not knowing about this sooner because Rusty's whereabouts and actions that night could be significant. Only tonight, in the last few minutes, have I realized how hugely significant they could be."

"Significant to whom?"

"Not only to you and me."

"Joe Maxwell's daughter?"

He kept his hands on his head but turned it toward her. She was fiddling with the fringe on a chenille throw, winding strands of it around her index finger meticulously, keeping her eyes on the needless twining instead of looking at him.

When she did peer over at him, she said, "One of my beauticians saw you at the hardware store. You had a roll of architectural drawings with you. The clerk you were consulting about paint colors remarked that the front elevation of the house looked like the Maxwell—"

"Okay. No need to go on." He lowered his hands from his head and laid it back against the cushions, as he'd done when he'd first arrived.

Crystal said, "Is she cute?"

"Cute" wasn't the right word.

"More than cute?"

Arden didn't have the perkiness that "cute" connoted. She was more serious and often looked sad. She was intriguing and infuriating, and there should be some kind of prize awarded for the sacrificial self-discipline he had exercised tonight by leaving her.

God*damn*. Why did life have to be so complicated?

"No comment?"

Crystal's question served as a prod away from thoughts of Arden and back to Rusty's actions that night. "You said it was later confirmed that Rusty's arm had been broken. When was that?"

"The swelling and discoloration got worse by the hour. I warned him that if he didn't have it seen to, he might get gangrene. I don't know if that's medically correct, but it scared him into agreeing to go to the emergency room. I don't know exactly what time it was when he left, but it was still dark, before dawn. I led him through the house and out the front door. Half-heartedly I offered to drive him, but he told me he'd left his car half a block away and that he could manage.

"A few days later—you were still in jail—Mom and I were at a gas station. He saw us, pulled in, and showed us the cast on his arm. He teased Mom into signing it." Scornfully, she added, "When he left, she remarked on what a nice, friendly young man he was."

All seriousness, she said, "That's the sum total of what I know about that night, Ledge. Since then, on the rare occasions that I've crossed paths with Rusty, he's never mentioned it, even in a subtle way that only I would catch the meaning of."

"But he keeps a close watch on you."

She made a gesture of dismissal. "I'm the one who got away. He can't get over that."

"I don't think his vigilance is that adolescent."

"What else could it be?"

"He wants to make sure you're accessible. He may need you yet."

She frowned. He asked her why.

"Well, it's just that . . . I've listened to everything you've said, and I would put absolutely nothing past Rusty. He's a moral cesspool and famous for his machinations."

"But?"

"*But* if he were establishing me as an alibi for some wrong-doing that night, why didn't he take me up on my offer to drive him to the hospital? Why didn't he parade me through the ER and make certain that we were seen together?"

"You were in place to use on an as-needed basis. The story about me, too. As it turned out, he didn't need either." After a strategic pause, he said, "It would be useful to know how Rusty explained his injuries to the ER staff who treated him. I was wondering if . . ."

Her brow arched suspiciously. "What?"

"If Marty might help me with that."

"Ledge—"

"I know, I know. Awkward."

As though on cue, they heard a car pulling into the drive. Ledge checked his wristwatch. "Twenty past eleven. Right on time." He looked at Crystal. "What about it?"

She sighed. "You can ask. But do so at your own peril."

They heard the jangle of a key ring, then the snick of the lock. Marty came in, dressed in blue scrubs printed with the Ghostbusters logo. She tossed her purse onto the entry table. "This is a cozy scene. Am I interrupting?"

Crystal said, "Actually, we were just talking about you."

"I hope it was something salacious." She crossed over to the sofa, bent down, and kissed Crystal on the lips. "Hello, you."

Chapter 22

Crystal smiled up at Marty. "Hello back. How was your shift?"

As Marty straightened up, she arched her back in a deep stretch. "Long. Depressing. I hate sick people."

"Great attitude for a nurse to have," Ledge said.

"When I chose my career path, I didn't yet know that I had an aversion to the afflicted. Now, I stick with it for balance." She weighed one hand against the other. "Misery at work. Happiness at home."

Crystal smiled up at her. "Pour a drink and join us."

She did so, then slumped in the upholstered chair adjacent to the corner of the sofa in which Crystal sat. She toed off her shoes and propped her stocking feet in Crystal's lap.

"You were talking about me? What about me? My pink stripe?" She shook her platinum, pixie-cut hair, showing off the neon strip in her bangs.

"Fetching," Ledge said. "I've thought about having Crystal paint one in my hair."

"Not your color. It would clash with that bloody cut on your face."

Ledge merely gave her wry smile. Under her breath, Crystal warned her partner that it would be best not to pursue that topic.

Ledge had come to like Marty Camp. She was one of the few people he was comfortable teasing with, but one had to tease back in order to survive her acerbic jibes.

She had moved to Penton after suffering through a contentious divorce. The root of the marital problem had been Marty's sexual dubiety. With her impeccable credentials, she had been readily hired by the county's largest and most reputable hospital, but was still living out of a suitcase in a motel when she'd gone into Crystal's salon for a haircut.

Meeting Crystal had been the end of her sexual incertitude. In a matter of weeks, she'd moved in with Crystal. Marty had made Crystal more content than she'd been in her life, and for that Ledge liked Marty a lot.

She had a repertoire of salty language, a droll sense of humor, and, while she was a more caring individual than she let on, she also took no shit from anybody. She understood the nature of Crystal's friendship with Ledge and was tolerant of it. But that acceptance could come to a screeching halt with the request he was about to make.

"Marty, I'm going to put you in a very awkward position."

"Crystal puts me in awkward positions all the time," she said, giving him a naughty wink. "But I draw the line at threesomes. Even if I were game, you don't have the right equipment."

"My equipment is right enough, thank you."

They all smiled, but Crystal laid her hand on Marty's arm to let her know that the subject wasn't conducive to cracking jokes.

"The hospital keeps records. For how long?" Ledge asked.

"Patient records? I'm not sure. Since I've been on staff, the ones I've had to access were fairly recent."

"How far back was the oldest?"

"Hmm, two, three years."

"Could you do some sleuthing in the records department?" Crystal said, "Without getting into trouble or crossing your personal ethical line."

"How far back?" Marty asked.

Ledge gave her the month and date. "Easter Sunday of two thousand."

She raised her eyebrows. In contrast to her hair, they were stark black.

"He would have come in shortly before dawn." He went on to tell her Rusty's full name. Crystal gave her a general description of the injuries he had suffered, then Ledge picked back up. "There must be a chart detailing his injuries. Can you get it?"

Marty pursed her lips. "You're asking me to violate patient privilege?"

"Yeah."

Marty looked at Crystal. "Is this important to you?" Then she waved her hand. "Strike that. Anything concerning Ledge is important to you." Going back to him, she said, "I'll think on it and get back to you."

"That's fair."

"Fair or not, that's how it'll be. Right now, I'm beat. I'm taking my whiskey into the shower with me, then I'm going to hit the sack." She stood and, carrying her shoes and drink with her, headed toward the bedroom hallway. "'Night."

Crystal called after her that she would be right in.

Ledge stood. "I can take a hint."

"Stay and finish your drink."

"Thanks, but no. Earlier tonight, I was on my way to a full-blown binge."

"You won't go back to how you were when you first got home."

"That's right. I won't, because I'm taking no chances." He went to the front door.

She joined him there and said, "The next time you run into Rusty, flip him the bird for me."

"Don't make light of this, Crystal. And don't underestimate him."

"I don't."

"He hasn't changed his spots since that night he climbed through your window, and I can't always be around to protect you."

"You protect me every day." She looked toward the hallway that led to the bedroom. "As long as everyone thinks that you and I keep the sheets smoking, Marty and I are free to—"

"Why do you care what everyone thinks? Why don't you two just go public?"

"I'll have to work up to it. It took me years to go public about Morg."

"Well, whatever you do, I've got your back." He pecked her on the cheek and reached for the doorknob.

She put out a detaining hand. "Ledge, I'm sorry you had to hear about that night from Rusty. I'm sure he gloated. I know how much you would have hated that."

"I did. He's a hyena. But I accept your apology. I can't stay mad at you for long. In all the time I've known you, I've only been mad at you once."

"When was that?"

"When I groped your boob, and you slapped me. Hard."

She laughed. "I had told you that no man was ever going to touch me that way again."

"I'd've been less than a man not to test you."

"You were sixteen."

"Still."

"Did I convince you?"

"I haven't tried since."

They smiled at each other, then she said, "You always alert me when you're having a *thing*, so that I'll be prepared when someone tells me, as a friend, of course, that you're cheating on me."

"A *thing*?"

She gave him a you-know-what-I-mean look, and he did know.

"Which makes me wonder why you haven't said a word to me about Arden Maxwell."

"Nothing to say. There's no thing. She consulted me about doing some handiwork. I'm working up an estimate."

"That's it?"

"Yep."

Crystal regarded him with the intuitive shrewdness unique to a woman, then she laughed. "If you say so."

"I just did say so."

"What about her baby's father?"

He raised his shoulders. "How would I know?"

"But she seems unattached?"

"As far as I can tell."

"And she's cute."

"I didn't say she was cute."

"You didn't say she wasn't. So...?"

"So nothing. I can't go there."

"How come?"

"It's difficult."

"How so?"

"Just difficult, all right?"

"Ooooh, touchy. That itch must be baaaad."

He shifted his stance. "Okay. She's attractive, and I'm..."

"You're...?"

"Curious. You know. I'm in that 'what if?' stage."

"Yes, I know that stage, but you're way beyond it."

"This coming from someone who knows nothing about how it works between boys and girls."

"I know about attraction. To hell with 'it's difficult.'"

"Spare me."

"Have you kissed her?"

"None of your damn business."

"Definitely yes. Have you seen her naked?"

"No."

"But you're dying to."

"Good night, Crystal."

"Another definite yes."

"Let me know if and when Marty comes through."

This time, she didn't stop him from leaving, but she was laughing lightly as she saw him on his way.

Rusty was in a bitch of a mood when he let himself into his house. Discovering that the alarm wasn't set pissed him off even further. "Stupid cow," he muttered, shooting a glance upstairs, where Judy was no doubt sleeping.

Alarm set, he made a beeline for his study. He locked himself inside, poured himself a drink, and flopped back into his easy chair. He didn't boot up his computer. Not even live-streaming sex shows held appeal in his present mood.

Burnet had been with Crystal tonight.

For a long time.

On his way home from a dinner with some pals, Rusty

had spotted Burnet's truck at the curb in front of her house. He'd driven a circuit through town. When he went past again, the truck was still there. And it stayed, even after Marty had come home.

To add insult to injury, Rusty had seen them together as Crystal was waving him off at her front door. The bitch had been laughing, as though she knew Rusty was watching her enjoying herself with Ledge Burnet. He'd wanted to kill her. But not before fucking her ten or twelve times.

"Cunt," he muttered and shot his drink.

His cell phone rang.

He didn't recognize the number. But he never knew when a call would be about something he needed or wanted to know. Like maybe Burnet had driven his pickup into a tree on his way home, and it had burst into flames, roasting him alive.

He answered. "Dyle."

A man identified himself as a deputy sheriff. "I worked for your daddy, and you after him. You may not remember me, though. I was low on the totem pole."

Still are, Rusty thought. His name had rung no bells. He snarled, "It's after hours, Deputy."

"I'm aware, sir."

"So this had better be damned important."

"It came down through the pipeline that if Dwayne Hawkins was caught engaging in dogfighting again you wanted to hear about it ASAP."

"That's right."

"Well, two of our vice guys got one of his cronies to rat him out. They busted Hawkins tonight."

Rusty smiled as he poured himself a refill. "Hawkins popped off at me a few nights ago, and I looked forward to teaching him a lesson in manners. I knew it wouldn't take too long for him to transgress, but I didn't expect it would be this soon."

"Hope you don't mind me calling you this late."

"Not at all, not at all. I'm obliged. What's your name again?"

The deputy stated it proudly, then went on to describe the arrest. "Hawkins attempted to make a run for it. Splashed through the bayou that runs behind his place, got stuck in the mud. That's how they caught him."

Rusty was told that Hawkins had put up a fight, assaulting one of the deputies so viciously, he'd broken his finger. "Didn't earn him any favors in this department, let me tell you."

Rusty had listened to the detailed account without interruption, drumming his fingers on the stuffed arm of his chair. When he failed to respond after several moments of silence had elapsed, the deputy said, "Mr. Dyle? You still there?"

"I'm here. Listen, I'd rather Hawkins not be booked until I read the arrest report and look into the case myself, okay?"

"Sure."

"Tell the deputies who brought him—"

"One's at the ER getting his broke finger set."

"The point is, keep Hawkins isolated. Let him simmer some of that meanness out. I'll come over first thing in the morning."

"Sure thing, Mr. Dyle."

"I owe you a favor, Deputy."

"Don't mention it."

"You took the words right out of my mouth."

"Sir?"

"You and I never had this conversation. Understand?"

"Yes, sir."

"I trust you do."

Rusty clicked off. Revived and feeling much better about the big picture, he threw back his drink and unzipped his pants. He was already hard.

Chapter 23

Lisa was in her home office, checking emails and reviewing her schedule for the day, when her housekeeper called to her from the kitchen, "Breakfast is almost ready, Mrs. Bishop. Can I make you a cappuccino?"

"Please. I'll be right there."

Helena had worked for Wallace long before his marriage to Lisa. She was an invaluable asset. She ran the household, leaving Lisa free to oversee the management of the company that Wallace had founded and had left in her charge of in his will.

Shortly after relocating herself and Arden to Dallas, she'd been hired by the commercial real estate firm where Wallace Bishop was CEO. Initially Lisa had been an assistant to an assistant, a glorified gofer. But she was a quick study and ambitious. Recognizing those qualities, Wallace had promoted her to work on an elite team personally overseen by him.

Their coworker relationship had led to romance.

He was fifteen years her senior but had never been married. He had welcomed taking on Arden as a dependent. However, he had stipulated that he didn't want other children. Lisa had accepted that condition, actually with relief. Had Wallace desired a child of his own, she would have reproduced, but forgoing motherhood hadn't been a sacrifice.

After they married, he'd encouraged her to re-enroll in college and earn her degree, a pursuit she'd regretted having to suspend when she became Arden's guardian. Wallace had made it easier for her by assuming some of her parental responsibilities. Over the course of those years when he was driving carpool and attending school events with Arden, she and Wallace had grown very fond of each other. They'd remained close until his death. In his will, he'd been as generous to her as he would have been to a progeny born of him.

Lisa often acknowledged that Wallace Bishop was the soundest decision she had ever made. She believed he would feel the same of her, and would be proud of how she had carried on after his death. The company continued to thrive under her leadership.

Now, she double-checked her day planner, then sorted through the stack of snail mail she hadn't gotten to yesterday. There were the usual invitations and junk, but one envelope caught her eye.

The stationery was a high-quality stock in dove gray. The return address was engraved on the back of the envelope, but it had been addressed by hand. To Arden.

"Mrs. Bishop?" Helena called.

"Coming."

Thoughtfully, Lisa tapped the envelope against her palm. Then, yielding to temptation before her conscience got the better of her, she opened it.

Arden,

Word reached me today about the loss of the baby. It came to me through channels too intricate to go into here, and how I learned of it doesn't matter. What does matter, greatly, is that I know how crushing this must have been for you. I wish you had notified me when it happened. I would have provided whatever consolation and support I possibly could, as inadequate as it would have been.

I realize I'm late to the dance, but is there anything I can do for you now? Before leaving Houston, you made it clear that you wanted to make a clean break. I understood and accepted your reasoning then, and I do now. But please know that I'm here for you if you ever feel the need to talk about it.

Jacob

P.S. I mailed this to your sister's address because it was the only one I had.

"I didn't want it to get cold."

Lisa turned and smiled at Helena, who stood in the open doorway holding a steaming, frothy cup of cappuccino. "Thank you." She laid the envelope aside, went over, and took the cappuccino. "I've had a sudden change of plans for the day, Helena. I'm afraid I'll have to forgo breakfast."

"Nothing bad, I hope."

"No, not at all. But I'll need the company jet today. Can you make that call for me while I cancel some appointments?"

"Of course. What's your destination?"

"Houston Hobby."

Helena left her.

Lisa sipped her cappuccino as she returned to her desk and reread the heart-stirring letter to Arden from one Jacob Greene.

Chapter 24

S hee-ut."

"Good morning, Dwayne," Rusty said cheerfully. "How's life treatin' you?"

Hunkered in the corner of his cot with his back against the wall, the Hawkins miscreant glared at Rusty. Rusty turned to the deputy who'd escorted him to the cell. "Leave us."

The deputy shot Hawkins a warning look, then turned away and ambled back toward his desk.

Rusty waved his hand in front of his nose. "I can smell you from here, Dwayne. Must be that lake water you got bogged down in last night while you were trying to evade arrest. Then you assaulted a peace officer. My, my."

"I ain't talking without a lawyer."

"Really? Gee, that's too bad. Because I think you would like hearing what I've come to discuss."

"Whut could you have to say that I'd want to hear?"

"Before we get to that, your disposition needs some re-adjustment."

"Whut's that mean?"

Rusty dropped his amiable grin. "It means, get over here and talk to me with respect, or I'll bring in someone to work you over good, and claim he was protecting me. When he's done with you, you'll be peeing blood and farting out your ears."

Hawkins mulled it over, then rolled off the cot and slunk over to the bars.

"That's better," Rusty said.

"Everybody says you're crooked as your ol' man."

"Do they?" Rusty chuckled. "Well, they're wrong. He was a pussycat compared to me. Which works to your advantage, Dwayne."

"Yeah? I ain't seein' it."

"You and I can work together to our mutual benefit."

Dwayne squinted at him with wary interest. "Doin' whut?"

"See what happens when you're courteous and cooperative? We're making progress already."

* * *

Arden had been at the courthouse when it opened for the day. After consulting the deputy manning the information desk in the lobby, she'd been directed to the second floor and the Sheriff's Office's Crimes Against Persons division. There, she'd made her request to one of the detectives, filled out the necessary forms, paid the nominal fee, and then had been instructed to return to the lobby and wait.

That had been almost an hour ago. She couldn't imagine why it was taking so long. Unless a certain amount of time was required to locate the investigation reports on twenty-year-old crimes.

Finally, the detective with whom she'd dealt arrived with a

sealed manila envelope and passed it to her. "Here you go. Sorry it took so long. I had to take a call."

"You've been very helpful. Thank you." She tucked the envelope under her arm and turned to go.

"Funny. We recently had somebody else request those particular reports."

Arden stopped and came slowly around. She had a feeling she wasn't going to think it was funny. "Oh?"

"I guess you moving back here kindled interest in these two investigations."

This wasn't welcome news, but she smiled as though unbothered by it. "Who besides me would be interested? Not a producer from one of those unsolved mystery TV shows, I hope."

He laughed. "Naw. Local boy. Ledge Burnet's his name. He was in here only a few days ago, asking for the same files."

"Did he say why?"

"Ledge isn't much of a talker, keeps his business to hisself."

But he was steeped in hers.

After his brief conversation with Dwayne Hawkins, Rusty passed the desk where the jailer was playing poker on his iPad. Rusty thanked him for letting him in, then left the cell block and took the stairs in favor of the creaky and notoriously slow elevator. He was practically jogging his way down. The day was young, and he was feeling very upbeat about it.

That was, until he saw Arden Maxwell in the lobby chatting with one of the SO's detectives.

That scenario stopped short Rusty's fleet-footed tread.

He'd seen Arden from a distance, but never this close. Sizing her up, he'd rate her an eight and a half.

He lurked there on the staircase until she concluded her conversation with the detective and left, taking an official-looking envelope with her. As the detective was on his way back up to his department, he met Rusty on the stairs.

"Morning, Mr. Dyle."

"Morning." He tipped his head toward the main doors. "Wasn't that Arden Maxwell you were talking to?"

"Yes, sir."

"What was she doing here?"

As the detective explained the nature of her errand, Rusty's lightheartedness of moments ago began to deflate. The detective must have sensed his displeasure.

He said, "There weren't any restrictions placed on those reports, Mr. Dyle."

"No, no, it's fine." To make a big to-do would only call attention to his interest. "I'm just wondering why she would want them at this late date. Did she say?"

"No, but I'd guess because of her daddy's alleged involvement in both cases."

"That's probably it. She was just a kid when all that happened. It's understandable, her wanting to learn what she can." He tapped the detective on his sleeve. "Thanks for seeing to her. Good public relations."

He tried to appear unhurried as he continued down the stairs. He exited the building and made his way along the sidewalk to the parking space reserved for him in the row nearest to the building. Arden was moving along the farthest row of the parking lot.

Wanting to catch her before she left, he quickly got into his car and drove it over to where she was unlocking the driver's door of a blue sedan. As he pulled up behind her car, she came around quickly.

Immediately, Rusty discerned two things about her. One, maybe she deserved a nine for the wreath of hair. It looked like she'd just gotten laid.

Two, his charm would be wasted on her. Her posture was rigid, and her expression was bitchy.

He didn't let that deter him, however. He enjoyed a challenge.

He put his car in park and got out.

"Ms. Maxwell?"

Arden had recognized the sound of the engine even before she saw the car. Her heart was thudding. Her mouth had gone dry. Trying to keep her breathing under control, she bobbed her head in silent acknowledgment.

"Hi, my name is Rusty Dyle."

Rusty Dyle? The district attorney. With whom Ledge had a long-standing grudge. Ledge's description of him had been inflammatory, but regardless of that, she would have instantly mistrusted the man's toothy smile. Her thoughts were rioting, but she replied to his greeting with as much composure as she could muster.

"How do you do?"

He walked toward her and extended his right hand. She was loath to touch him but shook his hand. Not to do so would have alerted him to her aversion.

He said, "I'd heard you were living here again."

"How did you recognize me?"

"Actually, I didn't. As I was leaving the building, the detective you talked to pointed you out and told me who you were. Anyhow, it's a pleasure to welcome you back to Penton."

"Thank you."

"Everybody treating you decent?"

"I can't complain."

"Good to know." He looked around as though assessing the town square. "Things haven't changed all that much since you and your sister moved away."

"Some things have changed quite a lot."

He came back around to her and flashed a grin. "Well, we did finally get a new fire station. *And* a Taco Bell."

She was expected to smile; she did so vapidly.

"Let's see, what year was that?" he said. "When you left, I mean."

"Two thousand."

"That long? Geez. That was the year I graduated high school. I guess things have changed. I'm district attorney now."

"I remember Sheriff Dyle."

He placed his hand over his heart. "My dear ol' dad. He died a while back."

"He sticks in my memory because he questioned my sister and me after our father disappeared."

"Oh, hell. Sorry about that. That whole business."

He shook his head with regret. *Seeming* regret. Arden didn't buy it.

He continued. "Daddy would've hated bothering you girls at such a tough time. But, you know, line of duty."

"Of course."

"Ever hear anything about what happened to Joe?"

"Nothing."

"Has he been declared dead yet?"

"Years ago."

"Huh. I'd lost track."

He was lying about that, too, and she couldn't wait to get away from him. "If you'll excuse me, I really need to—"

"They take care of you in there?" He hitched his thumb over his shoulder toward the building, then pointed at the envelope she carried. "Get what you came for?"

"Yes."

"Anything I can do to assist?"

"No, thank you."

"Well, if you think of something…" He reached into the breast pocket of his suit jacket, withdrew a business card, and passed it to her. "At your service. Anytime."

Arden thanked him with a nod and slid the card into her handbag. "Now, I really must go."

"Sure, sure, sorry to have detained you. I just wanted to say hi and introduce myself. You have a good day now."

Congenial smile in place, he went back to his car and got in. He gave her a little wave as he drove away.

Arden got into her car, tossed the envelope containing the investigation reports onto the passenger seat, then gripped the steering wheel with both hands, and laid her forehead on the backs of them. "Lost track?" Hardly.

As she'd told Ledge last night, she wanted answers.

She now had one. The individual routinely driving past her house was District Attorney Rusty Dyle.

Arden's initial impulse was to alert Ledge to her discovery. But, considering the hostility with which they'd parted the night before, she decided against calling him.

She must speak with Lisa, however. She needed to dismiss the remote possibility that their father was alive and well and keeping tabs on them.

Yesterday, Arden had been hesitant to bring up her childish dream that he would one day come back, afraid that

Lisa would either chide or pity her for clinging to such an implausibility.

Learning that Lisa had secretly shared that same vain hope had forged a stronger bond between them. It had been freeing for Arden to see proof that Lisa, the indomitable one, wasn't totally without vulnerability. She had left Lisa's office feeling that they had been equalized. The difference in their ages, all the differences between them, had been spanned by a common heartbreak.

But did she wish for Lisa to know that she had identified the district attorney as her "stalker"? Lisa would want to act on it immediately, notify the authorities, assemble the militia.

No. Arden didn't want to reveal what she had discovered about Rusty Dyle until she knew *why* he was spying on her. Since he and she had never even met, his interest couldn't be personal. Which meant it was official and must pertain to her father and two unsolved crimes, one a probable homicide.

She had obtained the investigation reports in the hope they would yield something she could use to defend against the accusations against her father.

By the time she got home, she'd decided on the tack to take with Lisa. She got herself a Diet Coke, sat at the table with the police files in front of her, and put the call through. When Lisa answered, the background noise indicated that she was on speakerphone in her car.

Arden said, "Evidently I've caught you at a bad time."

"I'm only running errands. What's going on? Did your pervert drive by last night?"

She wasn't certain Rusty Dyle could be classified as a pervert. Snake oil salesman, maybe. He had that kind of pointy-mustache leer and mannerisms. He'd clasped her hand a little too long for what should have been a polite handshake between strangers. Thinking about him made her shudder.

"Arden?"

"I don't know for sure if he came by last night or not. I was exhausted. The round-trip drive to Dallas and all." The "all" being her go-rounds with Ledge. Fighting with him, kissing him, fighting some more. "I was history the instant my head hit the pillow." She pushed on before Lisa could grill her.

"I've given a lot of thought to our conversation yesterday. Speaking for myself, and I believe for you, it was like undergoing open-heart surgery. Grueling and painful, but healing in the long run. I don't want to dim the afterglow."

"But?"

"I went to the courthouse this morning, the sheriff's office, and got the investigation reports on the Welch's burglary and Brian Foster's death."

"You did? Why? If you wanted to see those reports, you should have asked me for them yesterday."

"You have them?" Arden exclaimed. "Since when?"

"Since forever. I got them before I even moved us away."

"Why?"

"Why?" Lisa repeated, sounding dismayed by the question. "The investigators were alleging, and people were accepting, that Dad was guilty of both. I wanted to know what evidence they had to base such accusations on. Isn't that why you wanted the reports?"

"Precisely. Which makes it all the more flabbergasting that you never shared them with me."

"Arden, you were ten years old. The description of Foster's remains wasn't for the faint of heart. If either had contained something vital, I would have shared it with you. Neither did.

"There was no evidence placing Dad at either the store or where Foster was discovered. The authorities based their allegations solely on Dad being an embittered former employee, who had butted heads with Foster the day he was fired. That was their only substantiation."

"That wasn't the only substantiation, Lisa," she said softly. "Rather than answer to the charges, he vanished, and so did an estimated half a million dollars."

It pained Arden to say that, and her sister couldn't dispute it.

"True," Lisa said. "Those facts do point a finger at him. Collectively, it's compelling, but it's all circumstantial. Every scrap of it. When you read the reports, you'll see what I mean."

Musing aloud, Arden said, "I wonder what a prosecutor today would think of them. How much stock one would put into them?"

"Probably none if Rusty Dyle is still the DA."

Arden couldn't believe that Lisa had spoken the name that, not five minutes ago, she had determined not to mention. "What do you know about him?"

"Only that he's irksome. You remember Sheriff Dyle?"

"Yes."

"Rusty is his son. Growing up, he was a thoroughly obnoxious brat, always pulling pranks. Often cruel ones. He picked on the underdogs. Thinking of him as DA is enough to make one cringe."

Lisa went on to describe the man exactly as Arden would. "He had this sly grin that suggested he had the goods on you. You know the type."

Yes, Arden had come face-to-face with that type half an hour ago, but she was reluctant to tell Lisa about it, afraid she would go into orbit.

"He was odious back then, and I doubt he's improved with age. In fact, he's probably worse because of the power he wields." Lisa gave a light laugh. "I'm sure Ledge Burnet finds that hard to swallow."

For a second time, Arden was taken aback. Was Ledge's grudge with the DA common knowledge? "Why do you say that?"

"They were rivals over this girl. Crissy. Kristin. Something like that. I knew her only by reputation. She was a hot ticket. I wonder if she's still around. If so, those two might still be feuding over her favors."

"I wouldn't know," Arden murmured.

"Speaking of Burnet, before you left yesterday, you promised to call me after you had talked to him, but I didn't hear from you. What did you tell him?"

"That his services wouldn't be needed after all." She recalled the moment with embarrassing clarity. She'd wanted to flail at him, while at the same time wanting to throw herself against him and demand that he resume the make-out session they'd begun on the stairs.

"Ah, good," Lisa was saying. "That's one worry I can cross off. There's really no reason for you to stay there any longer, is there? Why don't you just come here? Please? I can tell by your tone of voice that you're troubled. What's going on?"

Arden drew her focus from near space to the investigation reports. "Lisa, in your heart of hearts, do you believe Dad committed those crimes? Don't answer as my guardian. We're beyond that. You've done me no favors by shielding me from knowing the more appalling aspects of all this.

"I've reached this low point in my life because I've been spared the worst. Please, from now on, be brutally honest with me like you were yesterday. Tell me true. Did he do it?"

Lisa took a long time before answering. "If the father that I knew *was* guilty, I think that rather than put us—all three of us—through the humiliation of a criminal investigation, a trial, and probable conviction, he would have chosen to make a clean break."

"So," Arden said quietly, "his running away could be construed as an admission of guilt."

Lisa hesitated, then asked, "What else would have compelled him to abandon his children?"

This answer was the most difficult for Arden to accept. "The money." She whispered the two condemning words.

"Yes," Lisa said. "Compared to Wallace's net worth, five hundred thousand would be a negligible amount. But to Dad, given his situation, his destitution, it would have represented a ticket out."

Or as Ledge had succinctly put it: *Flight.*

Chapter 25

That night in 2000—Joe

J oe had gotten through the entire day without taking so much as a nip. He'd tinkered in the detached garage, organizing tools that he never used anymore. He'd weeded the beds of his late wife's rosebushes, which hadn't bloomed since her death because only she knew the proper nutrients to feed them. He'd oiled every door hinge in the house, even those that didn't squeak.

He did anything he could think of to keep his mind occupied and hands too busy to pour a drink.

When Lisa had called him to supper, the first thing he'd noticed was the basket of Easter eggs on the dining table. The centerpiece had so reminded him of Marjorie, it had almost been his undoing. Somehow, though, he'd gotten through the meal without revealing his desperate craving for the anesthetizing effects of Jim Beam.

He'd even coaxed a few giggles out of Arden. Once a bouncy, chatty, and cheerful girl, she had become much more subdued after losing her mother. Her personality change was his fault, just as Lisa's increasing brittleness was. He was failing them as a provider and as a parent.

Lisa was competent beyond her years. She'd been unfairly burdened with new responsibilities, but was managing well enough juggling them and her studies. He had no doubt she would make her own future.

It was Arden he most worried about. She was still young and, to her great misfortune, dependent on him. With all his heart, he wanted to see that her future turned out to be much brighter than it portended.

After helping with the kitchen cleanup, he'd told the girls he was going out to the cemetery to tend Marjorie's grave. "I would like all of us to go tomorrow. I want to spruce it up before you girls visit."

Looking at him with scorn and suspicion, Lisa said, "What can you do out there? It's already getting dark."

"There's lighting at the cemetery. Enough for me to see by."

"It looks like rain."

"I'm not going to melt."

Lisa let it drop.

Whining, Arden asked if she could go with him. He reminded her that she had a new Disney film to watch. They'd picked it up in town that afternoon. "You don't want to miss that."

She'd looked dejected and rejected when he'd squeezed her shoulder and told her good night. He'd wanted to reassure her then that things would get better, but he lacked the courage to make that, or any, promise.

When he'd returned home hours later, only nightlights were on inside the house. He'd climbed the stairs and made it to his bedroom without being intercepted by either Lisa or Arden.

Once in his room, he'd opened the new bottle of whiskey and had begun steadily pouring drink after drink. Even so, he was still sober when his phone had buzzed and he'd seen Brian Foster's name in LED.

Why the hell would Foster be calling him *now*? With a sense of foreboding, he'd answered.

Then for several minutes, he'd listened to Foster blubber the reason for the call and explain why it was imperative. Joe didn't know the young man well, but Foster was an easy read. He was a nitpicker. He dealt with numbers. He thought in terms of exactitude, not fiction. He lacked the imagination to devise this story about Rusty Dyle's treachery, as well as the audacity to spread it.

Joe had no difficulty believing everything Foster told him.

At this point in his shaky narrative, Foster paused to take a deep breath. "In addition to insisting that he and I hide the money tonight, he also says that we should have a scapegoat in place. And, uh, Mr. Maxwell, he means it to be you."

Joe reached for his whiskey and took a slug directly from the bottle. "Let me get this straight. He plans to lay the burglary on me? He can't do that."

"He can. He will. He's certain that Burnet will blow the whistle, and the rest of us will be screwed."

"Burnet can't blow the whistle without screwing himself." Joe's hand shook as he raised the bottle to his mouth again. "He won't do that."

"I don't think he'll betray us, either, because of the pact we made."

Jesus, this guy was naïve. "Do you think that silly pact will carry any weight among a group of thieves, with half a million dollars at stake?"

Foster didn't say anything, but Joe could tell that the young man saw how ludicrous it was to hang his hopes on the honor of his accomplices. Joe almost felt pity for the guy and hated being the one to disillusion him.

"Look, Foster, I don't think Burnet will talk, either. Not because of a pact, but because he's too smart. The kid's been around. He'll realize that being charged for possession of marijuana is Mickey Mouse compared to being charged with stealing half a million. He'd get more than a few months in juvie for that. So he's not going to confess to the burglary. I just don't think he will."

Foster whimpered. "Well, it really doesn't matter what you think. Or what I think. *Rusty* is convinced that Burnet will turn, and he's taking precautions."

"By setting me up as the fall guy."

"Who better than the town drunk? I didn't say that, Mr. Maxwell. Rusty did."

Who better indeed? Rusty Dyle was a lot of things, but stupid wasn't one of them. "Did he say how he planned to go about it?"

"No. But it's almost time for me to meet him. What should I do?" The accountant's voice went shrill with near hysteria.

Joe rubbed his forehead. The whiskey had hit him hard, and it was probably the booze talking when he said, "You could call the cops yourself." He couldn't believe the words had left his mouth, but there they were, humming through their two cell phones.

"I thought of it," Foster said. "Before I called you, I seriously thought about it."

"Why didn't you? The pact?"

"No. I'm clinging to the hope that we'll actually get away with it, without...without somebody getting hurt."

Joe didn't think there was a chance in hell of that happening, but he didn't share that pessimistic outlook with Foster, who had continued to talk around sucking in gulps of air.

"But the real reason I didn't turn myself in," he said, "is because, if I did, I wouldn't live long. Rusty would kill me."

"He wouldn't—"

"He'd have it done. Even if I was locked up for my own safety. Deputies run the jail, you know, and they're all under Mervin Dyle's thumb. They'd probably stage my 'suicide.'"

Joe didn't doubt it, but he argued it anyway. "Rusty has browbeaten you into being paranoid and afraid of him."

"You're darn right I am. Aren't you?"

Yes, he was. More than a little. Rusty would have his daddy and the whole corrupt sheriff's department vouching for his son's whereabouts tonight, paving his tracks with alibis that Mervin would make certain were ironclad.

Out of the four of them, only three would be made to pay for their thievery.

Thinking about the likely penalty, and the effect it would have on his already fractured family, Joe almost barfed up his whiskey.

"You've got to tell me what to do," Foster wailed.

"Don't do anything. Don't show up at the meeting place. Leave the little bastard waiting."

"He will come after me."

The longer they talked, the faster Foster was unraveling. Joe had to keep a cool head, as hazy with liquor as it was. To panic was begging for a disastrous outcome. At the moment, disaster was only a possibility, a good possibility, but preventable if he could talk Foster off the ledge.

"All right, meet Rusty as scheduled. Hide the money. But then call his bluff."

"Wh...what...what do you mean?"

"Tell the asshole you won't be part of any scheme he has in mind for me. Tell him—"

"He would kill me!"

"He's not going to kill you. Think about it. He was the

ringleader of this. He originated the plan, made himself boss. Up to this point, he's pulled off a successful heist. He's sitting on five hundred grand."

Through his heavy breathing, Foster murmured agreement.

"So he's not going to do something now that would get him caught. Killing you would be a senseless thing to do."

Foster thought it over, then to Joe's aggravation he said, "No. I can't stand up to that guy. I just can't. It's not in me."

Joe didn't think Foster had it in him, either, which meant that he couldn't just sit here, getting drunker by the hour, waiting to see what trickery Rusty had in store for him. For all he knew, Rusty had already ratted out the rest of them, and arrests were imminent. That was a bleak but galvanizing prospect.

He had to act, and he saw only one option open to him. He asked Foster when he was due to meet Rusty.

"Half an hour. Well, now, twenty minutes."

"Where?"

Foster was about to answer, then stopped himself. After a beat, he said, "I took a big risk by calling and telling you."

"Yes, you did."

"What's to keep you from calling the cops and working out your own deal?"

"That's probably what I should do."

Foster groaned.

"But I won't. I swear to you that's the one thing I will not do."

Judging by the choppy sounds Foster was emitting, he was either retching or sobbing.

"Your time is running out," Joe said with forced patience. "Where are you meeting Rusty?"

Sniff, sniff. "There's a picnic area on the lake where he and I have met a few times to drink beer. It's gone to ruin. Only a few wooden tables are left and they're falling down. It's off the beaten path. There's a turnoff to it about a hundred yards east of that boat ramp with the bent flagpole."

Joe knew the spot. Years ago, he and Marjorie used to take the girls there, before the area had become overlooked and overgrown.

"What are you going to do?" Foster asked.

"I don't know."

"Will you be there?"

"If I can get there."

Foster sobbed for real. "We were all so stupid, weren't we, to be sucked in by him?"

"Yes. Very stupid. But let's try to salvage the situation before it gets worse. Okay?"

"Okay."

"Okay. Now listen. Starting now, we must be very careful. They check cell phone data. If we're ever asked about this call, our story is that you called to tell me how bad you felt over Welch's firing me, and to wish my family a happy Easter. Understand?"

"Yes, all right."

"Now, go meet Rusty. Take a flashlight. You'll need it out there. Keep it on as much as possible. Play along with whatever Rusty says for as long as you can."

"Then what?"

Then watch your back, Joe thought. But what he said was, "We play it by ear. Good luck."

He hung up before Foster could respond. He stared at the bottle of whiskey with bone-deep craving. Then he carried it into the bathroom and emptied it into the sink.

He took a dark-colored windbreaker from his closet and pulled it on over his white, short-sleeved shirt. He opened his bedroom door a crack and listened but didn't hear a sound.

He kept his footsteps light as he made his way down the hallway.

Being the coward that he was, he passed his daughters' bedrooms without looking in on them. If Arden woke up, he could ease her back to sleep with a white lie and a reassuring pat.

But not Lisa. She would see straight through any malarkey he tried to put over on her. The truth would come out. And then what would he do? What would she do?

In any case, he didn't risk an encounter. He descended the stairs, avoiding the treads that creaked, and left through the back door. He started across the field behind the house. It was a moonless night, sultry and still with the heavy scent of rain, which Lisa had forecast. He hoped it would hold off for a while longer.

The ground was uneven, and he wasn't that sure-footed because of the whiskey he'd drunk, so the walk to the cypress grove took him longer than expected, and when he reached it, he was leaking sour-smelling sweat from every pore.

He was glad to have the cover of the trees, although their density, and the darkness it created, made him claustrophobic. He didn't dare risk a flashlight.

Stumbling around in the marshland, feeling his way in the dark, he didn't find the rowboat right away, and, ever aware of the time constraints, his search for it became frantic.

His pants legs got soaked. More than once, he banged his shins on cypress knees. He walked into a clump of ghostly moss hanging from a low-lying branch, and smacked his forehead on another.

The discomforts did help to sober him up, however, and, eventually, he located the boat. It was a wonder he had, because vegetation had overtaken it, and it took some effort to pull it free.

Like everything else in his life, the craft had been neglected.

As a family, they had taken it out on the lake frequently. "Nature excursions," Marjorie had called them. They'd competed to see who could spot and name the most species of birds and wildlife. Whoever caught the first fish got the largest chocolate chip cookie from the picnic basket. Like that. How had his family deteriorated from that idyllic example of harmony to this?

Tonight, the boat looked as hopeless as regaining those happier days. He wasn't even sure that it was still watertight. He wouldn't trust it, except that going by car to the designated place would mean taking the long way around. Weaving through the intersecting bayous of the lake would take less time, but only for someone who had grown up doing it.

Joe had. Even in the dark, he would have no trouble navigating the swampy labyrinth. The future of his family depended on it.

He dragged the boat into the water and clambered aboard.

Chapter 26

Following her conversation with Lisa, Arden had determined that if she wanted to learn more about the ongoing feud between the smarmy district attorney and Ledge, a good place to start would be with the woman at the core of it.

Arden recalled Ledge telling her about his "friend" who owned the hair and nail salon where the errant squirrel had done damage in the attic. It hadn't been difficult to link his Crystal with Crystal's Salon on Main Street, a house that had been charmingly converted into a business. It was a white frame structure with pale blue shutters and purple petunias in window boxes.

Arden had planned to arrive just as the salon was closing for the day, and her timing was perfect. As she pulled into the shallow parking lot in front, a woman was locking the front door. Arden got out of her car.

The woman turned and smiled. "Hi."

"Hello." Arden continued up the walkway toward her.

"I'm sorry, the salon is closed," she said. "But I'll be happy to make you an appointment."

"Are you Crystal?"

"Yes."

It was easy to understand Ledge's enduring attraction. She was stunning. Her long, dark hair was as sleek as a seal's pelt. Her eyes were captivating, both in color and shape.

"I'm Arden Maxwell."

"I thought you might be."

"You've heard talk?"

"Around here, gossip is the number one pastime. I was hoping you would come into the salon one day so I could form my own opinion."

"What's your impression so far?"

Crystal smiled. "You've got great hair."

"Thanks. The humidity makes any attempt at control futile."

"I've got product that could help."

"I'm sure." Arden looked aside, then came back to her and said, "I was hoping I could talk to you about a private matter."

"Ledge?" When Arden reacted with shock, she added, "He told me you had consulted him about doing some handiwork."

"I did, but this isn't about that. It's about the bad blood between him and Rusty Dyle."

Arden sensed the other woman's subtle, cautionary withdrawal. "What do you know about that?"

"Not enough."

Crystal considered it for several moments before seeming to come to a decision. "That discussion calls for at least one glass of wine. My house is directly behind the salon." She pointed. "You can walk across the lawn with me, or drive around."

"I'll take my car."

By the time Arden had driven around the corner to the front of Crystal's house, she was standing on the threshold of the open front door. Arden hadn't expected her to be this agreeable to talking about Ledge. She'd even feared that when she stated her business, Crystal might tell her to get lost. She had envisioned the "hot ticket" being coarse and blowsy. Not as refined, or cordial, or overall appealing.

She couldn't deny a stab of jealousy.

"Thank you for this," she said as Crystal led her into a homey, pleasant living area. It was neat and uncluttered, but felt lived in. "I thought of calling ahead, but—"

"You thought an ambush would be more effective."

Arden gave her an abashed look. "Truthfully? Yes. Someone recently pulled a similar stunt on me."

"Ledge?"

"He, uh, wanted to demonstrate the inadequacies of my locks."

"Sounds like him."

Arden didn't take it further than that.

Crystal motioned her into a chair. "In any case, I'm glad you sought me out. Red or white?"

"Whichever."

"How about a bourbon?"

Arden laughed nervously. "Do I look like I need it?"

"A bit."

Once they had drinks in hand, and Crystal was sitting opposite her on the sofa, she said, "I heard about the loss of your baby. I'm so sorry."

"Thank you." Arden couldn't think of a graceful way to ask if Crystal had children or planned to, so she kept her curiosity at bay.

To break that solemn spell, each took a sip of her drink.

Crystal said, "I suppose you came to me because you're aware of my close relationship with Ledge."

"I don't believe it's a secret to anyone."

Crystal gave a wry smile over that. "What I want you to understand is that my loyalty lies with him. He's very protective of my privacy, and it works both ways. I won't betray any of his confidences."

"I wouldn't expect you to."

"Good." She settled more comfortably on the sofa. "What is it you want to ask me?"

"Ledge told me himself that he and the current DA have been in a grudge match for many years. But he didn't tell me why." She stared into the exotic pair of eyes. "Is it over you?"

Crystal looked down into her drink. "It was. I mean, they already disliked each other before I entered the picture, but it intensified when we got to high school and Ledge and I started hanging out. Rusty felt entitled to having anything he wanted."

"He wanted you, and you were Ledge's girl."

She gave a small shrug. "Rusty hated that."

"I know that Ledge enlisted in the army even before he graduated."

"He's told you quite a lot about himself."

"I twisted his arm. He told me about how he came to be a soldier and how long he served. That was a long time for the two of you to be separated."

"We were each busy doing our thing. I started out a beautician in the salon. When the owner got ready to retire, I got a small business loan and took it over."

"And obviously made a success of it." Wanting to get back to the subject of the hostility between the two men, she said, "With Ledge away, you were left free for the competition."

"Believe me, Rusty was never competition, but he took advantage of Ledge's absence. He tried numerous times to get something going with me, even after he married and started his family. Anywhere I happened to be, he would show up and make sure that people saw us talking."

"Insinuating that there was something between you."

"Exactly." She looked sorrowfully into the near distance. "Judy, his wife, believed there was. Still does. She despises me. Little does she know how much I despise him."

"Why don't you tell her?"

"Have a showdown? Her accusing, me denying?" She shook her head. "That would only spawn more gossip. But Rusty knows full well how much I detest him. I made it plain to him that I wouldn't have anything to do with him, even if Ledge didn't exist."

"He didn't take no for an answer."

"He *doesn't*," she said.

"He still pursues you?"

"Not as openly. He stopped doing that when Ledge came back. Ledge may be the only person in the world who intimidates him. Which, of course, makes Rusty even more resentful of him."

She paused before adding thoughtfully, "But their feud isn't only about me anymore. It's evolved over the years. It's over something that runs much deeper."

"What?"

"You'll have to get that from one of them."

Unsurprised by her evasion, but also frustrated by it, Arden said, "Do you know what it is?"

"Aspects of it. Not everything."

Arden covered her hesitation to continue by taking a sip of her drink. "I think their conflict has something to do with the night my father disappeared."

Crystal's eyes widened fractionally, indicating to Arden that she had knowledge of the night in question. Her guard went up again. "What would be the connection?"

"Ledge was arrested that same night."

Crystal replied with a soft yes.

"He claims Rusty set him up."

"He's certain of it," Crystal said.

"Do you believe that's the case?"

"I believe Rusty is that unscrupulous."

"So do I."

"I didn't know you had met him."

"Not until today. He intercepted me this morning as I was leaving the courthouse." She explained why she was at the courthouse in the first place, and then told her how the encounter with Rusty had come about. "He more or less trapped me between my car and his. That's how it felt, anyway. He poured on the charm, but I couldn't wait to get away from him. He gave off sinister vibes."

"I know the vibe you mean," Crystal said. "Once you've had experience with someone like that, you know to watch for it."

Arden was struck by the gravity of her tone and waited to see if she would elaborate. But she didn't, so Arden continued.

"But besides my meeting with Rusty, something else disconcerting happened while I was there. I learned from the detective who furnished me with the investigation reports that Ledge had acquired copies of them. Only days ago. Did you know that?"

"No."

"He's said nothing to you about getting those reports?"

"No."

Arden didn't believe she was lying, but she wasn't being

completely open, either. "Crystal, why would Ledge have any interest in them?"

"Why does it matter?"

"That's what I need to know. Why would Ledge care what was in those reports?"

"You'll have to ask him."

"I can't." The words came our harsher than she'd intended. Backing down a bit, she said, "It would be awkward for me to seek him out now. We had something of a falling out."

"When?"

"Last night."

"Over what?"

"I didn't hire him."

"Why not? He does excellent work."

"I'm sure he does. That wasn't the issue. It was a personality clash. We rub each other the wrong way."

The track of the conversation was making her distinctly uncomfortable, as was Crystal's sharpened scrutiny. Arden wondered if she perceived her guilt. Crystal's niceness made her feel wretched over those damn kisses. She had never poached on another woman and had a low opinion of women who did. She wouldn't be one of them.

"I apologize, Crystal."

"Apologize?"

For wishing you were ugly and crass and not Ledge's lover. "For placing you in the position of having to choose between being polite to me and breaching confidences. I had hoped you could shed light, but I realize now how awful it was of me to ask." She set her glass on the coffee table and stood.

"You don't have to go. We can talk about something else."

"Thank you. Another time, maybe."

"I'm sorry I couldn't tell you more."

"I understand completely."

Crystal walked her to the front door. "Will you be staying in Penton?"

"I haven't decided yet."

"I hope you'll try the salon. Some of my clients would kill for your hair color. But I don't think it can be duplicated out of a bottle. You have to be born with it." Smiling, she pulled open the door.

Ledge was standing on the other side of the threshold, one hand high on the doorjamb, as though he was about to push his way through it. He pulled off his sunglasses and gave both of them a blast of his icy blue glare before it settled on Arden.

"Well, hello there," Crystal said brightly. "Did you stop by for happy hour?"

"No." Without taking his eyes off Arden, he said, "Marty asked me to meet her here."

"I didn't hear your truck."

"I parked in front of the salon. Saw that it was closed. Walked over. Saw her car here."

It irritated Arden for him to refer to her in the third person when she was standing less than a foot away from him. "I was just leaving."

"What are you doing here?"

Crystal intervened. "Arden got here as I was closing up shop. I was so glad to finally meet her, I invited her over for a drink."

"It was very nice of you to have me," Arden said, turning to Crystal. "Thanks again. I'll stop by and take a look at those products. Bye."

Ledge stepped in her path. "As long as you're here, we've got business to settle."

"We settled our business."

"Except for the hundred dollars you owe me for working

up the estimates. Due upon receipt. That's printed in red on the invoice."

"I didn't receive an invoice and—"

"Have you checked your email?"

"—and furthermore, you told me we were even-steven."

"That was conditional. You didn't hold up your end of the bargain."

"I—"

"Here's Marty." Crystal eased around Ledge and went to greet whoever had pulled a car into the driveway.

A woman got out of it, then reached back in for a large, white paper sack. As they approached the house, Crystal said something to her that caused the woman to look at Arden with ill-concealed curiosity. Arden reciprocated. The newcomer was dressed in medical scrubs, but, from the neck up, she looked like a punk rock star.

When they reached the porch, Crystal made the introductions. "Marty, Arden Maxwell. Arden, my housemate, Marty Camp."

They exchanged hellos. Crystal said, "Arden already knows Ledge."

"Does she?" Marty looked her up and down, then turned to him and raised a raven-black eyebrow.

He said, "You're late."

"I stopped for Chinese." Marty hefted the sack.

"Well?"

She took a sealed letter envelope from the outside pocket of her cross-body purse and handed it to him, saying drolly, "You're welcome."

Without even looking at the envelope, he folded it in half and slid it into the back pocket of his jeans. "How did you—"

"Don't ask. And, anyway, I have no idea what you're talking about."

"Thanks, Marty. I owe you."

"You certainly do. Be afraid." She then looked at the three of them in turn and said, "This feels like one of those awkward situations you walk into and, for the sake of all concerned, should probably keep walking. If you'll excuse me?" She went inside but left the door ajar.

Crystal heaved a sigh. "This isn't only awkward, it's silly. So I'm going to be the grown-up. Last night, you," she said to Ledge, "and Arden today, came to me, talking about and around the same subject. She has questions that I can't answer.

"I think it's time for the two of you to go somewhere and have an honest conversation, while Marty and I carry on with our plan for the evening, which is to curl up on the sofa, gorge on Chinese, and binge watch a series about vampires. Goodbye."

She stepped inside and soundly closed the door.

Ledge kept pace with Arden as she walked toward her car. "What questions?"

"Go away." Reaching her car, she jerked open the door, then stood in the wedge, staring back at the house. "I don't feel right about this at all."

"What were you talking to Crystal about?"

She turned to him. "Why don't the two of you live together?"

"That's one of the questions you asked her?"

"No!"

"Then what was the subject you talked about and around?"

"Never mind." She was about to get into the car, but he hooked his hand in the bend of her elbow.

"You're not leaving until you tell me why you came to Crystal with questions that you wouldn't ask me."

"Because I don't trust you." She pulled her arm free. "And Crystal's faith in you is grossly misplaced."

"Oh. You're feeling guilty."

"You're the cheater. I don't have anything to feel guilty for."

He tipped his chin down and gave her a look.

"Don't," she whispered with distress. "I feel terrible. She was lovely to me. I pried, but she was steadfastly loyal to you. I can't believe she encouraged you to go someplace with me while she stays at home for a cozy evening with—"

The realization slammed into her. Crystal's total lack of animosity or jealousy over her dealings with Ledge suddenly made sense. She looked up into his face. "With *Marty*," she said. "They're partners."

The fact that he didn't react with a swift contradiction was an affirmation.

"How long have you known?"

He took her arm again. "I think you and I should go have that honest conversation that Crystal recommended. Your place or mine?"

"Neither. Someplace public."

"Scared to be alone with me?"

"Precisely. If we're alone, I'm liable to kill you."

Chapter 27

Ledge insisted that they leave Arden's car there and go in his truck. He drove them a few miles out of town to a wide spot in the road where two state highways intersected beneath a caution light. The axis didn't actually qualify as a town, although a portable building on one corner was designated as the post office. On the opposite corner was a restaurant.

"It doesn't look like much, but they actually grill a damn good steak." He got out and went around to the passenger side to help her down, but by the time he got there, she'd made the jump on her own. She hadn't spoken a word since leaving Crystal's.

When they walked into the restaurant, the hostess beamed and greeted him by name. Then she noticed Arden and sized her up. Her smile lost some wattage, and her generous bosom settled back into its natural position.

He didn't let on that he noticed. "Hey, Angie. We're having a business meeting and need quiet. Is the back corner booth free?"

Looking skeptical about the nature of the dinner, Angie led them to the requested booth. Along the way, Ledge surveyed the other diners scattered throughout. He didn't see anyone familiar.

He and Arden slid into opposite sides of the booth. He chose to sit with his back to the wall, facing out into the dining room. Angie placed two laminated menus on the table. "I'll be your server tonight. Can I start you off with your usual bourbon, Ledge?"

"Please."

"Double?"

"Single."

Arden ordered ice water. Angie sniffed disdain. "I'll be right back."

Arden turned her head to watch as Angie walked away. When she came back around, she said, "Friend of yours?"

"Not the kind that fits your inflection."

"A hopeful wannabe?"

"Forget her." He leaned forward on the table. "Why do you have a hankering to kill me?"

Her purse was beside her on the bench. She opened it and took out a manila envelope, set it on the table between them, and pressed her index finger in the center of it. "Copies of two crime reports. The two my father is alleged to have committed. I thought I'd had an original idea to ask for them."

He muttered a string of curses, which Angie caught the tail end of as she returned. She gave him an arch look as she served their drinks and asked if they were ready to order. They skipped the appetizers and went straight to the entrées. Regardless, it seemed to take an inordinately long time to order.

Arden apparently shared his impatience. As soon as Angie

was out of earshot, she sprang forward as though a tether had snapped. "If I had known you had these reports, I would have asked to borrow them and saved myself a trip to the courthouse this morning."

"Who spilled the beans?"

"The detective who helped me. He wasn't tattling. He didn't know I knew you." She gave him a probing look. "I don't believe I do."

For the time being, he let that pass. "Why did you want the reports?"

"That should be obvious and understandable. I wanted to see what, if anything, was in them that incriminated my dad."

"Nothing. Unless I missed a clue that only a family member would spot."

She shook her head. "I've read every word of both reports twice. I didn't find anything. Lisa had told me that it was a waste of time."

"So she's also reviewed them?"

"Soon after it happened. As a ten-year-old, I wouldn't have understood most of what I was reading. By the time I was old enough, years had passed. It never occurred to me to ask to see them. Not until last night."

"When you told me you would start looking for answers someplace else."

"Which would have been an ideal time for you to volunteer that you had done some sleuthing yourself."

"You didn't give me a chance to say squat."

"If I hadn't slammed the door on you, would you have told me?"

"Probably not."

"No probably about it, Ledge."

She picked up the envelope and returned it to her handbag. Or tried. It buckled. She wound up impatiently stuffing it in.

Then she pushed back a handful of her hair. She took a sip of ice water. He scooted his glass of whiskey toward her, she scooted it back, with enough of a shove to slosh some.

"All right. Clearly you're mad. Lay into me." He leaned against the back of the booth and folded his arms across his chest.

His complacency seemed to infuriate her more. "Don't patronize me. You keep me in the dark by talking in half-truths, riddles, and outright lies. *Why*? When are you going to be up-front with me?"

"What do you want to know?"

"What prompted you to ask for copies of those crime reports? After twenty years, what gives them relevance now?"

"Someone driving past your house every night."

"Oh. Right. About that. Turns out that it's your bitter enemy, the district attorney. Surprise!"

He took a sip of his drink. "No surprise there, except that you now know."

She gaped at him. "You knew it was him?"

"I suspected."

"All along?"

"Since the minute you told me about it."

"Why didn't you tell me?"

"Because I hadn't caught him at it. I tried."

"The camouflage and war paint night."

"I made no secret of trying to catch him."

"No, but you kept secret who you *suspected* him to be. Another of your lies by omission."

He didn't blame her for being pissed. If the situation were reversed, he would be, too. "When did you find out?"

"Today."

"Here you go." Angie seemed pleased with herself for having startled them. Neither had noticed her approaching.

"Filet for the lady. T-bone for Ledge." She set two sizzling platters on the table. Addressing Arden, she said, "I know how Ledge likes his. Want to cut into yours to see if it's cooked okay?"

"I'm sure it's fine."

Angie asked if they needed anything else, and when Ledge told her no, she left them. He picked up his knife and fork, and motioned for Arden to do the same.

"I'm too angry to eat."

"Force yourself." He cut a piece of steak, speared it, pushed it into his mouth.

"Why?"

"For appearance's sake."

"Don't you want to know—"

"Yes. But not now. Not here."

He looked around. No one seemed to be paying Arden and him special attention, but Rusty had far-reaching tentacles.

His steak was as good as usual, but he ate methodically, fueling himself without really tasting the food. He was more interested in the woman across from him, who took dainty bites of her dainty filet. She looked distraught, bewildered, anxious, and angry, all at the same time.

He wanted to tell her that everything was going to be all right. But he didn't know that everything was. Besides, what a fucking hypocrite that would make him.

They declined dessert and coffee. Rather than hassle with a credit card, he left cash on the table. Angie looked disappointed to see them go.

As they headed back toward Penton, he watched to see if anyone followed them from the area of the restaurant. No one did.

"Okay. Tell me," he said. "How did you learn it was Rusty?"

"I'd gotten the reports and was leaving the courthouse.

He pulled up behind me on the parking lot. I recognized the sound of his car's engine." She described the scene and recounted their conversation. "To tell it, it sounds perfectly harmless. But it didn't feel that way. My skin was crawling."

"With good reason. That detective didn't point you out to him. He's had you in his sights since you moved back."

"But why?"

"Hold that thought."

Well before they reached the city limits of Penton, he turned off onto a narrow side road that amounted to a rutted dirt lane. If one didn't know it was there, he would drive past without even seeing it.

Arden asked, "Where are we going?"

"To the scene of the crime."

Even at high noon, it was an ominous environment. After the sun went down, the threatening aspects were intensified by the encompassing darkness. Trees that competed for sunlight during the day formed a canopy that moonlight couldn't penetrate. Insects were intimidated into silence. Nocturnal creatures went about their business furtively. Fowl sheltered in their nests. The aura of menace was unrelieved.

When the road came to a dead end, Arden spoke his name with apprehension.

He said, "You should recognize the place by the description in the police report."

She undid her seat belt and leaned forward to peer through the windshield. Had the headlights not been reflecting dully on the murky water that channeled through the gnarled knees of the cypresses, she wouldn't have known the lake was in front of them. When he cut the headlights, it disappeared.

"This is where they found Brian Foster," she said in a whisper.

"Parts of him. In those cypresses." He pointed to the copse growing out of the lake.

She turned and looked at him. "What does this have to do with Rusty?"

"Rusty killed him."

Chapter 28

J udy Dyle summoned her family to the dinner table.

All three of the children were involved in sports and other extracurricular activities. Their after-school schedules required more coordination than the D-Day invasion. Furthermore, the schedule was constantly changing, making a set time for the evening meal impossible. Most nights, they ate in shifts, which suited Rusty just fine.

But Judy insisted that at least one night a week they have dinner as a family.

Tonight was the night. *Lucky him*, Rusty thought sourly. He took his place at the head of the table. At Judy's direction, their daughter mumbled her way through a short blessing.

Just as she pronounced the amen, Rusty's cell phone rang. *Rescue!* He pushed back his chair.

Judy said, "We agreed to ban cell phones at the dinner table."

"I didn't agree." Ignoring her glower, he left the table. As he entered his study and shut the door, he looked at the readout on his phone and answered. "Angie, baby. You horny for me?"

"You wish. Listen, we're busy, so I've got to be quick. I'm calling to ask a favor in exchange for some juicy skinny."

"You have it backward, sweetheart. You do me the favors. In exchange, I don't tell your boss that you dip into the till on a regular basis."

"He knows. He and I have worked out our own swap. Do better, Rusty. You'll want to hear this."

Her coyness annoyed him, but that steakhouse got a lot of traffic through it. Angie stayed attuned to the pairs, groups, and individuals who came in, and if she saw someone or something that she thought was out of joint and would be of interest to him, she reported it. She was one of his best informers.

"Okay," he said, "what can I do for you?"

"My kid sister is popping opioids like they're M&M's."

"Where's she getting them?"

"Her new live-in boyfriend. He's your basic lowlife, leech, and lecher. Put him away. My family will get her into treatment."

She gave him their names and where they were shacked up. Rusty promised to sic the SO's dope detail on the boyfriend. "Now, your turn. What have you got for me?"

"Ledge came in tonight."

"That's not exactly a news flash."

"No, but he usually comes in alone. This evening he had a woman with him."

"A woman not Crystal."

"Not Crystal."

Although Rusty figured he already knew, he asked what the woman looked like.

"Thirtyish. Blond. Bambi eyes. No muffin top. Pains me to

say, I wanted to scratch her eyes out. It's not like Ledge to cheat on Crystal, at least not out in the open."

"You know this because you've tried."

"Don't be tacky. Anyway, knowing how it is with the three of y'all, I thought you'd enjoy hearing that he was tomcatting. He said it was a business meeting, but, you know. He had hungry eyes, and not for his tender T-bone."

"PDAs?"

"No. A lot of talking, though, so maybe it was a business meeting. They had their heads together over an official-looking manila envelope. I didn't see any markings on the outside, or what was in it."

Rusty's face turned hot. He knew what was in it. "Thanks, Angie."

"My sister doesn't get touched. Just the asshole."

"Got it." He hung up, dropped his phone onto the desk, then pivoted and kicked the hell out of the ottoman in front of his easy chair. The steel tip on the toe of his boot left a dent in the leather.

Ledge and the Maxwell girl had their heads together over those police reports.

Judy opened the door without knocking first. "Are you coming back to the table or not?"

"Not!"

She pulled the door closed with a slam.

Any other time, he would have gone after her and taught her a lesson in respect, but she could keep. He had to get Burnet's attention without delay. Shock-and-awe style.

He went around his desk and opened the bottom drawer. Inside it was a small safe with a keypad lock. He opened it and took out one of several burner phones he used to make calls such as this one.

The number rang four times before a nasally voice answered with a surly, "Who's this?"

"Your worst enemy or best buddy, depending."

"Oh. You."

"Yeah, me. How soon can you be ready?"

"If you're waitin' on me, you're backin' up. Say where."

"Stand by. I'll let you know."

Chapter 29

Arden was looking at Ledge wide-eyed, but he wanted to make certain that she had understood him. "Rusty killed Brian Foster."

She leaned away from him until her back was up against the passenger door. Her mouth opened, shut, opened again. Then, "There's nothing in the investigation report to support that."

"There's nothing in it to support that Joe was the culprit, either."

"But Rusty's name doesn't appear anywhere in those reports. Dad's does numerous times. What caused you to suspect Rusty of all people? Is this payback for his getting you arrested that night? If he did."

"He did." The doubt in her expression made him angry. "Fuck it. Crystal wasn't convinced, either."

"You've talked to her about this?"

"Last night. She shared something I didn't know that lends—"

"You saw Crystal last night?"

Her voice had gone a little thin, and he enjoyed the tinge of jealousy it conveyed. "Yeah. Straight from you, I went to her." He relished her miffed expression for only a second or two, then pulled himself back on track. "She told me quite a story about the night Foster was killed."

"The night he died. According to the report, it never was determined if it was intentional or an accident."

"All right. The night Foster *died*, Rusty went to Crystal's house."

"A tryst?"

"You decide." He related to her everything Crystal had told him about Rusty's bizarre visit. He finished by saying, "At first, I was mad at her for keeping this from me for all these years. But I know how Rusty operates, how *persuasive* he can be. He convinced her that if she ever failed him, I would be the one to catch hell."

Arden asked, "*Had* you beaten up her stepbrother?"

"I plead the fifth."

"*Why* did you?"

"I had a reason. But we're not talking about that. We're talking about why Rusty needed an alibi that night."

"You didn't fight him?"

"No. But he couldn't have faked his injuries." He raised his hips in order to reach into his back pocket for the envelope Marty had hand-delivered.

"I wondered what that was about," Arden said. "It seemed very secretive."

"Rusty's medical chart. She filched it from hospital records. I haven't had a chance to look at it."

"I want to see, too."

He turned on the map light and spread the folded sheets open across the console. "Time of arrival in the ER, five fifty-two a.m. That's consistent with the time Crystal estimated he left her house."

He ran his index finger over the sheet. "X-ray on left arm showed a fractured ulna, fractured humerus. Contusions on face, neck, lower abdomen."

"Lower abdomen?"

"Can't figure that, either," he said, frowning. "CT scan of torso. No organ rupture or internal bleeding, but blunt trauma to spleen."

"What does that say?" Arden squinted at a notation. "Splinters?"

"Removed from palms of hands," Ledge said, reading from the attending physician's notes. "Treated for superficial scratches on arms and hands." He looked at Arden. "Sounds like defense wounds."

They went back to the notes. Rusty had been admitted. He wasn't discharged until Tuesday morning and was sent home with instructions to continue bed rest for several days, take prescribed pain medication as directed, and apply antibiotic cream to the scratches four times a day.

"I wonder how he explained his injuries to the medical staff. His parents."

"He's fluent in lying," Ledge said as he refolded the forms and returned them to his pocket. "Making up an excuse wouldn't have been a problem for him."

He glanced toward the lake, then reached across Arden's knees, popped open the glove box, and took out a large flashlight. "You want to come, or stay here?"

"Where are you going?"

"After reading the investigation report the other day, I came out here in daylight to do some exploring. But this is how Brian Foster would have seen it. In the dark."

"Maybe it was a full moon that night."

"It wasn't."

She gave him an inquisitive look.

"I remember from when those deputies made me get out of my car. As I was being frisked, I looked up at the sky, like 'You've got to be kidding me.' It was overcast. No moon to speak of. Drizzly off and on. Pretty much like tonight."

She looked through the windshield at the eerie surroundings, then gamely opened the door and hopped down out of the truck. However, she got no farther than the grill before Ledge took her hand. Aiming the flashlight onto the ground, he said, "I don't know if cottonmouths come out at night. Just in case, be careful where you step."

She hesitated, but then fell into step beside him, close enough that their hips bumped as they walked. "Why would Foster or anyone venture out here alone?"

"I don't think he did."

"But the report said that his vehicle was discovered on the highway."

"On the shoulder, near the turnoff."

"His were the only fingerprints found inside or out of his car. No other footprints to indicate a passenger."

"He came alone, but met someone here."

"Inspectors were able to cast only one shoe impression near the water. They determined that it was Foster's size shoe."

"The water is shallow enough for someone to have waded here and ambushed him."

"Defying water moccasins?"

"And alligators," he added grimly. "Someone was determined to make that meeting."

"My dad?"

"I saw in the report that you and Lisa were questioned about a boat."

"It was older than he was. A tub. He had stopped taking it out after Mother died, so I'm not sure it was still floatable."

"Did he know the lake well?"

She gave a soft laugh. "Like the back of his hand. He grew up on it. In his younger years, he was often called upon to help find people who'd gotten lost." Looking troubled by the implications of that, she said, "But he was no longer young and robust. The drinking had taken a toll on his stamina. I can't see him paddling a boat any distance, wading ashore, overpowering a much younger man, and then drowning him."

"It doesn't seem likely, does it? Rusty's injuries indicate quite a struggle." He shone the flashlight on the rough trunk of a nearby tree. "Splinters."

They had gone as far as they could go without having to navigate through the viscous water and around cypress knees poking up through the surface. "A hard fall on one of those knobs could break your arm in two places and bruise your spleen. I think Rusty was here with Foster."

Arden tugged on his hand, bringing him around to face her. "How did you make that connection? Injured spleen notwithstanding, it's a giant leap to conclude that Rusty was involved."

"I checked the county records. There was only one death over the three-day Easter weekend. Brian Foster's. Rusty had one hell of a fight with someone, like someone who was fighting for his very life."

"His body, enough of it, was retrieved from the animal for the medical examiner to rule it a death by drowning."

"That was the cause of death," Ledge said. "Foster could have drowned, or been drowned, before the gators got to him. They drag their prey down. He could've still been alive then, but not for long."

Arden placed her fingertips against her lips. "Lord, that's ghastly."

"Yeah." The horror of Foster's death was worse than some of the things he'd witnessed or heard about during battles that often lasted for days. "His parents left disposing of his remains up to the county. Nice folks, huh?" he said. "However he died, the guy deserves for it to be explained."

"*I* need it explained," she said. "How did the two of them even know each other?"

"Rusty makes it his business to know everybody."

"Yes. I sensed that today. He plays the role of hail-fellow-well-met."

"Right."

"Did you know Foster?"

"Not well. I'd met him. Couple of times."

"At the store?"

On the edge of quicksand here, he made a motion with his shoulder that indicated a semi yes. "Welch's was the kind of place where every time you'd go in, you'd bump into a dozen people you knew or recognized."

"Why did it go out of business?"

"The kids and grandkids didn't have the competitive spirit of old man Welch. When he died, so did the store. It happened while I was overseas."

"My dad wouldn't have had much of a future there even if circumstances had been different."

"Guess not."

"What was Brian Foster like?"

"He was a nerd. Timid. The anti-Rusty. Which I'm sure is why Rusty picked on him." He soothed his conscience by asserting that none of what he'd told her was an outright lie. She was thinking it over. He hoped her frown was one of concentration, not doubt.

He continued. "I don't how, or to what extent, Rusty was instrumental in Foster's death. I can't prove anything. But on the night Foster died a grisly death, Rusty, the walking wounded, showed up at Crystal's house in more urgent need of an alibi than emergency medical treatment."

"It's broadly circumstantial, Ledge."

"So is everything they had on your dad."

"All right, but circling back to motive, I understand Rusty being a bully who picked on a nerd for fun. But what would have provoked Rusty to kill him?"

Damn it. She'd given him another perfect opening to tell her why. But if she had knowledge of the burglary, and Rusty's motive to get rid of Foster, she would pose a real threat to Rusty. Bad things happened to people whom Rusty perceived as a threat. "Maybe Foster got sick of his bullying and fought back. Or, knowing Rusty as I do, he wouldn't have needed a motive. He would kill somebody just to see if he could get away with it."

"Based on the way he struck me today, I can almost believe that. Almost." As she looked out across the watery landscape, she blindly reached for Ledge's flashlight, and he relinquished it. She moved the beam across the panorama of the wetland. "The monotony of it has always frightened me. It all looks the same. How does one find his way? But Dad was never lost on the lake. He always knew exactly where he was."

Ledge didn't say anything.

"He had a boat. He also had a motive. Half a million of them, in fact."

Her extended arm dropped to her side as though the flashlight had become weighted. Slowly, Ledge took it from her listless hand. She turned and started walking quickly back toward the truck, stumbling over natural obstacles.

"Arden." He followed and reached for her, but she shook off his hand and kept walking.

He outdistanced her and arrived at the pickup first. He opened the passenger door. She reached for the handhold above the door, but he splayed his hand over her bottom and boosted her up. He went around, and, as soon as he slid into the driver's seat and cranked the engine, she said, "Please take me back to my car."

He turned the truck around and headed back toward the highway. "Don't jump to a wrong conclusion, Arden."

"Then why did you bring me out here? To see for myself how logical it is that my father killed that man? I would rather you have continued to delude, evade, and invent."

"*Invent?*"

"That crap about the district attorney."

"It's not crap. You saw the medical chart."

"All that means is that as a hotheaded young man, Rusty Dyle got into a fight."

"With Foster."

"You want it to be Rusty because of your silly feud."

"What would my silly feud have to do with Rusty's interest in you? Explain that."

"Explain *yours.*"

"My what?"

"Your interest in that night. Your obsession with Rusty, Foster, my dad, the whole thing. If anyone has unexplained motives for his actions, it's *you.*"

The truck bumped off the dirt road and lurched onto the highway. When it hit the blacktop, Ledge floorboarded the accelerator. He sped back to town without a word passing between them. Main thoroughfares, such as they were in Penton, were more heavily patrolled, so he stayed off them and took a backstreet route to Crystal's house.

With a short distance still to go, he pulled over to a curb that bordered a vacant lot, cut the engine, and turned off the headlights.

"Why are you stopping?" she said. "Where are we?"

"A couple of blocks from Crystal's house."

"Take me to my car, Ledge. Now."

"We can't do this in front of Crystal's house."

"Do what?"

"Either fight or fuck. Which?"

Chapter 30

───◆───

T hen we fight," she said.

"Okay. You go first."

She blinked. She took a swift little breath. She waited too long.

He leaned across the console and captured her mouth with his.

She remained stiff and unresponsive for a couple of heartbeats, then her lips became pliant, and her tongue engaged with his, and her hot, sweet body seemed to melt into the car seat.

He curved his right arm around her shoulders, and his left around her waist, and pulled her as close as the console between them would allow. She tunneled all ten fingers through his hair, angled her head, and held his fast as they continued a kiss erotic and evocative, a kiss that was a mind-blowing preview of what sex with this woman would be like.

She didn't kiss with the timidity of inexperience. But she also didn't kiss with the near boredom of a woman who had frequent lovers. She wasn't just going through the motions before moving on to the next step. She was into it, with an unabashed combination of pleasure in the kiss alone and a yearning for more.

He raised his head, looked into her face, pulled his arm from around her shoulders, and swept his thumb across her full, wet lower lip. "You want to know about my interest in you? It has a lot to do with this."

"Actions speak louder than words."

Holding her gaze, he slipped his left hand beneath the hem of her top, pressed his palm against her midriff, then moved it up to squeeze her breast and keep it plumped above the cup of her bra while lowering his head to nuzzle her.

He rubbed his face against those tantalizing breasts that for days—seemed like a lifetime—he had wanted to put his mouth to. His tongue dabbed at her nipple through her clothes.

She sighed his name. Her grip on his hair became tighter.

His mouth returned to hers while his thumb took up the brushing caresses that caused little catches in her breath. His mouth had left damp patches on her top like stamps of possession. They stirred the male in him to claim more.

He slid his hand from her breast to her waist, then between her thighs. Her slight, undulating shift in position granted permission and access. He pressed, stroked. She murmured something unintelligible, but whatever she said had desire behind it. She wanted to be felt, deep.

Her pants were made of stretchy denim that fit her like a second skin. Earlier he'd appreciated how the things molded to her incredible ass, but now he was frustrated by their tight fit. "How do I get into these?"

"Here, let me—"

The jangle of a cell phone froze them.

It rang a second time. "Mine's on vibrate," he said. "Must be yours."

Appearing as frustrated as he, her head flopped back against the seat. "It's in the outside pocket of my purse. Can you see who it is?"

He fumbled around on the floorboard until he located her purse, the outside pocket, her phone. He brought it up to where he could see it and, just as the phone stopped ringing, he read the caller's name.

He eased himself back across the console and resumed his place in the driver's seat. As she struggled to sit up straight, he extended the phone to her. "Somebody named Jacob."

"Oh." She held his gaze for several seconds, then reached for her phone and turned to face the windshield. "I'll call him later."

Seething, Ledge turned on the ignition and put the truck in gear.

"That sounds like Ledge's truck." Crystal picked up the TV remote and turned down the volume. "He must be returning Arden to her car."

Marty left the sofa and went over to one of the front windows.

"Don't spy on them," Crystal said. "They're not teenagers."

"I'm not spying. Just taking a peek." Marty raised one of the louvers of the blinds. "Yep, it's his monster truck. She's getting out on her own." Looking over her shoulder at Crystal, she reported, "No good night kiss."

"Hmm. I'm disappointed. I thought for sure there were banked fires smoldering."

"In the half minute that I was with them, I got that impression, too. Maybe they kissed in the truck. Maybe they did more than kiss, and a kiss would be anticlimactic. So to speak."

"But it's not like Ledge to—"

Marty interrupted her. "What the...?"

"What?"

"Crystal?"

"What's the matter?"

"Oh, my God."

Responding to the sudden alarm in Marty's tone, Crystal bounded off the sofa, and rushed to join her at the window. "What is it?"

"Are those *dogs*?"

<hr />

They had covered the two blocks to Crystal's house without Arden offering a word of explanation, from which Ledge inferred that Jacob couldn't be identified with nonchalance, such as that he was the octogenarian who'd lived across the street from her in Houston, or her first cousin, or her best friend's adolescent son hawking tickets for a fund-raising raffle.

By the time he pulled up behind her car, he was steaming. He put the truck in park but left it running, draped his wrists over the top of the steering wheel, and stared out the windshield, being a jerk and knowing it, but he was a guy with a three-day-old hard-on and he was fuck-all furious.

He said, "Jacob?"

"Is none of your concern."

"No?" He turned his head to look at her. "My stiff dick would disagree. It wishes we'd stuck to fighting."

She shot him a drop-dead look as she opened the door of the truck. She shut it with force and rounded the hood. The headlights spotlighted her as she dug into her purse, probably searching for her key fob.

Catching motion out the corner of his left eye, he turned his head. Two shadowy figures came streaking across the lawn across the street, a third not far behind.

He registered almost immediately what they were, what they signified, and, shoving open the driver's door, he burst out of it, yelling, "Arden, get back in the truck. Get in the truck!"

He'd telegraphed his panic, because she stopped in her tracks and looked toward him, but she was blinded by the headlights. She raised her hand to shield her eyes just as one of the dogs took a flying leap at him.

He jumped backward onto the hood and jerked his legs up in the nick of time. The dog hit the side panel with a loud thump and enough momentum to rock the vehicle.

Arden screamed.

"Go around, go around. Get in the truck!" Ledge crab-walked across the hood to the front of it, then jumped down. He grabbed Arden's hand, yanking hard, placing her behind him as another of the animals charged. Ledge kicked at it.

"Get in!" He let go of her hand and pushed her toward the passenger side, hoping to God she would do as he said.

He clambered back up onto the hood. The dogs continued to attack, trying to launch themselves high enough to reach him. They were snarling, barking a cacophony. Slobber flew from their maws in globs. His boot heel caught one in the muzzle and sent it backward. It landed hard on the pavement, stunning it, but only momentarily. Then it was up and throwing itself against the pickup again and again, maddened, frenzied.

He glanced behind him to see that Arden had made it into the cab, but one of the animals had targeted her and was repeatedly launching itself at the passenger door, its wide jaws snapping.

The front door of Crystal's house flew open. She and Marty came running down the steps. Crystal was screaming his name. He shouted for them to get back inside.

Then a blast of the truck's horn stunned him, the dogs, Marty and Crystal into silence.

Its ear-shattering blare continued. Then, above it, Ledge heard a shrill whistle.

So did the dogs. As one unit, they took off, racing in the direction from which they'd come.

Ledge gave no thought to pursuing them, or to anything else except Arden. Without even pausing to catch his breath, he slid off the hood and rushed around to the passenger door, where the window was streaked and gummy with canine saliva. He yanked open the door.

She was leaning across the console, her back to him. He didn't shout above the racket. Instead, he spoke quietly. "Arden, you can let up now. They're gone."

She turned and looked at him with a stunned gaze, but his words registered. She pulled her hand away from the horn activator on the steering wheel. The sudden, resultant silence was almost as deafening as the blare had been.

Her eyes still fixed on his, she sat upright in the passenger seat. He placed a hand on her knee. It was trembling. "Are you all right?"

"Yes."

"You weren't hurt?"

"No." Then, shaking her head, "No." She looked him over. "You?"

"No, but I was losing. Good thinking with the horn. Thanks."

"You're welcome." Her teeth began to chatter.

Crystal came running up to them, panting. "Are you two okay?"

"We're fine," he said. "Shaken, but fine."

"Good Lord, Ledge." Crystal splayed her hand across her chest. "You could have been killed."

"I think that was the idea."

She looked at him with dismay.

Marty joined them just then. She'd had the presence of mind to tell neighbors who'd come out to see what the commotion was about that everything was under control. She'd also collected Arden's purse, which she'd dropped when the dogs attacked. It had been trampled.

"Everything was spilled and scattered," Marty told her. "I gathered up what I could see. Your billfold is intact."

"Thank you." Arden took her purse but seemed indifferent to its battered condition and at a loss as to what to do with it.

Ledge took it from her and set it on the floorboard.

Marty said, "Should we call the cops?"

"It won't do any good," he said.

"But with a pack of wild dogs—"

"You heard the whistle?" he said. "They weren't feral, and they weren't on the prowl." He turned to Crystal. "Do you mind if Arden stays with you tonight? She shouldn't go home alone."

"Where are you going?"

"To run an errand."

This trio of women wasn't stupid. They shared a look among themselves.

Crystal said, "Of course; Arden can stay for as long—"

"Thank you, Crystal, but I won't be pawned off on you." Looking straight at him, she stated, "I'm going with Ledge."

"The hell you are. You're shaking like a leaf."

"I was. But the shock has worn off. I'm okay now. See?" She held out her hands, palms down to prove they were steady. They weren't.

"You're staying."

"No. I'm not."

Marty nudged Crystal. "I think we should leave them to hash this out."

Crystal looked indecisively at him, and then at Arden, then murmured, "Be careful," and went along with Marty.

Ledge waited until they were inside the house, then said, "Arden, I don't want to waste time arguing with you."

"Then you had better stop arguing."

"You could get hurt."

"You keep telling me that, but so far I haven't been."

"You can't go where I'm going."

"Which is where?"

"I don't even know yet. I don't know what I'll be up against when I get there. It will most certainly be dangerous. You can't go with me. That's final."

She stared him down, or tried. But he won. She capitulated.

"All right." She retrieved her purse and climbed down from the truck. But she didn't start in the direction of the house. She headed for her car.

"What are you doing?"

"I either ride with you or follow in my own car."

He erupted with a stream of obscenities, none of which fazed her. She walked back to him. "You believe Rusty was behind this, don't you?"

"It has his trademark."

"If what you told me tonight is true, and he killed Brian Foster, and he has let everyone think for two decades that my father did it, I've damn well earned the right to fight back."

His head dropped forward. He blew out a gust of breath. He counted to ten as he stared at the ground between his boots.

When he looked up at her, he said, "I gave you fair warning."

Chapter 31

As they drove away from Crystal's house, Ledge got on his phone and called Don. "The other night when Rusty ambushed me in the bar, there was a guy playing pool with some buddies. I didn't even turn around to look when Rusty hassled him about dogfighting. Rusty called him by name. Dawkins?"

Arden, in the passenger seat, heard Don say, "Hawkins. Dwayne Hawkins."

"Do you know where he lives? Or where he holds the fights? Rusty mentioned an old barn."

"You're not taking to that sport, I hope."

"Come on."

"Then why are you asking about it?"

"A friend of mine had a run-in with a vicious stray. He thought it might belong to this Hawkimans character."

Don said, "I'll ask around and get back to you."

"My friend needs to know now."

"What's the rush?"

"The dog may still be loose in his neighborhood. There're kids around."

"Then he should call animal control."

"I need that info, Don. Please?" He clicked off and propped the phone in the cup holder.

"You told a fib," she said.

"I edited the truth."

"A skill you've perfected."

He didn't respond to that.

She noticed that they'd driven past the same water tower twice. "We're driving in circles, aren't we?"

"For the time being, yeah."

"Why?"

"To see if somebody is tailing us."

"Is someone?"

"Not that I can tell now, but somebody had to have told Hawkins where we could be found. Rusty's got every deputy in the department in his back pocket. He had them on the lookout. Your car was spotted at Crystal's. Eventually, you would have come back for it."

"I could have been inside the house."

"To get to your car, you'd have had to go outside."

"I was the target?"

"Good. You're finally beginning to catch on." He turned into the parking lot of a closed business and brought the truck to a stop. "We'll wait here for Don to call back. I'm burning up gas, and I don't know how far we'll have to drive."

He turned off the engine and sat back in his seat, facing forward, staring at the brick wall in front of the truck. She did the same. Neither said anything.

Now that she'd had time to recover her breath and wits from the dog attack, her thoughts reverted to the fight they'd had just before it. The topic lay between them like a grenade whose pin had been pulled. No sooner had she wondered which of them would pick it up than he spoke in a grumble.

"That Jacob was the daddy?"

She glanced at him, then looked forward again. "Jacob Greene with an *e* at the end."

"Where'd you two meet?"

"I worked at Neiman's as a personal shopper. Jacob became a client. A good one. He spent a lot of money with me. I later became his patient."

"Patient? He's a doctor?"

"Yes, but by the time I started seeing him professionally, we'd gone beyond the traditional doctor-patient relationship."

"Obviously way beyond. How come you're not together now?"

"Well, for one thing, he's married."

"Ah. That's the crimp. Big one. The wife found out about his pregnant mistress and—"

"Will you shut up?" She turned to him then. "Jacob is a specialist in AI. Artificial insemination. He impregnated me, yes. Using sperm from an anonymous donor."

He held her gaze for several seconds, then bowed his head and rubbed his thumb across his eyebrow. "I feel like an ass."

"I can't imagine why." She didn't try to disguise her sarcasm.

He looked at her querulously. "Well, when I asked about the father, why didn't you just tell me?"

"I didn't even tell my sister. It wasn't any of her business, and it certainly wasn't any of yours."

"Right. So you've said."

Before they could take it further, his phone vibrated, rattling the loose change in the cup holder. He kept his eyes on her as he reached for it and answered. She heard Don say, "Okay. I've got the directions to his place."

"Gimme."

"I'd rather not."

"Then I'm sorry to have bothered you. I'll get the info from somebody else."

"This guy's no choirboy, Ledge."

"Figured that."

"You're looking for trouble."

"No, *he* was, and now he's got it."

Don hesitated, then muttered, "Hell."

The place looked almost too derelict to be real, more like a stage or movie set crowded with props to make it appear as squalid as possible. Floodlights mounted on metal poles formed a perimeter and shone down on the property, contributing to the movie set feel.

The house was as ramshackle as the various outbuildings, one of which was missing half its roof. The disemboweled, rusted-out vehicles scattered about were a cliché. Two mismatched upholstered chairs squatted on the porch under the overhang. Arden didn't even want to think about the vermin that nested in them.

Off to one side of the dirt yard was a row of cages, crudely constructed of weathered scrap lumber and cyclone fencing. They were filthy and overpopulated with dogs trained to fight to the death if necessary.

As Ledge drove the pickup into the clearing, the pack set up a ruckus so savage, it was bloodcurdling. Arden vacillated between pity for the animals over the egregious mistreatment and terror of them.

Ledge pulled to a stop and took several moments to assess the scene. Then he reached beneath his seat and came up with a leather holster. The pistol in it looked like something Wyatt Earp would have owned. He checked the cylinder to see that it was fully loaded, then set it on the console.

He reached behind him to the floorboard of the back seat and produced a rifle. With stern concentration, he went through a preparedness routine that involved several moving parts, a clicking of this mechanism, a clacking of that one. All of it he did with precision and caution and know-how, which was both assuring and disconcerting.

"Lock the doors behind me," he said, his features chiseled with resolve. "I'm going to keep the motor running in case you have to get out of here in a hurry. Do not hesitate. I mean it, Arden. If this goes tits up, get the hell out of here. No matter what happens, you are not to set foot out of this truck. If you're forced to use that," he said, nodding down at the revolver, "point it and pull the trigger. It's a hand cannon. If you don't hit something, you'll stop it in its tracks."

He gave her one last, hard look. "This son of a bitch tried to kill us, and he still might. If he makes a move, don't wait to see what'll happen next. Throw the truck into reverse and floorboard it."

He opened the driver's door and got out. He waited to hear the doors lock, then started walking toward the house, the rifle held at his side, barrel down. She marveled at his seeming calm. Her heart was pounding. She could barely draw breath.

The screen door of the house was pushed open, and a young man with stringy, shoulder-length hair stepped out onto the porch, barefoot. He was wearing a dingy white t-shirt and dirty blue jeans that hung onto his jutting hip bones by a thread. He carried a double-barrel shotgun.

When he snapped it up and aimed it directly at Ledge, Arden

made a small, fearful sound, which even she couldn't hear above the deafening barking coming from the dog pens.

Dwayne Hawkins walked as far as the uneven edge of his porch. "You're Burnet, ain't cha?"

Ledge didn't say anything, just continued toward the house in an unhurried, measured tread.

"You deaf or something?"

Ledge kept walking.

Hawkins stepped off the porch and walked toward Ledge, then stopped and assumed a belligerent stance. "You come here to shoot my dogs?"

"No, I came here to shoot you."

It happened in a blur of motion. Ledge swung the rifle up to waist level. The barrage lasted for only a few seconds, but it seemed to Arden to go on forever. The reverberation did. The dogs went crazy.

Dwayne Hawkins lay sprawled on his back in the dirt. The shotgun had landed yards away from his outstretched arm.

"Ohmygodohmygodohmygod." Arden didn't stop to think about Ledge's dire warnings and emphatic instructions. The door unlocked when she opened it and all but fell out. As she ran across the yard, she held her hands over her ears to mute the din coming from the cages.

Ledge seemed impervious to the dogs, to her, to everything. He walked over to Hawkins's prone form and pressed the muzzle of the rifle against the center of his forehead. In horror, she stumbled toward him, calling his name. He didn't react.

It wasn't until she got to within feet of him that she realized Hawkins wasn't dead. He wasn't even bleeding. He hadn't been touched. He lay between the arms of a V, neatly stitched into the dirt by bullets. His eyes were open and blinking rapidly. His rib cage was sawing up and down. Otherwise he was frozen with fright.

Ledge said, "You sicced your dogs on us?"

"I got nothing against you. Honest. Swear. Don't kill me," he pled, then began to blubber.

"Who put you up to it?"

"That asshole DA. Dyle."

"What did he pay you?"

"Nuthin'. We made a deal."

"What did you get in return, Dwayne?"

"He let me off for . . . I got this hobby."

"Dogfighting. Some hobby, Dwayne."

"You got no call to—"

"Did the DA tell you why he wanted to harm Ms. Maxwell?" Dwayne didn't move, but his eyes cut to her. "That her?"

"Did he tell you why he wanted—"

"No, no," he sputtered. "He said turn the dogs on y'all. That's all I know."

"*Y'all*? Both of us?"

"He said you two'd be together."

"How did he know that?"

"No clue. He said that sooner or later y'all'd show up at the house behind the beauty parlor and for me to be waitin'. I didn't mean to—"

"Sure you did, Dwayne. You meant for us to be chewed to pieces."

"I got nuthin' against you," he repeated. "Her, either."

"Well, I've got something against you now." Ledge's voice had the quality of an icicle. "Do you know what I did in the army?"

"Heard you was in the war, but—"

"Sniper."

Dwayne whimpered. His Adam's apple slid up and down.

"That's right, Dwayne. I could target your eye socket from a mile away. Any. Time. I. Want. And I swear to God I will if you don't disappear."

"Disappear? Run off, you mean?"

"That's what I mean."

"I cain't. Dyle said if I double-crossed him, he'd kill me."

"Then you're up shit creek, Dwayne."

"Dyle's got Mex'cans with cartel experience."

"And I've got a sniper rifle with a telescopic sight. If it's any comfort to you, you'll be dead before you hear the report. When you look at it that way, you're probably better off sticking around and sucking up to Dyle until—well, until I take a notion."

Hawkins hiccupped a sob, and snot trickled from his nostril.

Ledge hitched his head back toward the cages. "I ought to shoot you right now for animal abuse. But if you stay in the neighborhood, in the state, you're on borrowed time."

Ledge lifted the muzzle off Hawkins's forehead, walked over to the shotgun, and removed the shells. He put them in the breast pocket of his shirt. Giving Arden a fearsome look, he nodded her toward the truck.

She walked to it quickly. Ledge walked backward, keeping a bead on Hawkins as he picked up the empty shell casings. When he reached the truck, he got in, replaced the rifle on the floorboard, and put the pickup in reverse.

He said, "Rusty put him up to it. You heard that, right?"

"I heard."

"Do you believe me now? He killed Brian Foster." He thumped the steering wheel with his fist. "I goddamn know it."

Chapter 32

That night in 2000—Rusty

It never would have occurred to Rusty that the pipsqueak bookkeeper would turn brave in the amount of time between when the band of burglars had split up in the parking lot of Burnet's bar and now, when Foster arrived at their designated meeting place to hide the booty.

Even when Rusty had talked to Foster on the phone half an hour ago to tell him about Ledge's arrest and the jeopardy it placed them in, Foster had seemed his ordinary self. That was, uncertain and indecisive, anxiety and fear bringing him close to his breaking point.

Which was exactly where Rusty wanted him to be.

But as he watched from his hiding place on the other side of a narrow channel, he saw Foster plowing through the dark woods with less trepidation than one would expect. The beam of his flashlight danced among the trees and bounced over the marshy ground as he walked with a purposeful stride that was out of character with his scared-rabbit personality.

He didn't slow down or stop until he reached a barricade of

cypress knees in the shallows, where he stopped and shone the flashlight around. He aimed it at the grouping of picnic tables a short distance away, apparently believing that he would find Rusty there waiting for him, as he'd been doing the first day Foster had followed Rusty's instructions and had arrived with a six-pack of cold brew.

"Rusty?"

The dark, sultry stillness of their surroundings absorbed Foster's voice like a velvet muffler. He cleared his throat. "Rusty?"

On that second try, Rusty detected a trace of misgiving in his tone. He smiled, thinking, *That's more like it.* He stepped out from behind his cover of low tree branches, cupped his hands around his mouth, and called in a stage whisper, "Here."

Foster swept the flashlight beam across the channel, swinging it from side to side until it lit on Rusty, who raised a hand and made a staying motion intended to communicate that Foster was to sit tight.

"Where's the money?"

"Shh!" Didn't the idiot realize that sound carried over water?

Rusty unwound the line from around a sapling that he'd used to tie down the canoe, although there was little danger of it drifting. The current here was sluggish at best.

The canoe rocked when he stepped into it, but he maintained his balance. On his knees, he began paddling toward where Foster stood, still aiming the flashlight directly at him.

Speaking only loud enough to make himself heard, Rusty told him to turn it off. "You'll signal to somebody that we're here."

"Nobody's around."

"Kill the light, will ya?"

Foster switched it off. Rusty paddled as soundlessly as

possible, making shallow dips into the water. As he drew closer, Foster said in a whisper, "Can you see where you're going?"

"My eyes have adjusted. Catch this line."

He was about to pitch it when Foster said, "Hold on. Where's the money?"

"Right here."

Rusty pointed down to the bag in the hull. He grinned up at Foster. "Look familiar?"

"Open it."

"Waste of time, but if you insist."

Rusty heaved a sigh as though he were being unnecessarily inconvenienced, but he was playacting. He had counted on Foster being bright enough to ask to see it before committing himself wholeheartedly to this linkup. Leaning far enough forward to reach the bag, he unzipped it and held it open.

Foster flipped the flashlight back on and aimed it into the bag.

"Satisfied?"

"Yeah, okay."

"Then turn off that goddamn light."

Foster fumbled in his effort to click it off, almost dropping it.

Rusty couldn't resist taunting him. "How come you're so nervous? Are you afraid of the dark?"

"This place looks different in daylight. I've never been out here at night."

"Well, we'll have to remedy that." Now that he'd reestablished that they were accomplices and had regained Foster's shrinking trust, he needed to reel him in. "This is a great spot to have all kinds of fun."

"Like what?"

"If I confide, you won't tattletell, will you?"

"No."

"Me and my buddies come here and get stoned out of our minds."

"Oh."

"Next time, you'll have to join us." He hitched his head. "Those picnic tables? Great for making out on, if you remember to bring a quilt. But even if you don't. This girl Crystal?" Rusty smacked his lips. "Too many times to count, my friend."

"Crystal?"

At Foster's surprised tone, Rusty's eyes narrowed. "Yeah, Crystal. Why?"

"It's just that I overheard some of the women in the office talking about a Crystal. One's son has a crush on her, but she said she told him that he had just as well stop pining. He doesn't stand a chance with her because of Ledge Burnet."

Rusty ground his teeth. "Him and Crystal are over. She's with me now. Anyhow, enough of that. We'd better get moving. Watch your step as you get in."

"Get in? In the canoe?"

"I found a perfect spot to hide the bag." He thumbed over his shoulder. "Trees are so close together over there, you feel like Daniel Fucking Boone. You should've worn different shoes."

"Is there a road leading to it?"

"Sure. We're on it. It's what we locals call a boat road."

"I don't like the sound of that. What about a regular road?"

"It's a wilderness, Foster. A fucking swamp. That's what makes it an ideal hiding place."

Foster took an anxious look around. "Trees are dense on this side, too. And it has access to the road. Why not hide it over here? Temporarily, at least. It would be easier to get to in case we have to move it again."

"Also easier for somebody to find. Accidentally. Like I said, people come here to use the picnic tables. All we need is for some potheads to find this bag of cash and make off with it. Or a do-gooder who would hand it over to the law."

"I've never seen anybody else around. Not once in all the times we've met out here."

The accountant had acquired some courage, *plus* developed a stubborn streak, and both were beginning to grate. Had he taken a damn tonic or something? Rusty let his irritation show. He stood up, standing with legs straddling the bench so as not to tip the canoe. "What's up with you?"

"Nothing. I just think we need to think this through a little bit more."

"I've thought it through."

Foster flipped the flashlight back on and slid the beam along the side of the canoe from bow to stern. "Where'd you get the canoe?"

"That old tin shed at the boat dock down the road? Sheriff's office uses it to stow boats they've impounded for one reason or another. Usually because somebody was operating a craft while intoxicated.

"Anyway, whoever the offender was who owned this canoe never reclaimed it, so my daddy gave me permission to take it out whenever I want." He was still holding the paddle and motioned with it for Foster to get in. "I know what I'm doing. Don't be scared. Climb into the bow there."

Foster didn't move. He just stood there, then blurted, "I called Mr. Maxwell and told him everything."

Rusty's blood surged from normal temperature to an instant boil. "Come again?"

"You heard me. I don't need to repeat it. Mr. Maxwell knows you intend to set him up as our scapegoat."

Rusty didn't hesitate, didn't stop to think about it, just reacted with a burst of uncontrollable rage. He cut a horizontal arc with the paddle. Had it been a blade, it would have decapitated Foster. As it was, it struck him in the neck with such force, Rusty was sure it had crushed his windpipe. He dropped the flashlight, grabbed his throat with both hands, and attempted to make a sound. What issued from him was painful to hear.

Rusty watched calmly as Foster staggered forward a few steps before toppling facedown into the murky water amid an intricate, knobby sculpture of cypress knees, then lay still. Perfectly still.

The flashlight had landed in a few inches of water. It was still on, creating an unnatural underwater glow that was downright eerie. It even spooked Rusty a little, but he didn't retrieve the flashlight. Better to leave it.

It had been his plan all along to kill Brian Foster. No way in hell would he have lived through the night. However, Rusty hadn't planned to do it here, where his body could be so easily discovered by someone on an Easter outing.

Upon reflection, though, this unexpected turn of events wasn't all that unfortunate. In fact, it was better than what he had originally planned to do, which was to canoe to one of the deepest parts of the lake, whack Foster in the head with the paddle, and dump him.

He realized now the flaws in that plan. Once the body gassed up and resurfaced, a medical examiner would have determined that it had been a homicide. Of course nobody would ever suspect the sheriff's son of committing murder, but it would have created a hubbub that Rusty would rather do without.

This way, it would appear to have been a fatal accident. That would be an easy sell. Foster was new to the area. He was from up north someplace, had never experienced swampy terrain. He'd stupidly left his car on the road and walked—in wingtip shoes, for crissake—into the forest at night, completely unaware of the hazards it and the wetlands represented. The dumb schmuck had stumbled, crushed his windpipe when he fell, knocked himself unconscious, and drowned, his flashlight still on.

No relocating or disposing of his body was necessary. Leaving him where he'd died was much more efficient and less strenuous. He could simply paddle away. Which also saved time. Because now he had the additional complication of Joe Maxwell to deal with.

Addressing Foster's still form, he said, "Fuck you for that."

He used the paddle against a tree root to push the canoe away from the copse, then executed a one-eighty and headed for the dock with the shed where he would return the canoe.

He'd barely registered the splashing sound before Foster surged up out of the water and clouted him in the side of his head with a length of a fallen tree branch. It struck him in his jawbone, just in front of his ear. It stunned him. It also hurt like fucking hell.

Instinctively, he bellowed in pain and reached out for the jagged limb before Foster could wield it again. But Rusty missed, succeeding only in scraping the palms of his hands on the rough bark.

Foster, teeth bared and clenched, took another swipe with the natural club and caught Rusty just beneath his rib cage. Yowling, he bent double in an instinctual effort to protect the soft tissue from further assault. Taking advantage of Rusty's position, Foster grabbed the back of his neck and pulled him out of the canoe and into the water.

Rusty tried to catch hold of the side of the rocking canoe, but Foster kicked it out of his reach and sent it gliding across the surface, then relaunched his attack on Rusty.

They thrashed and splashed, kicked and clawed, each

trying to gain solid footing amid the network of gnarled roots both above the surface and below. The soles of Rusty's boots couldn't gain traction on the slimy lake bottom, and he fell hard, landing in a sculpted formation of cypress knees. A lightning bolt of pain sizzled up his left arm, went through his chest, and straight up into his brain. When it struck, he screamed.

But when Foster came at him from behind, he fought with a vengeance to stand, despite the agony and uselessness of his left arm. His right arm was working, though, and he jabbed his elbow backward into Foster's injured throat.

He felt the man's knees buckle and turned to see Foster crumpling. Foster tried but failed to stay on his feet. He stumbled backward, his arms flailing, as he fell into the water, face up. He went under.

Rusty stayed where he was, his breath rushing in and out, causing bursts of pain that had him blinking back tears.

Foster wasn't done yet. He made an effort to rise.

"Die, you motherfucker!" Rusty shouted.

Foster continued his struggle to pull himself out of the water.

And then, out of the corner of Rusty's eye, he saw motion.

Two dark forms moved with silent and lethal intent just below the surface, only their reptilian eyes catching the glow of the flashlight. They glided with deadly purpose toward the man flailing his arms in a vain attempt to save himself from drowning. Poor bastard was already dead and didn't even know it.

Rusty watched in petrified awe.

One of the gators lunged up out of the water, clamped Foster in his jagged maw, and dragged him under. He simply vanished. There was nothing to signify that he'd ever been there except for the swells that disturbed the surface, testaments to Foster's final struggle for survival.

Rusty stood there panting noisily until mere ripples remained on the surface. He had the presence of mind not to clamber onto the shore where he could leave footprints. He would have to stay in the water and hope to God the gators competing for Foster would be kept busy until he could get to his canoe.

He remembered the direction in which it had been sent drifting. He set out after it, plowing through knee-deep water. Every shadow on the surface of it looked like an alligator or poisonous snake, every shadow on shore a black panther sensing weakened pray.

He waded for what seemed like miles before he spotted the canoe. It was caught up in some aquatic vegetation. It was still a fair distance away. He feared going into shock before reaching it.

Cradling his throbbing left arm against his middle, which pulsed in pain, he slogged through the shallows, every step impeded by his heavy boots, his sodden clothes, and mostly by his increasing anxiety over what he was going to do about his injuries.

And about Maxwell.

At this moment, Joe could be drunk and quivering in fear that Rusty was contriving to have him implicated and arrested. Or, just as possible, he could have called the law already and was trying to negotiate his own deal.

But, not being a complete and utter fool, Joe wouldn't report this to the SO, which was Mervin's domain. No, he would notify another department of law enforcement. The Texas Rangers. FBI.

The thought caused Rusty to snivel worse than Foster.

A more rational section of his brain, however, insisted that a sot like Maxwell wouldn't do that. Before spilling his guts to any branch of law, he would want a guarantee of immunity, and none was going to grant that without hearing what Joe had to tell. He couldn't say a thing without risking that the sky would fall on his daughters, Lisa and the younger one. Destroy their futures? No, that would be too big a gamble for poor ol' Joe. He would never take it.

Rusty wanted to believe that.

Fear still niggled at him, though. It frightened him to think that tough cops, who went by the book and weren't impressed with the last name of Dyle, were on to him already.

One thing was for damn certain: He couldn't be caught with the money. Hiding it was priority *numero uno*. After the bag of cash was secured, he could deny any accusations thrown at him. His daddy would vouch for anything he said.

But just in case the unlikely happened, and he did fall under suspicion, and his old man turned contrary, Rusty also should establish an alibi. For the burglary. For Foster.

He hadn't actually killed the dipshit, but that could be a tricky technicality if he was ever accused of having done so. Best to establish a solid alibi for the entire night and avoid the whole mess.

By the time he reached the canoe, he had formulated a new plan. It involved Crystal, and it was brilliant for so many reasons, all of them self-serving. Eager to implement the plan, he covered the remaining distance to the canoe with a gush of renewed energy.

Getting into the damn thing with only one functioning arm was going to be a challenge, and he wasn't sure how to go about it. He was relieved to see that the paddle hadn't fallen out when Foster had tipped the canoe and pulled him into the water.

The paddle was lying in the hull.

All by its lonesome.

The money bag was gone.

Chapter 33

Ledge backed his pickup off Hawkins's property and out onto the road.

Dwayne hadn't moved. He still lay spread-eagled in the dirt under the glare of the floodlights.

As Arden got her last look at him, she said, "You won't really shoot him, will you?"

"I won't have to." He turned to her to make his point. "It's enough that he believes I will."

They'd gone only a short distance before Ledge placed a call to Don, who answered immediately. "Tell me you're okay."

"I'm okay."

"Hawkins?"

"Sniffling, but unhurt and grateful to be alive. But listen, the lowlife has dozens of dogs penned up out here. The conditions are criminal. I expect him to clear out tonight and, more than likely, abandon them. It would be dangerous to release them. Do you know anybody who's actively involved with the Humane Society or ASPCA?"

"Several people."

"Report it. Hawkins will probably be long gone by the time officials get out here, but those animals need rescuing."

"On it."

"Thanks, Don. Later."

"Hold it. Where are you? What are you doing?"

"Going home."

"Watch your back. Hawkins has brothers, don't forget."

"He won't breathe a word of this."

"You're sure?"

"Oh, yeah. I put a good scare into him."

He clicked off.

The drizzle that had begun to speckle the windshield as they left Hawkins's place had become a moderate rain. Lost in thought, Ledge hadn't even noticed until Arden suggested he turn on the wipers.

"What are you thinking about, Ledge?"

"Rusty and what I'm going to do about him."

"I've been wondering the same. His surveillance of me is creepy, but it's not illegal. If he was made to answer for it, he would harken back to my father, and I don't want that can of worms reopened."

"Unavoidable, Arden."

"I'm afraid you're right." She sighed. "Any questions raised about Brian Foster's death will lead straight to Joe Maxwell."

"You can count on Rusty to exploit that."

"So we do nothing?"

"I'm thinking of taking it directly to the attorney general's office." He sensed the look of surprise she gave him, but he kept his eyes forward. "Rusty has got to be put out of commission, and it won't happen on a local level."

"That's a big step, though. What about starting with another agency, outside the county?"

"Troopers, Texas Rangers? I've thought of that, of course. But they have their own cold cases. Foster's death wasn't officially deemed a murder. It wouldn't have priority. By the time somebody got around to looking into it, Rusty would have covered his tracks. I can't sit around and give him a chance to do that."

He looked over at her, adding, "He must be feeling pressure, because he amped things up tonight. That wasn't mischief, it was attempted murder. The time for fiddling around is passed."

"My moving back really stirred things up, didn't it?"

"I think you were the match that lit his fuse."

"I'm sorry."

"Hell, don't be. I'm not. For years, my fight with him has needed to come to a head. I'm glad it has."

He came to a crossroads, braked, and looked over at her. "I'm not taking you to your house. You shouldn't be out there alone. So back to Crystal's for the night?"

"Do you still have that bottle of whiskey?"

He was at a crossroads in the figurative sense, too. Being alone with her in a place with multiple horizontal surfaces, he didn't think he could resist the temptation to have her.

But his conscience wouldn't allow him to touch her again until he told her that he was a thief as well as a liar.

"One drink." He made a left turn onto the road that would lead to his house. A whiskey might make his confession go down a little smoother, but he seriously doubted it.

Dwayne lay there in the dirt, unmoving, until he could no longer hear Burnet's truck, then he got up and ran into his house. Dyle could give you pause, but he was a lot of swagger and not much substance, and everybody knew it. He got other people to do his dirty work.

Burnet, though. That guy you did not want to cross swords with. If Dwayne ever had thought otherwise, Burnet had shown him the light. He was a convert. To stay alive, he had to get gone. Like right now.

He scrounged around in the junk inside the house until he found the duffel bag he'd carried out of Huntsville packed with his meager belongings.

As he tramped through the rooms, he gathered up pieces of clothing that were strewn everywhere, and, regardless of which body part the article covered or its state of cleanliness, he crammed it into the duffel. He shoved his bare feet into a pair of boots, castoffs that the twins had given him when he made parole.

The waistband of his jeans was too loose to hold his pistol, so he poked it into one of the front pockets. He pried up a plank in the closet floor that gave him access to the crawl space where he kept mason jars full of cash. They were the last items to go into the duffel before he zipped it.

He was almost to the front door when his cell phone began playing the riff to "Bat Out of Hell."

He dropped the duffel at his feet and pulled the phone from his other jeans pocket. There was no caller ID, but he had a fair idea of who it was, and it weakened his knees. "Jesus."

If he didn't answer, Dyle would know something was up. So he swiped his sweating forehead with his forearm, then clicked on. Acting like he was put out over being disturbed, he said, "Who's this?"

"How'd it go, Dwayne?"

He forced his voice to sound laid-back. "Oh, hey. It went good."

"You found them all right?"

"Right where you said."

"Were they hurt?"

"Don't know. The dogs attacked, but during the fray, the girl managed to get back into his pickup. She leaned on the horn. Sounded like a damn freight train was coming. So I called the dogs off and got away from there before anybody could see me.

"Cain't say if either of them was hurt or not, but they got the bejesus scared out of them. Scaring them shitless would be good enough. That's what you said."

"Thanks for the reminder, Dwayne, but I remember what I said. You got away clean?"

"Yes, sir. No *problemo*."

"You haven't talked to anybody about this?"

"No, no. Not a word."

"Because this can't come back on me."

"I didn't tell nobody. Not even my brothers."

"Okay then, we're square, Dwayne. Nice work. Have a good night."

The DA hung up before Dwayne could wish him the same. He took a deep breath of relief and swiped his forehead again. His worry had been for nothing.

Phone in hand, he was tempted to call the twins and alert them to his abrupt departure, but he figured he ought to land somewhere first, where neither Dyle nor Burnet could find him, then notify his family of his sudden relocation and the reason for it. They would understand.

He picked up the duffel, killed the floodlights as he went through the front door, but didn't even bother to shut it. He would never be back. Whatever was left inside or out of the house, the next inhabitant was welcome to.

It had started to rain. He trotted across the yard but didn't forget to retrieve his shotgun. Burnet hadn't taken all his ammo. There was a box of shells in his pickup.

When he reached it, he looked wistfully toward the dog pens, where the animals were still acting agitated and bloodthirsty. Big money earners, those dogs. Trained to be killers. He hated like hell having to leave all that talent behind.

"Fuckin' Burnet," he muttered.

He opened the driver's door and tossed the duffel into the passenger seat, then climbed in. He was reaching for the ignition when a silky voice spoke from the back seat.

"If there's anything I can't stand, it's a cowardly liar."

They had to run through the rain to reach the porch. Ledge unlocked the front door and ushered Arden in, reaching around her to turn off the alarm.

"I've been promoted," she said. "Last time, I came through the back door."

"Last time, you weren't invited. You came in on your own."

"You didn't want me to follow you inside?"

"No, I didn't. But not because I didn't want you to be here."

She looked at him with frustration. "Another riddle. What does that even mean, Ledge?"

"Hard to explain."

"Try."

"A drink first." He turned toward the kitchen, but she stopped him by grabbing his sleeve.

"Let's wait on the drink and have this out right now. Is Crystal the hang-up, or not?"

"Not."

"You love her."

"Yes. But sex isn't part of it. Never has been."

"So is this some kind of unrequited love thing with you, like Lancelot and Guenevere? Crystal is off limits, so you make do?"

"As I recall, a kingdom fell because Lancelot and Guenevere screwed each other blind."

"You know what I mean. Are you pining after the unattainable love of your life?"

"Yes, I know what you mean. And, no, I'm not pining after Crystal."

She regarded him, her brow furrowed. "There's a story, isn't there? Something in her past?"

"It's Crystal's story to tell, not mine." No one would ever hear about Morg's abuse from him. Even with his uncle, he had hinted at it just enough to enlighten him so something could be done to stop it. She took a deep breath and exhaled it slowly. "You're very good at keeping secrets."

He damn sure was. He was especially good at keeping his own.

"You've been rained on." He motioned behind her. "The bathroom is down that hall, second door on your left. Grab a towel; grab two, one for me. I'll pour you a whiskey."

He turned and beat it into the kitchen before she could detain him again. He got the bottle of bourbon from the pantry, took two glasses from the cabinet, thought about cheating and taking a hit straight from the bottle for an added measure of courage, but resisted.

He poured an inch into each glass and added a couple of ice cubes. Leaving the bottle, he returned to the living room with a glass in each hand. Arden hadn't come back from the bathroom yet. He went over to the opening into the hall. "Did you get lost?"

The bathroom door was standing open, and the light was on. "Arden?"

Getting no answer, he walked down the hall. When he got even with his open bedroom door on his right, she said, "In here."

She was standing at the window, looking out at the rain. "You have a view of the lake from this room."

Seeing her there in his shadowy room, his heart began to thud with a mix of dread and anticipation. But he ignored the dread. Officially they hadn't had a drink yet. He'd made a vow to himself to tell her "after a drink."

He walked into the room and joined her at the window. "This view sold me on the house. When the mist rises over the water, it looks otherworldly."

"Hmm. A lot different from the landscapes of Iraq and Afghanistan."

"Like different planets."

"When you were over there, did you miss this?"

"Something terrible." He passed her one of the glasses, but neither of them drank.

"Did you buy this house as is?"

"No, it was a wreck. I fixed it up."

"By yourself?"

"Took me a couple of years."

"That involved a lot of labor."

"Yeah, but it gave me a lot of time to think, work through some postwar shit. It was my psychotherapy."

She leaned back against the wall. "Tell me something you've never told anyone else."

"About the war?"

She gave a slight nod.

"Arden—"

"Just one thing. Tragic or hilarious. Share a moment that stands out for whatever reason."

He turned his head and stared thoughtfully out the window.

"We, uh, went into an Afghani village that had been deci-mated. We were going from building to building, looking for survivors and injured, whether they were on our side or Taliban sympathizers.

"I went into this—you couldn't even call it a house. A dwelling. It was a mess. Carnage. Everybody was dead except for a young woman. Real young. Sixteen, seventeen. She was nursing a baby, an infant.

"I started toward her to help. But her face was uncovered. It flashed through my mind that I couldn't, shouldn't, let any of the surviving villagers know I'd seen her like that. It might have gone bad for her.

"She and I just looked at each other, frozen like, then I backed out without saying a word. It lasted maybe ten seconds at most, but of all the things I witnessed over there, it's seeing her with her baby that sticks with me. Not because it was the worst thing I saw, God knows, but because it was the most human."

"Do you know what happened to her?"

He turned back to Arden. "Before we pulled out, I saw her and the baby as they were being cared for by Afghani medics. Both were all right."

"Did she acknowledge you?"

"No. Hell no. She wouldn't have in any case, but, geared up, we all look alike. She wouldn't have known me from the others."

She gazed up at him for a moment, then whispered, "She knew you."

She set her glass on the windowsill and reached for his free hand. She turned it palm up and ran her fingertips over the calluses at the base of each finger.

"That morning when you came *uninvited* to *my* house, you ran your hand—this hand—along the bannister and across the mantel. Appreciatively. Like a caress. You probably weren't even aware of doing it. But it was so sensual, it took my breath. And ever since, I've fantasized you stroking me, just that way."

Lust as incendiary as lava coursed through him, overtaking everything. In its path, conscience, morality, and honor were consumed, and supplanted by unstoppable desire.

Glass of whiskey still in hand, he curved his arm around her neck, hooking it in the bend of his elbow, and growled, "Your fantasy is a helluva lot tamer than mine."

Chapter 34

He claimed her mouth.

Arden was vaguely aware of him letting go of her long enough to set his glass on the windowsill alongside hers, but he didn't break the kiss until he had to in order to pull her top up over her head. He reached behind her and unhooked her bra, slid the straps down her arms, then angled back and looked at her breasts with frank interest.

He flicked a glance up to her eyes. His reflected the raindrops that dotted the windowpane, but the light in them burned with a blue flame. The glimpse lasted for only a fraction of a second, but she read in it that he liked what he saw.

He slid his arms beneath hers, splayed his hands over her back, and drew her to him. He lowered his head. This time there was no cloth filtering the wet heat of his mouth. It tugged at her ardently but sweetly. She held his face between her hands and rubbed her palms against his scruff, loving its scratchiness in contrast to the sleek, fluid caresses of his tongue.

As she'd fantasized, he stroked her back from her shoulder blades, down past the dip of her waist to her bottom, then back up. She gave a little hiccup of delight at the feel of his calluses against her skin. His large hands made her feel slight, feminine, wanted. Desperately wanted.

He worked his hands into the waistband of her leggings. She squirmed in an effort to help him remove them, but he bracketed her hips and held her still. He nuzzled beneath her ear. "Are you okay to do this? It's been enough time?"

Emerging from a fog of desire long enough to translate his raspy whisper, she rubbed her lips against his, smiling. "Yes."

He mumbled something that might have been a prayer, then dived into another deep kiss that reignited the passion that had been put on pause. Together they got her out of her leggings and him out of his shirt. She unbuckled his belt; he undid the buttons of his fly. Then he lifted her and carried her over to the bed.

He set her on top of the covers. She lay back and scooted up toward the headboard. He pulled his belt from the loops and dropped it to the floor. He tugged off his boots. As the second one landed with a soft thud onto the floor, she hooked her thumbs into the sides of her underwear.

"No. Me."

He got onto the bed, standing on his knees between her legs. Every time she'd seen him, his physique had caused lazy currents of sexual awareness down low and deep inside her, but seeing Ledge shirtless caused a tidal wave.

He had a warrior's body. On the underside of his left biceps was a tattoo. His abs were a firm, solid six-pack. Just the right amount of hair fanned over his pecs. His yummy trail begged to be followed, because inside the jeans, now open and riding low, there was nothing except Ledge.

Planting his hands on either side of her, he lowered himself as though doing a pushup, dipped his head to her breasts, and again applied his mouth. He left her nipples beaded and flushed, the slopes of her breasts rising and falling with unsteady breaths.

He began working his way down the center of her body. He paved a damp trail of kisses in the hollow between her rib cage and around her navel, down to where his lips encountered stretchy lace.

But not for long. He finessed away that filmy barrier and sent it sailing over the side of the bed to the floor. His breath soughed over her as he whispered, "Blond everywhere," and planted the sweetest kiss there.

His thumbs scaled down the twin channels at the tops of her thighs to where they met. He uncovered that softest, most sensitive spot and stroked it with the tip of his tongue. Exhaling his name, she dug her fingers into his hair.

Then for the next while, he alternately tormented and gifted her. He was maddening in the way he teased, intuitive and deft in the way he responded to her slightest movement, pleading whimper, pleasured sigh.

Without resistance or hesitation, she followed the guidance of his hands to make readjustments in their position. He turned her over to kiss the small of her back, the dimples on either side, then lower where he took a love bite that he soothed with kisses.

As he turned her onto her back again, he paused to press wet kisses on the insides of her thighs. Then, sliding his hands under her, he scooped her up to his mouth and played over her with his lips and tongue until she came, ecstatically and without inhibition, while he stayed, lightly rubbing his lips against her, speaking in a low rumble words she didn't catch, but didn't need to in order to gather their meaning.

As she recovered, he retraced the kissing trail, this time making his way up her body, until he was levered above her, gazing down at her face when she opened her eyes. She mimed a thank you.

While she had been floating down, he had removed his jeans. He nudged her abdomen with his penis and growled, "We're not done yet."

"Oh, good."

He tried to smile, but it was strained, and his eyes were dark with intensity. "Take me. Guide me in."

She reached between their bodies and wrapped her hand around him. Her eyes widened in appreciation of his ampleness, which made him groan around another half smile. It turned into a grimace of pleasure as she stroked her way up, back down, up again.

Then she caressed the tip. It was full and taut, and already slick. The slow revolutions her thumb made to spread the moisture caused him to hiss and squeeze his eyes shut. "Damn, Arden. Now."

She did as asked and guided him. He pushed into her, but drew in a sharp breath over her tightness. "Jesus. Are you sure you—"

"Yes." She clutched his butt and tilted her hips up.

A profanity escaped on an expulsion of breath as he began to press and retreat in increments that stole her breath and accelerated his. When he was fully in, he paused as though to savor being imbedded in her, then the mating impulse overcame him.

He angled himself up so that every stroke was perfectly placed and brought her closer to another climax. When it washed over her, she hugged him tightly to her, chanting his name.

He buried his face in her neck, grinding against her and

maintaining that sublime friction until it became too much for him, too.

Arden was left breathless, boneless. In the aftermath, she surrendered to a delicious lethargy and settled deeper into the bed, loving the feel of him, his weight, his body heat, securing her there.

Eventually, he got up and went into the master bathroom. He washed himself and then brought a wet washcloth back to the bed. He bathed her stomach with it. "I should have gotten a condom."

"I wouldn't have welcomed the timeout."

"Me neither. That's why I didn't."

"I wasn't sure if that final growl was from ecstasy or frustration."

"Definitely ecstasy. Also a bit of frustration."

"I'm back on the pill."

"I didn't know that, and you're not supposed to risk another pregnancy for a couple more months. I read up on it."

She looked at him with surprise. "You read up on it?"

"Just in case I got lucky."

"You didn't get lucky. I practically begged you."

"Whatever. You did it good."

After cleaning her, he folded the cloth and set it on the nightstand, then placed his hand on the other side of her, bracing himself so that his arm bridged her torso.

He'd left the bathroom door ajar. There was enough light for him to see her in detail, but it wasn't so bright that it detracted. Rather, it was just enough to illuminate her skin and make it glow. He was even more entranced by the parts of her that were shadowed.

He used his free hand to explore. Her hair was a tangle on the pillow. The curls tried to ensnare his fingers. He pulled them free to trace the shape of her ear, to tug gently on the velvety lobe, outline her lips, and skate along the delicate ridge of her collarbone. He cupped her breast in his palm and lightly pinched her nipple. Its immediate response roused his resting cock.

Her hand found it and began a languorous caress.

And though her stroking caused a fever to spread through him, he continued his exploration of her in the same unrushed manner, venturing to even more seductive terrain that he didn't want to underappreciate because of haste.

She purred when he brushed his fingers through the hair between her thighs. They were relaxed and slightly separated. He noticed on the inside of one what he thought at first was a birthmark. Then he realized what it was.

"Oh, hell. I'm sorry. I didn't know that kiss was so rough."

"It wasn't rough, it was ardent," she said softly.

"Does it hurt?"

"Did or do you hear me complaining?"

In the deepest, darkest, basest part of his masculine soul, he was glad he had marked her, even if it was temporary. He rubbed the red spot with the pad of his thumb. "Arden?"

"Hmm?"

"I'm no poet, so I'll just say it."

"I'm listening."

"I like you naked and looking well fucked."

She laughed. "I like it, too."

She put one hand behind her head and lay there, studying him. "On some elemental plane, I think I knew it from the moment I saw you."

"Knew what?"

"That we, *this*, was bound to happen. When you turned

around and pushed the safety goggles up to your forehead, I...It was like a quickening. Here." She laid her hand on her stomach. "In spite of your being surly and trying to intimidate me."

"I wasn't—"

"You were."

He admitted it with a rueful nod.

"Why?" she asked.

"Because my 'quickening' took place a little lower than yours."

"Here?" Her fingers tightened around him.

He squeezed his eyes shut and breathed out. "Yeah, there. I'd seen you, yeah, but I wasn't ready for the stretchy t-shirt and blue jean skirt. I got instantly drive-a-nail hard. Scared the hell out of me."

"So your rudeness was a defense mechanism against the sudden attraction?"

"Not the attraction itself, but the unlikelihood that anything could come of it."

"If nothing was to come of it, you decided not even to bother being polite, but to act like a jerk instead."

"Something like that, I guess."

Pensively, she said, "That makes sense, because it didn't take me long to recognize in you something I've often been cursed with."

"What's that?"

"Loneliness," she whispered. "Your macho posturing made me mad. But I also came away thinking that underneath the tough-guy veneer, you were a lonely person, and that possibly your loneliness was self-imposed. I believe my intuition was right."

She removed her hand from his cock and placed it on his thigh, just above his knee, and rubbed it tenderly. And somehow that caress was ten times more intimate than the other. She was comforting and consoling him.

Which God knew he didn't deserve, and which she wouldn't be doing if she knew how badly he was deceiving her. He couldn't allow it. He lifted her hand from his leg and kissed the palm of it.

She touched his left biceps. "What's this?"

He turned his arm so she could see the tattoo better in the dim light. She traced the familiar figure eight with her fingertip. "Why the infinity symbol?"

Even after she withdrew her finger, he continued to stare at the marking that held such meaning for him. "Whatever we do stays with us forever. We can't shake it, can't escape it. It's eternal, there even after we die."

She frowned. "Wait. Aren't you the one who advised me to acknowledge the past, then to turn my back on it and move on?"

"I later said that was horseshit."

But she wasn't smiling at his quip. Her expression was serious and inquisitive. "What is it you can't shake or escape, Ledge?"

Tell her. Tell her now.

He looked toward the window where their bourbons remained untouched on the sill. The ice cubes had melted.

Selfish bastard that he was, he wanted to indulge in a few more minutes of this interlude before shattering her opinion of him.

The rain continued to come down, but not as hard as before. He said, "I have an idea."

"All right."

"You don't know what I have in mind."

"Do I have to move?"

"Not much."

He got off the bed and hiked on his jeans but didn't bother buttoning them up all the way. In short order, he had Arden wrapped in the coverlet and was carrying her through the house and out onto the front porch, kept dry because of the overhang.

He settled into the rocking chair with her in his lap, his arms encircling her.

She squirmed a bit to snuggle closer against him. "Did you make this chair?"

"Few years ago."

"Was our sitting in it together like this another of your fantasies?"

"The only one that didn't involve fucking."

She laughed and laid her head against his chest. Tweaking the hair on his pec, she said, "This is lovely. The sound of the rain on the roof. The scent of it."

"Um-huh."

After a short stretch of silence, she said, "Ledge? When you needed help tonight, you called Don, not your uncle. Why?" She must have felt him tense, because her fingers became still and she raised her head to look at him. "I know he reared you, but you don't talk much about him."

He leaned his head back against the slats of the chair and began to rock slowly. "My dad was Henry's brother, older by barely a year. My dad was in the navy, stationed in San Diego. He was about to be deployed to a ship that patrolled the Persian Gulf.

"I wasn't even two years old, so I don't remember any of this, but I'm told that he and my mom went out with a group of friends for one final fling before the men shipped out. They rode home with a guy who shouldn't have been driving. He plowed them into a bridge abutment. Killed everyone in the car."

She returned her head to his chest. "Unlike you, I at least have vivid memories of my mother. Although I'm not sure if that's better or worse."

"I can't say. My uncle Henry and aunt Brenda came out there to get me and brought me back to Penton, where they were trying to make a go of the bar. Life with them was the first one I remember. They treated me like their own. Maybe because they never had a kid.

"When I was six or seven, thereabouts, Aunt Brenda got really sick, really fast, and died of stomach cancer three months after her diagnosis. So then, my uncle Henry was stuck with me to raise by himself. But if he resented it, he never once, not ever, showed it.

"When I got my discharge from the army and came back, he was his same jolly self. Everybody's friend. But I noticed that he would be in the middle of one of his bad jokes and forget the punch line, and usually it was a joke he'd told a hundred times."

"Oh, no," Arden murmured. Again she lifted her head and looked into his face. "Alzheimer's?"

"I finally had to put him in a place in Marshall. For his own safety. It's a nice facility. He's well looked after. The staff—"

She leaned up and stopped his lips with hers. "You don't have to justify doing what is best for him and for you."

"You sound like George."

"Who's that?"

He told her. "He keeps an eye on Uncle Henry for me."

She returned her head to his chest, and they continued to rock for a time before she said, "It's because of him that you've stayed here in Penton, isn't it? Rather than pursue your ambitions."

"He's the main reason. When I was helpless, he didn't cut and run. I won't cut and run on him."

"That's very self-sacrificing. What one would expect of a hero."

"I'm no hero, Arden. Listen. There's something I've got to tell you." He tilted her head up to look at him. "Last night when you got mad at me for ending what we'd started on the stairs, you thought it was because of Crystal. Now you know better."

"You stopped because of Jacob."

He was so focused on what he was going to tell her and how he was going to phrase it that the name didn't immediately click. "What?"

"Because of my pregnancy, you assumed there was, or recently had been, a man in my life."

He shook his head. "No. Believe me, a phantom ex wouldn't have stopped me."

"Then why did you? Does it involve Rusty Dyle, Foster, my dad, all that?"

He drew a deep breath and let it out slowly. "Yes. It's about all that."

"Then can you please put it on hold?"

"No."

"Just until morning."

"We need to talk—"

"All right. But not tonight. Please? It happened twenty years ago, Ledge. A few more hours aren't going to matter. This chair is already crowded with the two of us. I don't want anyone else to join us."

She opened the coverlet, placed her leg over his, and straddled his lap. Sitting on his thighs, she undid the bottom button of his fly, reached in, and began to stroke him.

"God above, Arden."

He should stop her but knew he wouldn't. He wasn't going to ruin this. To stop now would be as unfair to her as it would be to him. That was a bullshit rationalization, and he damn well knew it, but...

He shut off his mind and just rode the waves of pleasure. Her small hand squeezed him, pumped him, mastered him. When she milked from him droplets of semen, his surrender was complete. And so was his damnation.

He lifted her onto him. She lowered herself with agonizing slowness until he was completely sheathed by her snug heat. He kissed her mouth with unforgiving and, as yet, unfulfilled hunger, then released it to rain kisses on her brow, her closed eyelids, her cheekbones.

When she tilted her head back and exposed her throat, he kissed his way down it and across her breasts, before eventually making his way back up. He placed his parted lips against hers, their breaths soughing in unison.

"I've lied to you, Arden. So many times. Continually."

"You're forgiven," she sighed, as he began rocking the chair.

He kept the pace languid, but with each gliding arc, he pushed in a little higher, reaching her where he hadn't before, and when she said his name on a near sob, he gathered her against him until there was no space between them. Nothing existed except her body and his, his hard and insistent, hers soft and inviting, his inside hers, a perfect coupling.

The chair rocked slowly; they spun out of control.

"But tonight I told you the biggest lie of all," he murmured against her lips.

As she began to come, she gasped, "Confess."

"This fantasy did involve fucking."

After a lengthy shower, where hands and mouths were never idle, they returned to the bed and spooned. He put his arm across her and drew her close.

Rubbing his face in her hair, he said, "When I called you Baby, over and over, I know better. That was my cock talking." He raised his hand to her lips and pressed them open with his thumb. "Who could think straight with you doing that?"

"Did you call me Baby?" She caught the pad of his tongue between her teeth and stroked it with her tongue.

"You don't remember?"

"I was preoccupied."

"Then I apologized for nothing?"

"No," she said, her shoulders shaking with silent laughter. She clasped his hand and tucked it with hers between her breasts. "I appreciate your chivalry. You are a hero."

His euphoria evaporated. Despair replaced it, pressing in on him from all sides. Against the back of her neck, he whispered fervently, "I'm no hero, Arden." But she hadn't heard him. Her breathing had become even and peaceful, her body soft and settled against his.

Over her shoulder he stared through the darkness at the two full glasses silhouetted against the rain-streaked window.

Chapter 35

Arden woke up alone.

She and Ledge had turned to each other once more during the night for a brief but hotly passionate bout; during it, they hadn't exchanged a single word. Language would have been redundant.

Feeling a bit let down because she had wanted to wake up beside him, she got up, showered in the master bathroom, which, in accordance with the man who used it, was large in scale. The materials were natural, masculine, and appealing.

After dressing, she followed the aroma of coffee into the kitchen, where Ledge was seated at the table, steaming mug at hand, the pages of the investigation reports spread out in front of him. His head was down, fingers pushed up into his hair, his forehead resting in his palm.

"What are you studying so intently?"

He raised his head and looked at her. He didn't say anything, but his eyes drew her toward him. When she was still steps away, he reached for her, pulled her between his legs, wrapped his arms around her, and pressed his face into her middle just below her breasts. Her fingers replaced his in the thick tangle of his hair. She bent her head over his. For a time they just held each other.

When he released her from the hug, he tipped his head back to look into her face. "Good morning."

"Good morning."

"How was your night?"

She shrugged, faked a yawned. "It was okay, I guess."

He smiled, but there was a restraint in his demeanor that she'd sensed the moment she'd entered the room.

"Coffee's still fresh," he said.

"I believe I'll have some. You want more?"

"More of you, yes."

Her tummy levitated like an untethered balloon.

But his sexy, gravelly tone, his suggestive squint, were short-lived. The reserve, which she couldn't account for, reappeared. "I don't know how you take your coffee," he said. "I've got real sugar and milk."

"That will do."

"Want breakfast?"

"Not just yet."

She went over to the counter and filled the coffee mug he had set out for her, then carried it to the fridge and poured a dollop of milk straight from the carton.

As she turned around, she saw through the wide window a car pulling in behind Ledge's pickup. Instantly she recognized the whir of the motor. She set her full mug of coffee on the counter. "Ledge?"

"Hmm?"

"Rusty's here."

He raised his head from the material he'd gone back to reading. "What?"

She nodded toward the window as she walked toward it. Ledge left the table and joined her there. At some point during the night, the rain had stopped, but it had left puddles in the yard. Rusty navigated around them as he made his way to the back door.

She and Ledge looked at each other with wariness, then he went to the door and had it pulled open before Rusty could knock. Arden moved up beside Ledge. It surprised her that he didn't issue Rusty a challenge, but she supposed his hostile and territorial bearing spoke for him.

Rusty gave them a smirking grin. "Morning, you two."

"What are you doing here? What do you want?"

"I want to be invited in, Ledge. Coffee smells good." Another smirk. "Unless I'm interrupting."

Ledge didn't extend any kind of invitation, just stood there, as impassable as a concrete wall.

"Ah, well," Rusty sighed. "Can't say as I'm surprised by your lack of manners. No one expects you to have any. Breeding tells, you know."

"Go. Away." Ledge made the two words sound all the more menacing by how softly he spoke them. "Don't ever come to my house again."

Rusty seemed unfazed. "What mischief are you up to out here, Ledge, that you would rather the *district attorney* not know about? I mean, besides screwing her." He hitched his chin toward Arden.

She took a lunging step toward him, but Ledge put out a hand to hold her back. "Don't buy into it."

"You're despicable," she said to Rusty.

"Me? *I'm* despicable? I'm not the guy cheating on his girlfriend. Speaking of whom, Crystal told me that both of y'all have been asking her all sorts of interesting questions about times gone by."

Arden felt Ledge tense. "When did you talk to Crystal?"

"Did I fail to mention that? If I'd been invited in for coffee, I would've—"

"When did you talk to Crystal?"

"I dropped by on her this morning before coming here." He leaned toward Ledge and said in an undertone, "One guy to another, just so you're braced for it, she suspects..." He wagged his index finger between Ledge and Arden.

"You're lying," Ledge said. "If you did see Crystal this morning, she didn't divulge anything to you."

"No? Then maybe it wasn't her who told me." He scratched his temple. "But I could have sworn—"

Ledge reached for the door and went to slam it in Rusty's face, but Rusty stuck out his foot and caught it with the steel toe of his cowboy boot. He pushed the door back open with such impetus, it banged against the kitchen wall.

Ledge bristled. The two faced off across the threshold, silently daring each other to make the first move. Arden held her breath.

Rusty was the first to capitulate. He relaxed his stance. "The point is," he said, stressing the words, "it's been brought to my attention that you two have grown real curious about the Welch's store burglary and all the bizarre goings-on that took place afterward.

"Now, as the top law officer of the county, I just wondered how come y'all are showing such avid interest. Especially you," he said, looking directly at Ledge. "Makes me question the smarts you're reputed to have. Trips to the courthouse, getting copies of investigation reports, all that. It's peculiar behavior, to say the least. Especially when you obviously have other, more pleasurable pastimes you could be engaging in."

Neither of them said anything.

"Nothing? No explanation for the amateur sleuthing?" His

eyes sawed back and forth between them, landing on Arden. "Does your big sis know about this recent hobby of yours?"

"My father's disappearance was a significant event in my life. I never got closure. Lisa understands that."

"Does she? Well, not me. I don't see that any good can come from dredging up crimes with mothballs on them. That is unless the culprit's kin turned up with the money he took." He gave Arden a cold and calculating look. "In fact, the amateur detective work could backfire and prove damaging to a person's health."

He paused to let all that sink in, before adding in a lower voice, "If I were you two, I'd leave well enough alone."

"Is that what you came to say?" Ledge asked.

Rusty nodded. "Pretty much."

"Well, now that you've said it, get off my property."

Rusty mimed doffing a hat, turned and took several steps, then snapped his fingers and came back around. "Almost forgot. I heard y'all nearly got mauled by some vicious dogs last night. Right outside Crystal's house. Close call. You were damned lucky to have escaped them."

Again, neither of them rose to the bait.

"In light of that attack," Rusty continued, "how'd you greet the news this morning?"

A sense of foreboding spiraled through Arden, but it was Ledge who said, "What news?"

"About Dwayne Hawkins. You remember. That piece of white trash I sent up for dogfighting? He was found dead this morning, slumped over the steering wheel of his pickup. Had a packed bag beside him on the seat. Looked like he was trying to make a quick getaway from that dump he lived in."

Arden leaned closer to Ledge. He shifted his shoulder to overlap hers.

Rusty continued. "Last night somebody tipped a group of

animal rights advocates to Dwayne's maltreatment of his dogs. They descended en masse on his property at dawn. Got the shock of their lives. Dwayne had met with a bad end, like his sort usually do."

Arden asked hoarsely, "How did he die?"

"Choke collar."

She took a swift breath.

Rusty flashed a grin. "I know. Terrible, right? It was one of those with spikes, the kind trainers use to turn their dogs into mean sons of bitches." He laughed at his play on words.

"The last call on Dwayne's cell phone only lasted a couple of minutes. They'll try to trace the number to the caller, but I'm betting they'll never discover who it was. What I think? Whoever talked to him scared Dwayne into hightailing it, and then ambushed him when he tried to leave.

"The lead detective told me it looked like his killer was waiting for Dwayne in the back seat of his pickup, wrapped that collar around his neck, and squeezed it tight till he died. Said there were deep puncture wounds all around his scrawny neck." He drew a line around his own.

Arden felt ill. It was all she could do to keep her expression impassive and not reveal her revulsion, not only for the scene he described, but for him. She sensed similar disgust and sheer rage pulsing through Ledge.

"Killed with a tool of his illegal trade. I call that poetic justice." Rusty gave them a wink and a foxy smile. Again, he acted as though he were about to leave, then paused and held up his index finger.

"Uh, one more thing. It might not go well for you two Nancy Drews if the detectives on Dwayne's homicide put two and two together. Y'all were attacked by fighting dogs on the same night that a participant in that sport got choked to death. See where I'm going with this?"

"If you were of a mind to suggest to the authorities that an unknown third party had put Dwayne up to siccing his dogs on you, I would feel compelled to inform the detectives that shortly after that potentially fatal attack, you were seen in Dwayne's neck of the woods."

"Seen by who?" Ledge asked.

Rusty's eyes glinted. "By someone who wishes to remain anonymous."

He let that settle before continuing. "But before I gave that info over to the sheriff's office, I'd feel obligated to share it with Dwayne's twin brothers. The pair don't have a whole brain between them, but they're meaner than sin, and, from what I understand from the poor deputy who had to break the news to them this morning, they're brimming with wrath over their baby brother's cruel demise."

He looked Ledge up and down. "I don't know their... inclinations. They may be too persnickety to take turns with you." He shifted his gaze to Arden. "But I shudder to think about the good time they'd have sharing her."

Ledge grabbed him by his necktie and shoved him backward a full arm's length before letting go with an added thrust. Rusty managed to stay on his feet but stumbled in order to regain his balance.

When he had straightened up, he looked at them and laughed. "See y'all." Then he turned and ambled toward his car.

Chapter 36

Ledge shut the door but kept his hand flat against it, watching through the window until Rusty had driven out of sight, then turned quickly to Arden. "Go get your purse. It's on the—"

"I know where it is. What are we going to do?"

"*You* are going to leave. We'll pick up your car at Crystal's. I'll follow you home, you can grab some things, secure your house, I'll escort you as far as the interstate."

"I'm not leaving now." She flung her hand toward the reports scattered across the table. "Not with this mess still—"

"Rusty killed that guy, Arden." He pushed his fingers through his hair. "Christ. I wanted to scare Hawkins because of what he did to us, but also to protect him from just this. I wanted to scare him into getting away from here, and out of Rusty's reach. He didn't run fast enough."

"Don't assume the blame for what Rusty did."

He made an impatient gesture indicating to her that she was wasting her breath.

"We've got to report Rusty to someone, Ledge."

"I am. I will. But, first, I'm getting you on your way." She looked prepared to argue, but when he chinned toward the bedroom and told her to hurry, she left him.

He called Crystal. She hadn't even gotten out a hello before he asked if Rusty had stopped by her place that morning.

"Where did you hear that?"

"From him. He said you had told him—"

"I haven't told him a damn thing. I haven't even seen him."

"I figured he was lying."

"When did you talk to him?"

"Right before I called you."

"What is going on? Are you all right? What happened after you and Arden left here last night?"

"I'll fill you in later."

"Marty and I were worried. I wish you had called and—"

"Crystal, stop. Listen." He paused, took a breath. "Our interest in the night Foster died has made Rusty nervous. He may start hassling you again about that alibi business, remind you that you're committed to covering for him."

"He'll get nowhere with me. I can handle him."

"No, you can't, Crystal. You *can't*."

"Okay, calm down. Warning taken. I'll be careful."

"Not good enough. This would be an excellent time for you and Marty to take a long weekend together."

"First of all, it's not the weekend. Secondly, we can't just—"

"That dog attack last night? Rusty's doing." That silenced her. "Then he killed the guy who did it for him."

He heard her exhale. "Good God, Ledge."

"Yeah. So please don't argue with me. Can Marty take off work?"

"I suppose. If she told them she was sick or something."

"Impress on her that I don't lose my shit easily, and I don't cry wolf. Cancel your client appointments. Make up some excuse for having to close the shop for a few days. Then get out of town."

"For how long?"

"Till I feel it's safe for you to come back."

"Rusty would have to be dead."

When he didn't respond to that, she said, "Ledge, that was supposed to be a joke."

"I'll call you when things have settled."

"What about Arden?"

"Right now she's with me, but I'm sending her packing, too." Sensing her hesitancy, he said, "Crystal, you know how Rusty works. He won't come after me. He'll hurt the people I care about."

Still sounding reluctant, she said, "I'll text you where we are."

He told her to be careful; she told him the same. They said goodbye. He gave himself a few seconds, then called Don, who launched into him the instant he answered.

"Ledge, what the devil? Dwayne Hawkins—"

"I've heard. Swear to God I didn't kill him. Rusty did. He drove all the way out here to my place to deliver the news in person." Talking in a shorthand he knew Don would understand, he summarized Rusty's visit.

Don breathed in, breathed out. "Is Arden okay?"

"How'd you know—"

"According to several of Crystal's neighbors who witnessed the whole thing, 'the Maxwell girl' saved the day by blasting the horn. You two were seen leaving together, and her car spent the night at the curb in front of Crystal's house. What else do you want to know?"

"Goddamn it," Ledge muttered.

"It's been circulating so fast, the cell tower's smoking. Folks don't know what to make of it, considering you and Crystal and all."

"I've got more important things than gossip to worry about. Arden is all right, but she was here when Rusty practically boasted of murdering Hawkins, which makes her vulnerable. I'm going to see her safely out of town."

"Ledge," Don said slowly, "sooner or later, even the dumbest detective will piece together that on the night you were attacked by a pack of fighting dogs, their trainer got choked to death."

Ledge huffed a dry laugh. "Rusty got that across to me, too. As soon as I get Arden on her way, I'll go see Uncle Henry. Just in case I'm unavailable for an unspecified period of time."

"You really think Rusty will lay this on you?"

"Likely. I did go out there to Hawkins's place."

"Against my advice."

"Don't piss me off by saying you told me so."

Don sighed. "We'll take it up later. What do you need me to do?"

"Top priority, take care of yourself. Carry on like it's any other day, but round up some longtime customers you trust. Good ol' boys."

"The ones who pack."

Ledge appreciated that Don didn't need it spelled out for him. "Nobody who has any ties or loyalty to Rusty or the late sheriff."

"There are a few retired Texas Rangers around, any of which would've loved to have had a crack at the both of them."

"Good. But no rough stuff unless it becomes necessary. Just have them hang around for a couple of days and nights, and keep their eyes and ears open. Have them covering your back and discreetly patrolling the property."

"I understand."

"Sleep with that shotgun."

"Even with the scattergun, I can't hit the broad side of a barn, you know."

"*I* know, but whoever you point it at won't."

"What's the plan after you've seen Henry?"

"To put Rusty out of commission."

"How do you plan—"

"Gotta go." He hung up before Don could ask how he intended to do that.

But Arden did. From behind him, she asked, "Are you going to do that by fair means or foul?"

"I don't know yet. I'll have to see how it plays out. You ready?"

She gave him a mutinous look as she shouldered past him and went out through the back door. He set the security alarm but, as he left, he wondered if his house and workshop would still be standing when he returned. Rusty might make good on his threat, except burn his house down rather than the bar.

By the time he got to his pickup, Arden had already climbed in. She sat as rigid as an I-beam, staring through the windshield, which was being speckled with fresh rain.

Ledge left her to stew and placed another call.

George answered with a cheerful, "Hey, Cap'n. How's—"

"Cutting to the chase this morning, George."

He reacted to Ledge's tone immediately. "What's up?"

"The dude?"

"With the boots?"

"I've got a situation with him."

"Tell me where. Give me an hour."

That was a friend. Ledge felt a tug on the inside. "Thanks, but I need you where you are. This asshole and I have a long history. He could soon drop a lot of shit on me, but he'll do it in a roundabout way. His practice is to prey on the defenseless."

"Like your uncle Henry."

"I'm coming to see him as soon as I can. I'll give you the background details then, but, George, I need you to keep a hawk's eye on him. When duty calls, please assign a staffer you know and trust to sit with him. Nobody who isn't authorized goes into his room."

"On it. What else?"

"Let me know if the dude, or anybody who doesn't belong there, shows up. I need to know immediately."

"Copy that."

"Thanks, man. Later." He clicked off.

"George is also former military?" Arden said.

He nodded. "Hard core."

"I could tell by the way you talk to each other."

"How's that?"

"Like combat soldiers." She motioned to his cell phone, which he'd placed in the cup holder. "I believe you've covered everyone."

"I haven't *covered* anybody. But at least I've put them on guard until I settle this with Rusty."

"What *this*, Ledge?"

Feeling the weightiness of her stare, he said, "I'll tell you when we get to your house."

The rain held off, but bluish, potbellied clouds made for a low ceiling and mistimed twilight. Arden unlocked her back door and went inside, but she didn't switch on the overhead kitchen light, leaving the room appropriately gloomy.

She set her purse on the table and turned to face him.

"Do you want to sit?" he asked.

"No."

"Well, I do." He pulled out a chair, rotated it, and straddled it backward. He clasped his hands on the back of it and addressed them rather than looking at her. "I was in on the Welch's burglary."

A gust of breath escaped her, but she didn't speak.

"Along with Rusty. It was his idea. He recruited the rest of us to help him execute his plan. That's why our digging into the crimes has him off the rails."

He looked up at her then, and she appeared to be on the verge of boiling over. Her chest was swelling and collapsing like a bellows. She had shut her eyes tightly. When she reopened them, they were shiny with tears of the furious kind.

"You...you—"

"I'm no hero. I told you that."

"It's the only truth you've told me."

She turned away from him and went over to the sink. Bracing her hands on the rim, she bent at the waist. He feared she was about to throw up, but her silence attested to a forced containment of emotions, and that was almost worse than retching or ranting would have been.

A drum roll of thunder shook the house. Fat raindrops began to slap against the window above the sink. His wrist-watch ticked loudly, reminding him that he should be well on his way to Marshall. But he couldn't just drop this on her and bail. She deserved time to absorb his revelation and grasp the pervasive dishonesty it represented. She deserved an opportunity to vent her rage.

Whatever form it took would be lighter than he deserved.

Eventually she turned on the faucet and scooped several handfuls of cold water into her mouth. Her movements angry and abrupt, she ripped a paper towel off the roll, blotted her mouth, and dried her hands. She left the towel balled up on the counter, came over and dragged a chair from beneath the table, and sat down across from him.

"You ingratiated yourself into my life."

"Yes."

"Why?"

"To protect you from Rusty."

She spurted a harsh laugh. "When you were the one I needed protection from."

He shook his head. "Rusty's been a monkey on my back for decades, and vice versa. We could have rocked along forever with our issues unresolved, and probably would have. That changed when you came back."

"So this is on me?"

"Not intentionally, but circumstantially. You showed up out of the clear blue, and it reminded Rusty that he still had a bone to pick with your dad. Joe had outsmarted him. Big time. It was like you were thumbing your nose—"

"I didn't even know—"

"Doesn't matter. That's how Rusty saw it. He doesn't let things like that slide."

She digested that but continued to simmer. "What about you? What did you think when I moved back?"

"When I first heard, I wondered what had prompted it, but I intended to keep my distance."

"You've admitted that you followed me into the super-market."

"Yeah. That was bizarre. Fate dumped on both of us that day. But you didn't know me, so I thought no harm had been done. Two months pass, and then I get a freaking voice mail from you. I couldn't believe it, but I wasn't going to call you back.

"The next day, you're in my workshop. God, you looked great. Knocked me for a loop, but... Like I told you last night,

I couldn't let it lead anywhere. I figured that if I acted like enough of an asshole, you for sure wouldn't want anything to do with me."

He paused, sighed. "Later that evening, Rusty came into the bar. He'd sought me out there." He gave her a bullet-point briefing of that conversation. "He'd been keeping tabs on you. I was afraid you would be a soft target for his retribution on Joe. Turns out, I was right."

She turned her head aside, rolled her lips inward as she thought on everything he'd told her. When she came back to him, she said, "You were here the following morning. When I told you about the car driving past, why didn't you warn me of Rusty? Why didn't you come clean then? Afraid I would turn you in as a thief?"

"Afraid you would turn me out," he said with a heat that matched hers. "And then you would have been completely defenseless."

"Instead, you deceived me into thinking…" She covered her face with both hands and spoke from behind them. "All sorts of things."

"Not everything was a lie."

She lowered her hands. "No? Which part was honest?"

"You know which part."

"Don't you dare mention last night." Her voice cracked on the last two words. She shot from her chair and headed for the room she slept in. "You know your way out."

He went after her, putting his shoulder to the door she tried to slam in his face.

"Get out of here! I've had it with you and your infernal cold war with Rusty Dyle. In my opinion, you two were made for each other."

"Will you please calm down for a minute and listen to me?"

"What for?"

"Because Rusty isn't done yet. Ask yourself why he all but admitted to killing Hawkins and threatened to implicate us? Hear me out. Please."

She hesitated, then backed up to the bed and sat down.

Ledge looked down at the floor and ran his hand around the back of his neck. "Several weeks before Easter of 2000, on a Saturday morning, Rusty cornered me in a diner. He laid out his plan to rob the store. I couldn't believe what I was hearing, and basically told him he was crazy and to fuck off. I was on the verge of leaving when he threatened me with reprisal if I didn't go along.

"He was sly, subtle, but his message hit me like a hammer. For all my badass attitude, I was convinced that if I told him no soap, he would punish me for it, and I would have to live with knowing that I had caused destruction or death to something or someone I cared about.

"So, weighed against my uncle's bar, his *life*, I chose instead to commit a felony crime. That doesn't excuse what I did, but that's the reason I did it. I wish I could undo it. I can't."

She looked in the area of his upper arm where she knew the tattoo to be. "Infinity."

"That's right. It's forever."

She assimilated all that, then sharpened her gaze on him. "How did my dad get away with the money?"

"I swear on my uncle's head, I don't know." He told her about Rusty's appointing himself keeper of the cash for six months, when they would divide it. "Minutes after we split up, I was arrested.

"I don't know what happened beyond that point, but Rusty somehow lost possession of that bag, because he's still bitter over being cheated out of the money. Bitter enough to get vengeance."

He walked over to her where she still sat on the bed. "Hate me. You're entitled. But don't underestimate him. You know firsthand what he's capable of. I think he has more in store. That's why I fear for your safety."

Startling them both, another voice intruded on their conversation. "How touching."

Chapter 37

Lisa stood in the open doorway, taking in the tableau with a frown of disapproval. "I knocked, but I guess you didn't hear me above the storm."

Ledge couldn't tell if she meant that literally or metaphorically. He looked to Arden to gauge her reaction. She stood but stayed where she was and didn't greet her sister with either a welcoming hug or even a smile.

Stilted, she said, "I wasn't expecting you."

Lisa slid a glance in his direction. "Evidently."

Arden motioned toward him. "This is—"

"Oh, I know who he is. His fear for your safety obviously extends to sharing your bedroom."

"Who I share my bedroom with is none of your business," Arden said. "Although I understand that you made it your business yesterday."

Ledge didn't know what she was talking about, but it was apparent that Lisa did. Defensively, she raised her chin a fraction.

"Jacob called me last evening," Arden said. "He left a voice mail, but I didn't listen to it until this morning. He told me that you had showed up at his house yesterday, unannounced, and that you created quite a scene when he refused to disclose personal information about me and my relationship with him." Arden paused to give Lisa time to comment. She didn't.

"He said you became so contentious, his wife threatened to call the police. Jacob persuaded her not to go to those lengths, but the upshot was that he had to order you, in no uncertain terms, off his property."

"All right, yes," Lisa said. "I tracked him down."

"After intercepting and reading a letter he sent to me. Who gave you the right to do that?"

Ledge reasoned that Arden must have listened to the voice mail before joining him in his kitchen that morning. Maybe if Rusty hadn't arrived she would have told him about it. But it was clear to him now why she wasn't overjoyed to see Lisa, who, even though called out, had retained her cool.

She said, "We should be having this conversation without an audience."

"Don't mind Ledge," Arden said. "He knows all about Jacob."

As Arden explained the nature of her relationship with Dr. Jacob Greene, Ledge witnessed the slow disintegration of Lisa's hauteur, and he enjoyed watching it.

Arden didn't let her off easily, either. "By accusing Jacob of adultery, you degraded me, him, his wife, but most of all yourself. You made a complete fool of yourself."

"No, *you* made a fool of me," Lisa fired back. "Why didn't you tell me you were having that procedure?"

"Because I didn't need your consent, and I didn't want to hear all the reasons as to why it was a bad idea."

"You misled me into thinking that you were carrying on with a married man."

"No," Arden said, dragging out the word. "You drew that conclusion without any help from me, and I wasn't going to defend myself against an assumption that was baseless and false."

She paused and swallowed hard. "My daughter, who I desperately wanted, was dead. Vindicating myself for how she was conceived—no matter how it had come about—was not a priority. I didn't care whether you approved."

As though to underscore that declaration, lightning lit up the room. The flash was followed by a crack of thunder that rattled the windows, calling Lisa's attention to the blistered paint on the sills. She took in the room as a whole, her critical gaze eventually drifting across him.

She said to Arden, "I thought you had told him his services weren't wanted after all."

He'd been leaning against the bureau with intentional indolence. Now, he pushed himself off it. "You don't need Arden to act as a go-between. You can speak to me directly."

Finally deigning to look at him straight-on, Lisa sized him up. "You've changed since I last saw you."

"Not you. You're exactly the same."

He hadn't meant it as a compliment, and she got that. She arched an eyebrow. "Your shoulders are broader, but the chip on them is still firmly fixed."

"That's not all I'm shouldering these days."

"Oh? What else is burdening you? Isn't that dive of your uncle's doing well?"

Arden stepped in. "That was uncalled for, Lisa. What's the matter with you?"

Ledge put up a staying hand. "It's okay. She can't think

any worse of me than she already does. Not that I give a shit what she thinks. In fact, feel free to share with her what I told you just before she got here, see how she reacts to that."

Arden looked at him with apprehension and gave a small shake of her head. "We'll talk more about that later. You need to go check on your uncle."

Lisa said, "Actually, I would like to hear what he has to say. Why is he fearing for your safety? Does he fear this roof will cave in on you, that a high wind will—"

"Arden is in danger from Rusty."

His terse statement shut her up. A tad more of her arrogance slipped. "Rusty Dyle?"

"That's the one."

She turned to Arden. "When we talked about him yesterday morning, you seemed not to know him."

"I didn't until half an hour before I called you."

Ledge looked between the two sisters. "You two talked about Rusty?"

Arden said, "Mostly in the context of your rivalry with him over Crystal."

"Crystal," Lisa said as though with enlightenment. "That was her name."

"Still is," Ledge said.

"Is the rivalry ongoing?"

"More cutthroat than ever."

"Aren't you two a little old to be feuding over a girl?"

"Crystal is a woman, but she's no longer at the heart of our feud. Rusty's main beef now is that he lost out on the money we emptied out of Welch's safe."

Lisa's features went slack.

"You heard right," Ledge went on. "I've confessed to Arden that I was in on the burglary."

Arden shot him a reproving look. "You didn't have to admit it to her."

Speaking softly and directly to her, he said, "Yeah, I did. For twenty years it's been eating at me. I'm glad it's out." They shared a look redolent with unspoken meaning, then he turned back to Lisa.

"Rusty coerced me into doing it. I should have bucked him. I didn't. We're long past being prosecuted for it, but that doesn't make me any less guilty."

"Why would you confess now?" Lisa asked.

"It's good for the soul. Besides, I plan to put Rusty out of business before he draws more blood."

"Draws more blood?" Lisa looked over at Arden. "What is he talking about?"

"It's Rusty who's been keeping a nightly vigil on me. I discovered that yesterday." She told Lisa about her disturbing encounter with him at the courthouse. "We, Ledge and I, believe that he, not Dad, killed Brian Foster."

Lisa looked even more shocked. "What?"

"Late that night, Rusty set up an elaborate alibi scenario with Crystal," Arden said. "Possibly for only the burglary, but it's more likely he needed an alibi for something else, some violent encounter."

"Like a fight to the death with Foster," Ledge said. "He also has a vendetta against your father. But he isn't here, so Rusty's going after Arden."

"How so?" Lisa asked, turning to Arden.

She described the dog attack and their showdown with Hawkins. She was blunt, sparing her snooty sister none of the gorier details.

When she finished, Ledge said, "There's a footnote. Hawkins was found dead this morning. You can guess who silenced him, and this fresh taste of blood has only emboldened him. Rusty all but confessed to us."

Looking queasy, Lisa backed up to the wall. "He's the district attorney, for godsake."

"Which only gives him license to do what he wants with impunity," Ledge said.

"Your fear for Arden's safety is justified, then."

"Thanks all the same, but I don't need your okay. Not for anything, but especially not anything concerning Arden and me."

Lisa gave him a dirty look, then turned back to Arden. "I told you repeatedly that moving back here was a terrible idea. You didn't listen."

"Because I had no idea of what I was walking into," she exclaimed. "I didn't know I had a built-in enemy. Did you?"

Lisa held her ground for a time; then her shoulders slumped, and she gave a small nod.

Arden regarded her with incredulity. "You knew about Rusty, his part in the burglary? All that?"

"Yes. All that."

"For how long?"

"From the night it took place."

Arden gaped at her. "You allowed me to stumble into this blind, Lisa. All those times you tried to dissuade me, why didn't you simply lay it all out?"

"I couldn't 'simply.' I couldn't warn you about Rusty without...without telling you that I saw Dad that night. With the stolen money."

Lisa abruptly left the bedroom and went into the kitchen, where she helped herself to a soda from the refrigerator.

Ledge and Arden followed her but declined anything to drink.

Ledge posted himself as lookout where he could see out onto the backyard as well as have a clear shot of the front door through the empty dining and living rooms.

The position also gave him a head-on view of Arden. He wanted to read her reactions to what Lisa had to tell her. She needed to hear it. At long last. But he dreaded the next few minutes for her. Apparently, she shared his apprehension. Seated across the table from each other, Arden was regarding Lisa as though she were a stranger she had never seen before.

Lisa fiddled with the soda can, idly turning it on the tabletop. Ledge wondered if she was buying time in order to fabricate a plausible partial truth that Arden would swallow. Or was she choosing words that would soften the blow of the hard facts?

She said, "I thought that by now Rusty would have given up the idea of regaining his booty."

"He hasn't," Ledge said before Arden could speak. "She's been in Rusty's crosshairs from the day she moved back. If you know anything about how Joe wound up with the cash and made his escape, now would be the time to tell us."

"*Us?* Whatever I tell my sister will be in private."

"Nuh-uh," he said. "I want to hear."

"Anything relating to our father is between Arden and me."

Arden said, "Lisa, Rusty has threatened to blame Hawkins's murder on Ledge. He deserves to know what you know about that night. He stays."

She relented. "All right. Where to start?" She took a sip of her soda, then began. "Directly after dinner, Dad left, saying he was going to the cemetery."

"I remember."

"You and I watched a movie. At bedtime, I tucked you in, secured the house, and went to my room. I worked on an assignment for one of my classes and didn't go to bed until after Dad came back. That's not when I saw him, though. He went straight to his room, I assumed to bed."

"What time was that?" Ledge asked.

"I don't remember," she snapped. "At the time, I didn't know it would be important to note."

He stared back at her but made no further comment.

She continued. "Hours later, I woke up to a noise downstairs. I got up and checked your room. You were sound asleep. I came downstairs, and when I got here to the kitchen, I was stunned to see Dad. I thought he was still upstairs.

"But he hadn't only left his room, he'd left the house without my being aware of it. His shoes were muddy, his pants legs were wet. Stickers and twigs were stuck in the fabric. He was also flushed and sweaty. He wouldn't have returned from the cemetery that way.

"Then I noticed a canvas bag, sitting on the floor, just inside the door. 'Where have you been?' I asked. 'What's that?' And he said, 'That's the cash stolen from Welch's store tonight.' Just like that.

"I thought for certain that I was having a nightmare. But, no, the basket of Easter eggs we had dyed was on the table. The faucet was dripping as it always was. I could smell the whiskey on Dad's breath. All my senses were sharpened, exaggerated. As much as I wanted to deny that it was actually happening, it was all too real to be a dream."

Ledge observed Arden. She sat rapt, barely breathing, taking in every word.

She said, "Ledge said that when the group split up, Rusty had the money. How did Dad get it from him?"

Lisa divided a look between them. "I can only tell you what

Dad told me, which was that Brian Foster called him with a warning. Rusty was going to use Dad as a scapegoat. Foster told him that you," she said, looking over a Ledge, "had been arrested for possession of marijuana, and Rusty feared that you would barter what you knew about the burglary in exchange for getting a walk on the drug charge."

Arden held up a hand to signal a timeout. "So, all this time, not only did you know that Rusty was in on the burglary, you knew that Ledge was."

He said, "She told you I was bad news."

Lisa jerked her head around to look at him. "You always have been and continue to be. If you had stayed away from Arden, she wouldn't have drawn Rusty's attention."

"If I'd stayed away from her, God knows what would have happened to her."

"Stop it, you two," Arden said. "Go back to that night, Lisa. To the phone call. What else did Foster tell Dad?"

"According to Dad, Foster was falling apart. Foster had agreed to meet Rusty and hide the money, but then he got cold feet. Dad persuaded him to keep that meeting so Rusty wouldn't be tipped off to his betrayal.

"Hoping to prevent a bad situation from getting worse, Dad sneaked out of the house, walked to the cypress grove, and used that old boat of his to get to their meeting spot. But he didn't make it in time. They were there ahead of him. Rusty was in a canoe. Foster was standing at the waterline.

"Dad overheard Foster—stupidly—inform Rusty that he'd told Dad everything, that basically the cat was out of the bag. With that, and just like that," she said, snapping her fingers, "Rusty hit Foster with a paddle. Dad told me he thought that Rusty had killed him right then. Apparently Rusty thought so, too."

She told them about Foster's rising up out of the water

and pulling Rusty out of his canoe. "Dad said their fight was brutal. Foster held out for as long as he could, but he never really stood a chance." Softly she added, "Certainly not against the alligators."

None of them said anything for a moment; then Lisa continued. "During the fight, Rusty's canoe had drifted close to where Dad was hiding in his boat. He spotted the bag lying in the bottom of the canoe. He snatched it and rowed away."

"Rusty didn't see him?" Ledge asked.

"There was no indication that he did. Dad said he didn't go across open water, but stayed close to the shoreline, in the shadows, under trees. He knew every square foot of this lake, all the bayous. Even pickled, he could find his way."

For a ponderous time, no one said anything. Arden didn't stir, then she got up suddenly and rounded her chair, placing her hands on the back of it as though to keep a grip on her temper. She was seething.

"Why have you kept this from me, Lisa? As recently as this week, when I came to your office and asked if you thought Dad was capable of committing the crimes, you talked around it, you dodged. You surmised. Conjectured."

"Arden despises liars," Ledge said.

"If I've lied," Lisa shouted at him, "it was to protect my sister from the ugly truth."

"It's a lot uglier than you're telling it," he said.

"You're a son of a bitch."

"And you're a liar."

Arden divided a frustrated look between them. To Ledge, she said, "What is she lying about?"

He looked hard at Lisa.

She sucked in a harsh breath, wheezing as she exhaled and said to Arden, "Dad wasn't the burglar. I was."

Chapter 38

That night in 2000—Lisa

Hey, Ledge, why do you think it is that Joe doesn't do his drinking here? Why doesn't he give your uncle Henry his business? Do you reckon he thinks nobody knows he's an alky?"

Rusty's taunt was the last straw.

Refusing to give him the satisfaction of her coming back with an angry retort, Lisa opened the door behind the passenger seat where he sat. After getting out, she slammed the door hard, hoping that the impact would shake loose his teeth.

She resented like hell having that prick lording it over her. She figured he knew how much she hated it, which was why he never passed on an opportunity to rile her.

But really, what had she expected when she agreed to participate in this misadventure? Courtesy and respect? She'd sunk to the level of Rusty Dyle, that witless accountant, and a juvenile delinquent. If she hadn't been desperate...

But she had. Her father had become increasingly inept and unreliable. He hadn't held a job since being fired from Welch's store. Judging by the number of calls and mailed notices from bill collectors, she knew their financial situation was rocky, but she hadn't known the extent of their indebtedness until Rusty had enlightened her. With insufferable smugness, he had disclosed exactly how dire her family's situation was.

He'd approached her on a windy weekday afternoon. After picking Arden up from school, she had dropped her at the public library to browse under the librarian's watchful eye while she ran some errands. She'd been returning for her when Rusty had materialized out of nowhere directly in front of her, blocking her path on the sidewalk.

"Hey, hotshot."

She hadn't seen much of him since she had graduated high school, but of course she recognized him. One couldn't miss that ridiculous haircut, and it was impossible to ignore someone as obnoxious as he. He wouldn't allow anyone to ignore him.

"Hello, Rusty."

She'd gone around him, but he'd fallen into step beside her. "How's college?"

"Fine."

"Gee, you're almost halfway through already."

"After this semester."

"I'll bet you're making straight A's."

"I'm holding my own."

"Must be tough, keeping up your grades and making that commute every day."

How he'd known that she commuted was a mystery, but she hadn't wanted to prolong the conversation by asking him for an explanation. "Nice seeing you, but I've got to dash." She'd lengthened her stride in an attempt to outdistance him, but he'd kept pace.

"Heard your old man got canned again."

That brought her to a halt. "What do you know about it, and what's it to you?"

"Ouch! The claws come out." He'd curled his fingers and pawed the air like a scratching cat.

"You always were and always will be an asshole, Rusty."

She'd tried to continue on her way, but he'd caught her by the elbow. "Don't turn your back on me, smarty pants."

She'd yanked her arm free. "I don't care if your daddy is the damn governor, I'll scream this town down if you ever touch me again."

"You're right. I'm sorry." He'd made an elaborate show of taking several steps back. "I don't want to get off on the wrong foot with you. Not since we're going to be business partners and all."

"Business partners?"

"That's right. We've got a lot to talk about, you and me."

"Guess again."

"Your first meeting with me is tonight."

"Are you out of your mind? I'm not meeting you tonight or at any other time."

"Oh, you will. You will *tonight*. You can't afford to miss this meeting." He'd leaned to one side to look beyond her toward the library. "You must've kept her waiting too long. I made note of the time when you dropped her off."

Lisa had turned to see Arden standing just outside the entrance to the building, the librarian watching from behind the glass. Arden had been holding a stack of books against her chest. She'd waved. Lisa had waved back, but it had been a conditioned reflex. She was thinking about Rusty's last statement. When she'd turned back to face him, he'd given her an insolent smile.

"Nine o'clock tonight. On the bleachers of the football field. That should be a nice and nostalgic spot for you, Miss

Homecoming Queen." He'd moved in closer and whispered, "Your little sister is gonna be a looker. She's already as cute as all get-out."

Then he'd turned away and sauntered off down the sidewalk.

The inflection in his voice when he'd referred to Arden had turned Lisa's stomach. For the rest of that afternoon, she'd tried to dismiss the comment and chided herself for paying any heed to it. Like father, like son, Rusty was reputed to be crafty and manipulative. He knew which buttons to push. She wasn't about to let him bend her to his will.

Nevertheless, at nine o'clock sharp, she had joined him on the bleachers.

He'd begun with irrelevant chitchat. "When Joe worked at Welch's, you were in and out of there quite a lot, right? You must've learned your way around, saw the operation of the store from behind the scenes."

"What is this about, Rusty?"

"It's about a lot of coin." He winked.

Then he'd told her his plan.

"I know what you're going to ask. Why enlist me? Well, see, Lisa, I need you to verify information provided by Foster. You know Brian Foster? The schmuck your dad tangled with the day he got fired? Him. The pussy.

"Don't get me wrong. Foster's smart with numbers, and he's sincere enough, but I need a guarantee that he's not feeding me faulty information. It would be awkward if alarm bells went off while we were hauling bales of cash out of there."

She had listened in disbelief. In spite of herself, she was amazed by his audacity and amused by his conceit. "You're talking madness. It's cold out here. I'm leaving. Don't ever bother me again."

When she stood up to leave, despite her earlier warning

about him touching her, he grabbed her hand and yanked her back down onto the bleacher.

"You'll go along, Lisa. Want to know why you will?"

With that, he had produced copies of overdue invoices owed by her father. She'd sorted through them with mounting dismay, and with another emotion that was foreign to her: humiliation. Her spring semester tuition was two months in arrears.

"One of these days your daddy is going to fall down in a gutter and not get up again," Rusty had said. "Where's that going to leave you?"

Whether knowingly or not, he had stoked her worst fear. Unless Joe had a miraculous turnaround, which there had been no signs of his doing or even attempting to do, she soon would have to support herself and assume sole responsibility for Arden.

That would mean sacrificing any hope of completing her education and fulfilling the ambition she'd had to leave this nowhere town and make something noteworthy of her life.

But *burglary*? "If I commit a crime, where will that leave me, Rusty? In prison."

"We won't get caught."

"You're delusional. Your scheme is preposterous. As desperate as my situation is, I want no part of it, and no part of you or those other two creeps. I'll figure out another way, an honest way, to pay our bills."

"Not so fast, whistle britches. You're in now, whether you want to be or not. You know the plan, you gotta do the deed." Then he'd given her a beatific smile and said, "Don't just think about yourself. Think about sweet little Arden."

Again, his tone, with its undercurrent of pedophilia, had sickened her. It also had frightened her. Obviously, he had been keeping track of her schedule. He'd followed them today to the library. Otherwise he wouldn't have known they were there and for how long.

She'd told him that she would think it over. But as she'd driven away from the football field, she knew her destiny had taken a steep, downward turn. She had made an irreversible pact with the devil.

Now here she was, in the parking lot of Burnet's pool hall, no less, the rubber soles of her blue sneakers crunching gravel and collecting mud as she left behind her three accomplices. As well as the money.

If Rusty thought she was going to sit by quietly for six months while he played watchdog over it, he had another think coming. Foster and that sullen Burnet boy might be gullible enough to believe in Rusty's integrity, but she sure as hell wasn't.

She didn't allow herself to dwell on the fact that she was now a felon. Even her righteous mother would have sanctioned the drastic action she'd taken. She had done what she'd had to in order to make a better life for herself and Arden.

In any case, it was done. Now, she must somehow figure out a way to best the psychopathic Rusty Dyle without tripping herself up. Having just left him, she was already trying to devise a way to beat him at his own game and reclaim her share of the take.

When her house came into view, she could tell even from a distance that it was dark inside, just as she'd left it. No cop cars in sight. When she got closer, she turned off her headlights, steered carefully into the driveway, and made the incline at a snail's pace.

The door on the detached garage was up. With relief, she saw that her father's car was still there. She'd had to wait until he returned from the cemetery before she could leave and keep her date with the other three crooks. She'd made it with little time to spare.

As she'd sneaked out of the house, it had occurred to her that her dad might run out of liquor and leave the house in search of a bottle, in which case Arden would have been left alone. That had been a risk she'd had to take, but she'd banked on the cemetery visit leaving her dad depressed enough to drink himself into a stupor before passing out.

The back door was locked, as she'd left it. That, too, boded well. She used her key and slipped inside. She smiled at the basket of dyed Easter eggs in the center of the table. She'd promised Arden that tomorrow they would bake a layered coconut cake using the recipe written in their mother's hand.

Please, God, for Arden's sake, let Dad go one day without drinking.

With that prayer, she silently climbed the stairs and went into her bedroom. It couldn't have gone any better, even taking into account that stupid confab Rusty had conducted in the ditch. She had left the house undetected, and had returned undetected.

She would figure out a way to get her money from Rusty sooner rather than later, but so far, so good.

Chapter 39

By the time Lisa had finished, Arden's knuckles had turned white, and she had to pry her fingers open in order to let go of the chair back. She looked over at Ledge. Throughout Lisa's account, he hadn't moved, either.

Her voice husky with emotion, she said to him, "You should have told me."

"*She* should have told you."

"But since she hadn't—"

"God knows I wanted to."

"But you couldn't without giving yourself away."

"That's not why," he said, looking pained that she would think that. "You had lost your baby. You have no other family. I didn't want to be the one who messed up what you have with her."

She held his steady blue gaze, then looked at Lisa, who sat with head bent. If she'd heard their exchange, she gave no sign of it. Arden said, "Lisa, what were you thinking?"

Lisa pushed the fingers of both hands up through her hair

and held it back for several seconds before letting it go. It resettled like a curtain framing her face. The hardness of her expression defied them to censure her.

"I was thinking how badly we could use that money to get us out of the red. I was thinking how helpful it would be to have that cash squirreled away when you became my responsibility, which was inevitable, considering the rate of Dad's decline. I was thinking that I was protecting you from Rusty's clutches as well as securing a better future for you."

"And *you*."

"All right, and me!" she shouted. "And why not?"

Then, reining in her temper and her tone, she said, "Dad wasn't providing. I was a college student with no income. The state could have taken you away. Would you have rather been placed in foster care?"

Arden rounded the chair and sat down. "Did you make up the part about Foster's phone call, catching Dad with the money bag?"

"No," she exclaimed. "My encounter with him here in the kitchen happened exactly as I described it. Everything Dad did after that phone call from Foster was just as I've told you, except that he was doing damage control for me, not for himself.

"Having recovered the money, he urged me to turn myself in. Giving back the money and turning state's witness against my accomplices might prevent me from being charged. Besides, that would be the right and moral thing to do, he said. Also, as a witness to Foster's death, he had an obligation to report it to the authorities.

"Of course, he was right on all scores. But in all honesty, his appeal to my conscience didn't affect my decision as much as learning that Rusty had had a hand in Foster's dying, whether or not he'd killed him outright. That shook me because it gave backbone to his threats toward you. He wasn't just a smarmy, spoiled brat. He was sick. Psycho. Evil. My worst transgression, even above the theft, was my naïveté regarding his depravity.

"So I agreed with Dad. However, he and I knew better than to call the sheriff's department. Dad told me that he would call the Texas Rangers, maybe even the FBI. But he suggested that we wait until daylight. He wanted to clean himself up, get cold sober and clear-headed. He said we had to place ourselves in the best possible bargaining position for my clemency.

"He told me to go upstairs and try to sleep. He held my face between his hands and apologized for all his shortcomings. He blamed himself for driving me to commit a crime, and told me he would make certain the authorities understood that desperation had led me to do it. He kissed my forehead.

"Obediently I went to my room. I was nervous and frightened. Even if I surrendered and threw myself on the mercy of the law, there was still a chance I would go to prison."

She reflected for a moment, then shook off her pensiveness and shifted her position in the chair. "I never saw Dad again. He'd seemed so contrite over his failings. There were even tears standing in his eyes. It never occurred to me that his *mea culpa* was a ploy."

No one said anything; then Ledge prefaced speaking by clearing his throat. "When did you discover that he was gone?"

Lisa looked at him, then at Arden. "When Rusty nearly beat down the door looking for him."

"You're lying."

"Rusty was here that night?" Arden asked.

She and Ledge had spoken in unison, but it was his accusation of lying that Lisa addressed. "I'm not lying! I was in my room, but it was a ridiculous notion that I could sleep. When the pounding on the door started, I was afraid it was lawmen, here to arrest me." She looked at Ledge. "I thought perhaps you'd done as Rusty had feared, that you had turned on the rest of us to save your own skin."

He gave her a baleful look but didn't comment.

She went back to Arden. "I was afraid that you would wake up and be terrified. Not even taking time to dress, I ran downstairs in my pajamas and answered the door. It wasn't men in uniform. It was Rusty, and he was a wreck. His clothes were filthy. He was all banged up and in obvious pain. He couldn't even stand upright, but he barged in, ranting, demanding to know where Dad was, threatening to kill him.

"I had to pretend to be shocked by his appearance, pretend not to know about his fierce fight with Foster and how it ended. I kept asking him what had happened to him, who had beaten him up, what had Dad to do with anything.

"He said, 'Foster told your old man about the burglary. He knew where I was going to meet Foster. He hoodwinked both of us and took the money. Where is he?' He told me that when he found Dad, he was going to kill him, and I believed him.

"He pushed me aside and hobbled into the kitchen here. There were Dad's fresh muddy footprints, and a wet patch on the floor where the bag had been. I gaped at them as though I didn't understand what they signified.

"Actually, at that point in time, I didn't," she said with a wry grimace. "I thought maybe Dad had seen Rusty's car coming toward the house and had sneaked out. Something like that. I was glad that he and the money were safe from this crazy person ranting at me. He went out the back door and into the garage. I followed, fearing Dad would be cowering in there. But he was nowhere to be found. Rusty was relentless, saying he was going to find him if he had to tear the place apart.

"When we came back inside, he went from room to room.

I kept trying to distract him by asking how he'd been injured. He was grunting and groaning in pain, but he dragged himself upstairs. He looked into your room," she said to Arden, "with me begging him not to wake you. If you had woken up and seen him in his condition, you would have been traumatized."

"No doubt," Arden said caustically.

Lisa plowed on. "Rusty searched in my room. That left only Dad's bedroom. It was empty. But what struck me then was that Rusty's muddy footprints on the stairs and along the hall were the only ones in any part of the house, other than those there by the back door.

"Dad had come no farther into the house than just inside the kitchen door where I had last seen him, remorseful, wringing his hands, tears in his eyes. The bag of money at his feet. It was then that I began to get a sick feeling in the pit of my stomach."

Lisa seemed to lapse into the memory. Ledge and Arden glanced at each other. He asked, "What was Rusty's reaction to finding him gone?"

Lisa roused herself. "He was like a man possessed. He pointed out to me that Dad's car was still in the garage, that my car was in the drive. He kept asking how he could have gotten away. I didn't dare mention the boat. But I did ask about Foster."

"And their secret meeting," Ledge said.

She nodded. "In that reeking ditch, Rusty had emphasized that we should act like virtual strangers if we saw each other. Why had he gone against his own advice and arranged to see Foster that same night?"

"How did he answer?"

"He didn't. But it was like I'd given him an electric shock treatment."

"He realized he needed to establish an alibi," Ledge said. "He went to Crystal."

"I didn't know about that," Lisa said. "Nor did I care. I just wanted him out of this house. He left with threats ringing in my ears. He warned me never to tell about any of it. He also said that if he ever discovered I was in cahoots with 'my old man,' he would kill me. Then he limped out of here."

"What did you do after he left?" Arden asked.

"Collapsed where I stood. I tried to absorb the shock of it all and figure out what I should do. My first priority was to protect you from what had already happened, and from whatever might be coming. After pulling myself together, I cleaned up the floors and straightened things Rusty had disturbed. By the time you woke up, everything looked normal."

"Except that Dad didn't come down for breakfast. You sent me up to his room, knowing that he wasn't there."

"I kept waiting for him to walk through the back door and explain his disappearance." She looked at the back door and gave a humorless laugh. "To this day, I'm still waiting."

She took a moment, then continued. "You and I baked our cake and had our Easter dinner, but you were dejected because Dad wasn't here. You asked to go to the cemetery, and I took you. Dad actually *had* gone the night before. There was a fresh arrangement of flowers on Mom's grave. I resented that pathetic gesture.

"If he had loved her as much as he professed, if he loved *us* so much, why had he left me to deal with Rusty alone? When he did slink back, I looked forward to calling him a gutless coward to his face. You see, I was still under the delusion that his abandonment was temporary."

She sighed. "On Monday, detectives from the sheriff's office came. It was clear from the outset that Dad was suspected of both the burglary and complicity in Foster's death. Can you imagine what it was like to be interrogated by Rusty's father? I wanted to blurt out what his psychotic son had done to poor, spineless Brian Foster. But I was afraid that if I breathed a word, Rusty would make good on his promise to harm you. Based on what you've told me about recent events, I still have reason to fear that. As you do," she said, looking over at Ledge.

After a time, Arden said, "They found Dad's boat caught up in cypress knees in a narrow bayou. There was a manhunt. Helicopters. Search dogs. Where did he go?"

Lisa raised her arms at her sides. "How he managed his getaway remains a mystery."

"Maybe he didn't," Arden said. "Manage it, I mean. Maybe he didn't survive that night. In his haste to get away, maybe he fell out of his boat and drowned."

Ledge reminded her that the lake had been dragged in search of his body.

"But only in the vicinity of where they found his boat, and around where Foster's remains were discovered. Maybe Rusty caught up with him after all, killed him, and hid his body, never to be found."

Ledge said, "It would have had to happen quickly, or his arrival at Crystal's house wouldn't time out."

"And he was so badly injured," Lisa said. "I think he would've lacked the strength."

"Also," Ledge said, "if Rusty had caught up to Joe, he would have reclaimed the money. He wouldn't still be bitter over losing it."

"He wouldn't have hounded me for years."

Lisa's statement took Arden by surprise, and Ledge, too, it seemed. He said, "Fill us in."

"I had made arrangements for Arden and me to relocate as soon as the school semester ended. This would have been almost three months after Easter, and still no sign of Dad. Days before we were due to leave town, Rusty came here to the house and repeated his vows of vengeance if he learned that Dad and I had plotted to screw him out of the 'haul,' as he called it.

"Then for several years after we were in Dallas, he would show up periodically and issue the same threats. But he could see how modestly we lived, at least until I married Wallace. After that, I guess Rusty gave up hope. He stopped the surprise visits."

She reached for Arden's hand. "Marrying Wallace gave me a sense of security, but I never forgot Rusty's threats. I knew he hadn't forgotten them, either. *That's* why I was so adamantly opposed to your moving back here. I panicked when you told me you had interviewed him to do repairs." She tipped her head toward Ledge. "I never wanted you to know any of this."

"But I should have known, Lisa. I've lived in denial that Dad took the money and ran. You enabled that. You let me cling to the hope that he was innocent."

"I couldn't bring myself to tell you differently and shatter that illusion."

"I'm not that fragile. I've built up an immunity to having my illusions shattered." She looked at Ledge. Although his eyes shone very blue in the dim room, his expression was unreadable.

Lisa took a drink of her soda, which must have gone warm. "Now that we've bared all, what do you plan to do?"

"Shut Rusty down," Ledge said.

"We're going to take everything to the attorney general's office," Arden told her. "All of it. Foster. Dwayne Hawkins."

"The burglary," Lisa said, looking resigned.

"I'm sorry," Arden said. "But all this started with that."

"It's time I paid the piper for an egregious mistake."

"You can't be prosecuted."

"No, only persecuted. Which," she said, drawing a deep breath, "is no less than I deserve for being so stupid."

"We're both guilty of that," Ledge said.

"Did Wallace know?" Arden asked.

"God, no," Lisa said, looking horrified at the thought. "He put me on a pedestal. If he'd ever found out, I couldn't have borne his disappointment in me." She gave a wistful smile. "Before this goes public, I'll resign my position at the firm to spare the board having to demand my resignation. Wallace left me a rich widow. I won't suffer anything except the humiliation of having been a thief." She turned toward Ledge and regarded him for a long moment. "You surprise me."

"How's that?"

"You didn't break the pact." She gave a terse laugh. "Honor among thieves?"

Before he could reply, his cell phone rang. He pulled it from his pocket. "Hey, Don." He listened, then said, "Oh, shit. Did she say—Wait, this could be a setup. Did you check the caller ID? You're sure?" Then he hissed, "Son of a bitch. Yeah, yeah, I'm leaving now." He looked at Arden, who was already on her feet. "She's doing all right. Yes, yes, I will. I promise. Gotta go." He clicked off.

"What?"

"A staffer at the memory center called the bar, asking for me. She talked to Don on behalf of George, who was on his way out of the building in a dead run, giving chase to some guy who pretended to be a friend of the family there to see Uncle Henry."

Arden said, "I'll come with you."

"No." His tone brooked no argument. "Not this time. You two stay together, but leave here as planned. Soon as you can get gone, go." He looked over at Lisa.

As unflappable as always, she said, "I've taken care of her for twenty years."

Coming back to Arden, he said, "I'll keep you updated if I can. If not, Don will be in touch."

"Ledge—"

"I've got to go, Arden."

"I understand. Hurry."

He left through the back door, but Arden went out behind him. Beyond the steps, the downpour was as heavy as a drapery. He hovered beneath the eaves to fish his key fob from his pants pocket. He flipped up the collar of his jean jacket. Arden had crowded in behind him on the top step.

He turned and reached for her hand, squeezing it hard. "If you were paying attention last night, you know everything you need to know." He punctuated that with a firm kiss, then hurdled the lower steps and ran through the torrent to his pickup.

Arden stayed and watched him drive away before going back inside.

Lisa was standing at the sink, gazing out the window. "It's really coming down."

Arden shut the door forcefully. "That's what we're going to talk about? The weather?"

Lisa turned, looking defensive. "Weren't you better off not knowing?"

"No."

"What difference would knowing have made?"

"I would have been free of doubt. I would already be well past this stage that I'm in now."

"What stage is that?"

"Infuriated."

Lisa shook herself as though throwing off a cloying garment. "We have a lot to talk about. Most of it will be painful for both of us. But it would be beneficial if we presented a united front when we take all this to the attorney general, or whomever. Don't you agree?"

Arden turned her head aside, raked her fingers through her damp hair, and murmured, "Ever practical."

"And you're ever impassioned."

Coming back to Lisa, she said, "Yes. I take things to heart, I feel deeply, and I refuse to apologize for it." Having reached an impasse, she turned way. "I'll pack."

"I haven't been upstairs since you've been back. I'm going to take a look around."

Not caring if she sounded snide, Arden said, "Make yourself at home."

She went into her room, took her suitcase from the closet, and opened it on the bed. She packed only what she would need for several days, not by any means intending to stay with Lisa indefinitely.

After folding several changes of clothing into the suitcase, she opened the closet and bent down to get a pair of shoes. When she straightened up and turned around, she came face-to-face with Rusty, who was leering at her.

Before she could make a sound, he raised his hand to the side of her head, and the lights went out.

Chapter 40

———◉———

Ledge drove at a speed that would have been incautious on dry pavement. It was suicidal on wet. His windshield wipers were on high, and it was still like driving through a car wash. He steered with his left hand while using his right to place a call to George's cell, holding out little hope that he would get an answer.

He was shocked and relieved when George answered with, "Yo. Cap'n. You all right?"

"Yes, but how are things there?"

"Under control."

"You caught him?"

"Caught who?"

Ledge's heart bumped. He braked, causing his truck to hydroplane and fishtail. He maneuvered it onto the shoulder and stopped. "Somebody from the center called the bar, said that you were chasing a guy from the building, that—"

"Cap'n, I'm sitting here with your uncle Henry. We're watching a rerun basketball game on ESPN."

"*Fuck!* I mean, damn, I'm glad you're both okay. But, oh, fuck, George."

"You were suckered."

"Big time. The dude got to somebody there on staff to fake an emergency call."

"I'll find out who and make them cry for their mama."

"For now, stay with my uncle. Don't leave him alone until you hear from me personally."

"Copy."

Ledge didn't let himself become distracted by either his temper or self-castigation. He went into combat mode and focused on the job at hand.

He wheeled his truck around, barely avoided getting stuck in the ditch on the other side of the road, and was soon speeding in the direction from which he'd come.

He thumbed his phone to call Don, who answered immediately. Without any preamble, Ledge asked if any of the retired Texas Rangers were within shouting distance.

"All of them."

"Dispatch them to the Maxwell place. Like *now*. I'll need witnesses who'll bear out that I was given no choice."

"To do what?"

"Kill Rusty."

"Arden?" Lisa called.

Where Arden lay with her ear against the floor, she could both hear and feel the vibration of her sister's footsteps as Lisa entered the kitchen from the direction of the living room.

Rousing, Arden tried to sit up, but she was dizzy and off balance. Her hands were bound behind her back. Flex-cuffs, she thought.

"This place looks even worse upstairs, if that's possible," Lisa said as she came through the kitchen.

Arden tried to warn her, but only managed to croak her name.

"Are you—" When Lisa pushed open the door, she froze in place on the threshold and gripped the doorknob for support.

"Hi, Lisa."

Arden's synapses were operating sluggishly. From where she lay on her side on the floor, she looked up and blinked Rusty into focus. He was wearing disposable gloves. Her nine-millimeter looked very dark and menacing against the bright blue latex on his right hand.

Her own gun was aimed at her? How and when had Rusty gotten it?

Lisa said, "Don't, Rusty. Please don't."

"Don't pull the trigger, you mean?"

"Please."

"Look at that, Arden." He nudged her hip with the metal toe of his boot. "Did you think you would live to see the day that this bitch would beg?"

He bent down and hooked his free hand in Arden's elbow, then yanked her to her feet with a suddenness that made her nauseated. He shoved her down onto the side of the bed. She sat, swaying, but raised her chin and gave him the fiercest look she could muster.

"Ledge is on his way here. If you hurt us, he will kill you."

"Ledge is speeding in the opposite direction to rescue his poor ol' senile uncle Henry." He poked the barrel of the pistol between her breasts. "If you move, you're dead."

Lisa raised her fingers to her mouth and whimpered. "Arden hasn't done anything to you."

"Not yet, but she and Burnet are cooking up a bad batch

of hassle for me. The only reason I haven't killed her yet is because, first, I want to expose her to the devious bitch you are."

As he said that, he reached into his shirt pocket, then opened his hand so they could see what it held. "These little buggers are the best invention ever. You stick them someplace like underneath a kitchen table, and you can hear conversations clear as a bell. Well, not quite *that* clear, especially with this damn weather. But clear enough.

"Unfortunately, I didn't get this one planted soon enough to be privy to everything Arden and Burnet have been discussing over the last few days, but I'm guessing they've been plotting my never-gonna-happen downfall.

"However, I did get it in here last night after taking care of some other, rather urgent business." He winked down at Arden as though they shared an inside joke. Dwayne Hawkins. "While I was here, I helped myself to this." He brandished the pistol. "So when I kill her," he said, indicating Lisa, "it'll look like you did it before shooting yourself."

"What a foolish plan," Arden said. "Nobody will believe that I killed my sister. I have no reason to."

"Yeah, you do. You just don't know it yet." He gave her a wide grin. Then going back to Lisa, he said, "Where was I? Oh, the bug." He bounced it in his palm, then returned it to his pocket. "Luckily, I successfully planted it last night. Because, today, I caught you lying through your pretty porcelains."

"I confessed that I was in on the burglary, not our dad."

"Oh, I know. I heard. And it was touching. Truly. But, no, see, what I'm referring to came later in the conversation, when you were telling her and Burnet about me coming here, ranting and raving like a man possessed. Et cetera."

"Do you deny it?"

"No. Not at all. If I'd've found Joe and the money that

night, I probably would have killed him, and you with him, taken the money, and been a happy camper."

He pursed his lips and frowned down at Arden. "Wouldn't have made a very good Easter morning for little Arden, though, would it?" Then his features became taut with malevolence as he turned back to Lisa. "Did baby sister's welfare cross your mind when you were murdering her daddy?"

Arden's stomach heaved. She had to swallow quickly to keep from spewing bile.

Lisa fell back a step, her spine landing hard enough against the door frame to make a knocking sound. "You're demented."

"I'm crazy like a fox is what I am. I pick up on things. Like when you told your appreciative audience that I went into the kitchen there, looking for Joe, and all that was left of him were muddy footprints just inside the back door and a wet patch where the bag of money had been."

"So?"

"There were no footprints. No wet spot."

Arden looked over at Lisa, whose lips had gone as white as her fingers still gripping the doorknob.

"When I heard that," Rusty continued, "it got me to thinking that the rigmarole about you hearing him come in, finding him in the kitchen with the money, and telling you the jig was up, yada yada, was bunk. He never made it back to the house that night, did he?"

Lisa's throat worked. "I told Arden the truth. Dad—"

"Okay," he said, cutting her off. "Have it your way. One thing you did tell the truth about, I did warn you that, if you betrayed me, I would kill her with you watching."

"No!" Lisa cried as she thrust her arm out toward him.

Arden surged to her feet and raised her knee, trying to knock the pistol out of Rusty's hand, but dizziness made her uncoordinated. She did no harm to Rusty. He secured her around the waist with his free arm, pulled her back against his chest, and jammed the pistol up under her chin.

He yelled at Lisa, "Now, I don't care that you killed the old drunkard, I just want the money!"

"It's gone, you idiot! I spent it!"

Hearing that from Lisa caused Arden's knees to give way. She sagged against Rusty, making it an effort for him to hold her up. "Stand up," he demanded and jabbed her under the chin with the gun barrel.

She forced herself to remain upright, but that endeavor was secondary to trying to grasp and accept that Lisa had done what Rusty accused her of. It couldn't be true. Could it?

Yes. Guilt was inscribed on her sister's face. It was on display in her slumped posture, starkly evident in her eyes. It emanated from her. How had she managed to mask it so well for all these years?

She spoke in a hoarse voice. "It was an accident. I swear."

Arden could only look at her. What was she expected to say?

Lisa wet her lips. "I was so relieved that I had made it back to the house without something dreadful happening. I actually went to sleep. I woke up when I heard Dad going out the back door.

"I went downstairs to see what he was doing. Through the window, I saw him in the far distance, walking toward the cypress grove. I thought, he's drunk, and decided to let him be. But it had gotten foggy. There was drizzle, and it was dark. I was afraid he would injure himself, stumbling around out there. So I talked myself into getting dressed and going after him.

"He had already pushed off into the water when I caught up to him and asked what the hell he thought he was doing, taking that boat out in the middle of the night. He told me about the call he'd gotten from Brian Foster." She raised her hand and rubbed her forehead.

"He knew about my participation in the burglary. I was humiliated, ashamed. He didn't scold, but said he had to try to prevent the situation from becoming worse. Since it was my fault we'd been dragged into it, I couldn't let him act alone. I had to make reparation myself. I got into the boat with him."

"You were there?" Arden said.

"I witnessed Rusty and Foster's fight."

Arden felt Rusty's body tense. Before she could warn Lisa not to say anything more, she continued. "I was the one who actually spotted Rusty's canoe, caught in some low branches. Dad and I paddled over to it. I lifted the money bag out. We got away unseen and started our way back.

"I kept urging Dad to hurry. I knew that once Rusty realized the money was missing, he would come looking for Joe Maxwell. We needed to beat him to our house. You were there alone," she said, meeting Arden's gaze. "I was so frightened for you."

Arden didn't acknowledge that. "What did you do to Dad?"

Lisa choked up. "All the way back, he talked about making things right, keeping me out of prison. We would give the money back and make a deal for clemency for me."

Rusty sneered, "But you were thinking finders-keepers."

She ignored him and kept her eyes on Arden. "I suggested alternatives."

"Like keeping the money," Rusty said.

Lisa shot him a dirty look. "I suggested that we should consider the ramifications of my confessing. What if it backfired? Dad began to lose it. In the space of a few hours, he'd learned that his firstborn had committed a felony. He'd watched Foster die in a ghastly manner. He'd rowed that damn boat for God knows how far.

"When we reached our cypress grove, we were still arguing about what our next move should be. I held the money bag while Dad dragged the boat onto solid ground. When he got ashore, he tried to take the bag from me. We had a tug-of-war."

"You won," Arden said.

"He fell down, on his back, and rapped his head on a cluster of cypress knees. I thought he would come out of it in his own good time. In the meanwhile, I had to get to the house. I ran back, went upstairs, and changed into my pajamas. No sooner had I done that, this lunatic arrived." She glared at Rusty.

"Forget him," Arden said. "Tell me about Dad."

"After Rusty left, I went back to the grove. I was exhausted."

"I don't care," Arden shouted. "*Tell me about Dad.*"

"He was dead." She said it with benumbing finality. "He was exactly as I'd left him. I couldn't believe it, but..." She raised her arms helplessly at her sides. "There was nothing I could do, Arden."

"Except to let everyone think badly of him instead of you."

"Yes! It seemed a perfect answer. A solution that was so...neat."

"No fuss, no muss."

"If I had been sentenced to prison, what would your life have been like?"

There was nothing Arden could say to that. "What did you do with...him?" She swallowed thickly.

"Put him in the boat. Weighted him. Then—"

"Stop. I don't want to know."

Lisa looked like she would protest, then said softly, "He loved the lake."

After a beat, Rusty whistled. "You had a busy night, gal. You had a body to dispose of, and a bag of money to hide."

"You walked all around it, Rusty. You came this close." She

made an inch with her thumb and index finger. "I was holding my breath."

It seemed to Arden that his temperature rose several degrees within seconds. "And later? What did you do with it?"

"I told you. I spent it." She smiled. "Every last cent."

He flipped his aim to her and fired.

Shock registered on her face.

Arden didn't even realize what had happened until her sister pitched forward and fell to the floor.

Then Arden screamed.

While driving with heedless ferocity, Ledge had placed repeated calls to Arden's cell phone. They'd all gone to voice mail. So he wasn't surprised when her house came into view and he saw Rusty's car in the driveway, blocking in both her and Lisa's cars.

His impulse was to roar up in his truck and barge in. But without knowing what kind of shit show was going on inside, not knowing what kind of danger Arden was in, he left his pickup at the end of their drive. As he alighted, he saw other vehicles speeding from different directions toward the property.

The cavalry. God bless Don.

He didn't wait for the backup, but proceeded up the drive on foot, revolver drawn. It was still loaded from last night when he'd left it with Arden to defend herself while he'd dealt with Hawkins.

The only light on inside the house was coming from the window in the room where Arden slept. Running in a crouch, he approached it cautiously, now glad for the pelting rain that helped obscure him.

Through the window, he saw the three of them in an arrangement that nearly caused his heart to burst. Rusty was holding Arden with a nine-millimeter crammed into the soft tissue under her chin. She could die. At any second.

But no sooner had Ledge processed that dreadful thought, Rusty suddenly turned the gun on Lisa instead and pulled the trigger. Ledge reacted as he'd been conditioned. He fired. The bullet shattered the window and accomplished exactly what he'd intended: It startled Rusty into releasing Arden.

The instant Ledge saw an infinitesimal space between them, he fired a second shot. It struck precisely where he had aimed.

Rusty was neutralized.

Ledge crashed through what was left of the window.

Rusty released Arden so abruptly, she reeled into the wall, bashing her elbow. But she was impervious to the pain and only dimly aware of two additional gunshots reverberating in the small space, the racket of glass shattering, the thud of footsteps.

She stumbled over to Lisa and dropped to her knees, but she was helpless to touch her because of the hand restraints. Frantically, she pulled her hands against them in a maddened attempt to break free.

A voice she had come to know well said from behind her, "Be still." She looked over her shoulder. Ledge was kneeling behind her. He snapped the restraints apart with his pocketknife.

Then gently Arden and he turned Lisa onto her side. When Lisa blinked, Arden sobbed in relief.

Ledge, who'd located Lisa's wound, raised his eyes to Arden, and what she saw in them made her tremble.

He said, "Ambulance is coming up the drive."

She looked back down at Lisa, who was moving her hand in a restless, groping motion until she found Arden's. Realizing what her sister was attempting, Arden hooked their little fingers together. Lisa closed her eyes momentarily, then reopened them and gave Arden's finger a tug.

Arden leaned down, placing her ear directly above Lisa's lips, but what she managed to utter was gibberish. Arden leaned back in order to look into her face, but Lisa's eyes were already partially closed and unseeing.

Arden sensed commotion behind her and, at the same time, Ledge placed his hands on her shoulders and pulled her up to stand. "Give them room."

Paramedics crowded into the space. One immediately began administering CPR on Lisa.

"Lisa?" Arden hiccupped a sob. "Lisa?"

Ledge placed his arm around her and drew her close.

Lisa was still receiving CPR when they placed her on a gurney and carried her to the ambulance. Arden was given a hand up and climbed in. The doors were shut, and it sped down the drive toward the road.

Ledge had seen in the eyes of one of the medics who had attended Lisa what he already knew. It had been a belly shot. Her chances of surviving were remote. He wanted to be with Arden.

But she might not want to be with him.

The rain had stopped. The men Don had sent to assist if necessary were circled around in the yard, chawing among themselves over what had happened, and giving their statements to the law officers who'd arrived with the ambulance. Some were from the sheriff's office. Some, Ledge was relieved to see, were from other agencies. They would be impartial.

One of the retired Rangers noticed Ledge and brushed the brim of his hat with his fingertips. Ledge bobbed his chin in acknowledgment but didn't join the group. He stayed on the steps at the back door.

Soon, Rusty was carted out of the bedroom, through the kitchen, and out the door where Ledge had been waiting.

The .357 had blown Rusty's right shoulder joint to smithereens. The medics had stanched the hemorrhaging blood vessels, but Ledge knew it hurt like a mother. It wouldn't kill him. Ledge hadn't meant it to.

He hadn't been looking Rusty in the eye.

Rusty was cursing the paramedics who carried his gurney. When he spotted Ledge, he tried to sit up, straining against the straps holding him down. "Fuck you, Burnet. You crippled me."

"Maybe."

"I'm not done with you."

"Oh, you're done, Rusty."

"I'm going to kill you."

Ledge did something he never thought he would do in the presence of Rusty Dyle. He smiled. "I don't think so."

Epilogue

———◆———

A pair of headlights swept across the living room windows before going off. A door was shut. Footsteps sounded on the porch, then the new lock on the front door was unlatched with a decisive snap, and the door swung open.

Ledge stood silhouetted against a twilit sky.

Arden stayed as she was, seated on the second step of the staircase, bare toes curled over the edge of the next tread down. Her high-heeled pumps lay on the floor where she had stepped out of them. The darkness inside was relieved only by two candles, which she'd placed on either end of the mantel.

"Hi."

"Where did you get a key?"

"I bribed the locksmith." He said it with no sign of embarrassment or remorse.

She let it go. "How did you know I would be here?"

"Just figured."

It had been four days since Lisa was pronounced DOA at the hospital. During that time, there had been formalities, legal and otherwise, that had kept Ledge and her apart. She hadn't sought him out. He'd made no attempt to see her. They hadn't even spoken by phone.

He must have been sensitive to her need for time and distance away from him in order to contend with everything that had been disclosed in the final hour of Lisa's life.

The crime scene tape had been removed from the house today. She'd been cleared to return, and she'd felt that she must go back. But after getting the candles from a kitchen drawer, she had gone into the living area, even though it was the least comfortable room without a place to sit.

She would never go into the catch-all room again.

When she'd left with Lisa in the ambulance, she'd taken nothing with her except her handbag. Everything she was wearing, she'd had to buy. The new black dress was appropriately funereal.

Ledge closed the front door and walked toward her. As he got closer, she caught him looking at her legs. Her hem rode several inches above her bent knees, but she didn't want to tug it down and call further attention.

He lowered himself onto the step beside her. They didn't look at each other or speak for a full minute; then he said, "You buried her today?"

"You heard?"

"You can't keep a secret in this town."

"You can. You did. Lisa certainly did."

He exhaled a breath laden with regret. "I heard about the worst secret she'd kept. God, I'm sorry, Arden."

He'd missed hearing that shocking revelation by seconds before he had shot out the window glass. "Who told you?" Arden asked.

"The detective who took my statement. He'd also taken

yours." He turned his head to look at her. "Do you want to talk about it?"

"No. I'm weary of it."

"Fine by me."

They sat in silence. Then she said, "Our appointment with the attorney general...?"

"That's in abeyance. A prosecutor in Rusty's office—young, idealistic, no love lost for his former boss—is treating the public disgracing of Rusty Dyle like a crusade. He's already charged him with two counts of first-degree murder—Lisa and Hawkins. That doesn't include Brian Foster.

"He said Rusty had taken crookedness to new heights and promised that heads will roll in the sheriff's department, the county court. That's just for starters. In light of all that, the burglary of Welch's store way back in 2000 is at the bottom of his to-do list."

"He and the attorney general would probably be content never to reopen that investigation."

"Probably. But I want my admission to go on the record, even if it's by deposition. I also want to make an official apology to you. Here and now." He held her gaze. "Arden, I'm sorry I didn't confess my part in it sooner. I should have leveled with you the day you came to the workshop. My intention was good, but maybe my judgment was lousy."

The seriousness of his expression was emphasized by the play of candlelight and shadow across his features. "Yes, you should have," she said softly. "But if you hadn't gotten here when you did, and acted, Rusty would have killed me, too. In exchange for saving my life, I can forgive you the other."

He looked like he wanted to say more, but he had apologized, she had accepted, so before he could belabor the point, she changed the subject. "Thank you for contacting the demolition company for me."

"You've heard from them already?"

"This morning. The foreman is coming tomorrow to walk through the house to see what will be involved. Goodwill is taking all the household items and my belongings. I don't want any of it. I didn't have much here, anyway."

He looked at her through his perceptive squint. "It's not too late to change your mind."

"No, it needs to come down."

He looked over at the piano. "What about that?"

"I've already notified a day care center that it's theirs for the taking."

"Nice."

She took a deep and weary breath. "I also must see to Lisa's affairs in Dallas. There's a multitude of them."

"That's what the lawyers on retainer are for."

"I know. But there will be so much I must personally handle. Sorting through her effects, and what's left of Wallace's. The house will have to be sold. I can enlist Helena to help, but, largely, decisions on how to dispense with it all will fall to me. It's exhausting just thinking about it."

"Then stop thinking about it. It'll get done. Operating capital won't be a problem for you. You're going to be rich."

"Yes."

"Try to contain your happiness."

She acknowledged that he was being facetious. "Wealth was Lisa's ambition, not mine. I'm grateful for the financial security, but I'm going to make a business of giving large portions of it away."

"Hmm?"

"I'm going to establish a foundation that will benefit a number of charities."

"Yeah? That's great. Can I make a pitch for veterans' organizations?"

"Submit a list. They'll be first in line for consideration." She smiled at him, but her thoughts were serious. "There's a lot I'll have to learn. It will be a full-time job, but it so happens that I need a full-time job, and overseeing something like this excites me. It feels right, like this is what I've been seeking, like this is what I was intended for and just didn't know it yet." Her throat tightened. "I just wish this epiphany hadn't come about the way it did."

He gave her a moment, then said, "Well, before you start giving away your fortune, don't forget that you owe me a hundred bucks."

"Eighty-five."

"How's that?"

"I'm knocking off fifteen for the house key you entitled yourself to." They smiled at each other, then she said, "Enough about me. Have you been to see your uncle?"

"Yesterday for about an hour. I took him a pint of Blue Bell, which he didn't share. He's greedy with his ice cream."

"What about the staffer who raised the bogus alarm?"

"George sniffed her out in no time. She was young, green. Rusty had flirted with her the morning he was there, and had made an impression, so when he called and asked her to help him pull a prank—"

"A *prank?*"

"Well, she didn't know any better and meant no harm. She learned a lesson, though. George is pushing for the center to adopt a stricter security policy."

"I trust George will get it done."

"Oh, you can count on it."

She hesitated.

"What?"

"I wish I could have known your uncle Henry, before."

"So do I. You would've liked him. Everybody did. I miss him."

His expression was wistful and sad, and it broke her heart for him. Looking away, she stretched her neck and shoulders. She was so very tired. "Are Crystal and Marty back yet? Do they know that Rusty is over and out?"

"They do. They're celebrating in New Orleans."

"Is New Orleans braced for Marty?"

"I doubt it. She got a piercing."

"On what?"

"I was afraid to ask."

Arden smiled, then asked quietly, "Did you tell them about Lisa?"

"Yes."

"Everything?"

"Yes. I figured you would rather me tell them than for them to hear a distorted version through the grapevine."

"Yes, I would. Thank you."

"They sent their condolences."

Nodding, her gaze went back to the flickering candles on the mantel. They reminded her of a church altar, which prompted her to say, "Maybe I should have had a clergy-man there today. Under the circumstances, it didn't seem appropriate."

"I don't believe there are any rules about what's appropriate in a situation like yours. Even if there are, it was your decision to make."

"There were just the three of us. The funeral director, Helena, and me. For the homecoming queen."

Her voice cracked, and she tilted toward him. His arms caught her, pulled her against his chest, and tucked her head beneath his chin. "You've asked about everybody else. How are *you*?"

"Very glad that you showed up just now."

"Really?"

"Yes."

"I didn't know how you'd take to me. After knowing."

"I take to you, Ledge." She hugged him tighter.

"Yeah?"

"In a big way."

"Thank Christ."

He tipped her head back, ran his thumb over her lower lip, then kissed her like his very life depended on it. She curved her arm around his neck and, pulling her mouth free of his, gasped, "Lay me down, Ledge."

They got to the floor. He worked her skirt up over her hips and peeled her panties away. He was only halfway done with his fly when she impatiently pushed his hands aside and finished the job.

They mated fast and feverishly, and, when she cried out his name, he gave one final push and grafted himself to her.

When both were spent, he settled onto her. Gradually they regained their senses as well as their breath. Her fingers drifted through his hair and cupped the back of his head.

"Am I a horrible person?" she whispered.

He raised his head and looked down into her face, brushing back strands of hair that were stuck to her cheek. By tears. "What's the matter?"

"I buried my sister today. But more than anything I wanted—needed—this."

"Sex."

She began to cry in earnest.

He gathered her close and turned them until she was lying on top of him. "You need this, too."

And he held her to him, his large, capable hands stroking her while she mourned.

———◆———

An hour passed before they finally got up and righted their clothing. She collected her handbag and her shoes, then went up on tiptoe and gave him a tender kiss. "Thank you."

Possessively, he curved his hand around her neck and brushed her jawline with his thumb. "It was my pleasure."

She placed her hand on his chest. "I got your shirt wet."

"Anytime."

She rested her cheek on his chest again. "Lisa did a terrible thing, but it doesn't cancel all the wonderful things she did for me. Essentially she gave up her young adulthood for me. I loved her, and I know she loved me."

"No one could argue that." He kissed the top of her head, then leaned away from her. "How do you like that cabin you've been staying in?"

"How did you know—" Then she laughed. "Never mind."

"Will you let me take you home—to my home—give you a bourbon and a bath? I have a tub for two."

"You have a tub for twenty."

"That's a yes?"

"With an exclamation point."

He gave a one-shouldered shrug. "And, if you like it there tonight, you could stay indefinitely."

She arched her brows. "Is that an invitation?"

"No strings attached. It's just that soon you're not going to have a roof over your head." He glanced toward the dining area. "I hope they start the demolition with that chandelier."

She laughed again, more lightly than she had in ages. "Actually, I like the idea of having strings attached."

"Good. Me too. Let's get started." With their arms around each other's waists, they walked to the front door. "Oh, the candles."

He walked over to the fireplace and ran his hand along the carved wood mantel. "You sure you don't want to salvage this?"

"Do you? If so, it's yours."

"Thanks. I'm doing a remodel where I think it'll add some character." He stepped back and assessed the plain brick chimney. "The rest of it has none."

Arden had been watching him with adoring eyes, when suddenly she was yanked from her mooniness. "Chimney." Ledge had cupped his hand around one of the candles, about to blow it out. "Wait! Ledge. She said chimney."

"What?"

"Lisa. Just before she died, remember? She whispered something to me, but I didn't get it." She raised her fingertips to her lips. "She said chimney."

They looked at each other with a significant question mark between them.

He said, "Flip on the light."

She did. He kneeled on the hearth, opened the damper to a shower of soot, and looked up into the flue. "Got a flashlight?"

"In the kitchen." Arden rushed into the kitchen and re-trieved it from a drawer. She carried it back to Ledge, who shone it up into the flue.

"Is there something up there?"

He didn't say anything, but repositioned himself, edging farther into the grate, and reached up with his right arm, clenching his teeth as he strained. He gave several hard yanks, then withdrew his arm and scooted out just as a canvas bag dropped into the grate.

Dusting his hands, he came slowly to his feet and said under his breath, "I'll be double damned."

Arden whispered, "Is that it?"

"That's it, and it's still full."

The two of them stared at the bag as though expecting it to start breathing.

"She told Rusty she had spent the money. *Every last cent*," Arden said, imitating Lisa's spiteful tone.

"That would've been a trip wire."

"Yes. He shot her instantly." She continued to gaze down at the bag. "Did insurance cover the Welch's loss?"

"Yes. At the time, that relieved my conscience a lot," he said.

"Then what happens to stolen money that's recovered?"

"I'm sure that young, fire-breathing prosecutor will know."

"Hmm." After a moment, she added, "Imagine the paperwork that will involve, and he's already got so much work ahead of him."

Ledge looked at her askance. "What are you thinking?"

She took a deep breath and let it out slowly. "I'm thinking what a befitting donation this would be to launch my foundation. Something that caused so much grief being used for something good. It should be earmarked for a particularly worthy cause. Say, Alzheimer's research and treatment."

He swallowed hard and said huskily, "I like the way you think."

"Good. We're agreed."

He placed his arm around her waist and pulled her against his side. "This explains why Lisa didn't want any work done on the house."

"It explains more than that."

He looked at her inquisitively.

"I didn't understand the last word she spoke, and, even if I had, I couldn't have grasped the implication of it. Not until now."

"What was the word?"

Softly, Arden said, "Penance."

About the Author

Sandra Brown is the author of seventy-two *New York Times* bestsellers. There are more than eighty million copies of her books in print worldwide, and her work has been translated into thirty-four languages. In 2008, the International Thriller Writers named Brown its Thriller Master, the organization's highest honor. She has served as president of Mystery Writers of America and holds an honorary doctorate of humane letters from Texas Christian University. She lives in Texas.

———

For more information you can visit:
SandraBrown.net
Facebook.com/AuthorSandraBrown
@Sandra_BrownNYT